THE END
AND
THE BEGINNING

JIM OLESON

Outskirts Press, Inc.
Denver, Colorado

Outskirts Press, Inc.
http://www.outskirtspress.com

ISBN: 978-1-4327-6120-2

Library of Congress Control Number: 2010931363

Outskirts Press and the "OP" logo are trademarks belonging to Outskirts Press, Inc.

PRINTED IN THE UNITED STATES OF AMERICA

ACKNOWLEDGMENTS

Building the background for this imaginary tale took me to places I have never been before. I am most appreciative of the many people and places that protect and nourish our history and share it willingly.

To the public libraries in Marietta, Chillicothe, Toledo in Ohio and Amherstburg, Ontario.

To the Campus Martius Museum in Marietta, Ft. Meigs Museum and Visitor Center in Perrysburg, Ohio. The River Raisin Battlefield Visitor Center and the Monroe County Historical Museum in Monroe Michigan and the Ft. Malden National Historical Site in Ontario.

I would like to thank my family; Kit, Cori, Jon, Steve, Rachael and Nick for their encouragement in this adventure and in fond memory of my dear friend Rex who always told a good story.

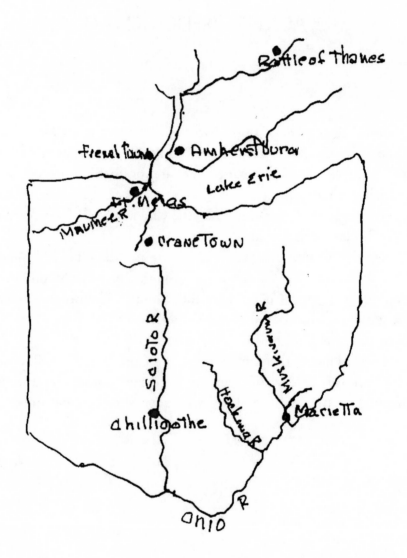

PROLOGUE

The Territories of the Northwest were like no other land: great endless rivers, flowing south, north and west; fresh streams of great abundance with sweet waters, providing for a world of wildlife of all forms and dimensions; endless dark forests covering hills and plains, bold and formidable, to be entered with caution; flat grass lands where great herds of buffalo and antelope benefited from their harvest; enormous lakes of profound beauty and danger.

A proud land; forever in time, going through its own seasons repetitively, predictably. The living creatures of this wild land know its motions and moods, and are content. For the eons the land has prospered in its present form, managing whatever nature gives. For eons, trees only fell as nature prescribed; only recently have they felt the violence of the steel ax.

The boundaries of this vast land included the Ohio River to the south and west; the Ohio River flowed into the Mississippi River basin, which in turn went north to its headwaters and the vast Canadian forests. The great lakes—Superior, Michigan, Huron and Erie—separated the northern boundary from the British-owned Canadian colony. The Appalachian Mountains presented a natural, formidable barrier to the east, discouraging the western migration of non-indigenous peoples. This enormous tract, representing the heartland of the continent, was created as a political entity for the government of a new nation for the control and settlement of its people and the harvesting of its resources. It was the destiny of a new nation. Change had come and the lands of the great northwest were no longer whole.

The northern Europeans have appeared. Before them and because of them, displaced originals have come unwelcome to this serene land. Removed from their tribal territories on the seacoast, plateaus, and mountains of the eastern seaboard, pushed relentlessly west, the clans of the Delaware and Wyandotte, Shawnee and Mohawk, the entire Algonquin culture forced from their lands and villages in just a few decades. The displaced tribes came through the river valleys of the Alleghany and Monongahela, over the Appalachians and Berkshires, following Nemocolin's path and other trails of Indian commerce. They came reluctantly, with great resentment, and in continual conflict as they sought to stop the relentless movement of the man of the white skin who took, changed, and destroyed all things precious. The Northern Europeans did not rest; they closely followed the eastern tribes as they continued westward, overcoming the physical barriers and the violent resistance of the natives. The originals saw this migration as an unstoppable malignancy that destroyed all in its path. Some knew they could move no further; they needed to take a stand to ensure their existence...

This unspoiled land was a new battleground of cultures with the outcome already determined; survival, however, is a powerful driving force, and the originals would take a stand, however hopeless, to preserve their way of life and protect its friend the earth from destruction.

South of the great river that formed the southern boundary of the Northwest Territories, another migration was underway. The northern Europeans who inhabited the southern states were also moving west, looking for new opportunities in the wild and unsettled lands of the Tennessee and Kentucky River valleys.

They too forced the originals out of their way as they claimed all lands that appeared prosperous. To exploit the land and maximize personal gain, they brought with them the African slave who for three hundred years in this land of freedom and democracy was the engine that drove the southern economy. Black people did not come to this new land willingly. Many were sold to masters who more often than not were brutal and cruel men. These slaves knew that the burdens and hardships, already intolerable in the civilized plantation culture from which they came, would be unendurable in the raw and savage world they were about to enter. Settling the land, building the masters' domiciles and industry would fall on their backs. They were the beasts of burden that would make the Europeans wealthy. To labor in the tobacco fields was, next to the developing rice and sugar farms of the Mississippi Delta, the most torturous and lethal industry of their world.

For those who marched westward, word was beginning to spread from one slave camp to another that there might be hope, a cautious hope, a desperate hope. Across the wide river was the new state of Ohio, a free state; if you could somehow cross that body of water. White folks would help you go north to the country called Canada where any black man could live free. Around the evening fires, in the fields of their labor and in the hovels of their homes, they asked the river to show them the way. In the second decade of the nineteenth century was the beginning of another transition. The Europeans' cruelest institution was to be challenged, amid great conflict, and ultimately overthrown.

So it would be in the Northwest Territories in the year of 1812 that great events were about to unfold that would define the American identity. In conflict and turmoil, one great civilization would be forever destroyed and another would begin to breathe the life of freedom.

PART 1
THE END

CHAPTER 1

Marietta, Ohio
June 1812

"*Our great patriot lies herein, resting now for all time, his worldly duties done. General Jonathon McGuire in every way a founding Father, creating this great country three score years ago. He fought the king on the streets of our fair cities, on the trails and byways of our country side, the greens and commons of our villages, in the halls of our government, on the battle fields of our great war. His deeds forever remembered when and wherever patriots gather. The General has earned his rest and all yee here on this day the 22nd of June in the Year 1812 is witness to his legacy.*"

Rufus Putnam, an old war friend, leader of the Ohio Company of Associates, and founder of Marietta, closed his Bible and put his notes into his coat pocket. He had helped bring McGuire and his family to this territory in 1792. They shared a lifetime of tragedy and triumph, and had known each other in the War of Independence and years thereafter as politicians and entrepreneurs. They were in many ways brothers. He found his brief words fitting. *The older one gets the less needs to be said, the general would want it this way,* he thought as he threw a handful of dirt onto the coffin. Rufus would miss his dear old friend; he worried for a moment of the great debt the general left behind and how it would be resolved The hundred or so friends and citizens of Marietta attending the funeral service walked slowly past the gravesite, located on the McGuire property, overlooking the river. They dispersed to their carriages and horses for the short trip back to the farmhouse where refreshments were waiting. It was a fairly sunny day with light breezes. The general's daughter would serve outdoors on the front lawn.

The last decade of the general's life revolved around his 1,240-acre farm, located in the hills over the mighty Ohio River. Several miles southeast was the rural hamlet of Marietta, a prosperous community of one hundred and twenty dwellings, a bank, two churches, and several hundred people, and supporting an active boat building enterprise that provided transport for travelers going west to Cincinnati, the Mississippi, and beyond. General McGuire came to the Ohio valley in 1792, his years as a local Pennsylvania business man, politician, and war hero over. With Maggie, his wife of thirty years, he secured a military land warrant with the assistance of Rufus Putnam of the Ohio Company of Associates. The McGuire's thrived on this new opportunity, building and creating a most prosperous farm to be envied by everyone in the county.

This all changed one April evening when Maggie, in her happiest days, suffered a stroke while sitting on the front porch enjoying the sunset over the Ohio. The general referred to the seven years since her parting as his resting and weeping time. His interests in the day-to-day operations of the farm diminished; he spent more time in solitude, healing as best he could from the loss of his beloved, and gradually reviving his interest in literature and language.

Eventually, he would turn over the commerce of the farm to

his only child Virginia and her husband Joshua Sprout, oldest son of Ebenezer Sprout, a hard working and proud frontiersman who, through his industry, was able to cast off his squatter heritage and purchase a small plot of land that kept his large family in modest but honest means. Unlike his father, Joshua was not of pleasant disposition. He was a selfish, angry, blaming man, who seems to have resented his father's reputation as a self-made citizen, respected by the New Englanders who founded Marietta in 1788 and the more recent frontier settlers who shared the community. The general was disappointed in Virginia's choice of a husband and felt that her rebellious nature was at the root of her decision. Joshua's lack of curiosity and scholarship was a barrier between him and the general that had been difficult to overcome.

No one understood Joshua's disposition and attitudes, so different from the rest of his family. He did work hard on occasion and, under the direction of the general and the quiet management and manipulation of Virginia, he contributed to the bounty of the farm. The family's industry however was productive and the farm continued to flourish.

Upon Maggie's death, the general retired to his cottage, a small three-room cabin with a small loft; this was the original home built by the couple in their first years on the land. This was the home of his best memories. It served him well these last years, as he focused his energies on writing his memoirs, corresponding with old friends, and entertaining the occasional reporter who sought out his remembrances of the war and his experiences in building a new country. There had been increasing interest in his past on the part of others in the community in the last year, with the talk about a second war with the British Empire.

His greatest enjoyment however was tutoring and mentoring young Jim, who had come to the farm as a homeless waif seven years ago. An abusive, violent stepfather forced his mother to give over her son to save his life.

The general loved his rolling land of soft hills and gentle valleys. The hills that surrounded and occasionally intermingled with a large tract of tillable soil, laid out like a serpent through the center of the property, were heavily wooded with hickory, maples, oak, and ash. The four hundred and twenty acres under cultivation raised a multitude of crops: wheat, corn, potatoes, and beans were the staples. The farm had another two hundred and twenty acres of lightly wooded rolling pasture. In good rain years, this was enough to maintain an ample number of cattle, horses, and pigs, both feral and domestic. A small creek flowed out of the forested woodlands and led quietly to the Little Muskingum River. This creek, several wells, and in most years, adequate rainfall provided ample moisture to meet the many demands of all the farm's enterprises. The living area was centered on twenty acres, on a small hill at the southwest end of the property. A short walk through a small stand of maples led to the bluff overlooking the Ohio River, while the Muskingum ended its journey several miles to the west. The bluff was several hundred feet above and a mile from the river bank. After the spring runoffs, the flood plain was rich in vegetation and a provided a common summer pasture for the hamlet's livestock.

The rugged northern and eastern acreage of the property included a small stream that flowed through a narrow gap in the dense hills and spread out into small drainages that meandered across the property, creating deep bottoms. The opening also included a small path that followed the stream as it fought its way into the "Thickets," a large tract of heavily forested, rugged, and impenetrable land that defied civilization. The stream and accompanying trail meandered for many miles in a northerly direction. The thicket began on the general's property as rolling forested hills that continued in an easterly and northern direction, turning quickly into steep ridges and deep bottoms that rolled relentlessly to the hazy blue and grey mountains of the Appalachian plateau. The ridges were smothered in dense vegetation, thick forests, occasional meadows of wild flowers, small creeks, and impenetrable swamps and marshes. The dark thicket, as it was referred to by the settlers, was for the most part left alone.

The trail to the north was both narrow and difficult, working its way over steep ravines and deep valleys, through the large stands of hardwoods and dense underbrush that was still untouched. On the remainder of the property, sufficient timber was still available from the forested hills for those in need of prime lumber, a major winter industry of the general's enterprise.

The farm was located on the edge of the western foothills of the Appalachian Mountains. It was a rich and prosperous land, shared over the last two decades with many bands of displaced Indians, primarily from the eastern states, representing numerous clans and tribes in conflict with the original inhabitants and the never-ending flow of white settlers taking and destroying everything in their path.

The general felt that he was probably walking down the lane for the last time; his breath was short, there was pain in his chest, mostly he was very tired, and he paused several times between the main house and his cottage only several hundred yards away. The path was next to an apple orchard that he and his beloved Maggie had planted sixteen years before. He was too disconcerted to enjoy the green buds of his prize Belvidere Apples filling out the branches. The sun, low in the western sky, was casting ominous shadows that guided him home. *I need to take care of my unfinished business,* he thought. He reached his cottage, his home for the last eight years, fell into the chair, breathed heavily for several minutes, and waited for some energy to return. "Digger, get young Jim, bring him here." The hound dog, still eager after all these years to be a part of the general's life, ran to the shed as he had done many times before to bring the student to see his teacher.

Several hours later, exhausted, McGuire slowly forced himself upright and sought the comfort of his bed, using all his energy to stay focused and he wrote on his bed desk.

Journal Entry
Jonathon McGuire
Maggie's Hill
June 1812

> *I have done my work, it is late. I fear this will be my last entry. Young Jim is on his way. It was difficult but most prudent, he knows little and I have protected him so. He is ill equipped to take on his enemies here. He was given old Buckskin, my Kentucky rifle, plenty of shot and powder, and twenty silver coins to see him through the hard times. He will determine his prominence on the northern frontier, war is near; he will grow to be a man. I worry he is not well prepared...I do expect and it is my hope that he will return one day to this land of ours. I have not talked with Virginia. I will miss her so. I am so tired. I rest my pen.*

The General fell into a coma in the early morning of June 19th. Digger whined softly, lay down with his chin on the general's chest, and awaited the dawn. Their times together were over.

A clouded moon provided Jim a grey light as he traveled through the thicket; he had to walk cautiously the first several miles, leading Buckskin down a path very familiar to both. The darkness, however, kept him focused on the trail; he would have several hours of waning moonlight to distance him self from the land and world he loved.

Tears flowed freely as the sadness, fear, and confusion overwhelmed him. Everything so fast, so confusing, saying good bye to his beloved general, not understanding fully what was happening, leaving forever on a moment's notice, without saying goodbye to anyone else.

The general's words swarmed and raced through Jim's mind, devastating to his innocence: "Leave…danger…you will be harmed…little time…go north, seek your fortune…find general Hull…don't come back." *What do they mean? Why do I have to leave? Is the General dying? Will I survive?*

The first recognition that terrified him was that he was all alone. Forced back again into the wilderness, Jim continued to walk, leading his horse for several hours over the difficult trail, almost unaware of the steep ridges and thick forest that reached skyward, black and ominous. The first faint light of dawn brought Jim to the first clearing; he would now be able to ride Buckskin, who was restless from several hours of being led down the dark trail. They went at a short gait and would gallop when the trail allowed. They continued in dense forests canopied by great trees. In many areas, little if any daylight could trickle down to the forest floor. Occasional glades and small meadows appearing in early light were the only sign of day. There would not be any evidence of human activity until he reached the Muskingum River road, several hours west and north.

Jim tried hard to clear his mind and control the panic. He tried to recall word by word all that was said at the general's bedside only a few hours, a lifetime ago.

"Jim, you need to listen now and hear everything I have to say, do not miss a word. You have to leave now, there is danger here and I am no longer able to protect you. Joshua will harm you and you are not ready to challenge him. The war is soon to start. Here is a letter of introduction to General Hull, who is to lead the American army of the Northern Frontier. Go to Detroit, find the general, he is an old friend. He will assist you. Take Buckskin, he is sound and able and knows the trail. Take my Kentucky rifle over the mantle and my shot and ball, and here is a small purse of silver. Use it wisely. Remember all that we learned together; you have great promise."

"Go by the thicket and follow the Appalachian Indian trail north; this is still wild country with no habitation. Follow the Hock hocking River to the trace road and then west to Chillicothe on the Scioto. If you encounter Indians, share my name and you should secure safe passage. Several miles north on the east bank at Stony Creek is a farm with two large oaks near the homestead. There, they will assist you on your journey. Do not share who you are until you meet and know Jed Hicks. Be careful here. I will tell your friend Anna and your mother of these events; they will find a way to communicate in good time. Get stronger and wiser; your inheritance will await your return. Farewell my dear, dear friend. Now get your things and go."

Jim strained to remember if anything else was said. *What did I forget?* The fear rose again as he began to realize that the general was dying. The sense of loss and loneliness overwhelmed him and poured out in great sobs, tears reappeared on his cheeks. The feelings of desolation equaled that terrible summer alone in the thicket.

He rode Buckskin slowly now, continuing north; eventually the path widened with occasional breaks in the tall trees and dense undergrowth. The day brought a cloudy sky and rain. He felt somewhat better in the light of day with surroundings that were still familiar. In the summer of his eighteenth year, he began a new life, much as he had as a child, alone and afraid those seven years earlier.

Joshua Sprout's heart was in his throat as he ran from the great house down the lane to the general's cottage. *The old bastard may finally be gone, this is too good, too good, it will be all mine now.* Just minutes before he had heard Penelope the kitchen maid running from the cottage and up the lane, yelling; "Someone help, the general isn't talking, he's not moving." She had found him moments before, lying on his bed, breathing heavily but not responding.

Joshua was winded when he reached the open cottage door. His wife Virginia, the general's only child, was already there crying hysterically, slapping her father's face. "Wake up daddy, wake up!"

Joshua stood and observed for a minute, offering no assistance. He assessed the situation and walked back outside. Mingo, an itinerant laborer of mixed breed was working the pigs near the sty. Joshua ordered him to saddle a horse and fetch Dr. Jabezz True in Marietta and not to overheat the horse. He walked back to the cottage, trying not to show his excitement.

Virginia, even in her grief, quietly took the general's journal and several unfinished documents, hiding them under some blankets to pick up later.

The general labored hard in his illness all day, breathing heavily, sweating profusely, unresponsive to his surroundings. He spoke periodically in mostly inaudible mutterings; names of old friends and places were occasionally recognizable. Virginia stayed by his side and did not allow anyone else to come close to him; she cleaned his bed, washed his body with cold water and liniment, and talked to him quietly, speaking of wonderful times together and urging him to return.

Dr. Jabezz True arrived in early afternoon, performed a brief exam, listening to McGuire's breathing and looking into his eyes for any sign of clarity. After several minutes he told everyone to leave, except Virginia. "He will be gone at any moment," he said. "There is nothing medicine can do now. You need to be strong. You have great responsibilities and many will depend on you."

Virginia was still holding the general's hand, tears in her eyes.

"Yes I will," she said, more to herself than Dr. True.

"Are his papers in order?"

"Yes, they are at the bank. Daddy said Mr. Putnam will handle everything," Virginia said. "Please stay with us until the Lord takes him."

"Yes of course," he said.

Joshua was interested in other things. He desperately wanted to search the general's cottage, but realized he would have to wait until the old man was gone. It wasn't until several hours after the alarm was raised that he realized Jim was not to be seen. *I can get rid of both them at the same time.* He knew his time had come; his dreams and schemes of controlling the farm and eliminating his worst enemies were now possible. He walked to the corral, determined to find out where that bastard Jim was. He did not intend to waste any time. Jim would be the first to go.

Anna Erickson, the farms laundress and Jim's best friend heard the news only after her first loads of laundry were hung to dry. She ran first to find Jim, looking in the shed and barn and gazing over the fields. He usually tended the general's horses at this time of the morning. Coming to the corral, she saw that Buckskin was missing. "What's happened?" She was filling with panic, trying to sort out what was going on. She ran back up the lane, looking for signs of her best friend, protector, and future husband. She reached the cottage, where most of the farmhands and helpers were milling about, waiting for word from the general's daughter. The fate of their beloved patriarch would determine the fate of the farm and all those who depended on its bounty and his benevolence. If the general died, would Virginia be able to control her dictatorial, abusive, and domineering husband? No one wanted to think about that.

Anna noticed almost unconsciously that Mr. Sprout was searching the shed where Jim lived and studied rather than inside tending to his stepfather and wife. The door was open and she could see him, tearing through Jim's belongings. She stopped, struggled to control her emotions. *The men I love are gone — this is happening to fast—I need to think.*

After searching Jim's room, and the cottage, the fine Kentucky rifle was no longer on the mantle over the fireplace. One of the field hands also noted that Buckskin, the general's favorite horse, was nowhere to be found; his saddle was also missing. Joshua had more than enough evidence and was eager to report this to the sheriff.

Joshua Sprout then told Mingo who was saddled up and ready to leave to also seek out Deputy Sheriff Micah Miller while he was fetching the doctor. "Crimes have been committed and they need to be addressed now",

Joshua had spent most of his ten years of marriage resenting the general's dominance on the farm and in his relationship with his wife. All of his ideas were discounted and of little value. Virginia sought her father's counsel and company more than his own. The father and daughter spent much time together, often in the presence of the general's young student. When Jim practiced his new language skills, sometimes the three of them would speak in French or Spanish, excluding the unlearned Joshua entirely. Many times, decisions were made without his input.

He knew he was not Virginia's first choice for a husband; she struggled with intimacy while providing Joshua with his sexual rights and privileges. One child, Elizabeth, was born in the first year of their union. She gave her father comfort and companionship, but seemed to enjoy the company of others more. He resented them all, and had dreamed of the day he would take over the farm and impose his rule. Well, Joshua's time had now come.

Deputy Sheriff Miller arrived in the late afternoon and went to the main house and listened to the list of crimes allegedly committed by young Jim. Influenced by the intensity of Joshua's need for action and intimidating posture, he agreed over some cider to file a warrant for Jim's arrest in the morning. Deputy Miller, replacing Sheriff Timothy Buell, who had enlisted as an officer in the U.S. Army, was a timid, quiet and tentative man who tried to please everyone. He left the farm without mentioning his intentions to Virginia or the doctor, still by the general's bedside.

The general died at 11:05 that evening. At first light, Joshua rode hard to the sheriff's office in town and got his warrant.

Wanted
Jim Morgan for felonious Acts of theft of property and Livestock from the state of General Jonathon McGuire

By order of the sheriff of
Washington County, State of Ohio
Suitable reward for his apprehension

19th day June 1812

Joshua withdrew some funds at the Marietta First Mercantile Bank to have posters printed at the Marietta Western Spectator. He would have them distributed by postal carrier throughout the new state of Ohio.

CHAPTER 2

Washington County
Ohio
June 1812

Buckskin was fresh and responsive to Jim's lead. They continued onward for a few hours, crossing the Little Muskingum and several creeks, following the banks of a marsh. Although little used by anyone except the local Indians, the trail was easy to follow and Jim remembered its major features from previous travels, both by himself and with the general. Around mid morning, he saw signs of civilization; a wisp of smoke from a distant fire where wood and brush was being burnt; a few fields, rich with corn several inches above the ground, two farm houses and several outbuildings on his approach to the post road, all offering a sense of order and purpose to this wild land.

He didn't know why for sure, but he felt it best that he wasn't seen. He waited among some trees while an empty wagon pulled by a team of dark horses and a mule behind passed, heading east. The driver was talking and swearing to no one except his weary animals.

He found the trail going west easily, several miles north of the post road; the farm land turned quickly back to forest as he rode east down the path. From here on in, he would now encounter new and unfamiliar territory. He paused, looked back, and tried to convince himself that he would be okay. Like the thicket trail it was well marked but little traveled. Jim continued on for most of the day, vigilant in the new surroundings, looking for signs of life and activity.

With Buckskin slowing down and showing signs of fatigue, Jim found a meadow with good forage and stream, and unsaddled, watered, and hobbled his horse. Tired now, he laid down under a large oak to give more thought to his predicament. He fell to a hard sleep almost immediately.

The morning shadows were beginning to form when he was awakened by his horse chewing close to his head. He awoke hungry; the little bit of cornbread and jerky that he had hurriedly gathered from the general's kitchen would only last the day. "What do I do now?" he said, trying to control the panic and grief that overwhelmed him.

Jim thought back to his wonderful days with the general. All the years they were together. *Now it is gone…* His fear and desperation were not unlike how he felt during his days alone in the forest seven years ago……

Journal Entry
Jonathon McGuire
July 3rd, 1806
Maggie Hill Farm

> *"A most interesting morning late. I was in recluse at the pond reading Charleston's recent accounts of the battle of Cowpens when a young man, more like a boy appeared over my shoulder and asked to what I was reading. I was startled and observed a young man clothed in animal skins. I thought him to be Indian. He appeared to be in wretched*

condition: clothes torn, his hair matted and quite long, and, most disconcerting, an emaciated body and face. He was accompanied by a hound dog he called Digger, young of age who appeared in better shape than the master. I regained my composure, closed the manuscript and replied, 'A summary of the war of freedom.' We then began a most remarkable conversation. The boy, who appeared to be ten or eleven, was, as I said, wretched in his appearance. I inquired as to where he came from and he calmly replied in a strong voice, 'The thicket.' He didn't volunteer any more information, but asked if I had fought in the war. I replied that indeed I was a member of the revolutionary army. He inquired as to my role, what battles I fought in. I shared without elaboration my participation.

"I was most intrigued as to his poise and countenance, as he appeared to be fighting for his very survival I inquired of him how he came to be here. 'I live in the thicket, been there since spring,' he replied in a most matter-of-fact way, 'I went to school once. I wanted to learn my letters. I try to read whenever I see writing but it is hard when you don't know the letters.' I asked him to sit and offered him the two apples I had in my purse. He took only one, ate with gusto, and gave the core to his companion.

"I asked his name and he replied, 'Jim Morgan, my father was Patrick Morgan.' He then asked my name and stated that he had heard of me and everyone said I was a good man. Upon further inquiry, he told me that he has been living in the thicket for nearly four months, spends some of his time at the Councils Keeper's village and sneaks home to see his mother on occasion. I immediately recalled the story. He comes from a family of squatters, His father died on the Ohio several years back and his mother married Samuel Kirkwood's oldest boy Elizur, a no-account roust

who made life most miserable for those around him. One night early this spring, Elizur in a drunken stupor was beating upon Jim and his mother. In the course of events, Jim applied an ax to the villain's back, causing serious but not mortal harm. Word has it, as I now recall specifically from a visit with Madelyn Moody at the congregational church, that young Jim ran away and has not been seen since. Elizur has vowed to seek Jim out and bring his dead body back to his mother.

"Most everyone thought young Jim went down river where some relatives are reported to live, probably near Cincinnati. As I was recalling these events, I asked him how he survives in such an inhospitable world. He replied, again in a most casual manner, that he has several camps set up where he sleeps, and 'I fish, mostly over at the birch creek and trap rabbits and Water Bird of the Council Keeper clan feeds me when I am very hungry. It will be easier when the crops ripen.' 'How long do you plan to live in this manner?' I asked 'Until I kill Mr. Kirkwood. He is searching for me ever since I destroyed his whisky maker.'

"We conversed in this manner on several subjects well into the afternoon. He was of a curious nature and most inquisitive. We agreed to meet again soon. He made his good bye and walked back, with his dog at his side, into the thicket from whence he came.

"I must say I look forward to getting to know this young man."

And so it was that a remarkable relationship began. Several times each week, Jim and his dog would walk out of the thicket. Jim would lay his pack made of rabbit's skins on the ground next to the old rocking chair that the general had placed there for his own comfort and contemplation many years before, and the three of them would share time together underneath the large virgin hemlock near the fish pond. They quickly became comfortable with one another, sharing the lunch that the general would always bring, enjoying the warm summer days and conversation on many subjects. The general on some occasions would bring two old cane poles and freshly dug worms, Bass and catfish dominated their catch and Jim would take half the fish with him when he returned to the woods.

The general always brought a book or newspaper with him. He was a voracious reader and, enjoying his own voice and mastery of the English language, recited to an audience at every opportunity. He possessed a large library; some say the largest in Washington County. For the first few weeks, Jim listened in quiet contemplation as the general read. He quickly developed an interest in contemporary American literature; J. Hector St. John De Crevecoeur *Letters from an American Farmer* by, Ebenezer Cook *The Sot Weed Factor* by, and *The Narrative of the Life of Olaudah Equiano* introduced Jim to a larger world. The general's ability and patience in explaining the literature to the young man generated great interest and curiosity. Jim would ask many questions, his imagination and speculation far exceeding his comprehension. The general wondered how such intellect and inquiry could have sprung from Jim's squatter parentage.

The hours they spent together always included lunch, which Jim would share with Digger. He would eat whatever was offered and never asked for more. Sometimes the three of them would walk around the property, discussing the land and all the ideas and improvements that were implemented by the general and Maggie, who had departed several years ago.

When the harvest season began, the young boy offered to assist and soon became a valued hand. On long days he would sleep in the apple orchard, wrapping himself in his blanket and sleeping on the hard ground with his dog by his side. He worked most days, but although he would disappear on occasion into the thicket and be gone for a day or two, he always returned. Jim began his labor with the wheat harvest, followed quickly by the potatoes and corn and in September, the apples.

Jim was a quick learner and soon mastered most of the jobs that needed doing. When the apples were harvested and the cider made and shipped, General McGuire visited Jim's mother and asked for her permission to bring Jim into his household. Molly, Jim's mother, anxious for her son's welfare was most grateful; her prayers had been answered and she cried with joy. An old tool shed was cleared out and made habitable, and this became Jim's new home.

Maggie was only several years gone and the general's grief would occasionally surface. Jim listened to his sad recollections, usually without conversation, and it appeared that the general managed his melancholy in the acceptance of this eleven-year-old boy. In October after the harvests Jim asked if he could be taught his letters and, thereafter, the general devoted an hour or two of each day to teaching him to read. He progressed under the general's tutelage and, by early spring, his reading and, to a lesser degree, writing showed some competency.

Jim and McGuire occasionally took walks out to the bluff overlooking the river, where the teacher would share great adventure stories with fascinating conclusions. They relived the general's role in the Revolutionary War on these walks, with the general sharing all of his experiences, including his cowardice at Brandywine Creek, which had haunted his soul these many years. On rainy days, they retreated to the general's cottage, where Jim was introduced to more great literature.

McGuire realized how empty his life had been since the loss of Maggie; His daughter and only child whose recent marriage to an angry and jealous man left little opportunity for the two of them to spend time together. The general knew that Jim filled many of his

Needs; he worried of becoming dependent on this unique young man. He needed to be cautious.

At first Jim resisted sharing anything about his own life. Even though the teacher was adept at inquiry, the student appeared more interested in the wide world around him than in himself. Eventually, and with encouragement from the general, they would take hikes into the thicket and Jim would show him wonders that not even the general had seen: a freshwater spring well hidden in dense undergrowth; populated by all forms of wildlife and stands of enormous hardwoods with a secluded camp site, where runaway slaves or other fugitives may have hidden in times past.

The young man showed him a way through the bogs and swamps that dominated the lower part of the thicket bordering Blue Creek, which eventually found its way to the wetlands of the Ohio. In only a few months, Jim had become more familiar with the thicket than even the Indians. He had maintained several camps, all close to water sources but well concealed. His primary camp included a small cave, well hidden behind a fallen oak in a deep and almost impenetrable hollow. The other camps were temporary, mostly hidden groves of birch and maples trees; he had made use of bushes and ground coverings which were easy to disperse. The general was amazed at this young man's ability to live and, to a degree, flourish in such an alien world.

Jim opened up over time and told the general of his summer living as an orphan of the forest. He talked about how he ran into the wilderness to avoid the abuse of his stepfather and how, in his first days he approached and was befriended by Water Bird the sister of Council Keeper, Chief of a Shawnee Clan who had been granted a small tract of land east of the Muskingum and north of the Ohio in the Treaty of Harmar a decade before. She provided him with food, basic tools, and clothing. On one occasion, Jim and McGuire visited Council Keeper's village, and the general observed the close bond between Water Bird and his new friend.

Water Bird had been taken from her family by missionaries from Pennsylvania at a young age to learn the white man's ways. She spent several years in a rigid world of Methodist religion, education, and everything non-Indian. When she was old enough to manage on her own, she returned to her brother's family and struggled to readapt to a tribal culture. She took two men, both warriors; the first died in a conflict with the Pawnees, and the other was lost in the Battle of the Muskingum. She birthed two children; both died from the white man's disease. Water Bird eventually accepted a lonely life with her brother, managing his village and its relationship with the ever-menacing white world. Over time, she found solace and comfort in this role.

The day Jim walked into the village in early April of his eleventh year, she saw him standing in front of the long house, staring at the open entry way, asking in English for something to eat of anyone who walked by. "Food, please, food," he said, holding out his hands. The villagers gathered and watched, but avoided any contact. Summer Fish made motions for him to leave, and several of the native youth began to taunt him. Torn clothes, bare feet, infected mosquito bites, and hundreds of spring wood ticks covered much of his body. His hair was disheveled and clogged with dirt. Water Bird walked over to him; Summer Fish and the children walked away and watched from a distance. She looked down upon this wretched figure for several minutes and then asked his name in English.

"Jim. Jim Morgan, ma'am," he said, his hand still out. "Come with me," Water Bird said as she handed Jim a piece of jerked beef. They walked to an outdoor fire pit near her shelter where some coals from previous fires still had life. She blew the fire to a flame and made the tip of a stick red hot. She took off his clothes, a torn and dirty shirt and a pair of pants held up by a piece of rope, and began the long and tedious job of burning off the bloated, blood-filled ticks.

After several hours, when all the ticks that she could find had popped and sizzled to their demise, she walked the naked Jim to the bank of Blue Creek. They followed the water upstream for a mile to a mud wallow used by passing buffalo to cool off in the hot afternoons and rid themselves of parasites. She laid him on his back and packed his entire body with the wet mud. "Stay as you are and let the mud dry, I will be back for you," she said, and returned to the village.

Jim had not spoken since Water Bird had approached him. He felt a great sense of safety and relaxed his vigilance, hoping that she would protect and care for him. The mud began to dry and soothed his burnt and inflamed skin. He soon relaxed and dozed off; only the pangs of hunger kept him from a restful and needed sleep. Water Bird returned as the sun was casting long shadows over the peaceful scene. She stood him up, walked him to the river and instructed him to clean off his mud-caked body. Jim was weak and feverish and had difficulty standing. Eventually, and with much effort he washed himself free of the mud. She handed him a worn but clean deer skin shirt and a pair of grey wool pants, both too large for his frail body. She had also brought a long strip of leather, which she tied around his waist to hold up his pants. "Time for you to eat" Water Bird said as they walked slowly back to the village. She brought him to a small shelter facing a fire and open on one end, where he ate greedily of smoked venison and dried corn and drank of the fresh water that was offered him. It was dark when he finished; Jim was still feverish and overwhelmed with fatigue when Water Bird handed him a blanket and told him to sleep in the shelter. He lay down; a brief hope that he would survive floated through his mind as he fell immediately into an exhaustive slumber.

The sun was warming the campsite when Jim was awakened

by a large, elderly, heavy-set Indian, who stared at him for several minutes and said in broken English, "I am Council Keeper. Do you go to your people now?" Still groggy, Jim replied that he couldn't go home or he would be killed by his stepfather.

"How long you in woods?" Council Keeper asked.

"Six or seven days," Jim responded.

"You must leave now," said Council Keeper as Water Bird approached her brother.

"I will see to the forest boy's necessities and provide him with assistance so he can be on his way," she said, leaving no doubt as to her authority and intentions.

"He needs to go, he brings big trouble from the white man," Council Keeper said as he turned and walked away.

Water Bird watched Jim intently. "Do you have a home?" she asked. Jim briefly told his story. "Can you not go to town and talk with the sheriff?"

"Mother said that we cannot trust the sheriff and that if I went to town Elizur would find me and I would be killed," he said.

"Do you have other family that you can go to?"

"Only my mother and Daisy my aunt; my father drowned three summers past," he said.

"Here eat this" said Water Bird, and handed him a bowl of corn mush and a dried sweet potato. Several villagers were standing around, telling her to get the boy out of camp.

"Wait here, I will be back," she said, and walked to Council Keeper's lodge. She returned in less than an hour, saying "Pick up your blanket, we need to go." Jim, still somewhat in a daze, feared that his short period of sanctuary was ending. Water Bird headed out of the village along the Blue Creek trail, handed him a pack made of skins filled with various items.

They didn't talk as she led him down a well-worn trail; Water Bird carried a deerskin pack on her back with a leather strap that fit naturally on her forehead. Following her was a young female hound of medium size in various tones of brown and black. She made no noise and walked close to Water Bird, keeping to the trail. After several miles, the trail faded into underbrush and thick foliage. The party proceeded silently into the forest away from the river; there was no visible path as Water Bird made her way through the underbrush. Soon they began climbing steep ridges and then down into deep ravines. They continued along this exhausting path for several hours, stopping on occasion as if to get their bearings. The dog was now leading the way and it was clear that both she and Water Bird knew where they were going. It was hard work as they made their way through grape vines, bushes, and shrubs, stepping over and around fallen trees and brushing away saplings. They walked the small creeks in the ravines, climbed up the sharp ridges and resting when necessary. Totally immersed in the wild, they eventually came to a small open area in a deep hollow with a spring hidden by heavy growth and unseen by anyone who did not know of its presence. A massive oak, recently fallen in a storm, lay almost across the spring, its many branches providing great opportunity for shelter, the space where it had stood creating an opening in the canopy for the sun to reach the ground. It was a restful, peaceful place and Jim felt its comfort. Behind the tree, covered in underbrush, was a small cave elevated from the spring; its opening was high enough for Jim to walk in and sufficiently deep and wide to lie down and move about. It was dry and, with some clearing away of vegetation, a comfortable place to sleep.

Water Bird walked slowly around the area, looking for any signs of habitation. She cleaned some of the fallen debris and undergrowth from the spring and found that it still supplied adequate water; she took a small drink and appeared satisfied. After several minutes she said, "You will stay here. It is safe. Watch and learn from what I do." She went to work preparing a small shelter in front of the cave; Jim helped her collect leaves and small branches to provide a ground cover for his sanctuary.

He watched and assisted as best he could; in less than an hour, they had prepared a small but well-protected shelter. Water Bird showed Jim how to use saplings and branches to camouflage the immediate area. She collected dry grasses and fallen leaves, and then started a fire with her flint and stone, making Jim watch closely.

When the fire was going Water Bird sat down and took some smoked venison and parched corn out of her pack. They ate in silence and, when they finished, she showed Jim where and how to set a rabbit snare. They walked down the hollow for a short distance to a small creek and fished with a string and hook made of bone, with bits of meat for bait. Together, they caught a few small trout. Upon their return to the camp, Jim made his first fire using her tools; they sat mostly in silence while the dark night and bright stars took over. Water Bird rolled into her blanket and fell asleep instantly. Jim watched her for awhile, wondering what would happen in the morning. *Will she stay with me? Will we go somewhere?* His eyes got heavy and he also fell into a deep, dreamless sleep.

Water Bird woke early and had Jim make a fire, clean and cook the fish; a snare had caught a rabbit in the night and she showed him how to dress it. They ate a quiet meal; she then looked at Jim directly and said, "I give you food to last for many days if properly rationed, a blanket, moccasins, ax, bear fat, knife, snares, fishing line, and my fire starter. If you are brave as a warrior, you will survive. Be strong. I will leave you my dog; follow her, she knows her way and will let you know of danger. Leave no trace, and stay off the trails. I will return to you here in a week's time. Come to me if you are in great need, but come quietly and at night. I will get word to your mother that you are safe. I will leave you now." She then got up, walking back out of the clearing the way they had come. Stopping for a moment, she said, "I will forever call you Forest Boy," then quickly disappeared into the dense forest. The dog watched and whimpered once but made no effort to follow. Jim was alone again. He leaned over and petted the dog slowly along her neck.

Water Bird would write later in her journals that she needed to finish mothering and that Jim was in dire need of assistance.

Jim moved to other sites during his stay in the thicket, continually fearful of his stepfather, who had vowed to deliver his lifeless body to his mother would find him. On occasion, he would hear the bellowing of Elizur's hound as his drunken master searched the forest for the young man who destroyed and threatened his livelihood. On several occasions, when the dog's howling got too close, Jim would wade out to the middle of the swamp on Blue Creek and spend the night very alone and afraid. These were his darkest moments; a sense of hopelessness would overwhelm him and he yearned for his mother's embrace. Jim tried his best to conceal his presence, remembering everything he was taught. He lived primarily under the cover of the thick canopy of large deciduous trees, close to the marsh and swamplands so that he could escape if necessary. He stayed away from the few animal paths that crossed the thicket and where travel was the easiest. Over time, as he became more secure and confident, he spent most of his time at the sanctuary.

He filled up his days moving about the thicket, learning all of its secrets and becoming familiar with the wild life he saw frequently; several deer and a fox became almost daily acquaintances. He named his dog Digger for her enthusiasm in going after ground squirrels, and depended on her for her vigilance and sense of direction. He never had to worry about getting lost in this dense, rugged wilderness as she would always bring him back to a familiar place. They ultimately developed the ability to talk to each other. He gradually became confident that he would survive as he mastered the many challenges of living in the wild, starting fires, catching fish, snaring rabbits, and accommodating his loneliness and desperation.

Jim always seemed to be hungry, no matter how many fish and rabbits he caught. He visited Water Bird several times that summer; she would feed him and mend or replace his clothes with new moccasins, a deer skin shirt, and leggings. With his sunbaked skin, long hair, and animal clothes he could be mistaken for an aboriginal. One night in June when Elizur was attending his still, Jim visited his mother, who hugged and held her son, tears falling down her face. Jim felt her warmth and wanted desperately to stay; they talked quickly and quietly, he told her that he was doing well in the thicket with Water Birds help. He enjoyed some fresh bread and cheese and awoke his sister to share a moment. Nothing was said about how long he would stay in the forest but he knew that he would not be coming home; understanding how fearful she was of her husband.

It was still night when he left, his mother sadly watching him disappear in the darkness.

Jim's occasional visits to Water Bird occurred at night lasted only a few hours. He would share his experiences and she offered advice and wisdom on how to survive, He always left feeling more confident and less desperate and lonely.

One day, his roaming brought him to the edges of the McGuire place, and he came back often to watch with envy and curiosity the routines and daily events of an active and prosperous farm. He observed the general several times before he confidently walked out of thicket. Thus began a mutual friendship of trust and affection rarely recorded on the American frontier.

CHAPTER 3

On the Hock hocking River
June 1812

Buckskin was well fed, rested, and ready to move; Jim saddled and rearranged his packet and roll. This was new territory. Jim had never gone beyond this turn-off in his frequent journeys with the general. Others at the farm and in Marietta had said that several Indian hunting camps were located on this trail. There were reports that some Shawnees and Delaware, refugees from the battle of Tippecanoe in the Indiana territory the previous year, had returned and reestablished themselves. They were not friendly and were causing problems in the nearby settlements; resentments continued and vigilance was required.

The ground on the trail was hard, as it had been a dry summer. Jim rode with caution and some anxiety. He had spent a lot of time with Indians growing up in Marietta, and many days over the years with Water Bird and her clan of displaced Shawnees. She taught him the basic language of the Algonquin culture, which influenced all northern tribes, and developed an intimate knowledge of the aboriginals' customs. This should be of help when he encountered them. The country around him was still heavily forested, but the undergrowth however was not as dense as the thicket and he was able see some distance when there were breaks in the trees. He rode for several more hours before reaching the Hock hocking River; he found a sheltered cove where he would spend a cold, dark, restless, and hungry night. He unsaddled and watered his horse, collected edible grasses and bushes for him, and tied him to a nearby tree. "I will deal with tomorrow, tomorrow," he said as he wrapped his blanket roll around himself on the cold ground, listening to the drifting river.

Jim awoke at first light, having had little sleep. A slight morning breeze from the east kept the mosquito's down to a tolerable level. Buckskin needed water and pasture; Jim needed food. He went to riverbank with the horse following, noticing no life on the river; he relieved himself, washed his face in the stream, made up camp quickly, saddled up, and journeyed across the river. Here, the current was slow, the water two hundred feet or so across. Jim didn't know how deep it was but he and the buckskin had crossed many a river; neither was hesitant as the water rose to withers height before receding. They quickly picked up the path on the far side and continued to head west. *We need to find pasture and provisions today,* he thought, trying hard not to let feelings of fear and catastrophe overwhelm him.

The ride was uneventful over several hours as they proceeded down a worn path, only wide enough for a horse and rider. Jim noticed the fresh hoof marks of several ponies, and anticipated that he would eventually run into Indians that were using the trail. Although apprehensive, he felt confident that with his comprehension of the native Algonquin language and familiarity with Indian culture he could manage almost any encounter.

The path eventually widened where the dense forest of ash, oak, and hickory covering the hilly terrain of the Appalachian foothills gave way to views of scattered birch and poplars with fields of marsh and swampland. Birds were plentiful and Jim enjoyed their carefree and busy music. He was also watchful for wildlife and opportunities to shoot any form of wild game. His stomach was developing the soft ache he remembered so well from his hunger days. The day was uneventful and Jim and the horse traveled into the evening, crossing several creeks and making another lonely camp.

Jim wondered about the sudden turn of events, some beyond his understanding. There were more questions than answers, and he struggled to control his fears. *I need to be a man, I need to be brave.* The thought rang hollow. *I will do what the general says.* Thoughts of the general dying brought bouts of sadness and grief that left him weak and confused. He awoke early and continued on his journey.

By late morning the sun was warm on his body, encouraging Jim to drift off as he tried to stay alert. Sometime in the early evening on his fourth day of travel, several Indians stepped onto the path several feet in front of him from the shadows of a glen of young poplars. Buckskin was alert and nervous, but stopped at Jim's command. The natives stared at Jim for several moments, unspeaking, observing his posture, demeanor, and the quality of his horse. Jim, fearful, remained silent, maintaining, he hoped, the impression of confidence.

"What business brings you to our land?" The Indian, speaking in good English appeared to be the eldest of the ten or so warriors who had quietly appeared on the trail.

"I am bidding the due of General Jonathon McGuire of Marietta on the Ohio.

I am passing through your territory to labor for a family on the Scioto near the sacred burial grounds of your people." Jim paused, hoping that his words were understood. "I am called Forest Boy by Council Keeper, leader of the Shawnees on the big river."

The men and horses were gathered in a small, cluttered, temporary hunting camp, several yards off the trail where a handful of hutches made of bent willows covered with skins, bark, and mosses were spread randomly in an open meadow next to a large marsh. Several deer were dressed out and hanging from the limbs of a large hemlock. Catfish were being dried on low bushes adjacent the marsh. It was a busy place.

Further away, several women surrounded a grid made of branches on four Y-shaped sticks sitting a foot off the ground, with a smoldering fire underneath. There were pieces of buffalo meat on the grid, being turned by the female attendants. When properly dried, this would be the jerked meat that was the staple of the frontier. Not far away, hanging over another fire, was a boiling pot filled with the fat of a recently killed black bear; this was being rendered to serve mostly as mosquito protection. The boiling blubber presented an offensive stench that was difficult to tolerate.

The spokesman appeared to be the leader of this small hunting party until a much taller man with a slight limp walked up from the marsh. He washed his hands from a gourd of water and approached Jim and the other warriors. He was tall and erect, with a strong presence, although much younger than the elder. He wore a beat-up beaver hat with a white plume, faded, dirty red wool shirt, and deerskin leggings. His long hair hung out of his hat; the streaks of grey suggested a man older than he was. His eyes were dark and deep set, and a strong nose dominated a face with a small scar along the left cheek, which gave him both a distinguished and sinister appearance. A long knife was secured in his leather belt; some bone jewelry around his neck and a bracelet of a dark copper were his only adornments

Jim spoke first in the Algonquin dialect, learned over the years from Water Bird. He hoped it would be understood. The tall aboriginal spoke quietly in a similar dialect.

"Do you seek the war of the northern frontier?" the leader asked, looking at Jim's Kentucky long rifle, a coveted firearm.

"I seek only to fulfill my master General McGuire's wishes

and provide labor for a family in need," Jim said.

The warrior met Jim's eye but didn't speak for some time. "Do you have anything to trade?" he asked.

"I have meager possessions, only sufficient for my survival; I have nothing of value for barter," Jim said. The warrior walked slowly around the horse, on which Jim remained sitting.

After another period of silence and observation, the elder said, "Sit with us; share our pot, for you travel with no provisions."

Jim said, "I have nothing to offer in return, so I am thankful for your generosity."

The tall Indian turned and walked to the cooking pot, where he was handed a bowl of boiled venison. The others followed and joined him around the fire.

Jim dismounted, keeping his rifle in his possession, secured his horse so that he could graze on some bushes, and followed the men to the cooking fire. *Do I trust this man and these people?* He wondered, his heart beating hard. He knew from his years of interaction with originals that he had to show confidence without fear in order to be treated with respect.

A small pot was hanging from a makeshift tripod. The men gathered around the fire,

A young woman poured the food into wooden bowls using a large wooden spoon; the stew was tepid and foul smelling. It included pieces of fish, venison and rabbit in a greasy liquid. Jim tried to eat calmly, but finished his bowl quickly; he did not ask for more and none was offered. They ate for some time without conversation.

When the meal was finished and the women picked up the bowls and wooden spoons; the tall leader wiped his hands on his leather breeches and said, "We too are people of the big river and know the Council Keeper and the general of the white man's war; speak of what you know of recent events. Tell us what the general says about the war on the northern frontier."

Jim talked for some time, mentioning that there had been constant conversation in Marietta over the last three months speculating that President Madison would declare war on Great Britain and attack Canada. Jim, hoping to ease his tension, talked about how the General and his old friends would gather on Saturdays at Bracket's Tavern and talk jokingly about joining up for one last battle. He spoke of the militias marching every Sunday after religious services; how military commerce on the river had increased significantly this spring and government recruiters were trying to enlist young men into the American army, with little success. They were all listening to his words and he was sure that they understood his dialect.

The tall Indian asked if many cannons had been seen on the river since the spring floods. Jim mentioned that he had seen twelve field pieces several weeks ago on flat boats that tied up but only stayed a night; he did not know their destination downriver.

He then asked, "How did you learn our language?" Jim told his story of how Water Bird, Council Keeper's sister, spoke to him in the dialect of the Algonquin language spoken by the Council Keeper's clan. He mentioned his use of the native language with other tribes and clans that passed through or traded in and around Marietta, as it was common to many northern cultures. He knew by the men's dialect and use of words that he was speaking to another Shawnee clan.

The tall leader then spoke again: "The Council Keeper of the Shawnee holds the Paper of the Harmar and thinks he is safe from the white man's greed. He will be a homeless chief in need of the white man's charity. Your general is a good man and always a friend of the Shawnees; he was most generous during the starving years. I call him my friend. We know of you, Forest Boy and you will have safe travel to the sacred mounds and your family."

Jim felt great relief that he would be able to continue his journey, thanked the man for his safe passage, paused for a moment, and asked, "May I know the name of the general's friend so that I too can call him friend?"

The Indian looked at Jim, paused for a minute, and then said in the native dialect, "I am Tecumseh chief of the Shawnee Nation. If you go to the northern frontier and fight in the war, you will find the sons of Pucksinwa and you will be our enemy." He looked into the fire and gestured for his pipe.

Jim knew of the Battle of Tippecanoe November last when the Shawnee suffered a serious defeat and their settlement of Prophet's Town was burned down. It was not his place to ask about this. Jim observed that their hunting appeared successful, and the elder said after a prolonged silence, "The salt lick provides abundance in deer, the marsh water birds, and the creek, many fish."

The men were brought tobacco in a large leather pouch with an assortment of wood and clay pipes. Once they were lit, the smoke hung low and moved slightly in the light breeze. The tall man looked at Jim and said, "You have the General's rifle."

Jim said, "He gave it to me when he sent me on my way. He has owned this rifle since the Great War, a gift from General Greene, after Yorktown. It is old and little used but well cared for and holds its line."

The warriors sitting by the fire talked amongst themselves, no longer showing any interest in the white stranger. Tecumseh stretched out, his back resting on a fallen log, inhaled deeply, and continued to talk, blowing the smoke from the side of his mouth.

"I have sat at your general's table and him at my fire many times for many seasons. He understands the red man's trouble and a fair man who asked of me how the white and red man could live in peace. I told him of my father who died at the hands of the white man when I was a boy; our father was a man of much wisdom who spoke at many fires and with many clans that he feared the white man. He foretold that they would kill the Great Spirit, take our lands, and destroy the forests. The only way to stop this evil is for the red man to unite in claiming common and equal right in the land, as it was forever and should be now. Pucksinwau was the only prophet of the dancing tail clan, when he died I was raised by many: Cheeksaukalo, my brother who let you live today; Tecumpase, my sister; and Black Fish the great chief."

Tecumseh puffed hard on his pipe and continued;

"They all taught me my father's way: work hard, speak and act with honor, a warrior's death is honorable, torture and abuse of your enemy is not the warrior's way. I honor my father's code. He also said the only good white man is a dead white man." Tecumseh chuckled to himself for a moment and there were a few grunts of approval. He paused again while he prepared a second pipe; all the other warriors were now listening intently.

"Soon there will be war; I have raised an alliance of many tribes from all the regions of the land. We will soon join the red coats in Canada and stop the President's army from taking more of our land. In time, the foul General Harrison will die at my hands and Tippecanoe will rest in peace." Jim sat stunned, afraid to reply.

There was silence for a moment, and then Tecumseh raised himself, stamped out his pipe, and said to Jim, "Shoot us a deer with the long rifle at the lick. We go at the moon rise." The warriors left the fire to get ready for the hunt.

The hunters, hiding in the shadows, saw the doe and her yearling in the moonlight, as it broke from the scattered night clouds, coming slowly and quietly to the marsh where the salt was easy to access. Jim readied his weapon, waited for a good shot, and fired. The doe dropped. Her yearling was shot as she desperately bolted away.

They returned to the camp late in the night after killing two more deer and dressed the game by firelight. When they were done Tecumseh told Jim to leave at first light. Dirty and tired Jim eventually rolled into his blanket near his horse, hoping to get some sleep before morning.

Jim arose before dawn and, without any goodbyes, rode Buckskin out of the hunting camp, slowly heading west. He was overwhelmed by the experience. *I know of this great Shawnee and his efforts to bring all the original tribes together to defy the white man. I sat at his fire—the most powerful and dangerous chief in the Northwest Territory.*

He had heard many conversations between the general and the other town folks who took their leisure at Bracket's Tavern and on the green on Saturday after market. They had talked of the Dancing Tail Clan and their leader Tecumseh; or he who walks across the sky; the great leader of all the tribes in the Northwest Frontier. Feared by all as a threat to white settlers who had taken possession of his lands, his brother the Prophet had led and lost the battle near the Tippecanoe River in the Indiana territory the previous fall.

He thanked his good fortune that he did not inquire about the battle that the Indians lost, caused primarily by the Prophet's poor leadership. He knew the clan had broken up after their village, Prophet's Town, was burned to the ground by the victorious and vengeful General Harrison. There was much shame in the clan at this time.

Jim also recalled the General telling stories about the starving years, when he and several area farmers took several sled loads of corn, potatoes, and frozen beef to the Shawnees near Greenville during the bitter winter and spring of 1802.

Tecumseh and his group of hunters would finish their labors this day. They had no more interest in the foolhardy young traveler. Another day at this site would provide ample fish and game, properly smoked and dried, to last the clan for several months.

Other family groups of the Shawnee were doing the same across northern and central Ohio.

Soon the Dancing Tail clan would unite with all the other Shawnee families on the Maumee River, then travel to Fort Malden near Amherstburg in Canada at the confluence of Lake Erie and the Detroit River. There they would join the British and many other northern tribes for the long-awaited war against the occupiers. Here, too, they could take vengeance for the shame of the Tippecanoe.

All the aboriginals knew the peace was a temporary arrangement, tolerated by the white man, and would not last long much longer.

"The white man wants all land, everywhere, forever," wise leaders of the many clans and tribes said as they looked into a bleak future.

Jim did not see any more originals in his travel across this unsettled territory, except for another hunting camp that was some distance from the trail. The Indians stood and watched but made no move to communicate and he continued on without stopping or speaking. Signs of white civilization became more visible as he approached the Scioto. Several farms on the riverbanks were active in their summer dress; others were abandoned or burnt out, standing stark and forsaken in this green land, victims of Indian raids in previous years.

Jim and Buckskin traveled two more days in warm summer weather before reaching the Scioto, crossing and resting on the Licking River for a half a day, where pasture and easy fishing for catfish replenished their energy. The path was wider now and easier to follow as the landscape flattened out to smaller rolling hills, with dense forests mixed with open meadows and marshland. Jim was on disputed land from here to the Scioto. The general had told many stories and often talked about the Indians' continual push west ward, forced by the white man's unrelenting and encroaching civilization.

White settlers had established homesteads in this area west of the hills, which was still populated by a mixture of several tribes and clans, many of which had been forced back from the coastal areas years before. The combination of indigenous natives and settlers resulted in an uneasy arrangement that frequently broke out in territorial skirmishes. Remnants of Iroquois, Delaware, Pawnee, and Shawnee groups integrated into hunter/gatherer communities trying to maintain the only life they knew, struggling with a violated culture and the omnipresence of the occupiers.

The hatred between them resulted in two decades of violent conflict, with many white and Indian casualties. The land, however, was prosperous and less dense than the foothills as the land flattened; dark, rich soil and flowing water generated an abundance of game and grains to sustain the populations.

Jim did not stop to meet the inhabitants, as he was anxious to find the Hicks' home; here, he hoped to find shelter and hospitality among the friends of the general. He would then have time to think out his future. He passed several farms and homesteads then came to a creek that entered the Scioto from the east without much notice; this must be Owl Creek. He had followed it upstream for less than a mile when he saw the two oak trees sheltering a small homestead. This was the place. He recalled the general's words: "Be careful here, make sure you know Jeddah Hicks before you share your identity"... Jim wondered at the secrecy and worried about being careful.

CHAPTER 4

Scioto River
June 1812

Journal Entry
Jonathon McGuire
February 2nd, 1806
Maggie Hill

'*Twas introduced today by Mr. Moody at the 1st Congregational church to an engaging family that is most interested in our endeavors and expresses curiosity in our cause. Jed Hicks and his wife Abigail, a couple in their mid years, have purchased a 240 acre parcel north of the capital on the Scioto River; they are staying with the Maxton family and preparing to continue downriver to Portsmouth town and then upriver to their homestead. They appear to be a most serious, industrious, and very well educated couple with two offspring approaching adulthood, both with a serious countenance. Her father is the Parson at the Chillicothe Methodist Church. They expect to be on their property in late April and, with the help of the preacher and his flock, will prepare themselves with ample shelter and sustenance. They hope to have a kitchen garden and some acreage this summer to help them through the difficult winter. They have done our work in the aid and abetment of our dark friends and, in time, will be ideally situated to be of great assistance. I told them I would visit on my next trip to Columbus.*

"It was dark and brittle today and caused my knee much discomfort. A cold wind with snow is now adding to this long season. It is best this day is over."

It was late afternoon when Jim approached the front door of the modest but well maintained house; he remained saddled, awaiting a response. Soon, a comely lady of modest proportions and middle age opened the front door and stepped out cautiously.

"What is your business?" she asked suspiciously.

"Pardon the intrusion, ma'am," he said. "I only inquire as to your need for some common labor. I am competent in most agricultural functions and fully able to perform them. I seek only some grain and pasture for my horse and some provisions for myself."

She observed him in a speculative, untrusting manner for several moments. "What is your name, where do you come from and your destination?" she asked.

"Jim is my name, ma'am," he said. I have traveled from the Ohio to enlist in the army of the northern frontier, for there is war coming."

She continued to observe him for several more minutes. "There is work, to be sure. If you are the man you describe, then I welcome your assistance," she said. "Walk your horse to the barn. You will find water, barley, and hay; I will be by shortly to make your acquaintance and show you to your duties."

Jim walked Buckskin into the corral; two horses in modest condition were standing idle, waiting for their daily hay ration.

The barn was of modest proportions, one story, with a loft that was nearly empty of forage and would need more before the present crop was harvested. He unsaddled the horse, led him to water, found the grain, and fed all three animals. When they were settled, he surveyed his surroundings. The buildings appeared to be recently constructed. The barn was made of rough-hewn wood, sixty feet in length with a height of only ten feet. The one story had an elevated section six feet above the main floor and covering half the length of the barn. This area stored the hay and straw while the lower level had twelve stables that housed six cows on one side and six horses on the other. There were no oxen to be seen.

A corral, small in size, bordered the main entry into the barn. The horses, now curious, watched Jim's every move; four Guernsey cows stood idle in a nearby overgrazed pasture adjoining the corral, soon to be milked.

Adjoining the barn was an empty hog pen, with no sign of any recent activity; a well built hen house was active at this time of day with a good twenty fowl conducting business. A smokehouse, also well constructed, was near the well halfway to the house, which stood on a small hill, surrounded by a dozen hemlocks that provided a windbreak and shelter. A vegetable garden, also in need of attention, was located on the south side of the home.

Jim could see that, in all aspects, this farm needed labor. He had seen only the woman and wondered where her husband and children were. Most noticeable was the over forty acres of corn, almost knee high but in dire need of cultivation. If not dealt with soon, the entire field would be overcome by weeds. There were still several hours of daylight; Jim needed to burn energy, sweat, and labor, to get back to the things he knew well, and to find some purpose to occupy his anxious mind. He did not wait for the woman to return. He searched the barn and quickly found the working harness. The horses were excited at the opportunity to be harnessed and he led them to where both a one-handled and a corn plow were stored. He selected the corn plow, best used for cultivation and easily managed with a two-horse team. He hitched them up and proceeded to the field. He felt the soil under his feet; took the lines in his left hand and guided the plough with his right.

The horses were well trained and instantly felt confidence in Jim's direction; they moved easily. Jim focused on his labor and took comfort in the familiar smells and activities. For a few hours, his fears would be set aside.

Abigail Hicks stood on her back porch and watched this young man, filled with energy and competence, as he walked the rows. He spoke hardly a word to manage the horses, who responded well to his controls. He worked until dark and, in the last of the shadows, returned the horses to the barn and prepared them for rest. Abigail had already milked and serviced the cows and returned them to pasture. She waited until his chores were finished and walked to the barn with some cold chicken, boiled potato, and cider.

Who is this young man? Why did he come here? She wondered. But her initial fears subsided as she began to feel confidence in his presence.

"I have brought you dinner and some soap and towels for your comfort. I see you have your own blanket; the loft offers a good sleeping quarter. Draw your water from the trough, it needs to be replenished," she said. She felt herself talking faster, with more authority than usual, and wondered why. The young man stood silently, nodding his head at her comments. She watched him eat. "What is your age, Jim? Do you have family?" she asked. He took a long drink of the cider. I am eighteen years old, ma'am," he said. "My mother is known to me, although I have not spent much time with her due to unfortunate circumstances."

Abigail was going to ask another question and thought better of it. "I am at the house if you are in need of assistance," she said.

She started to leave when Jim said, "Thank you, ma'am, for the food and lodging. I will continue to cultivate tomorrow if you wish."

"Please continue, but do not overwork the horses. Good night," she said from a distance. Jim felt good. Sweat, sore muscles, and fatigue were welcome to him; it gave him comfort to be productive and of value. He would sleep easy this night.

Jim was in the fields at first light, hitched and ready to plow. The soreness in his body left quickly as the plow broke the earth and turned over the weeds to reveal a rich soil. He could do two or three acres a day if the weather and horses held up.

He worked steady into mid morning, then rested and watered the team. Abigail watched Jim work and admired his energy. She brought a lunch out to the field when he took his break. , "I believe I can work these horses for about six hours a day. They respond well but fatigue fast and may need a day off every several days. The hay and pasture are good, but you will run out of grain in a week or so. Should get the field cultivated in ten to twelve days if there's no rain." Jim said.

"So you plan on staying for awhile then?" Abigail asked.

Jim said, "There is work that needs tending to: the root cellar, fencing on the front pasture, cleaning out the pigs and cow sheds…"

She pondered for a minute. "You're welcome to stay and work. I cannot pay wages for labor but you have a roof and provisions from my table; if that agrees with your intentions?"

Nothing more was said for the moment. Jim hoped he had a new home. He had lived with a constant fear due to the ever-present threats of his deranged stepfather, who vowed to kill him, and the memory of his lonely summer in the thicket. These fears continued to reappear in spite of the sanctuary provided by the general over these many years and Jim did not want to return to the solitary existence that he had known so long ago. If the general was no longer a part of his life, he would try to find someone else he could care for and who would care for him. He did not want to be on his own, to fight a war with strangers. He wasn't ready yet.

"Would you be Mrs. Hicks?" Jim asked quite spontaneously after dinner that evening.

"I would be her and how do you know my name?" she asked.

"General McGuire sent me to seek your refuge and to be of service to you and Mr. Hicks. The general was quite ill when I left, he sent me north away from Mr. Sprout." Jim was talking fast now, all of his thoughts pouring out. "I am not to return. He directed me to find my fortune with the army of the northern frontier, for there is to be war soon.

He gave me his Kentucky rifle and the buckskin I rode in on. The general was very ill; I am afraid he was soon to pass, and I left without any goodbyes, in the dark of night. He was so insistent." Jim wanted to cry and scream out his fears. He held back, however, trying hard not to show his feelings.

Abigail was silent as she absorbed and comprehended all that was said. "So you are Jim, the general's student?" She already knew the answer.

"Yes, ma'am," he said. "You know of me?"

"He talked of you frequently, with great affection and was quite proud of your accomplishments. I am saddened by the thought of the general's death." She paused for a moment and continued in a quiet voice. "My husband Jed took fever and left us in March last. My son is on a mission with the church; I have sent for him and desperately await his arrival. My father, the proctor of the Methodist Church in Chillicothe, sent two hands to assist me; they both ran off after planting. My daughter of seven-teen years is with her husband, a trader in Cincinnati. I refuse to leave my land. This is my home. So; Master Jim, you have come at a good time. You do know of your mentor's mission to assist the black slaves of the south?" Jim replied that he knew that the gen-eral and others in Marietta were active in helping slaves, but they were very secretive and did not share much information; the gen-eral disappeared on occasion for several days at a time and would only say he had been working for freedom and liberty. "There is more to talk about, but it will wait for another time. There is work to do now," said Mrs. Hicks. She then turned and walked back to the house with great anticipation. *He comes at a critical time. This is most opportune,* she thought.

CHAPTER 5

Maumee River, Ohio
June 1812

The Shawnee hunting party that Jim had left a week before broke camp and left late on the following day. Tecumseh left earlier than the clan, preoccupied with his mission to bring as many Indians as he could to join the British in this new war. The Dancing Tail Clan trekked north along the trails established by the aboriginals generations ago to facilitate travel and commerce. The days were long and without incident. They followed the Muskingum, carefully crossed Zane's Trace and then followed the Licking River in a northwesterly direction. They traveled through open plains, woodlands, and occasional stands of virgin forests; they crossed numerous creeks and several rivers. The party encountered a few whites who nervously watched them go by their small farms and hamlets; the few travelers that crossed their paths made wide berths, neither side interested in a confrontation.

On the fifth day, they paused on the Sandusky River, resting the horses for the arduous journey through the great swamp. It was June and the water level was low; the horses would be able to walk through the deeper sections. The bear grease would provide some relief from the unrelenting swarms of mosquitoes that could drive both man and beast crazy. The travels spent only one night in the heart of the swamp; two long days brought them to the northern boundaries, where the clan rested for a day. Cheeksuakalo now led his people at a faster pace, pushing harder to reach their destination. On the eighth day they reached the great Indian gathering grounds on the banks of the Maumee River and settled in to await their leader. The smoke of the Shawnee nation fires hung low under grey skies. Hundreds of warriors were gathered with their women, children, and elders. They were prepared to fight the foreigners one more time.

Tecumseh reappeared early on the second day. He came from the west with two score warriors and was well worn from several days of hard riding. The camp became electric upon his arrival as they rallied around him, waiting to hear his great words. "Stay busy with your business; get ready to move at the dawn. I will meet with the leaders at the fire," he said. He stood erect and strong on his six-foot frame. His dress on this day was simple: a deerskin vest over a red cloth hunting shirt, with a leather breech cloth, knee-high leggings, and soft moccasins. His belt held a pistol, hatchet, and long knife. He met with his clan, gave instructions to others, bathed in the cold waters of the Maumee, and then slept for several hours.

The camp immediately busied itself with preparations; the women and young boys speared the sturgeons that gathered in the shallows this time of year and prepared the fires for a fish boil. The men attended to their horses and weaponry, the youth talked of the travels into unknown territory and speculated on the courage, aroma, behavior, and gifts of the king's white men. The night sky was old when leaders of the twenty-seven clans that made up the Shawnee nation gathered close around several small fires. Tecumseh stood tall and talked loud for all to hear. Only the leaders were allowed close to the fires; the others stood farther away, trying to catch an occasional phrase of the great leader.

THE END AND THE BEGINNING

"*The family of mighty Pucksinwau welcomes you, my brothers of the many clans that make up the Shawnee nation. Only Dark Hoof stays in his village, awaiting the dominion of the white man. Many of our brothers from the west have already joined us north of the great Lake. I come to you to tell you of great victories soon to be ours against the Americans.*

"*Brothers the only way to stop this evil is for all red men to unite in claiming a common and equal right to the land, as it was at first and should be now—for it was never divided and belongs to all. Selling our country to another is not of our understanding. Why not sell the air, the clouds, the great sea, and all the forests. The Great Spirit, the master of life, made this earth for the use of all of his children.*

"*I have traveled for many sunsets far to south of the great river to have our brothers the Creeks, Cherokees, and Pottawatomie to join us. They too choose the dominion of the white man, soon to be destroyed and enslaved.*

"*My brothers of the many fires, I have talked to the king's generals and they claim they do not seek to own the land, only to use it as we do. Brothers, hear me: I know of the king's treachery. Trusting in his words is like allowing the wolf to sleep with our children. The British seek our assistance in this new war against our enemies and, when victorious, will sign a paper that honors the wishes of the Great Spirit. The northern nation awaits us at Fort Malden with food, weapons, and many gifts. My brothers, leaders of the great Shawnee nation, we go north at first light to join the redcoats in this Great War. We will avenge for all time the shame placed upon us by the Patriot leader and his people.*"

It took a day to cross the Maumee; they then sailed by boat, supplied by the British, to reach the British encampment at Fort Malden. Over two thousand Indians from Canada and the North West Territory joined the army of the redcoats.

The American Army did not actively recruit native warriors and only a handful of scouts were with General Hull when the first shots of the war of 1812 were fired at Fort Detroit.

CHAPTER 6

Marietta, Ohio
June 1812

Anna noticed Digger lying in the sun on the side of the cottage; she was beginning to accept the reality that she, too, had lost everything. She called and Digger slowly walked to Anna's side. She hugged her for a moment and they shared their grief. Digger would spend her days at the general's grave site; Anna found the time to bring food and water, in which she showed little interest, and sit with her for awhile. After dark, Digger walked back to the cottage and lay by the door. Over time, Digger spent more time with Anna, watching her as she went about her work. On occasion, she returned to the gravesite and spent a large part of a warm afternoon sleeping on the new grass; Anna often wondered what they were talking about. Early in the morning and some evenings, she would notice Digger sitting on the bluff, looking out over the Muskingum River where it enters the Ohio, as if to see if her friend Jim would be returning. Both of them took some comfort in being together and sharing their loneliness; they became inseparable.

Anna struggled through the summer. The general's daughter, Virginia, tried hard to keep the farm operating smoothly. The help, both indentured and hired, worked deliberately but cautiously, watching for any signs that Joshua would take control of the farm. Conversations among the help were quiet and private. They discussed what would occur with all of them concerned about their futures. Anna often labored into the night, helping Virginia in her kitchen and laundry; they spoke little of the traumatic events that changed their lives on that June day. Anna desperately missed both the general and Jim. Digger was at her side most of every day, but disappeared whenever she smelled the presence of Joshua.

The general, Anna felt, had saved her life several years prior when he purchased her indenture from the Mowatt family of Pleasant County, Virginia, who owned a laundry. The Mowatt's were miserable people among whom drunkenness was a common occurrence. They worked very little. Most of the labor was performed by Anna, who would carry heavy pails of hot water to the wash tubs and then scrub, wring, and hang clothes by hand. The hours were long and the additional work of cleaning the house and carrying for two younger children gave her no respite or hope of anything but misery for many years to come. The Mowatt's labor focused mostly on the making and consumption of corn whiskey. From the beginning, Anna fought off almost daily sexual assaults from both the oldest son, Jerkin, and his father.

She ran away frequently, and was always treated abusively upon her return. She was fifteen years old when she ran all night and for the last time, from their miserable hard scrapple homestead to the Ohio River and then across on a leaky and rickety fishing skiff she found tied near the landing at the Potters' fishing camp. She tried her best to get across the river, but heavy currents from recent rains forced her further downriver. It was a little after dawn when a solitary fisherman tending his lines, seeing her struggle, brought her aboard and rowed hard for an hour to the shelter of Marietta. He was a young man, quiet, and didn't ask any questions. Anna didn't volunteer any information, saying only that she wanted to be put ashore anywhere on the Ohio side.

He rowed up to small pier on Marietta's waterfront. "Go to the congregational church up Harbor Street and ask for Mrs. Moody," he said. "She will assist you. I will return the skiff to the Potters. Good luck." The fisherman, whose name she didn't know but whom she would always remember, left her there, wet and all alone.

Anna's life had never been easy. She was born in the province of Varmland, Sweden, one of three girls and two boys who, with their parents and one grandparent, lived as crofters on a small plot of rented farm land where the family, after sharing the meager harvests of potatoes and other garden vegetables each fall, would not have sufficient provisions to carry the family through the winter months. Her father, a quiet, non-complaining man, worked when he could as a woodcutter. Her mother took in laundry and served as a midwife when called. It was a bitterly poor home, where starvation always threatened, particularly in the winter and early spring. The family had little time for anything but survival.

When Anna was ten, her father took ill with consumption and became bedridden. Her mother turned Anna over to the poor relief authorities as a parish pauper child, and she was soon auctioned to an American family as an indentured servant for seven years.

The price at auction covered Anna's transport to America and a month's ration of food for her family. On the day she left her home, her father was crying from his bed. They hugged briefly; it was the only embrace she ever remembered from him. Her mother, with desperation in her voice, encouraged her to work hard and find a way to bring the family over before her father died.

Anna upon her arrival in Marietta and with the help of Mrs. Moody found work as a washerwoman at Medlien's Boarding House on Picketed Point at the confluence of the Muskingum and Ohio rivers. It was difficult in the wild, violent, and abusive world on the riverfront. After Anna survived a serious assault, she was attended to by members of the 1st congregational church where Virginia befriended her and brought her to the general's farm to recover.

The last three years had been the best of her young life. She labored primarily in the kitchen and laundry, and developed a warm and trustful relationship with Virginia as they worked together on many household projects. They shared a common interest in animals and flowers, particularly Maggie's roses. From the beginning, she was an outspoken girl with a witty demeanor, making her quite popular with the other farm laborers. The general was fond of her and encouraged her curiosity and inquiry. She had a way with animals and he accused her in jest of stealing Jim's dog Digger from him. She cherished the infrequent moments when he would read to her from books of particular interest to the general at the time. Her favorite moments were when she could spend time with young Jim, whom she knew, would be her life's companion. He had no idea of course, but that was okay. They had time. Joshua Sprout was resentful of her popularity and endless energy. She felt uncomfortable feeling in his presence and avoided any interactions with him.

CHAPTER 7

Washington County Court House
Marietta
July 1812

Virginia and Joshua Sprout rode down the hill in their one-horse buggy to the Washington County Court House. The cool morning was beginning to give way to a humid and hot day. It has been a month to the day since the general's death, and Joshua was impatient to get this business over with. He did not know the contents of the general's last will and testament, but he was confident that everything would be left to Virginia. Joshua would then control one of the most prosperous farms in the Muskingum and Ohio River Valley. He would be a powerful man, respected by everyone.

His ambitions were endless and he was anxious to begin. At the time of the general's death, he had been told by the county judge, Heywood Mather, not to make any changes or sell any property until the estate of General Jonathon McGuire was settled. Judge Mather's reading of the last will and testament this morning should give him this power.

Joshua paid little attention to Virginia, who had not been herself since her father's departure. She was mostly quiet and subdued, but worked tirelessly in the management and daily operation of the farm. She had still not spoken more than a few words to her husband since the general's death, and spent as much time as possible with her friends at the Congregational church, escorted on some of her trips into Marietta by the laundry maid Anna Erickson.

I will show everyone; Virginia will come around when I take over, Joshua thought as the buggy pulled up to the courthouse entrance.

Upon completion of formal introductions and an inquiry as to any questions, the Magistrate, Henry Wooten, removed the official document from the safe and opened it for all to witness. He informed the group that, in response to the general's wishes, his last will and testament would be read aloud. Guests at the proceedings included Virginia, Joshua, Sheriff Micah Miller, bank trustee Willford Connor, and Rufus Putnam, executor of the estate. Mr. Wooten handed the document to Judge Mather.

My final Will and Testimony

I begin my last worldly task by thanking all of you invited to bear witness to the disposal of my material wealth. You have all benefited me; permit me to express my profound gratitude. I have many wishes and desires that I beg to have fulfilled on a day that is unbeknownst to me.

All my documents and correspondence of value to persons present and future I will to the Washington County trustees for placement and safekeeping within the library. I ask that this same body deliberate and act wisely in the maintenance and distribution of these documents.

To all the maidservants, indentures, and helpers on my properties, who labored tirelessly on behalf of my family and contributed to our prosperity, I disperse my resources in the following manner. To Charles Sumner and Wendell Petrol, who have been with us since the beginning, one hundred

American Dollars. To Penelope Merritt and Henry Pennmetter, loyal ser-
vants, fifty American Dollars to each and To Anna Erickson, fifty American
Dollars my books of poetry, and the collection of butterflies that we both
so admired. Any who may still be beholden of an indenture ship or other
contract of labor that may restrict their freedoms, I release from said debt and
wish them god speed and benevolence. I do, however, require that they remain
in the employ of my daughter for one year from this date in order to receive
the aforementioned inheritance.

To the Church of the Congregation of Marietta, I offer the sum of
five hundred American Dollars to sustain their effort to provide sanctu-
ary and welfare to any and all fugitive slaves who may request assistance,
and to promote their efforts toward the Abolition of slavery in our great
country.

To Madam Elva Johnson, Proprietor of Becket's Tavern and Inn I
bequeath the sum of fifty American Dollars to offer to all friends and associ-
ates a serving of rum until such funds are exhausted.

To Mr. James Morgan, my faithful student and honest friend, who gave
me more than I could ever offer him, a sum of 240 acres of deeded and
secured property commonly referred to as the Thicket, for him to husband
and develop in such a manner that assists in his prosperity. The said section
of land has been surveyed, dated, and documented for this purpose by the
firm of Henry Montague. Mr. Morgan will be required to take possession
of said property no later than four years from the date of the execution of
my estate. Upon possession, He will be prohibited from selling or financing
said property until the day of his majority. If he fails to claim the land as
set forth herein, it will be placed in the governance of my family as directed
in this document.

To my dearest daughter and most precious friend, Virginia, I bequeath
all of my remaining assets and treasures in her name only to manage and
perform in her best interests and at her discretion.

I have appointed General Rufus Putnam as trustee of my estate to
oversee its dispersal and to provide such assistance to my daughter as deemed
necessary and to determine the time and place at which she will assume full

fiduciary responsibility.
  I trust in the gracious God and his mercy.

John McGuire
Brigadier General
Continental Army

Joshua sat in disbelief, his knuckles white as they grasped the arms of his chair, his face red with rage; it was only a moment until he roared with frustration and anger: "He can't do this; I have slaved on this land and will not be without value. I have legal title to this land. This is my farm and they owe me everything." His voice was loud; he began to rise from his chair. Sheriff Miller moved forward somewhat tentatively, urging him to calm down while trying to escort him to the door. "And that bastard kid getting the Thicket; He is a wanted felon and will come to justice. He can't do this." The Sheriff asked him to hold his temper. Joshua ignored the sheriff and stormed out of the courthouse.

Upon Joshua's departure, Virginia rose quietly from her chair and approached the large desk. She signed several documents that ensured her inheritance, shook the hand of all present, nodded a thank you, and turned to leave. She walked out of the courthouse to the horse and buggy and, with a gentle flick of the reins, began the journey back to the farm alone.

Joshua spent the afternoon in McIntosh's Tavern on the point, drinking rum with several of his cronies and ranting over the general's injustice and how the town leadership was out to get him. The more he drank, the more he talked and bellowed his frustrations and anger. After several hours of rampage, while buying patrons an occasional round to keep them as an audience he started talking about revenge. He rambled through a litany of actions and individuals who would experience his wrath; the patrons quietly scattered, not wanting to be a party to his threats.

Eventually, Mack McIntosh, the long-suffering innkeeper, encouraged Joshua to leave; it was late afternoon when he staggered out the side door wobbled down Front Street to Connor's Stable, borrowed a horse over the protests of the stable boy, and headed over to the little Muskingum River to seek out Elizur Kirkwood and his whiskey maker. For many years Joshua and Elizur would gather at the still and go on heavy drinking bouts usually lasting several days.

The still was several miles up the creek, hidden in a small gully in a heavily wooded area. Joshua, who had spent a great deal of time with Elizur in his earlier years, developing a taste for his homemade corn liquor, knew the trail almost by heart. The shadows were deep when he approached and hailed the whisky maker. Elizur stoked the fire, poured the whisky, and they settled in for a long night.

For years, Elizur, one of the original squatters on this land, had roamed the forests north of the Thicket that abutted the Little Muskingum River. He had lived a solitary life since several years earlier when Molly, his wife of two years and Jim Morgan's mother, left his violent beatings, drunken stupors, and indolent behavior and sought the comfort and relative safety of her recently widowed sister Daisy. Molly and Elizur never divorced, but led separate and independent lives except for the husband's uninvited visits to his wife and sister's farm and the ongoing threats to harm her son who was now safely in the care of general McGuire

Daisy Whitney's husband, Alfred, was an industrious man who had recently died of consumption. He had spent all of his time on the small piece of bottom land given to him by Amos Calvin for two years of labor, clearing land and building a grand house. Daisy inherited forty acres of well-developed creek side land with a good well, ten acres in pasture and another ten in cultivation. The property had a small but well-maintained house, barn, and several other modest buildings. The sisters worked a sizable garden, and husbanded several cows, pigs, and a large flock of chickens while raising Jim's younger sister, Amy. Their labor allowed them to scratch out a modest and frugal living.

Their sanctuary, soon after Molly moved in, was threatened by the occasional and unwelcome visits of Elizur, who managed to disrupt their lives with his abusive threats and demands for sexual gratification. His drunken behavior was tolerated for a time but, as his visits increased, they knew that his threats of violence would soon become very real.

Elizur came one evening, whiskey jug in hand, determined to force his dominance, to have his woman and take her home. She refused his demands and, when he smashed his fist into Molly's face, he felt the cold end of a musket pointed in his ear. Daisy was determined to eliminate this threat from their lives. Molly, quickly recovering from the brutal blow, stood close, her face bloody, pointing a knife to his throat. Her words were brief: "Get off our property and never come back." He was sober enough to recognize the seriousness of his situation and backed slowly away, leaving the property quickly and quietly. The sisters knew there was more work to be done this night; they hid Amy in the woods that bordered the farm and prepared for Molly's husband's return. As expected, Elizur came back later in the darkness to seek his revenge. He drunkenly approached the house, staying in the shadows, protecting the firebrand he had cupped in his hand. Molly was well hidden along the fence where they knew Elizur would approach the house. She was the first to attack, hitting him on the shin with the back of the long-handled ax; as he fell, both sisters were upon him. Molly with the ax handle and Daisy with a wooden club made of birch. The attack lasted for several minutes, with all the rage from years of abuse and humiliation pouring out of the sisters. Elizur fell helpless; overwhelmed by the intensity and violence of the blows upon his body. The beating stopped and there was silence except for the heavy breathing of the sisters and barely audible moans from the victim. They dragged his thin, beaten, and bloodied body down to the creek trail and left him there, semi-conscious and barely alive.

Their adrenaline spent, they walked quietly back to the house. Amy ran out from hiding and the three hugged for a long time. When they had regained their strength, Daisy asked, "Should we kill him?" Molly thought for a moment and said, "No. This is enough for now."

Elizur lay without movement for some time. Eventually, he was able to get his bearings and crawl away. He revived himself in the creek, wiped the blood from his battered face, and made his way painfully to his run-down, dilapidated two-room shack on Martin's Creek. He spent the better part of a painful month recovering from numerous contusions and lacerations. His hand was broken and he suffered from blurred vision. He nursed his wounds, plotted his revenge, and made his whiskey.

One night a month after the assault, with his wounds healed and his vision restored, he came back to the sisters' farm. Standing on the creek trail, he took aim and shot one of their cows, the best milker.

The sisters recognized then that the feud with Elizur was not over, and that it would soon lead to severe consequences. They discussed all of their options in great detail. They knew he would never leave them alone and, short of murder, they had few alternatives. Going to the law was not seriously considered. The sisters had come to this land as squatters and grew up in a hill culture that was suspicious of authority; neither lady trusted any government representative, particularly Deputy Sheriff Miller, whose history of temerity and inactivity in difficult situations and his enjoyment of Elizur's whiskey meant that he could not be trusted. Furthermore, no one from town would be of assistance to a family of squatters.

After much deliberation, they finally decided to visit General McGuire and request his help. The general had intimate knowledge of the history and circumstances of the bitter and vengeful Elizur, primarily due to his sponsorship of young Jim at age eleven, three years earlier. They would go in the morning.

The general had had a few encounters with Jim's stepfather over the years. The general himself had threatened his life and livelihood if any harm came to Jim or his mother. Elizur stayed away but, whenever the whisky and an audience allowed, would make violent threats against the general, his own estranged wife, and young Jim.

Elizur's recent actions had violated the previous understanding. The plan the sisters proposed, however, was somewhat unorthodox.

Journal Entry
Jonathon McGuire
Maggie Hill Farm
September 1808

> *"I must say it was most unusual day. At 10:00 this a.m. I was writing a letter of Commerce to the Cider Works of Cincinnati to explore the purchase of a new apple press when I was interrupted by Young Jim's mother Molly, her older sister Daisy, and Jim's sister Amy standing in my doorway, most nervous and fidgety. I asked of their health, arranged for refreshments, talked about Jim's well being, and awaited their business. It seems that they would like me to mediate a feud between the sisters and Molly's husband, albeit estranged. I knew somewhat of the hostile engagements that have been occurring these past two years since she left him at the time of Jim's escape into the thicket with nary a blanket or coat...*

"I recall my one visit with Elizur, a most repulsive man, who if not for the quality of his fine corn whiskey, all of his reputable customers in the county, and his long-suffering mother, would be put off the charter land he squats on. My objective at that time was to ensure that he would desist in any malicious or felonious activities directed at Jim, whom I had just taken into my guardianship. I was most explicit of the repercussions that Elizur would incur if he failed to comply with my directive. He agreed and ceased with all threats and aggressive action against my student.

"The ladies and I walked outside to enjoy our cider when I observed the aforementioned standing down on the thicket trail with his misbegotten mule and tired old hound dog. Molly, in a most nervous state, told me about the violent encounters that had occurred this summer, and asked that I protect them from Elizur and the evil deeds he has been perpetrating on them. I inquired as to her marital status and Molly confirmed that she continued to have legal duty to her husband. I suggested that this creates a most difficult circumstance.

"Molly and her vocal sister presented a plan and asked that I negotiate with Elizur; they felt that he is in fear of me and will agree and comply with all expectations.

"I mentioned that this was an unconventional contract. Molly was prepared to provide and perform her wifely duties on limited conditions, and to provide provisions and laundry once each month. In return, Elizur would do no harm to the sisters' persons or property.

"I asked Wendell to secure a stronger jug of cider and, upon its deliverance, walked down the path to where the other party was waiting. Mr. Kirkwood was most accommodating; he accepted the cider that was offered, listened to the offer as I presented it, and only asked how often he could

visit with his wife. I informed him that oral contracts were binding and, if he violated any part of the agreement, I would see that he was removed from the grant land where he was in illegal habitation and engaged in elicit commerce.

"Upon his agreement, he left, leading his mule into the thicket. The sisters and I spent some time in chatter; they expressed great relief and appreciation for my humble effort. I do hope for their sakes that the ruffian mends his ways. Jim came by and they had a warm chat before the sisters and family departed.

It was a most unusual negotiation; I dare say it was a bountiful day."

So it was agreed by the sisters and Elizur that he would come to the sisters' farm and have his way with Molly, who felt it was still her duty as a married woman to meet the sexual desires of her husband. This would occur, however, only if he presented himself sober and with acceptable hygiene.

He, in turn, agreed not to injure any animals, and to refrain from destroying any property and bothering any of the sisters' family at any time and for any reason. Visits could not occur more than once per month. He was required to announce his arrival at the end of the lane that came off the creek trail, wait an hour, and Molly would come to him. He would then be served a hot meal in the yard, given a sack of provisions, and expected to leave.

There was no written document that defined the agreement, as Elizur could not read at all and Molly very little. The arrangement, however, worked for the most part; over the past three years, the sisters felt some degree of safety, although there were times when they knew Elizur was in the cottonwoods near the creek, watching them going about their daily labor.

Elizur always wanted to stay longer during his visits and enjoy some social time with his wife; none was offered. He generated hatred and disgust in these two determined women who, he knew firsthand, had the desire and wherewithal to do him bodily harm. He always left without lingering, knowing that there was a musket pointed at his back most of the time he was there.

Molly felt good that her son Jim was in the safekeeping of the general and would be until his majority; she was, however, envious of the special relationship they had, and she regretted the lack of time she had with her son, as he had become a busy and energetic boy with a curious mind. Their visits were becoming more infrequent and never lasted long enough for her.

She would frequently recall that terrible spring night long ago when Jim, still a young boy of eleven to protect his mother from another brutal beating by her new husband, his stepfather, swung an ax into the shoulder of Elizur. The blow went deep in to the flesh, leaving a large gash that nearly killed him. Filled with fear for her son, Molly told Jim to run into the woods and hide from the drunken Elizur, who was soon able to rise to his feet. He stopped the bleeding by filling the long, deep gash with mud from the creek, and wrapped it awkwardly in an old grain sack. He staggered to the creek and buried his head in the cold water, searching for some sobriety. In a few minutes, he grabbed Molly by her hair and told her "your son is a dead man" He rested for a few minutes, finished his jug with several hefty swigs, and entered the forest to hunt the boy down.

Jim had spent a lot of time in the dense woods, creeks, and marshlands that surrounded the small farm that Jim's dad had built before his death. He was comfortable being alone, and was able to find his way in the thick undergrowth and on the few trails that provided for transport. Molly trusted that Jim would be able to live in the woods much better than in town. She came from second-generation squatters, who moved from the Shenandoah Valley in Virginia in 1785 and defied every effort by the government to chase them off the free land of the Ohio. They were burned out twice but her family, of Scot-Irish descent, kept moving further back into denser hollows and eking out a living with a few pigs, small clearings where corn was planted in mounds Indian style, and all the game they could shoot. It was a hard life, but these families of hill people would seek no other.

Upon leaving his mother, Jim ran as fast as the darkness allowed to Elizur's still, where he proceeded to pick up an ax and, in a night with little moon, did his best to destroy the coils, buckets, and tubs that Elizur kept there. After several minutes in a tearful and rage-filled assault on the evil whisky maker, he threw down the ax, exhausted. He left the site to begin his sojourn in the wild. Molly survived the attack and left immediately with Amy, the two cows, and a few personal belongings to find refuge at her sister's farm. Elizur would spend the summer nights, when he wasn't making whiskey with his repaired still, searching the thicket with his old hound dog to find and kill young Jim Morgan.

Molly was most grateful when the general and Jim came to her on an October day and proposed that the general assume the guardianship and provide for the welfare of her son. She placed her printed name on the document and cried great tears for this answer to her prayers. Her son would be safe.

When Daisy and Molly heard the news of the general's death they gathered together with Amy, said a prayer, and the fear returned. *What do we do now?* They asked themselves silently. They did not have an answer.

CHAPTER 8

Scioto River
July, 1812

Jim settled in with hard work and long days. For several weeks
he attended to numerous projects; from sunrise sometimes to
dark, he found things to do. He worked independently, with little
supervision or direction from Mrs. Hicks. She brought him meals
and, on many occasions, they sat by an overturned barrel or at the
table under the oaks near the house and engage in lengthy discussions, mostly about Jim's life with the general; she was surprised
at how educated and conversant he was in language and literature
and he, in turn, found out about the Hicks' commitment to the
abolition movement and learned more about the general's active
role in the Marietta anti-slave efforts. Jim knew of the general's
passion for Africans and his abhorrence of slavery; he now had
a greater understanding of the general's sudden disappearances
for several days at a time, and the meetings with Matthew Curley,
Reverend Robert Moody, Rufus Putnam, and others that Jim did
not attend. These reminisces about the general almost always resulted in the sadness associated with the loss of his guardian; on
these occasions, Jim went back to work until his mind refocused
on the task at hand.

At other times, they discussed work around the farm and

Mrs. Hicks' son's return from his mission. Jim observed that Mrs. Hicks was highly educated and very formal in her demeanor and language and seemed out of place on a poor farm in the wilds of Ohio. , Jim noticed on many occasions Abigail watching him from a distance and was curious about her intent; at times, he was startled by her unannounced presence. He went about his business, comfortable in the security the farm and Mrs. Hicks provided.

Abigail watched Jim in his labors and felt stirrings in response to his strong and muscular body; he was attractive and desirable in his youthful presence. She thought about him now almost continually, and knew that it would be time soon. How it would be managed was her only concern.

With some assistance from Abigail, Jim had fixed up a small area in the loft well away from the hay and dry feeds. He had a bed made of several bales, a cloth blanket as a sheet and his own travel blanket, a cover, a small table with a water basin, and enough candles for Jim to read several books that were brought to him from the house.

It was almost dark when she came to him. Jim had lighted a candle was washing up from a day's work. She stood silently for a moment in the flickering light, staring at his bare chest. "Have you enjoyed the pleasure of a woman in your young life?" Abigail asked as she walked slowly toward him and touched his flat, muscular stomach.

"Yes, ma'am I have," he said. "Clara Wagon who was a scullery maid at Bracket's and two Indi—"

"You don't need to tell me who they are, Mr. Morgan," she said. "I have a lustful appetite and am in need of your maleness, if you are of a similar feeling and thought." She spoke formally, with confidence she touched him and he was already aroused. Nothing more was said as they both lost themselves in the intensity of their pleasure.

Abigail did not linger very long and, as she was dressing, she said, "I have carnal appetites, as you can tell. I have not been with my husband since long before his passing. Our behavior this night will not change our habitation; I will come to you on occasion with desire and, if you agree, we will continue. Do not expect any more intimacy than this." Jim said nothing; he reached for her but she was gone into the darkness.

The rest of Jim's summer settled down into a comfortable routine of hard work, his labors were showing results as well-timed rains brought the corn to an abundant maturity and the meadows were rich in the grasses and grains that would see the farm through the winter. Mrs. Hicks came to Jim frequently; little was said in their lovemaking, and Jim soon found himself mostly indifferent to her passions. They spent much of one rainy day together in his bed as he listened to her recall and retell her life and all of its trials and triumphs. Jim found that she was a strong, independent woman who was determined to stay on her land. She was appreciative of Jim's hard labors, gave ample provisions, and offered little in supervision and direction in his work. He was content with his life at this moment, and had no desire to find the war in the north.

Abigail's father, sister and several members of her father's Methodist Church came to visit in early August, in a buggy and a wagon filled with hardware and provisions. They stayed for several days, worked in and around the house, and invited Jim to eat with them outside under the large oak trees.

On the first morning of their stay, Preacher Morton asked Jim to talk with him; they walked down the lane to the cornfield and he observed Jim closely. He inquired of Jim's background and history and wanted to know everything about the general, especially in the days and weeks prior to his leaving. Jim shared all that he knew.

"My friend Jim, I do bring sad news," the preacher said. "The general is dead. He went into a coma soon after your abrupt departure and did not regain consciousness. His daughter attended him and ensured his comfort. He was buried at the farm next to his beloved Margaret. Mr. Putnam and the good folks of Marietta laid his body down on the 22nd of June."

Preacher Morton paused, allowing Jim to absorb the news; hearing what he already knew did not change his sense of devastation and abandonment. He had hoped that somehow he could return to the farm and continue his enchanted life. He was numb and wanted to be alone, to let his mind wander and remember all the good times. Jim stood with his head down, his two arms outward, leaning against a tree. The chirping of far-off birds, buzzing of several bees, and quiet rustling of a gentle breeze were the only interruptions to his thoughts. After several minutes, the preacher placed his hand on Jim's shoulder and broke the silence. "In his will, he left in your name his acreage in the thicket. All that is required is that you claim possession before your twenty-first birthday.

"Jim, there is more news that brings concerns. It seems that Mr. Sprout has warranted your arrest for the theft of property and livestock." He handed Jim a copy of the handbill. Jim read it in disbelief, confused and overwhelmed. He began to speak but the preacher interrupted: "We believe in your honesty and good name. We will be of assistance at your request. Let us know in good time of your plans and intentions; we are your friends." Jim remained silent but raged internally; the general's warning of dangers now made sense. He had another enemy and someone other than his stepfather that he could hate. Urges to return to clear his name and seek revenge interplayed in his mind. The grief over the loss of his mentor fueled his anger.

Jim wondered about Anna and the farmhands that he had grown up with, and thought little about the generous gift of thicket land on which he had spent much of his life. He worried about his mother, Amy and Aunt Daisy, and hoped that they would find a way to be safe from the drunken and violent Elizur.

From that moment, Jim chose to be alone with his feelings of loss and sadness. He distanced himself from most family activities, but participated in discussions regarding slavery and the new war. Detroit had already been taken by the British and its Indian allies; Hull had surrendered, the eight hundred villagers left at the mercy of Tecumseh and his alliance of marauding Shawnees and Delaware. The remainder of the American army and militias had returned to Ohio, awaiting more troops and a new commander.

The next day, after the outside dinner table was cleared, the preacher assumed the posture of one about to deliver a sermon and stated in a clear, strong voice, "There is great fear that Tecumseh and his alliance will return to Ohio and slaughter the white settlers, and there is no army to stop him. You need to abandon this farm, Abigail, and return with us to Chillicothe. There is protection with us; we can do our work from the church." Abigail mostly ignored her father's pleadings, insisting on maintaining the farm. After several efforts to change her mind, the preacher became silent and sullen.

Jim stayed out of the talk. He was glad that he had not shared the letter of introduction to General Hull that the general had given him during their last fateful meeting. He kept to himself and performed his labors. Mrs. Hicks did not in any way recognize their relationship, either to her company or to him.

The family left the following day. There was no more talk of war; as the harvest was upon them, a young indentured from the preacher's parish came to assist in the labor. They worked very hard, morning to nightfall, through the several weeks of harvest. When it came, it was bountiful and abundant. Abigail did not enjoy Jim's bed after her father's visit.

The harvest was put away by mid September; the labors of summer were over; Jim's had enjoyed his labors and for now was quite content. He had no desire to leave the serenity and security that he had made for himself.

This time of peace ended very abruptly soon after. Jim awoke late one night to the sound of hooves, murmured conversations, and frenetic activity.

CHAPTER 9

On the Ohio River
July, 1796

Journal Entry
Jonathon McGuire
Ohio River
July 2nd, 1796

'We commence our 2nd week on this river, one day out of Wheeling, Virginia territory.

"Both Maggie and I are distressed this day. Our boats harbored at Wheeling for 2 days to allow our stock to re acclimate and replenish in the rich marshlands south of the city. It was a decrepit town and we had to be mindful of our livestock lest they be taken by the many ruffians who idled on the banks. Maggie and I were walking around mid day through the market in the center of town. We heard a commotion and walked toward many people who were congregating near some cattle pens. Among them, we witnessed a coffle of two score or so black slaves standing two together with iron chains around their necks and wrists. Several large men of white color were standing over these wretched souls, whips at hand and guns belted. These creatures were almost

all young women and children; many of the children were naked or dressed in rags.

"Several of the children younger then our Virginia were moaning with great wails of grief and pain. A white man of the slave trade was walking one of the women, clearly the mother of some, to a wagon nearby where she was placed, still in her neck and wrist irons, into bondage with another slave. I will forever hear the penetrating heartache of her soul as the Waggoner ordered his mules forward. Soon thereafter, the wretched custodians began to whip the crying children into silence.

"The beatings on these 3 waifs were merciless. Their small frail bodies were torn apart by the cruel lash. Most of the casual observers and pedestrians quickly walked away, sickened I trust by the beastly deeds. My dear Maggie could take it no longer and, with anger and disgust, was moved to storm her way to the offender and order him to stop the beatings. Her voice was louder than I have ever heard from my small gentle lady. The ruffian stopped, looked around, put up his whip, and left the children in the dirt, bloodied and near death. A kind soul brought the urchins a cup of water. It was quiet after this episode and I could hear from far away the wailings of a grievous mother who would never see her beautiful children again. My Maggie has not said a word since this ordeal; our lives will change I am sure; a Christian person cannot be idle in witness of this terrible event.

"We floated on down the great river, our animals and stores properly cared for. Wendell and John are custodians of our flat boat that follows and, with good water, we will see Marietta in several days. This part of our journey no longer holds any adventure. We want only to be away from the gloom and despair that we feel so strongly.

"In God's mercy,

Jim walked out of the barn and watched the activity near the house. There was sufficient moonlight on a cloudless night for him to make out objects. One horse stood silent as two figures came out of the house with Abigail; there was muffled, almost frantic, conversation lasting several minutes. Then the rider, a male tall in profile, remounted and rode off in haste. He disappeared in the dark, heading toward the post road. Mrs. Hicks and the small stranger went back into the house.

Jim did not move; he knew somehow that he would become involved. In less than a half hour, they both came out of the house. Mrs. Hicks was holding a sack in one hand and holding the stranger's hand in the other. She saw Jim standing silently in the barn doorway and they walked toward him.

"Jim," she said, "I want you to meet Libithia. She is a runaway slave who is urgently in need of our assistance. That was my son, Jacob, who came with her; he is as we speak riding north on the post road. The child is being followed by slave catchers who are close behind. I suspect they will be here very soon, looking for our fugitive."

Jim observed the young girl, no older than fourteen years. It was hard to make out her features in the shadows. She was wrapped in a tattered blanket and held a small cloth bag. Mrs. Hicks said, "It is of great necessity for you to provide escort on her journey. Protect her and present her to the next safe house."

Resentful of the demand and angry that he was not included in the events, Jim said: "This is a most unusual request; I am not prepared for this endeavor."

The smack across his face was hard and loud; the slave girl pulled back inside her blanket, keeping her head low, trying to disappear. "You have no say," said Mrs. Hicks. "The general sent you here for this very purpose. You need to go now. There is little time. Go by the river; stay off the roads—the canoe under the dock is used for this purpose: take it and travel only by night. Are you listening to me?"

Jim, stunned, didn't respond. "Get your rifle and belongings," said Mrs. Hicks. "I have set aside some provisions and other necessary things for the two of you. Travel only by night; hide as best you can along the banks. It is two nights by river to the Circleville landing. Go to the new mission seek out the Moran's; they will care for her from that point. Be very aware of the slave catchers. They are devious and diligent; they will soon know of our deception and be on your trail. On your life, do not allow Labithia to fall into their possession. Do you understand?"

Jim quietly went to his loft, retrieved the Kentucky rifle, a pouch with some writing materials, the letter of introduction to General Hull, and the coins given him General McGuire. He came back out into the shadows; he had a strong urge to just leave, abandoning both the girl and the responsibility.

Mrs. Hicks' anticipated Jim intentions. "Do this now, Jim," she said, "and do not shirk your duty. Do not come back here upon deliverance of Labithia; go north and join the army of the Northern Frontier. They are in need of you. Go now."

For reasons unknown to him at the time, Jim chose to accept responsibility for the life of a slave girl. He said nothing to anyone, and started to walk down the river path. Mrs. Hicks hugged Labithia briefly, pushed her in Jim's direction, and whispered, "Jim is a good man. He will care for you." Labithia ran without hesitation, quickly catching up and falling in behind her new master. They disappeared into the darkness.

Abigail stood and watched for a few moments, then turned and walked to the house, anticipating that Lucas Williams and the half-breed Pelitah Moon would soon be at her door. "I will deal with these rascals and trust that her son will lead them away from the young child and her reluctant protector." With building anticipation, she went inside and erased any evidence of the slave girl. She paused for a moment, her mood becoming melancholy.

"What a fool I have been. I am forty years old," she said. She could feel the soreness in her nipples as they rubbed against her cotton undergarment.

It was midmorning when the slave catchers arrived at the Hicks farm. They came quietly and slowly, vigilant, looking for clues to determine if this family was participating in the new but ever-growing practice of slave sanctuary and rescue. When they called at the house, Abigail forced her musket out of the front window and asked their intentions. Lucas took his time assessing the potential danger of this spirited woman who appeared to know the workings of the firearm that was pointed at him. He spit some tobacco juice. "My name is Lucas Williams of Kentucky Territory. We are under lawful governance of the state of Ohio, seeking the whereabouts of a nigger fugitive that may be passing this way. Have you seen or know this runaway.

Abigail lifted the gun slightly so that its barrel met the eyes of the slave catcher. "I have no truck with your business or your profession," she said. "I will share no information; now get off my property this minute." Lucas took a moment, surveyed the property again; knew immediately that she was a not only sympathetic to anti-slavery but active in providing sanctuary.

He was more confident now. "Harboring runaway slaves is a felony in this state," He said, "and be obliged to cooperate with sworn officers of the peace such as myself. We will look about your property."

"You will die if you do, it is your choice," said Abigail from the window.

"What be your name and where be your husband?" Lucas asked. There was no answer, only the musket aimed at his head.

The slave catcher and his partner chose not to challenge this determined woman. Quietly and slowly, they turned their horses and headed off the property. On the way back to the main road, Lucas noticed several horses pastured near the barn. He paused for a moment and said to his partner, the half-breed Pelitah, "I know that horse, the buckskin. It belongs to the nigger loving general in Marietta. They are on the river. We are close." Moon did not respond, but nodded his head in agreement. They headed north on the Chillicothe post.

Labithia was very tired. She had had almost no sleep or rest for the three days since she left Marietta. She was the only one left of a group of four slaves who escaped from the Breckinridge tobacco plantation in Henry County, Kentucky. Two had drowned in the river when the makeshift raft that was left for them fell apart several hundred yards from Ohio and freedom. Othello, Labithia's best friend and protector, was caught outside of Marietta in the early morning light as he looked for a safe trail to the village. A laborer at the boat works took him to the sheriff in hopes of a reward. Labithia hid all that day in the undergrowth and marshy banks of the river and waited well into night for Othello, who did not return. Desperate and determined, she moved in the dark shadows of Marietta, where she found the church with the white steeple and weathervane where, it was told, white folks would help her. She hid in a flower-covered corner at the back of the congregational church where someone would find her.

It was first light when Madelyn Moody, the parson's wife, made her daily early morning walk around the church property. She came upon Labithia, still crouched in the corner of the church.

"Wuld you be Ms. Moody? I sek sanctary," said Labithia.

"Come child." Mrs. Moody reached for her hand.

The runaway slave spent two days in the attic of the parish home. She was provided with a bath and new clothing, ate as much as she wanted, and slept a peaceful sleep, unlike any she could remember. Most of the time, she was left by herself and told to be very quiet. Mrs. Moody came at night and discussed many things with her, mostly relating to her future. She could not stay in Ohio and would have to go to Canada.

Arrangements for her journey were made. Labithia asked many questions: "How far tis Kanada be? Who take me? Will the slave catchers find me?" The parson's wife reassured her without giving her much information. On her third night at the church, she was awoken, introduced to Jacob, and they departed quietly.

"I knows how to be quiet, master Jim. Don't you go telling me things I already knows," she said. They were in the canoe; it was a moon filled night, and Jim's strong strokes pushed steadily up the slow flowing and meandering Scioto River. Jim had mostly been silent since they left Mrs. Hicks'.

He had mentioned that they would paddle until the pre-dawn light allowed them to find a hiding place along the bank; here, they would stay all day without talk or movement. Nothing else was said. The night was quiet and uneventful. They passed several homesteads, the barking of a dog, and a fisherman with candled light on the far side of the river; these were the only signs of civilization. They passed without being noticed.

Jim thought less about past events and more about the seriousness of his situation. He recalled conversations with the general and his friends about the evil of the fugitive slave act that permitted slave owners to enter the Free states to capture and return their property. Most repugnant were the slave catchers who now roamed Ohio with impunity and arrogance. Their violent natures and cruel dispositions were well documented in stories of captured slaves who were brutalized and, on occasion, killed. The slave catchers were both scorned and feared by many Ohioans. Jim knew he had to be careful, and took some comfort in the knowledge that the general would be proud of him.

He was careful in selecting a place to hide during the long day; in the early light, he located a spot in a thickly forested area that came down to the river's edge. He covered the canoe with the thick undergrowth that overflowed the bank and found a dense spot where they could be hidden from sight in all directions. "You need to rest here all day, don't move or make any noise," he said to Labithia. "I'm leaving you my water and the food. I need to check things out and I will not be far away. Don't move for any reason."

Labithia grabbed Jim's shirt sleeve: "Don't leave me, master Jim. Yu is al I hav" Her voice was both pleading and demanding.

Jim reassured her and repeated that he would keep her safe. "I will be watching you," he said. He took his rifle and disappeared into the brush. He walked back to the water, looking for a suitable place where he could watch the river and its traffic from out of sight.

He spent a long day watching for the two men Abigail Hicks said were looking for them. Labithia stayed very still in her hiding place, taking a few drinks from the water container, but saving the food for when her protector returned. They did not see or speak to each other all day.

They were on the river for several hours on a bright moonlit night when, paddling slowly, they came around a bend and could make out the shadows of a pier extending six to eight feet into the river. Behind a small hill and in between the cotton woods, Jim could make out the silhouettes of several buildings, facing each other and raised from the ground on the Hope Well Indian mounds. He was confident that this was his destination. Cautiously, Jim back paddled and decided to survey the area on foot before going to find the church. He secured the canoe a half mile downriver and had his companion hide near it. He proceeded to walk carefully back to the Circleville Landing on the well-traveled river trail. His fears were heightened, but he hoped the slave catchers were not here.

He froze when he saw the shadow, several yards ahead off his right shoulder, a barely discernable movement. He stayed in place, trying to control his breathing, which sounded to him like the continual rolling of thunder. The shadow began to move, turning and walking toward him; he saw the profile of a hat brim, and there were several whispered words to another unseen person. The shadow then turned but came no closer. The second person came out of the darkness; both shadows were near enough that, for a moment in the moonlight, he could see the darkened, bearded face of one of the men. Jim could not move, frozen by fear, his heart pounding; he wanted desperately to run, but felt paralyzed; it took his entire will to slowly, very slowly, move backward, cautiously, quietly, retracing his steps.

He retreated, hoping in the dead silence of a moonlit night that he made no noise, to escape this terrifying situation. He found Labithia where he left her. She felt Jim's fear and hugged his arm desperately. His panic slowly subsided and together, very quietly, they returned to the canoe and floated downriver to a safe distance to await the setting of the moon. Calmer now, Jim decided they would go to the river's far side and then proceed north around the landing, abandoning the Circleville Sanctuary and toward a destination and future unknown to him.

Jim wondered and worried later about his fearful and panicked reaction in this dangerous situation; his fear of cowardice would stay with him and he wondered whether he would react in the same manner when future events were presented to him.

They waited until the moon lost its light and then started upriver, slowly at first but, as they passed the landing and got out of hearing range, Jim powered his strokes and paddled. They kept going for hours, until the grey of dawn forced them to take shelter on the far side of the river. Jim felt confident that he had placed sufficient distance between them and the slavers; they could hide and rest for the day. He needed time to think through this predicament and decide what to do and where to go.

Jim spent most of the next day well hidden. He slept some, but his vigilance and indecision kept him a wake most of the time.

Labithia found a comfortable spot among some bushes, well hidden from the river. Jim thought of going straight to Canada, but he knew little of the journey and wanted to be rid of this slave girl as soon as possible. He decided to continue north, to seek out other communities and find churches where someone may assist them.

It was after midnight the following night; very quiet with a rising moon. Jim, vigilant, was silently paddling upriver, keeping close to the west shore to be protected by the shadows of the large cottonwoods and smaller undergrowth. Suddenly, he saw the silhouette of a person standing silently about twenty-five yards upriver, chest high in the water, holding to a branch of a fallen tree to keep his balance in the current. Jim quickly back paddled, panicked. The shadow spoke in a quiet but distinct whisper: "Jim Morgan, I am Jacob Hicks."

Upon hearing Jacob's voice, Labithia immediately rose from her resting position in the front of the canoe, and said, "Mastr Jacob, we is bein chased by dem slave catchers." Jim touched her shoulder to encourage her silence and back paddled to hold the canoe in place.

"Lucas Williams is on your trail," Jacob said. "He knows you are on the river. He is watching for you several miles up river below the Columbus bend." Jim's fear subsided and he paddled toward this friend he had never met. Jacob held the canoe with one hand when it came within reach. "They were supposed to be following me, but abandoned my trail to follow the river," he said. "I am perplexed as to why that happened."

Jim was able to observe Jacob close up, and saw that he was tall in stature and shivering from standing in the cold water. Jim, wanting desperately to be absolved of his duties and trusting his instincts, asked, "Why are you standing in the river? "

As Jim gently turned the canoe, Jacob said, "It was the only way I could think of getting close enough to you without risking alerting the slavers of our presence. It is cold now; can we go to shore here and discuss our predicament?"

Jim assented without comment, and pointed the canoe toward shore, led by the shivering Jacob. They walked the canoe several hundred feet into a shallow marshy area and secured it to some bushes.

Once on shore, Labithia hugged Jacob and said, "Mastr Jacob has don com back to save me from dat devil. I be safe yu protec me."

Jacob said, "Let's move away from the river, out of earshot." They walked slowly in the soft moonlight, following a small and overgrown trail. After several minutes, Jim heard the breathing of a horse and instantly stopped. "That will be my horse," said Jacob. "I posted him here while I tried to find you and it is most fortunate that I did." Jim was now glad to be in the company of a fellow conspirator; although Jacob was a stranger, Jim needed a friend. He also hoped that Jacob would take over the task of rescuing the young fugitive.

"How did the slave catchers know we were on the river?" Jim asked, talking fast. "It was only luck that I saw them last night before they observed me. I could see no other opportunity but to continue up river; I was not informed of any other sanctuary other than the church at Circleville." Jim's frustration was apparent. Jacob took a bed roll off the back of the horse, removed his wet shirt, and replaced it with one from his bedroll.

"Is I safe now, master Jacob? Is I safe?" Labithia asked. She was tugging at his belt.

Jacob hugged her and said, "Not yet. We still have a long way to go. Jim and I need to talk; there is some dried jerky in my bag, take a small amount for yourself." She found it immediately and sat down tearing into the strip of beef with gusto, more secure in the presence and care of two protectors.

"I sure is hungry," she said. "Thnk yee, mastr Jacob."

Jim and his new friend walked several feet into the dark shadow of a large cottonwood, away from the hungry fugitive. "I am so glad I found you," Jacob said. "I was quite frantic when Lucas did not follow me into Circleville and beyond. We were hoping to keep him following me for several days. He is a determined man; I am told that he never gives up, and regrettably very few of our refugees ever get to keep their freedom once he pursues them. He gets help from people who do not share our beliefs, and there are many of them." His shivering subsiding. The nocturnal solitude was only broken by the quiet rushing of water, the chirping of crickets, and the occasional bellow of a bullfrog.

Jim asked, "What do we do now?" Jacob was quiet for a few more minutes, moving Jim a small distance away from Labithia's earshot.

"There is another concern that needs your attention," Jacob said. "Virginia McGuire approached me when I was in Marietta arranging for Labithia's passage; she told me that her husband, Joshua, had met and spent considerable time with Lucas Williams at the farm. One of the workers overheard Joshua offering Lucas fifty gold coins if he would bring back the hair of Jim Morgan. Jim, these are dangerous men; they intend to kill you and return her to captivity. Be vigilant and do not allow them to approach you. Shoot first if it comes to that."

"I believe I should take the canoe upriver, get their attention, and have Lucas follow me; you can take the horse and go west and north, away from the river." Jim was silent; he had hoped that he would be excused from his responsibility and allowed to go north to the war on his own. Jacob continued, "You cannot get to Canada with Libithia. The war has stopped all transport. There is a sanctuary among the Wyandot nation on the Sandusky River past the treaty line; they protect black fugitives and provide for their safety. It is a journey of three days in good weather.

"Once you are there, seek out Charles Walker, who runs the

trading post and acts as the tribe's agent. He will accept her into his care and provide a safe haven until the war ends and she can continue on her journey."

Jim thought for a moment. "How do I know this Walker can be trusted?" he asked.

"Some years ago, your mentor brought a fugitive slave to his mission," said Jacob. "He thrived in his custody until he moved into Canada last summer."

"Would that be the slave also named Jacob?" Jim asked. "I know of him."

"Yes," Jacob said. "We do not have much time; we need to move soon."

They split up whatever food they had left and Jacob provided directions for moving west on the present trail and then north on the Amity road, following the big Darby River.

"Follow the road," he said. "You will cross the Scioto; when you get to Mill Creek, you should, if you are in need of rest and nourishment, seek out Samuel Cuthbertson's farm. He is building a small mill there. They are reported to be sympathetic to our efforts."

Labithia, her hunger now minimized, was anxious about her fate; the two men sat with her, and Jacob gently and sympathetically explained the circumstances and the plan that would take her to freedom. It was clear that she felt much safer with Jacob. She was glad, however, that she was out of the canoe and off the river. Although he did not answer her many questions, Jacob assured her that she would be safe.

"It is time to go," Jacob said. "I will paddle upriver and distract them as long as I am able." He turned and walked toward the canoe, but stopped and turned back. "Mrs. Moody told me to tell you that Anna sends you her best wishes and is taking good care of Digger. Write to her when you are safe." The mention of Anna's name brought warm feelings and an urge to return to the farm. Jim was glad that his dog of many years was in good company.

"Jacob," Jim said, "if you go to Marietta, tell Anna of my circumstances and plans. I will find a way to correspond when I am able."

They departed in silence, Jim leading the horse in the darkness and Labithia walking alongside. He pushed back his intense longing to return to Anna and the security of the farm and his previous life; however, he did not have much time for regrets. Jacob pushed the canoe into the stream, going north; he was very anxious about his mother and whether the slave catcher had done her harm.

Jim led the exhausted horse with his charge asleep in the saddle; he, too, was weary. It had been three nights and four days since they left Jacob on the Scioto. They had seen several signs of the slave catchers in the last twenty-four hours. Labithia and Jim had moved almost continually since the sightings, both in daylight and darkness, to stay ahead of their pursuers.

Jim had observed their movements when he was able from the occasional vantage point of a small hill or large tree. It was only a matter of time before they would be observed, overrun, and captured. The fugitives had moved with little or no sleep and nothing to eat for the last twenty-four hours; Jim had lost his sense of vigilance and caution as fatigue eroded his mind and energy. He would need to find refuge this day. The thought of abandoning Labithia never occurred to him as they continued on; his only hope was that he could find safety with the Wyandotte or confront the slave catchers. Strangely, he no longer had a great fear of them, more confident now that he could, if necessary, kill them. He almost looked forward to an encounter, and knew this would happen one way or another.

They had been walking down a well used path along the Sandusky River for most of the night and early morning. All the signs now indicated they were in Wyandot territory, and Jim was hopeful he would soon encounter some Indians and hoped to secure their assistance in providing refuge for Labithia. Jim was anxious to find the slave girl sanctuary and divest himself of this responsibility. He tried not to get to close to her but, in their seven days and nights together, he had developed a paternal fondness for this small, sad, pathetic girl who had a tenacious will to live and live free.

Her thoughts and the ongoing conversations they shared during quiet moments of their journey were filled with optimism and hope. She asked a hundred questions about things she didn't know or feared, and created many wishful scenarios in which she lived a wonderful life in a free society. She wanted to know everything about white folks and how they lived their lives, and wondered about life in Canada. Jim began to enjoy her stories and her positive and hopeful countenance. Over time, he warmed up to her, overcoming his resentment over the responsibilities that had been forced upon him. He became determined to provide safe passage and freedom to this small, thin slave girl.

Jim was leading the horse along the path and into a clearing where the river meandered and flattened out into a meadow when he saw three Indian children watching from a rise a short distance away. Jim kept walking, more excited now, leading the exhausted horse. He did not wake the dozing Labithia. Hopefully, his journey would soon be over. As the path climbed out of the meadow, he saw several wigwams and a toiled field where maize, squash, and beans had recently been harvested. The corn hills had been left to rot; already they had turned into brownish vegetation. A family of pigs roamed and rutted in the spoilage, and several dogs barked, announcing the arrival of the slave girl and the fugitive. Smoke from a fire hung low in the trees.

The villagers; women and children only, watched them approach; seeing a small black girl they took her off the horse and without saying a word and escorted by two women, moved quickly toward a heavily wooded area a mile or two away.

A few moments later, a young boy jumped on a pony and rode quickly away. Jim asked the elder of the group where the warriors were, but she did not answer. Jim was now alone; his horse could go no further, her endurance spent; *safe for now.* Jim felt a great relief.

He led the horse to where several others were loosely tethered. He unsaddled, watered, and brought her some feed from the communal stock, rubbed her down briefly, hoped that she would survive.

He walked out of the camp the way he came and found a well-secluded spot in a stand of willows and chestnut trees with sufficient undergrowth to remain hidden but with a good view of the trail and the village in the distance. He made himself comfortable, prepared his rifle, watched and waited for the slave catchers and fell into a deep slumber in spite of his best intentions.

It must have been the snorting of a horse that awakened him; Jim became alert immediately. He quickly looked in all directions, through the trees and down the trail, until he saw a slight movement. He waited with a thumping heart; late afternoon shadows were darkening the landscape and his hiding place.

Two horses and riders were moving very cautiously, coming slowly in his direction. They paused when they saw the village in the distance. One of the riders brought his binocular to his eye and surveyed the camp for a long time; the two riders talked for a moment and started to move forward. Jim quietly and slowly brought his long rifle to his shoulder; several more feet and they would be in range. He hoped that Labithia was well hidden somewhere in the forests of the Wyandot Nation.

As he lay in wait, Jim was unable to control his heavy breathing and pounding heart; he swallowed to drown his rising panic and desperately hoped that the slave catchers would turn around and leave. He didn't know if he could kill someone but knew that he would have no choice. *They will kill me if they have the opportunity.* In spite of his fears, Jim realized that he would only be able to take one shot; if he stayed where he was, he would be shot before he could reload. He would have to run into the dense trees and hope to reload his rifle. He decided to shoot the white man closest to him first. *Stay calm,* he repeated to himself as he carefully wiped his sweaty hands on his pant legs. All he could hear was his own breathing and the rustling of the leaves of the cottonwoods and sycamores. *Such evil in such a peaceful place,* he thought.

The riders stopped again. Pelitah Moon pointed toward the village and they talked in whispers as Lucas searched the camp with his binocular. Jim's long rifle was very heavy as he sighted the head of Lucas Williams; it would be an easy shot if he could pull the trigger. He waited.

Jim heard the sounds of horses moving at a gallop before he could see them. Quickly, several riders came into view, Indians accompanied by a tall white man. They rode hard through the village and halted suddenly several feet in front of the slave catchers. The horses made a commotion as they were reined tightly. All the riders were carrying weapons and the Indians looked menacing; they were close to Jim's hiding place and, listening closely, he was able to hear the exchange of words.

The white man spoke first. "Who be you and what is your business with the Wyandot Nation?" Lucas sat tall in his saddle, looking at the party halting his progress.

"I be Lucas Williams," he said, "deputized by the state of Ohio, legally searching for a runaway nigger whom we have tracked to this location. Who be you and what is your purpose here?"

"I am Charles Walker," the white man said, "legal representative of the sovereign nation of the Wyandot. You have transgressed beyond the Greenville treaty line and have no jurisdiction here. We do not recognize nor engage in any form of business with individuals not chartered or contracted by the nation; neither will we respond to any inquiries on any matter. Your business is finished here. Long Hair and his deputies will escort you out of our jurisdiction." The Indian deputies moved forward, rifles raised.

"Now you hear me, you bastards," Lucas said. His voice rose and he spoke with great authority. "The state of Ohio does not recognize the Indian Territory when crimes have been committed. I am a sworn officer of the court and am performing legal business. Do not resist my authority to seek and return private property and a wanted felon. I possess judicial orders that assert my authority. If they be in your possession, you are harboring fugitives and in violation of state and federal laws. Back your horses away, allow us to pass and pursue our lawfully sworn duties, or I will see to your arrest."

A long pause ensued, the two sides glaring at each other and searching for signs of fear or reticence. Long Hair moved forward, his rifle aimed at Lucas's head. The Indians sat silent on their horses, eyes focused on the slave catchers. After a brief moment of stare down, Charles Walker restated his intent. "You will leave now or be shot dead." Another moment of angry silence ensued.

"Do not threaten an officer of the court," said Lucas. "Hear me: I will not be stopped. I have the law to support me. I will be back to collect this property and seek my revenge." Slowly, Lucas and Moon turned their horses and rode off with the escort following a few feet behind.

Jim waited for a few minutes, stood up, and walked out of the thicket and introduced himself.

"Welcome to the Wyandot Nation," Charles Walker said...

CHAPTER 10

Marietta, Ohio
August 1812

It was an early July morning, the sun still hidden behind the grey hills and forests east of Marietta. A night rain welcomed the morning with the promise of a humid and uncomfortable day. Rufus Putnam, Acting Sheriff Micah Miller, a disappointing man, and August Sprout, Joshua's oldest brother, rode out of town on the little Muskingum River trail. They rode into the hardwoods, hills, and marshes that dominated the terrain northeast of Marietta. Rufus Putnam, now seventy-one, still rode tall and easy in the saddle. The mission of the three men on this day was not to be pleasant. Putnam was mostly irritated that his relationship with his beloved friend and partner had come to this. His death was most untimely; he had needed Jonathon's energy and determination to ensure a profitable harvest so that the proceeds of the McGuire farm could pay off the large debt that had accumulated on the account over the years. As the president of First Mercantile Bank, Rufus was responsible for the bank's solvency; his unwise lending to Jonathon McGuire had placed a difficult burden on the bank and a blemish on Putnam's reputation. Joshua Sprout was an unpleasant man, but he had to be found; his labor was needed to ensure a bountiful harvest. *These are challenges for a man much younger than me,* thought Putnam.

The road was well maintained for the first several miles and little traveled on this morning. Several miles upriver, they turned off the main road onto the Stony Creek trail, and climbed into the dense hills that were home to Elizur Kirkwood and his whisky maker. They could smell the pungent odor of brewing corn meal mush before they saw the smoke of the fire. The barking of the blue hound alerted the camp to the intruders; it was a cluttered, disheveled encampment that the three riders saw as they rode down and into Elizur's Hollow. Several men and two Indian women were in various states of intoxication and unaware of the visitors. Joshua Sprout was sitting on the ground and, trying to get up, stumbled and fell over several empty jugs and one of the women.

August was appalled at the sight of his brother and angrily cursed and threatened him. "Get your sorry ass out of the jug and get on this horse," he said. "You got work to do and a family to keep."

"I go where I want," Joshua said, still stumbling and unsure of himself, trying in his foggy condition to figure out why these men had pursued him to his retreat.

Rufus edged his horse forward toward Elizur, who was standing further away, close to an old shotgun leaning against a tree. "Mr. Kirkwood," he said, "I see that you are still in habitation on the company's property and engaging in illegal commerce; a most difficult situation you find yourself in."

The whisky maker, defiant, said, "I been here for near seven years and no one has ever thrown me off. I guess I've earned some title to this here property." Rufus looked around at the squalor, and then directly at Elizur. He paused for a minute and said, "Sheriff Miller has a subpoena on his person and it accuses you of trespass and illicit trade. I do believe we should place you in chains and escort you to the county jail." Elizur, agitated, started walking around the camp with his head down, mumbling to himself, disengaging from the visitors.

Mr. Putnam and the sheriff watched for any sign of aggression but only saw only fear and confusion Rufus said in his most authoritative voice; "I do believe you should clear your camp. Send those squaws back to the Harmar and these other ruffians back to the swamp. We will accompany Mr. Sprout back to the McGuire farm to assume his responsibilities. Clean this place up, Mr. Kirkwood. The sheriff will be back in a week's time to determine your fate."

It was late evening when the party of four came up the back trail, approaching the house in single file. Anna walked out to greet them. Putnam was in the lead with Joshua bringing up the rear, slouched in the saddle and looking most bedraggled.

"Pray, why bring that man here Mr. Putnam?" said Anna. "He is unwelcome and carries only misery in his veins. We are getting along quite fine, sir, without his company."

Rufus continued on toward the house. "Now Anna, this is not for you to decide," he said. "We have business with Mrs. Sprout."

"She has no use for him either," said Anna, her voice louder. She paused and then ran to catch up with the leader. "Sir, please, do you have any word from Jim?"

"You will be the first to know, Anna, when we hear something," he said. Anna watched as Virginia came out on the porch. She and Rufus talked for awhile as the sheriff and August helped Joshua off his horse and led him to the rain barrel to clean him up. Rufus escorted Virginia back into the house.

"We are in for trouble now," Anna said to the other hired help that had come to observe the events. Everyone quietly went back to their business.

For a week, nothing much happened. Virginia never left the house; sad and dispirited, she spent her time with her daughter

Elizabeth, reading, sewing, and looking at various mementos of her mother and father. Mostly, she sat in her favorite chair in her bedroom on the second floor. The room overlooked the farm buildings and apple orchards that faded into the grey haze of the Appalachian Mountains. Virginia talked very little and, when Anna asked about farm-related business, all she would get was a slight nod or quiet words informing her to do what she thought was best.

Elizabeth, visibly worried, began to spend all of her time with Anna; crying and holding onto her whenever she could. "What is wrong with mummy? Why is mummy sad? Is she dying?" These were questions Anna dealt with continually as she went about her business and tried to provide some comfort to the frightened eight year old. Of equal concern was the disappearance of Joshua; he was nowhere to be seen and was not performing any of the daily duties and routines of the farm. Anna would catch glimpses of him on the far side of the house in the small growth of hemlocks that overlooked the Ohio, cleaning and occasionally shooting his various rifles and pistols at birds and other targets, always with a jug at his side. He made no effort to talk to Anna or any other laborers, made his own meals, and generally avoided contact. On some days, he rode out in the early morning and did not return until after dark.

In the meantime, harvest season was upon the farm and much work needed to be done; the hands continued in their labors with a great uneasiness, fearful of the future. More and more, they came to Anna asking questions that didn't have answers. Anna was encouraging, saying the Virginia would be herself again soon. She needed more time to mourn the loss of her father. Slowly, Anna was becoming the manager of the farm; it was a responsibility she didn't want.

Early on a humid morning late July, Wendell Petrol and Charles Summer sharpened their long, curving scythes and walked down to the acres near the creek where the wheat always ripened first. Anna watched as they worked together, making long arching cutting motion, and the wheat fell to the ground. Anna was always amazed by how Wendell, with only one arm, could somehow maneuver the scythe to his will; the men moved smoothly, cutting an acre in the first several hours. A moment of melancholy passed over Anna as she remembered Jim working with them; with his strong shoulders and abundant energy, the three of them could cut five acres of wheat on good days. She willed the sadness away and went about her duties. Soon she would call Penelope and they would follow the cutters, raking and stacking the wheat in the windrows, allowing it to dry so that it could be stored later. It would take a lot longer to harvest the wheat without Jim, Joshua, Virginia, and the general helping out. Corn would be ready for picking before the wheat was thrashed and bagged. *There is so much work to be done; it will not be finished,* she thought. More help would be needed.

Anna was pleased to see the two veterans of the Great War, Wendell and Charles, taking charge of the chores. It was so unlike them. They much preferred to be told what to do and then complain about it. How they must be suffering with the loss of the general and the disappearance of their good friend Jim. *These changes must be confusing and fearful to them,* she thought as she went to get Penelope.

She reluctantly realized that she would have to do something. Without help, the farm would fall apart all too quickly. She went back to the house, placed a piece of Virginia's stationery on the table, took quill and ink, and wrote as best she could.

Dear. Mr. Putnam,

Forgive me my rudeness but I have to tell of events at the Maggie hill farm. We have not seen Mr. Sprout since you returned him here 3 weeks last, Ms Virginia continues to mourn the loss of the general and shows little interest in the farm and poor Elisabeth cries all the time. The hands are continuing to go about their duties but are most fearful of what is to come. I write to you for I know of no one else who could help us.

A most humble servant.
Anna Erikson

She folded the letter, put it in an envelope, and walked down to the dairy barn to talk with Henry. Mr. Pennmetter had been in charge of the dairy since before her arrival; he milked the twelve milch cows, made the cheese and butter, gathered the eggs from the ducks and chickens and slopped the hogs, fed all the animals, and slaughtered in season. Once a week, he took the dairy and produce to the market in Marietta. He was an older man, of strong features, a disheveled appearance, and an odorous presence. Most unusual, however, was that he didn't talk; he said very little to anyone and did all of his labors by himself. He worked all the time, resisted assistance, and led a solitary life. He protected his livestock vigorously, not allowing anyone to interfere with his efforts. The general had said on numerous occasions that Henry had given up on people; his life was his animals and this may be best for him. No one knew much about his history and, whatever the general knew, he never shared.

Henry lived in the far corner of the barn, away from the milking stanchions. He had made himself a humble residence: he possessed a cot, small table, lantern, pipe, and his shotgun, which was with him most all the time. Whenever someone sought to engage him in conversation, tell him what to do, or interfered with his animals, he pointed the shotgun directly at them and waved them away. Somehow, he had managed to survive since he joined the farm 10 years prior. Anna wondered how he was handling the loss of the general; he continued to do his jobs as he always had but to her knowledge, he had not said anything to anyone since the general's death.

"Henry," said Anna, "would you be so kind to take this letter to Mr. Putnam at the Mercantile Bank after market tomorrow? I also have some late tomatoes and onions from the garden for you to sell." Henry looked at Anna as though he was about to say something, but he only grunted, took the letter, and walked out to the pasture. .

Early the next morning, Henry hitched Cotton, his favorite mule, to the small wagon and made the two-hour trip to the market in Marietta. After the market, he went to the bank and handed the note to the teller.

It was the Sunday next when the carriage owned by the Mercantile Bank climbed the hill to the farm; Rufus Putnam, the bank president, Willford Conner, August Sprout, and Virginia's close friend from the First Congregational Church, Madelyn Moody, disembarked. Mrs. Moody, holding a large picnic basket, knocked on the front door. Rufus saw Anna, who stood watching some distance away, and gave her a small nod. Henry came forward and took the horse to water and rest.

Several hours later, the party left the house; Elizabeth was with Madelyn and they were carrying a carpet bag. They left without talking to any of the hands.

Early Monday morning, Joshua was looking over the corn fields, assessing the forage and the shape of the beef cattle grazing in one of the pastures. He walked through the un harvested acres of standing wheat. Selecting a scythe from the several stored next to the supply wagon, he sharpened it and began to work. He said nothing to Wendell and Charles, who had been cutting for an hour or more. They watched him with great interest.

At the house, Virginia came out of her room, and looked at Anna and Penelope, who were standing in the kitchen. She said, "I am most sorry that I have abandoned the two of you during these hard times. We will work together just as before. Elisabeth is staying with the Moody family for the rest of the summer; I will be visiting her on Sundays." She picked up a broom.

The Maggie Hill Farm returned to its usual commerce: the wheat was threshed, the corn was picked. The apples were harvested; cider was fermenting and would soon be ready for shipping. The swine and cattle grew fat from the fields. Life returned to normal, but it wasn't as before. The work got done and everyone knew their jobs, but a silence had fallen hard over the farm. Everyone felt the loss and it didn't get better over time. Fall changed to winter; they brought twenty swine and twelve cows to the slaughterhouse in Marietta. The war had brought good prices to the local market; the army was buying up all available meat. They did not have a threshing or husking frolic, and there was no mention of a cattle drive.

CHAPTER 11

Upper Sandusky
Wyandotte Nation
November 1812

Jim was welcomed; shelter and board was provided at Mr. Walker's trading post on the Sandusky River, near the Indian community of Upper Sandusky, which was close to the southern boundary of the reservation. After an exhausted twelve-hour sleep, Jim made himself useful by doing a full inventory of all the commodities at the trading post. In addition, his familiarity with the Wyandot dialect meant that there was another voice to facilitate commerce between Charles Walker and the locals. Jim's sleeping quarters was in a small shed. The work was not hard and Mr. Walker was a quiet gentleman who did not demand much from his tenants. The work they did was for the room they shared and the meals that were taken at the large table in the middle of the trading post. The table was also used for inspecting pelts that were brought in by the local Indians.

One day early in Jim's stay, a short, well-built Indian with a strong nose and thick neck walked into the trading post. Jim immediately recognized him as Long Hair, the man who forced the slave catchers to leave the nation. He approached, shook Jim's hand, and said, "I want to learn the white man's words." They spent the next two weeks together; teaching each other everything they could.

They went fishing, hunting, and trapping. Jim would read from books found at the trading posts. The trader also spent time with them around the big fireplace, involved in the discussions of the day and the reading sessions. This was the quiet time of year and business was minimal. Charles Walker had been the chief trader for six years; he was a well-educated man with much knowledge of the Wyandot culture. He enjoyed the presence of the two young and curious men of different cultures, exploring each others worlds.

The late November rains had continued for three days; gray skies hung low in the forest and blending with the morning fogs. There was a persistent mist on this brisk morning as Jim and Charles Walker left his small mission to attend the great conference of the fifteen clans, called together by the Grand Sachem Tarhee, holder of the calumet and unchallenged leader of the Wyandotte for over three decades. He had resided at the village called Crane town since the Treaty of Greenville fifteen years prior.

Jim was initially impressed with the activity and commerce that supported the twenty or more dwellings of rough hewn logs and shingled roofs, shelters of willow saplings covered with the birch and poplar bark, and small hovels made of trees and branches. The dwellings were spread over several littered acres without form or fashion. Gardens of beans, squash, and maize, presently lying fallow, were dispersed throughout the clearing. Pastures surrounded the community in which horses, sheep, and cows were busy grazing; pigs and chickens randomly appeared throughout the settlement.

The riders' destination was the council house; a large rectangular building rounded at the corners and maintained in the original ways of the eastern nations. Sixty feet long and about twenty feet wide, it had three large entryways, equal distances apart, facing south. The interior was supported by bent saplings; the exterior was covered with large sheets of bark stripped from elm and chestnut trees. Three large fires were warming and providing light to the hundred or so Indian leaders who had gathered this day, the smoke lifting slowly out the smoke holes in the roof. Outside, under a large canopy of deer skins, the women were preparing a feast of fowl, deer, fish, and recently harvested squash, maize, sweet potatoes, and beans. The smoke hung low, in keeping with the weather, and the mixed aroma of burning wood and boiling meats was welcoming and hospitable. Charles and Jim had been riding for two hours and were well soaked.

Tarhee, at the advanced age of seventy, still maintained a lithe and straight body; he stood tall at six feet, four inches, and dominated the gathering. His uncovered long dark hair with streaks of grey flowed randomly over his deerskin tunic; he wore few adornments but, as was his custom at important events, he had the Medal of Honor given to him by General Henry Harrison for his efforts to bring the hostile and renegade tribes together to secure the Treaty of Greenville. His talk this day, however, would be of war. He took his place in the center of the great hall, sitting on a raised platform covered with animal pelts; gathered around him were chiefs and sachems from the many surrounding villages. His voice was still strong and true, and it carried throughout the length of the council house. The audience became quiet in anticipation of the great leader's speech.

Only the distant barking of a distressed dog broke the silence and, around the doors of the council house, many children of all ages jostled for a position where they could see the shaman. He remained sitting as he began to speak.

"The great spirit above has appointed this day and this house for us to meet together. I shall deliver my sentiments to you of the many fires. So many seasons past, we lost our people and our hearts at the great battle of the fallen timbers, betrayed by our allies the British who cared not for our people and abandoned us in a time of great peril. I was born in the great forests of the north, but will never return to the land of my spirits.

"I have buried the long knife into the heart of the white man of the red coat. Brothers, hear me tell you of the treaty made at Greenville on the banks of the Scioto. Many great chiefs of many tribes, the six nations of the Iroquois, the Delaware, Ottawa, Chippewa, Pottawattamie, and the Wyandotte sat at that fire and made our peace with the American invaders. Brothers, it was not an easy peace and we suffered for our lands and our ways.

"The Americans took pity on our suffering and have honored some of the provisions that were agreed to; but in the times since, we have struggled. We have not seen the many silver dollars, provisions, and annuities promised us at every harvest moon.

"Our great spirit has seen us through many hard seasons. In spite of these hardships, we have hope and promise. Our lands then settled have not been violated, and a peace has flourished throughout our great nation.

"Hear me, leaders sitting at our fires: another war between the British in the north and our colonial keepers began in the season just passed. Battles have been fought and already the American leader General Hull has surrendered at Fort Detroit to the British and their allies, the Shawnee clan of the Dancing Tail and our brothers Round Head and Walk in Water, who lead the Wyandotte of the north. They have made their choice and we must make ours here today.

"We have all lived in fear of attack from the northern white man, as there is no protection on the frontier from the lake of Erie down the Sandusky River. We stayed on our land and will not leave it. Brothers, the friends of General Harrison have now promised us provisions of grain, forage, and cattle that will provide for our families so that they can see the coming of spring. I know it is a small portion of all that is owed to us. The great generals expect that the Wyandot Nation will provide scouts for his army and join General Tupler in marching north to the fields of war. It is now our duty to honor our agreement.

"Brothers, hear my voice as you have in the past; I speak from the heart and with truth. I do not care to fight again for the white man. I pray to the spirit that they should kill themselves and leave our land to its original people. Hear me also say that I do not trust this new general; he speaks lies as all the others have done, and his words are not true."

His speech was interrupted with the chants and whoops of warriors expressing their support and feeling the intense desperation of a crumbling world. Tarhee's voice got stronger as he continued.

"It is only of necessity that our nation should fight this war that is not ours, for only then will the foreigners continue to honor the treaty and allow us to keep our lands and maintain our ways. It is our only way.

"I speak with truth when I tell you of the great battles of the Wyandot nation The Great Spirit has given the Wyandotte power in battle. We fought with the great Shawnee chief Corn Stalk in the Dunmore war, with Pontiac at Fort Sandusky.

"The Wyandotte have long been brave warriors. Tecumseh, my friend and a great Shawnee chief, has spoken to other tribes and clans from the great river to the south and the mighty water of the sun going down are joining this war to fight with their white brothers of the north.

"Already, the Shawnees of the Dancing Tail clan, Tecumseh, and his brother the Prophet have left our lands and gone north to the fort on the river Detroit to take up the warrior's ways again. Already they have great victories over the Americans. General Hull has surrendered his army and shamed his country. General Harrison is now greatly in need of our spirit to rally his troops.

"Great warriors, I also know that Round Head and Walk in the Water, great chiefs of the Brown Town Wyandotte, have joined the British and are camped at Fort Malden. They have chosen what they see favors them. They will never be able to return to our lands. They will be our enemy.

"Our life is here. I am an old warrior who has seen much. It is best for us now to fight with the Americans. The general Harrison has asked us to send warriors to scout for the Americans. I go to war again. Call your warriors to join me at the Maumee."

Energetic debates followed the Grand Tarhee's speech. Many of the clan leaders were opposed to another war, and feared that Harrison would take over the land once the warriors left. The arguments on both sides were loud and angry and lasted for several hours. Tarhee left the long house when the debates were most heated; the tribal women listened intently from outside the long house, expressing their fears and disapproval with wails and outbursts. Over the next few hours, the leaders came to an agreement that satisfied both sides. The warriors and families would not leave the Wyandot Nation until the provisions of food stocks, forage, weapons, and ammunition were given as promised by General Harrison.

Twelve warriors, mostly young and led by Long Hair, Jim's friend since his day of rescue, would report to the American Army's encampment on the Maumee and act as scouts. Tarhee would stay on the Sandusky. Once the decision was made, they all feasted, sang, and danced their rituals of war throughout the night. Jim and Walker returned to the trading post the next morning after a warm night on the floor of the long house.

The scouts would leave in about week's time; they hoped for a cold spell to freeze up the great black swamp and make travel much easier. Jim would leave with them to enlist in the army of the frontier.

CHAPTER 12

Upper Sandusky Ohio
December 1812

*D*ear *Anna,*

I trust you have received this letter in confidence. I regret not being able to write for such a long time. I think of you and the farm often, wondering what events have occurred since my sudden departure so long ago. I believe you have knowledge of why I left and have not returned. I know of the general's death and the warrant for my arrest, although I know not of the felonious deeds for which Mr. Sprout seeks my apprehension. In any event, I have followed the General's direction as spoken to me when I left. It best be said that my time away has been most eventful and is better to be told in detail in your presence. I am curious about your life in my absence. I hope that Virginia is attending to the business and enterprise of the homestead and is able to control and manage her husband.

I think fondly of you and Digger attending to each other and I worry less. I hope that my blessed mother has been removed from harm's way and is not under the threatening presence of her husband.

I expect that Eldore Thermolay has shared my present situation and circumstances with you. May I add that I am in good health. I leave Crane town in the morning to join the army of the Northern Frontier on the Maumee River. I will write again when I am able.

If you desire to correspond with me, please post to the attention of Charles Walker, Indian Agent for the Wyandot Nation at upper Sandusky, State of Ohio. He will know of my circumstances and arrange for your letter to find me.

Give my solicitations to all the hands and helpers. Anna, I know not what events will occur. I wish for the day when we are in company again.

With affection and in anticipation, your humble friend,

Jim

Labithia had spent her time the last six weeks in the care of Lebanon and Millie Parker and their five children. The Parkers were emancipated blacks who had migrated from Virginia to the upper Ohio six years previously in search of a freedom and security not easily found even for the free blacks of the north. They found their peace here in the Wyandot Nation. They took over an abandoned two-room log cabin on Necessity Creek and, with industry and skill, turned the property into a modest and self-sustaining homestead. Lebanon replaced the fallen roof, put in wood floors, and added a small loft and an additional sleeping room on the first floor; he was a skilled carpenter and bartered his services to the occasional construction projects that needed his craft. Two years ago, he had rebuilt the Indian Agency and Trading Depot. The Parkers were industrious in many ways: several chickens turned into a breeding pool of roosters and hens that were much sought after. They found sufficient pasture to provide sustenance to two milk cows and were able to harvest several feral pigs each fall. Millie created a summer garden on two acres where her corn, beans, and squash grew abundantly and provided sufficient vegetables for the long winters. Through these efforts, the small homestead prospered and the Wyandot welcomed and admired their commerce and friendship.

Labithia worked alongside Millie and the two oldest daughters in performing all the domestic duties that were required on the modest farm: cooking, washing, collecting and cutting firewood, and tending to the youngest child, two-year-old Petaluna, were duties that Labithia performed with energy and eagerness. She relished her acceptance in this generous and happy family "It's sure amazing what freedom can do to one's disposition," Millie commented on several occasions as she watched this spirited young lady enjoying her state of emancipation. Deep concerns shadowed this serenity—both Millie and Lebanon knew that the slave catchers would not give up. It was only a matter of time before danger would reappear and most disconcerting was the inability to move the young fugitive northward into Canada due to the state of war that now existed. No one was available to make this journey and no one was available in Canada to receive her. They would need to find her a place to hide.

Several weeks after their rescue, Jim delivered provisions from the trading post to the Parkers. He stayed for dinner and would sleep on the cabin floor before returning. Labithia was excited to have her rescuer pay her a visit. Jim admitted to himself how much he enjoyed the young lady now that he was no longer responsible for her; after the dinner was cleared, they sat around the fire enjoying a bowl of tobacco. Labithia, who was sitting near the fire learning the intricacies of mending, suddenly started to talk about her life as a slave. She had not shared much of her life that Jim knew about... She didn't look at anyone, but stared into the fire as if talking to herself.

"I loss my mommy when dem speclators grabbed me from de field and took me from master Cartwrights. All de slaves just loked and didn't say nothin, dey put me in chains around de nck and we walked all de night. They grabbed two mor niggahs. Rosco, who be old and didn't walk well, he and I wr bound together for many a day as we walk. We came to a big city called Weelin and stayed there with no food for a long time. Both Rosco and me were purchased by another speclator and went on a flatboat down de big river. Dey say we go to work a tobacy place.

"We be sittin and watchin the river when a white man standin near by say that be the Ohio River and th other side be free land where whites would help slaves get to Kanada. Eh man wern't talking to us, but I herd all hy say. I no forget. All the tme I watched tat land and told Rosco we go to tat free land. We don stop de next day and wer marched to the tobacy farm ownd by Master Breckinridge. He treat us mean" we don run far away to Ohio

She stopped at that point, looked deep into the fire, and said, *"I never see my mummy again."*

Jim slept little that night; he had saved Labithia's life. He was beginning to realize what that meant for the little slave girl. His thoughts wandered to the general and Maggie and all the slaves they must have helped. He wondered why he was not included in these noble deeds. He got up before the day began and went over to the sleeping Labithia and kissed her on the forehead.

In 1808, the Parkers quite suddenly and unexpectedly received their first fugitive slave. It was early in the evening on a hot July day when Mr. Walker approached the house and asked to visit. He was harried and exhausted, but quite direct, "time is critical and we have a great need; will you provide shelter for a fugitive slave from Kentucky who is over yonder in the bushes and in need of food and rest"

Without comment or question, Lebanon and Millie accepted this dangerous request and became one of the very first sanctuaries in Ohio that would give the enslaved peoples of the south a sense of hope and a taste of freedom.

CHAPTER 13

Maumee River, Ohio
January 1813

Jim was the only white man that accompanied Long Hair and the twelve warriors going north. All were mounted and they had an additional string of supply horses. Rations were meager; corncobs to provide forage for the horses represented much of what they carried. They were promised ample rations when they reported to General Winchester.

The American Army encampment on the Maumee River near the rapids was full of chaos and confusion. They reached it on their third day of battling cold, blustery and dark weather that chilled to the bone. After twenty straight hours of enduring the black swamp, even the hardiest of the travelers were looking forward to shelter, food and warmth. At the center of the encampment, soldiers were building wood huts and a picketed stockade, of which only one side showing any sign of progress. Efforts appeared disorganized and chaotic. Several homes and barns in the immediate area had been taken over by the Officer Corps; flags were flying and horses, wagons, and other supplies were arranged in an orderly fashion. The smoke from the chimneys brought envy and thoughts of better times for the cold and hungry contingent from the Sandusky.

It was clear that the army had only recently come to this encampment; the recruits were disappointed in the lack of housing or adequate shelter of any kind. Several cabins were scattered throughout the area, but these were poorly built, many with canvas for roofs and doors and rough-hewn log sides that varied in height and length. The fields around the encampment were filled with tents of several sizes and styles; these appeared to be the primary domiciles for the several thousand enlisted men gathered there.

As they struggled to erect lean-tos and makeshift cabins, the soldiers appeared to have been left on their own to make the best of their situation. There were many fires with men standing idly by, warming themselves with no apparent duties or activities.

The regular soldiers were dressed in blue formal wool uniforms, with tall, ill-fitting hats that had no apparent purpose. The volunteers, for the most part, were clothed in their own home-spun garments of wool and cotton that varied in their condition and the warmth they provided. They all possessed a government-issued gray blanket that gave a little warmth and comfort. The officers were uniformed in their winter attire, well suited for the cold Ohio weather.

Long Hair and his warriors rode through the disorder, heading to the buildings, where several flags and ensigns were whipping in the wind. A uniformed sergeant walked over to Long Hair and ordered him to halt. The warriors remained on their horses and, in a few minutes, General Tupler and several of his aides came out of a farmhouse. They approached and welcomed the Wyandot scouts; after several minutes of conversation, the chief and two warriors were invited into the officers' quarters while the remainder of the scouts moved out of the encampment, dismounted, and built a fire as they awaited their leader. Long Hair returned from his meeting and led his men out of the encampment. They rode west on the north side of the river to find a more satisfactory camp, choosing a cluster of cottonwoods several miles away from the chaos.

The sergeant that had greeted the warriors now noticed Jim "What are you doing here white boy?" he asked.

"Joining the army," Jim said.

The sergeant looked him over for a minute and said, "Get your ass off that horse and follow me." A uniformed orderly took the horse, stripped off the bedroll and saddlebag, and tossed them at the feet of the recruit. "This horse is now government property," said the sergeant, "and so are you. Follow me." Jim picked up his belongings and followed the sergeant to an open area, where several large elm trees supported a canvass tarpaulin sheltering two makeshift tables and a few chairs. The open area was warmed somewhat by two fire pits that were kept fueled by a large pile of cut wood that served as the northern wall of the compound. It was clearly a temporary shelter unsuited to a winter climate

Jim was surprised and disappointed by his immediate impression of the great American Army. He thought he would be welcomed into an organized and structured encampment where he would be treated with courtesy and respect.

"Stand at attention you idiot. You're in officer country," said the sergeant. The recruit made an ineffective effort to stand straight. "A new recruit, sir," the sergeant said to a young officer who was preoccupied with the papers and parchments on the table in front of him. The lieutenant looked up but did not stand and surveyed his new recruit.

"Where are you from?" he asked.

Jim said, "From Ohio."

He was immediately clobbered across the side of his head by the sergeant, who faced him and said, "You refer to officers as sir always."

Jim could feel his anger rising and the impulse to assault his attacker was strong. With difficulty, he maintained a compliant presence. The lieutenant ignored what had happened and asked, "Where in Ohio?"

"Marietta, sir."

"What are you doing with the Indians?"

Jim paused wondering how he should answer finally said "Resting on my way here, sir."

The lieutenant continued to ask questions. "Are you on the run from any crimes or circumstances that would make you unfit for military service?"

"No, sir," was his answer that was less than truthful but seemed to be the response the lieutenant wanted.

"Very well," said the lieutenant. "Go to that table and be sworn in with Corporal Hewitt. He will give you the information you need. Stay out of trouble and you will do well." The officer returned to his papers.

The corporal was serious as he filled out an official-looking document, name, age, date of birth, county of residence and next of kin. Jim answered all of the questions and gave his mother's name, saying she resided in Washington County, Ohio. The corporal took a great deal of time to complete the form. Finally, he stood tall and, with his most authoritative voice, addressed the recruit.

"You are signing up for a one-year enlistment in the army of the United States of America. Your rank is private; your pay is 6.66 American dollars per month. Payable at the pleasure of the U.S. Army. You have no rights or privileges other than those granted you by your superior officers. If you desert or in any other way fail to fulfill your duties as ordered by your superiors, you will be summarily disciplined to the extent of death by firing squad if so ordered. There are no uniforms to provide you with at this time and you are to use your personal firearm if you have one in your possession. Sign your X at the bottom of this document."

The corporal handed the document across the table. "Place your x on the bottom

Jim took a minute, read the information carefully, and asked if he could sign his name instead of an X.

"You know how to read and write?" the corporal asked. Jim said he did. "The Commandant may want to talk to you."

Jim's enlistment in the American Army began. He was assigned to General Winchester's command and took up residence in a wooded area, where he joined the 2nd company of the 3rd Ohio Infantry. He was immediately assigned to gather firewood and work with several other recruits in building a structure out of roughly cut timbers, fallen branches, and patches of canvas, to provide them with a crude shelter.

Jim awoke to a cold blustery morning; the early January wind was bitter as it blew the snow in sheets across the open fields and whistled through the woodlots. The weather continued cold and dismal over the next several days. The shelter, when finished, provided nothing more than four walls and a leaky roof. The food was worse than the shelter and consisted of hard biscuits, jerked beef, and salt pork; meals were sporadic, and only one meal was served on most days. The recruits were overseen by an indifferent, intoxicated corporal who was seldom in sight. Most of their first days were occupied in standing sentry, gathering increasingly scarce fire wood, and trying to keep warm. In a very short time, Jim, was bored, lonely, hungry, cold, angry and disillusioned. They were always wet in their shelter and the recruits huddled together to secure some warmth from the fire pit at the front of the cabin, which did not provide consistent heat. Jim wondered why his General would speak so often and so reverently about the army and its glory. He could see none of it.

The young soldiers who shared the shelter immediately wanted to be somewhere else; they talked of home and better days. There was no longer any sense of adventure, just tedium, hunger, cold, and loneliness. These were hard times for Jim; he thought often of the warmth, happiness, and friendships back on Maggie's Hill, of the general, Anna, and Digger. He hoped his mother and sister were safe.

On the seventh day, a sergeant appeared and ordered all the new men to form up; forty recruits were introduced into the company. "Get ready for war," said the sergeant. "We are moving out tomorrow."

Jim and the others had just finished a breakfast of some heated corn meal mush and corn flour biscuits when an officer's orderly seated on a steaming, prancing dun-colored horse approached the bivouac and said, "Private Morgan, I am in need of Private Morgan. Where is Private Morgan?" Surprised to hear his name, Jim responded, and the orderly said, "It is my orders to fetch you to General Winchester's quarters immediately."

Jim began to ask what for, but the orderly said, "My orders are to bring you to the general. That is all I can say. Join me on my horse this moment." Jim reluctantly used the orderly's arm to swing up behind the saddle; the horse rode powerfully for about a mile, mostly in a foot or more of snow; Jim was dropped off at the open end of a barn, where several blue-coated officers were standing.

Some distance away, several Indians were gathered, sitting on their haunches, holding the reins of several of their horses. Jim stood alone for several minutes before an officer approached him and asked his name. "You are the friend of Long Hair?" said the officer. "He seeks your counsel. Go and do what is right for the U.S. Army." Jim followed the officer into the dimly lit barn.

As soon as his eyes adjusted, he could see several officers sitting in chairs facing Long Hair and two of his warriors. The officer escorting him said, "This be Private James Morgan of the 19th Ohio, sir."

General Winchester, sitting casually, asked Jim, "You know

this Wyandot Long Hair?"

"I know him, yes sir," Jim said in his best military manner.

"It seems this young warrior doesn't trust our interpreters and has requested your services," said the general. "Do you know his language?"

"Yes, sir."

The general asked, "Are you literate in both reading and writing?"

"Yes, sir," Jim said.

Jim was then ordered to talk with the Indian scout; he walked over to Long Hair and they walked out the open barn door to their horses, where a small fire was being managed by the remaining scouts. One of the army's interpreters followed along; he was quickly dismissed by Long Hair, who spoke angrily in the native dialect. "The general wants us to spy with Colonel Lewis on his journey to French Town," he said. "I have not received our rations, forage, or weapons as promised when we left the Sandusky. We will not go with this army without our supplies; I trust you, my friend, to tell the general my exact words. He needs to know my intent." Jim nodded turned and walked over to the general and his party.

"Sir, Long Hair requires provisions, forage for the horses, weapons, and munitions," he said. "He will not escort Colonel Lewis without the supplies that were promised." Jim continued to stand at attention; the general's party looked toward their leader to see how he would react to this insubordination.

"You tell that no good red bastard that he will get his supplies when I give them to him and that he is ordered to go on this expedition," said the general. "They all will be shot if he refuses. Tell him."

"Yes, sir," said Jim, and walked out of the barn. He thought for a moment before he said, "My good friend Long Hair, I repeat what I was told. Trust my words to be his intent." The warrior stood without speaking. "The general does not accept your request for the supplies you were promised. He orders you to obey his order or you and your men will be shot."

There was silence for a moment. Long Hair looked into Jim's eyes, smiled slightly, and said, "My friend Jim be brave as a warrior. We will meet another time."

The Indians got on their horses and rode quickly out of the encampment, disappearing in the forming mist. Jim returned to the general and stood quietly at attention. "What say you private?" asked the general. "What was his response? What did he say?"

"He said nothing of your order, sir," said Jim.

"He talked, what did he say?" asked the general, aggravated.

Jim said, "He told me to be a brave warrior, sir." The general stood up and stormed out of the barn, his adjutants close behind. Jim stood formally and quietly alone, not knowing his role; he eventually left the building and began to walk back toward his unit.

He was soon called back by the general's adjutant, who said, "The general wants to see you now." He was hurried into the general's quarters, a crowded living area in a small house. He entered and stood at attention. The general was preoccupied with numerous documents; he continued to read and sign them as he asked Jim, "Where did you learn the redskin language?"

"I was taught by the Shawnees when I was very young and I have used it with frequency for years," Jim said.

"How many dialects do you know?" asked the general.

"Most of the northern tribes, sir," said Jim, "All that are Algonquin, sir."

"What did Long hair say to you before he left? Be honest now?"

"He told me to be a strong warrior, sir," said Jim.

"Do you know him well?" asked the general.

"I lived with the Wyandot nation during the fall and we hunted together, sir."

The general didn't respond right away, reading a letter that had caught his attention. After several minutes he said, "I may have some use for you. You're to be transferred to my detachment. Report back to my adjutant and you will be assigned a billet. You're dismissed."

The next day, January 18th, on a windy, blustery evening, General Winchester, heavily wrapped and riding in a sleigh pulled by a team of strong and energetic horses with his headquarters company on horseback, and three hundred troops of Ohio regulars on foot, moved down the Maumee River and onto the frozen ice of Lake Erie to march north up the Detroit River to the River Raisin and the small community of Frenchtown. Here, an advanced contingent of mostly Kentucky militia had routed a small company of British soldiers and their allies two days prior. The general, always an opportunist, was anxious to secure his name to a victory and pushed the men hard. With less than three weeks in the army and with a company of strangers in a strange land, Jim marched with them.

CHAPTER 14

Journal Entry
September 12, 1777
Jonathon McGuire
Brandywine Creek
Pennsylvania

I'*am most reluctant to write and, thereby, to recollect all the thoughts and memories of that terrible day. I think sometimes it would be best not to record the events of the battle of the Brandywine four long and bitter days ago. My pen will not be able to express or convey the pain and humiliation upon this person by my own actions and those of my troops. I seek not to remember but to forget those events; I yearn to return to the field of battle and re-create events as they should have occurred. This night at this time is the first opportunity to apply my history to paper, a task not welcomed but most necessary. I recite this shameful experience with great difficulty but my narrative is accurate in detail and honest to my recall.*

"The 200 men and 12 officers of my command, earnestly recruited from the fine men of Bucks County, left their families and livelihoods on June 17th, and marched across the hills of Pennsylvania and flat pine forests of

New Jersey to the patriot army and the great general en-
camped in Morristown. We reported to duty on July 1ˢᵗ,
1777. I was given the rank of Colonel by the good governor
of Pennsylvania. We were assigned to General Green's com-
mand and familiarized ourselves to the rituals and practices
of military life. Although limited in drill and formation,
we learned eagerly all that was offered and awaited the call
to battle.

"My meetings with General Washington and his sub-
ordinates were frequent; I found him to be a serious man
of few words. He appeared preoccupied and contemplative
much of the time. He was, I must report, always courteous
to his staff and his junior officers. This was a time of high
spirits. Food and dry goods were abundant as the French
supply ships were discharging there cargoes on the Delaware
landing. There was a bounty of new volunteers as eager as
we to seek combat with our enemies.

"We marched out of our encampments on the
Morristown heights on September the 2nd and proceeded
south to defend Philadelphia from General Howe, who
had landed a most formidable force at the Head of Elk
on the Chesapeake. We provisioned at Chester for several
days. My company was then attached to General Sterling's
Regiment and we moved forward to Brandywine Creek, a 2
day march from Philadelphia.

"The briefings indicated that Howe and Cornwallis
would attack us on the 9ᵗʰ. My company was placed on the
right flank of Sterling's skirmish line, on higher ground on
the creek's west side. We all were determined to show our
courage and to fight an honorable battle. The order given to
me by Gen. Sterling was to protect at all costs the skirmish
line from any flanking movement or other trickery that the
devious British might attempt.

"I recall the sunrise to be set with fog with a most humid day to follow. I must confess that in anticipation of my first violent engagement, I was quite calm. The men endured a dry breakfast, most anxious and excited about the pending battle.

"The noise of war began early and, in time, became overwhelming. General Greene had engaged the Hessians several miles down the creek and the sound of cannon and musket fire was clear and ominous. We stayed in position, awaiting orders and action.

"'To your flank, move to your flank. Damn you, protect our flank.' The general was staring at me with a furious look in his eye. 'The redcoats will be attacking behind you, they are moments away, move your men.'

"I realized that I been motionless in both thought and deed; I ordered my officers to move to the right and quickly formed a skirmish line across the road adjoining the river facing north. I could hear the drums and the fifes, the marching feet and the cries of halloo from the red enemy marching at fast time 6 abreast; cannon shells were now bursting around us. I moved my horse, drew my sword, and recalled that I had told my men to be steady. The first volley was most deadly, and the most horrible events I would ever experience were upon me. My loyal horse, King Royal dropped headless from the direct burst of a cannonade, blood spurting, filling my eyes and mouth with his blood and brains. I found myself on the ground, in a panic and most confused, trying to find his head. All around I could feel the fear and chaos, the smell of gunpowder, the screaming of men and horses, men running, dropping their weapons, falling dead to the ground, The British front was just yards away, coming toward me. I must most solemnly admit to my journal my mortal fear; my only desire was to live and be away from

the death and carnage. I was thrown clear of my horse and, with my sword in hand, I confess I was running only to get away, to save my life. I ran for a great distance as fast as I could until my lungs were ready to burst. I felt the power of musket volley after musket volley. Ball and shot were exploding all around; the redcoats continued to pursue us. Men were running, falling, screaming. Someone was standing looking down on me, 'Stand, man, rally your troops, return to the battle.' One of my officers was grabbing my arm and yelling in my ear. 'Get up, men are waiting for you, get up, lead us.'

"I got to my feet; someone was helping me. Exhaustion dominated my being; my men were walking in retreat. Someone ordered rally to Birmingham Hill—I noticed that my sword was broken in two. Cannon fire was all around, some patriots were shooting back.

"We fell behind a skirmish line. I, most regrettably was unable to get control of my faculties. I lay on the ground, my men around waiting to fire and stop the advance. I recall that we volleyed several times, a host of men were fallen, blood turning black, remnants of flesh and bone, some in great pain. A most chaotic, fearful condition, a most wretched, pathetic creature was I. Someone yelled 'Fall back, in orders of 3.' My men picked me up and assisted me to the next volley line. I was still unable to offer assistance, to take command, to manifest anything other than cowardice.

"It is my best recollection that the line held, the mercenaries stopped their advance, we sat where we were, exhausted, the explosions abating, the terrible screech of war diminished. Smoke began to clear. A commander unknown to me, atop a horse, stood over us. 'Take your officer to the rear,' he said, 'we have no need of him here.'

"I tell my story, never to be told again. I admit to my

fears and inadequacies only in these pages and to myself. My burden will be long. Forever I will suffer my failure and humiliation.

"I met with General W. this p.m. He had just returned from a ride and was seated outside his headquarters alone under a large oak; he was without coat and hat, and was enjoying a cup of cider. His staff were about, busy with other things. Captain Tilighman escorted me to a simple chair facing the General and made introductions. The general inquired as to my health and talked of the weather, it being a most balmy and calm September afternoon.

"He remained quiet and preoccupied for a time, looking eastward at the Delaware not too distant. He then inquired about my civilian life back in Bucks County and said, and the words will in my shame be forever remembered, 'Colonel, you failed your men and yourself this date and that will be your burden to manage as best you can. I too failed my men and my country: I did not respond sufficiently to my advisors that told me of the encirclement. I too carry a burden of failure. It is the price of command.'

"He was most respectful when he told me that the remainder of my company would be transferred to another command and that I have been reassigned to the commissariat and ordered to report to Commissary General William Buchanan at Coryell's Ferry on the Delaware. Here, I am to become a purchasing officer. They have found me a horse and I will escort 3 empty wagons with teamsters at first light. I have kept my rank but

My days of command are over; failure is now final. I have no words to express my sorrow and my shame."

CHAPTER 15

Frenchtown
Michigan Territory
January 1813

General Winchester marched his three hundred men all through the night and came off the ice on the south bank of the River Raisin in mid afternoon. There was jubilation as the new troops were welcomed by the victorious army of General Lewis and his Kentucky volunteers, who had routed a small group of British and Indian troops the previous day. Winchester's reinforcements were instructed to prepare a defensive line in an open area just north of the river and on the right flank of the Kentuckians, who were well protected behind a puncheon fence that protected the gardens of the Frenchtown inhabitants, and to prepare for an assault that was expected the following day. The general then retired to the pleasant and spacious residence of Peter Navarro, a mile from his troops on the south side of the Raisin. Requests by his aides for the general to stay with his men, to send out patrols, and to reinforce the picket lines were ignored as he took his leave.

Jim's only thoughts were of getting out of the cold; hours of numbing marching had left him exhausted and with little interest in his surroundings or the upcoming engagement. He only sought replenishment, warmth, and shelter. The new troops were stationed exposed in an open field on the right flank, outside the picketed defenses that Colonel Lewis had established earlier in the day. The line was parallel to the Raisin about a mile north. The men were put to work building a line of defense as best they could in anticipation of a British attack.

The new troops were distributed and billeted amongst the thirty or so houses and out buildings that defined Frenchtown. Fires were built in an abandoned barn back from the skirmish line and the troops of Jim's company would in turn warm themselves throughout the night. Frozen cobs of corn that were stored in the barn to be used for forage for livestock were roasted and consumed by the nearly famished men.

It was early morning, still dark. Jim was standing in the open on his tour of sentry duty when the assault began.

The drummer was beating reveille when the loud crack of several sentries' muskets permeated the sleeping village. Jim saw the first flashes from the enemy's rifles; he immediately ducked as bombshells and canister shot screamed over his head and overwhelmed the space around him. He crouched, immobilized for several moments, gasping for air and desperately looking for protection. Other troops were coming from their shelters in small groups, taking position on the skirmish line. In a moment the sounds of musket fire and cannonade were deafening, mixed in with the ear splitting cries of the Indians. Jim began to see their movement among the smoke of the rifles and the shadows of the early morning.

He watched as if he wasn't there until a man next to him cried out in pain and fell face down in the snow. He then lifted and aimed at a moving shadow coming toward him; he fired and watched the shadow fall, oblivious to the reality that he may have killed someone. He clumsily reloaded and set his second shot.

Someone yelled, "To the picket fence." A few men retreated hastily, then after more sporadic musket fire, Winchester's entire relief force broke and ran. Overwhelmed with fear and in the middle of a wild and desperate pack, Jim ran through the snow, aware now of the war cries of the hundreds of warriors of Tecumseh's alliance running among the gardens, trees, and fields that bordered Lake Erie. Like the others, Jim was overtaken by a terrible panic; fear was his only feeling, escape his only thought. The Wyandotte and Pottawatomie surrounded them and poured musket fire into the retreating troops, taking a deadly toll. Running fast through the woodlots, they were soon able to outflank the beleaguered company. Explosions from the cannons and the whistling of the musket balls intensified and added to the chaos; Jim only wanted to be away from the noise and violence, to find protection and silence. The mob of frightened and stricken men continued to run in several directions. Some reached the frozen River Raisin and crossed. Jim, running as fast as he could, fell on a patch of bare river ice; still in a panic, he regained his footing and ran amid the chaos, trying to escape the enemy.

Jim was shot in the shoulder as he climbed up the south bank of the river; he fell down from the force of the musket ball and confused and bewildered, lay on the ground. He felt no pain but saw the crimson stain of his blood on the snow around him. He thought of death and began to sob. A Kentucky militiaman who had left the picketed defense line to support the retreating troops grabbed him by the shoulder and yelled at him to get up and run. *Get to the houses, regroup there.* Oddly, Jim felt embarrassed, as he had soiled himself; he got up on one knee, staggered for several steps and followed other retreating soldiers for several hundred more yards to the village. There, he took shelter behind a small farmhouse.

I lost my rifle; oh my God, I left the general's rifle. Injured and terrified, it was all he could think about.

Jim sat for several moments looking at the blood that covered his shoulder, not knowing where to go or what to do. He watched in horror and disbelief as many of his retreating comrades who had fallen or were trying to surrender were tomahawked, shot and scalped. All around him men were dying. He closed his eyes; fear overwhelmed him and he sat helpless, his back against a wall, awaiting death. Eventually, a medical aide came by and looked at the blood-soaked wound. He yelled at Jim to get up; he was forced to his feet and taken to the Parvy house not too far away, where many of the wounded were gathering.

The low-ceilinged room was crowded and filled with the smells and cries of the injured. In the middle of the room, under the dim light of several lanterns, bloodied men were standing over a blood-stained kitchen table, cutting, mending and sawing into the flesh of their patients. The smell of men dying, blood, feces, and urine was overwhelming. Someone cut Jim's shirt open and forced a bandage onto his wound. He was awake but very tired, and not fully aware of where he was. He could feel the pain in his shoulder now, but even that seemed far away. He sat in shock; everything he saw or heard seemed to be in slow motion and far away. He soon realized that he had run in fear and panic from the battle, lost the general's long rifle and soiled himself. He felt his blood-stained shirt and his fear increased. He desperately wanted to get up and leave, to escape from these horrors, but he was unable to move. Everything became blurry; Jim drifted away.

The many wounded were unaware and uninformed of the events that were occurring around them. Not long after Jim was shot, General Winchester and Colonel Lewis were made prisoners by Chief Round Head at a bridge about a mile from the village. They were stripped of their clothes down to their pantaloons, shirts and boots and taken to the British Commander, Colonel Proctor. Winchester unconditionally surrendered his entire army, even though the Kentucky volunteers under major Graves and

Madison were holding their line and confident of winning this battle.

Jim slowly became aware of someone talking close to his ear as he sat on the floor, his back against a wall. "Soldier, listen to me," he said. "I am Dr. John Todd. You have been shot; a musket ball is lodged in your shoulder, just below your collar bone. I have to go in, find it, and get it out, and it has to come out now. Just nod if you understand. We will move you to the operating table; this will hurt. You need to be strong; these men will move you and hold you." The pain was white and streaked across his soul; he faded into darkness.

It was late afternoon when Jim became aware of the lengthening shadows as they slowly crossed the room. It seemed much quieter now. He could hear the moans of broken men, several calling for their mothers. He felt the pain in his shoulder, his arm wrapped tight against his chest. He was desperately thirsty and called repeatedly for water. A medical orderly eventually stopped and placed a cup against his lips; Jim drank it greedily, relieved.

"You will need to walk soon," the orderly said. "We need to move you to another house. I will be back to help you." He hurried on to other patients. Jim sat and waited; his clothes covered in blood and sweat, absent of thought and drained of any feelings, unaware of time or place.

Several hours later he was helped to get up and walk. Water was provided and he moved to another house about a hundred yards away; other wounded soldiers were already in the house, resting as best they could.

He felt cold as he entered; his room had a fire that provided both warmth and light, and soon an orderly put a cup of laudanum to his lips. "Drink this," he said. "It will help you sleep." He slept again for several hours, conscious only of his pain and the sound of death. .

In the grey light of dawn, the tireless Dr. Todd spoke to the twenty or thirty wounded men packed into three rooms of the modest farmhouse. "We are waiting for sleds to come for us from Fort Malden," he said. "We will be moved this morning and taken to the fort as prisoners of the British; we will leave as soon as the British sleighs arrive. Mrs. Godfrey the owner of this house has provided us with some beef broth and dry bread; nourish yourselves and rest as well as you can. Those of you who are able will need to walk; I will make my rounds and attend to your wounds shortly." The men who were alert enough listened in disbelief; word quickly passed around the rooms that General Winchester had surrendered his entire army. The men were indeed at the mercy of the British and their Indian friends; fear was now added to the pain and suffering.

Before dawn, Dr. Todd had been called outside by his frantic associate, Dr. Ezra Bowers. "The British are leaving; see for yourself," he said. The doctor was able to make out Major Reynolds, the British officer who was left behind to control and protect the wounded prisoners, leaving the village with his entire complement: three interpreters, a dozen enlisted men, several sleighs of wounded British soldiers, and a handful of Indians heading down the Raisin River toward the lake, where they would turn north to the Detroit River and Fort Malden. Dr. Todd immediately began to run toward the departing group, with a sense of panic and foreboding. "Major Reynolds, I need your attention," he called as he ran. The major initially ignored the calls, but eventually stopped his horse and waited for the doctor to arrive; Todd called out in an angry and desperate voice, "You are leaving us. We have no way of transporting our wounded. You were left here to protect us from the savages. We are your prisoners; it is your duty to provide safe transport."

The major listened for only a moment and said, "I have my own men to care for, I can't be burdened with yours."

"You are a criminal if you leave us now," said the doctor. The

Indians will slaughter us; they will soon be upon us. How dare you leave?"

Major Reynolds, now irritated and impatient, said, "So be it." The British gentleman turned and clicked his horse; the conversation was over.

The devastated doctor watched them disappear into the darkness; the fear of annihilation was upon him as he turned and walked back to his doomed patients.

It was mid morning; the crystal fog was settled around the forlorn town. Jim was now standing unassisted outside the home where he and other wounded soldiers had spent a fretful night. The doctor had told him earlier that his surgery was successful; his injury was not severe and he would recover.

The pain was tolerable and he was able to stand leaning against the porch railing; his thin blanket, however, did little to protect him from the chill and gusts of frigid winds. The Indians had left French Town the night before and moved north to their encampment on Stony Creek after the surrender ceremonies the previous afternoon. The assaults and killing of the fleeing soldiers had ceased the previous day upon the order of General Proctor, the British commandant. The wounded prisoners under the care of the two Kentucky doctors now looked to the north with fear and trepidation; they could see through the patches of fog and swirls of snow that several hundred Indians had returned and were busy painting their faces with lamp black and orange ochre, the colors of slaughter and revenge. The wounded soldiers, their doctors and the orderlies were subdued as they began to realize their situation and contemplate their fate.

In the distance; standing away from the face-painting warriors, were several chiefs who appeared to be holding a council. Several of the prisoners were able to identify the chubby profile of Round Head and the much older and taller Walk in the Water, the Co-Chiefs of the Brownstone Wyandotte. Other members of the council were less familiar. The parley went on for most of the morning. Eventually, several of the council mounted their horses and set off in single file, coming slowly toward the Americans who were congregated outside the Godfrey house. Dr. Todd and Bowers joined the small contingent of wounded and quietly watched the twenty or so riders approach. As they got closer, Jim was able to recognize Tecumseh and members of his clan; the horses were well ridden and the men appeared tired, wrapped in robes and blankets against the cold.

Without much thought, Jim walked up to Dr. Todd and told him that the warrior on the lead horse was Tecumseh and that he knew him, could talk his language. He asked permission to approach the chief. He was surprised that this young private knew of the great chief Tecumseh, and granted permission with a nod of the head; Jim walked slowly away from the group and waited for the approaching riders. When they were close enough, he began to speak in the Shawnee dialect.

"Tecumseh, great chief of the Shawnees," he said. "I seek to parley." Tecumseh rode abreast of Jim, then pulled up his horse and stared down at the prisoner. "Great chief," Jim said, "I am Forest Boy. I was welcomed at your fire during the season of long days when camped at the salt marsh on the Hock hocking River." Tecumseh looked at him without speaking. Jim continued; "We are injured prisoners who have been abandoned by your white allies and are unable to protect ourselves. I inquire of your intent and request your protection."

Tecumseh looked at Jim for several more minutes and, without any sense of recognition or change of expression, said, "Forest Boy, you have become a warrior. A warrior's fate awaits you."

Jim asked, "Will we have safe passage to Amherstberg?"

Tecumseh looked about and said, in English and loud enough for the doctors to hear, "This is Round Head's battle and Walk in the Water's victory; they will decide the outcome and the fate of the injured."

Jim, anguished, said, "Great chief, you can stop the slaughter. Where is the honor that you speak of?"

There was a long silence. Tecumseh looked back at Jim and, with irritation in his tired eyes, said quietly, "You know not of honor. War and sacrifice await you; then you may know of what you speak." Tecumseh turned about on his horse and watched the gathering of Round Head's Indians for a moment. He turned back and looked directly at Jim. "Tell your doctor, if you can walk you will live."

The horses moved on and the parley ended. Jim watched in silence as they rode by, heading to the east, with only the gusts of cold wind protesting the slaughter that was about to begin. As Tecumseh's party rode on, Jim also recognized the Prophet and Cheeksauhaloslo, his elder brother, who nodded in recognition.

The doctors approached Jim, anxious to hear what the great chief of the alliance had to say; Jim, now very exhausted and wanting to sit for a minute, said, "Those ones who can walk will live."

More aware now of the throbbing pain in his shoulder and the first sweats of a fever, Jim walked as best he could out of Frenchtown; he was one of forty ambulatory American wounded with no protective escort except for several of Round Head's northern Wyandotte warriors. He was at the back of the group and didn't believe he would make it the eighteen miles to Amherstburg. The journey would take all night, with no place to rest or take shelter. It seemed impossible.

The walking wounded were subdued, stunned, shocked, and enraged at the slaughter they had just witnessed. For more than an hour, two hundred face-painted Wyandotte and Potawatomi led by the two chiefs had rampaged through the village of Frenchtown, taking up where they left off the previous day, plundering, killing, and scalping the wounded Americans who were left behind, unable to walk or protect themselves.

Jim and the others watched in horror as they burned down houses with wounded men inside. They heard horrific screams of terror and agony as many were burned alive. Those able to escape out of the windows and doors were eagerly and wantonly slaughtered. Skulls were broken open, throats slashed, and the victims' warm innards poured out onto the snow as tomahawks and axes did the brutal work. All were scalped for the generous rewards that awaited them at the fort. All of the homes and out-buildings in French Town were burning. Flames and dark clouds swirled about in the gusty wind as the walking wounded moved as quickly as they could east on the Raisin River to Fort Malden. The group moved down the frozen river in silence with rage in their hearts.

The terrifying image of thirty or more freshly mutilated bod-ies spread randomly on the blood-stained snow, many with the steam from the warm bodies rising and then fading into the colder air was fixed in Jim's mind. The smoke and flames from the burning homes, providing an evil silhouette to the devastated town, left him almost without feelings. Many of the Indians, still drinking the spirits found in Jerome Jerasume's cellar, continued their rampage, taking anything of interest and destroying every-thing else. The cries of the helpless victims violated Jim's soul.

Most of the residents of Frenchtown had left the previous day, heading back to the Maumee and the protection of General Harrison. There may be no one to tell the world of the slaughter of the helpless wounded soldiers on the River Raisin.

Eventually, Round Head and Walk in The Water's warriors followed the walking wounded on their way to Fort Malden, kill-ing any prisoners who could go no further and fell along the way. There was no order or authority to provide control; initially, there were words of encouragement amongst the injured prison-ers. But efforts to help those who could no longer walk gave way quickly to the realization that it was every man for himself as the wounded fought personal fatigue, pain and cold in a star-filled night. They had no energy to help their comrades; there were no healthy bodies to carry the burden, only the encouragement of Dr. Todd and his two aides to lead the men in the right direction. Behind them were the Indians; boisterous predators, waiting for the weakest to fall and fail. Many did.

Jim's body was exhausted, pain and fever draining his energy. His fear of faltering and being slaughtered pushing him forward. He could hear the drunken cries of the Indians mixed with the cold gusts of the west wind. As he plowed onward, he realized that, in the last twenty-four hours, his life had changed once more. He now knew the violence of war, the overwhelming fear, the need to escape, the lack of honor, his own cowardice, the brutality.

As he huddled inside his thin blanket, his head down, following the footsteps of the others, Jim realized that he was now of another world. Anger and rage soon dominated his feelings; he thought of revenge, to live to destroy the enemy, who were now very real and very close. He walked with the dull pain in his chest, the fever of his body, the thirst, fatigue, hunger, and cold. He vowed that, if he survived, he would over come his fears, be his own man. He would seek no one else's protection or care. He would choose his own course.

It was a grey dawn when the wounded stragglers walked off the snow and ice of the Detroit River and into the hands of the British and captivity. Amherstburg was a small community consisting of a few residences, several public buildings, a small stockade called Fort Malden, and a dock and shipyard with several ships in various states of repair. In the distance was the Indian supply center, several one-story log structures where the inducement and provisioning of the Indian alliance took place.

The wounded who survived the march waited outside in front

of the stockade for most of the morning. The doctors went inside to determine the willingness of the British Medical Corp to provide needed attention to the exhausted men. Eventually, they were brought into a small building used for storing military supplies; there was just enough room for the men to lie down and no heat in the building on this cold day. The collective heat of the men soon brought some comfort. Several aides in red coats and a doctor moved among the men, providing bowls of a hot stew and cups of water. Efforts were made to clean and dress the soldier's wounds. The exhausted men were in terrible shape. Dr. Todd moved around the room, tirelessly administering the medicinal supplies provided to him by the medical proviso. *There will be many deaths this day,* he thought.

The bowl of rich broth with small bits of meat warmed Jim's body and a cup of cold water quenched his terrible thirst and fed his spirit; an aide came by, cleaned the pus that was now beginning to flow from his open wound, and applied a clean bandage. Exhaustion took over; Jim's eyes closed. The soldiers' deep slumbers were broken by painful calls for their mothers and the soft breathing noises of death as men began to succumb to their injuries.

Jim awoke from a coma-like sleep; the smell of urine, feces, infection, and unwashed bodies welcomed him back to his cramped world. Shafts of light coming through the poorly constructed supply room walls told him that he had survived the night and morning hours. He felt the throbbing ache in his shoulder and decided that it wasn't any worse; that was an improvement. Within a few minutes, as Jim waited for strength to return to his body, Dr. Todd knelt next to him, their faces nearly touching.

"Private Morgan, how do you feel?" asked the doctor. He didn't wait for an answer. "Your wound is healing. We put a clean bandage on early this morning; the infection is under control and your fever is waning. You have slept well for eighteen hours."

Jim, now more alert, said that he was feeling better and asked for water. He wanted to get up and away from the smells and moans of the wounded.

"We need you to do something for us if you are able," the doctor said. "We do not know if anyone saw and reported the massacre of our wounded at Frenchtown. If you are strong enough, we will send you back to our lines to report this atrocity to General Harrison. You will have to walk alone, without a weapon; do you have the strength and the courage?" The doctor paused, looking intently at Jim.

"Where do I go?" Jim asked; still not alert enough to fully appreciate the request.

"Across the ice, the way we came," said the doctor, "toward the Maumee until you find American soldiers."

He paused again and Jim, without thinking, simply said "Yes."

"Good," the doctor said. "We will get you ready. You leave tonight." He quickly walked away. The aide gave Jim a drink of icy water from a cup and helped him to go outside to the corner of the shelter, where those who could stand and walk relieved themselves. Jim was moved to another corner of the room where he was told to rest the remainder of the day; there seemed to be more space available and less moaning. He stretched out fully and tried to make himself comfortable. Thomas, the aide, left but returned shortly with a bowl of milk, rich stew, and ample portions of beef, corn, and onions. Through the course of the day, Thomas returned, first with a pair of winter moccasins in much better condition than his own and a British army–issued field blanket that was far superior to its American counterpart. Jim slumbered through most of the day. He got up on his own on one occasion to go outside to relieve himself.

Dark had returned when Dr. Todd brought some biscuits, jerked venison, and a canteen of water. "We will come for you in an hour when we remove the soldiers who died this day," he said. "You will be carried out as a corpse and left at the gravesite awaiting burial. Be very still. When we leave, wait several minutes until the guards return to their posts. There should be enough light to see the river and the way across. Stay south of the island. Take this document and give it only to General Harrison. We wish you God's speed." Jim only nodded, not truly aware of the difficult journey ahead.

The doctor walked away, paused at a several boxes piled atop one another that served as a desk, opened the ledger that he used for recording deaths and, in the light of several candles, wrote down: James Morgan, Private, Ohio regulars, 17th Division, died of wounds, Jan 27th, 1813.

Jim had made good progress, walking in a cold and silent night down the west side of the Detroit River and following the Lake Erie shore. The escape was remarkably easy with the indifferent security demonstrated by the British militia. He waited for only a few minutes, saw no sign of any guards, rose from his grave and headed in the darkness to the Detroit River. The eight hours of continuous walking was now beginning to drain his strength, and he could feel the clammy dampness of his fever returning. He would need to rest, eat and drink from his canteen, which he had been hoarding all night. He knew that soon he would be nearing the River Raisin and the slaughter of several days past. He put that thought aside, as he was more interested in finding a sheltered place to rest. He welcomed the morning light.

In another hour, he approached the mouth of the river and walked cautiously inland to find shelter. Exhausted and sweating profusely, he knew that his fever and the infection that caused it were returning; he would need medical attention soon. For now, he only wanted to rest. The lonely and bleak silhouettes of numerous brick chimneys that, until a few days ago, were warm and inviting homes were standing in a forlorn line facing the river.

As he approached he noticed the many small mounds of snow scattered about the ruined village and knew that underneath were the frozen bodies of the slaughtered soldiers. Jim looked around, hoping to find some human life, local residents who might have returned home, but he only saw a few ravens pecking at the remains and he was sure the coyotes and wolves had feasted on the human carrion. Why had no one returned to provide a proper burial? Jim walked slowly to the west through the desolation and came upon a ruined house where part of a wall and a small section of the roof had survived the fire. It would provide adequate shelter from the wind and cold; he made himself as comfortable as possible, thawed some of his water by holding it against his body, ate some jerky, wrapped himself in his British blanket, and, completely fatigued and numb, fell into an exhausted sleep.

Jim felt the cold and heard the snort of a horse at almost the same time. From his prone position, he could only see knee high, and observed the hoofs of several horses and the moccasin feet of their riders. He knew they were Indians and could see that the leader was following his footprints from the previous day, which were still recognizable in the light snow. Jim had no weapon and no strength; he was helpless and anxiously awaited his fate.

It only took a minute for Long Hair to recognize the shaking, huddled body. He bent down, looking into his eyes. "Forest Boy, what brings you here?" he asked. Long Hair quickly realized that Jim, unresponsive, was in very poor condition; one brush of the back of his hand on his fevered forehead and Jim was placed on the saddle of Long Hair's horse. Riding double, they headed for the Maumee River.

The ride was long and lasted throughout the day. Jim slipped in and out of consciousness; he did his best to stay on the horse, but only the strength of Long Hair kept him from falling. When they arrived, the winter shadows were long on the Wyandot encampment located several miles upriver from the American stockade.

The healer saw and heard the commotion and realized that he would be needed as the tired riders came into camp. Small Tree was excited and pleased that Long Hair had brought his white friend to him instead of the white butchers. *I can show my father, the great shaman of all the Wyandotte my skills, and he will be boastful,* the young healer thought as he cleared out some room in his small lodge of strips of bark placed expertly over bended saplings. A small hole over the fire pit carried the smoke away to the spirits to let them know of his powers. The healer gathered and organized the tools of his trade as the scouts lay Jim on the small mat of furs; he felt Jim's body and knew what he needed to do.

The next day, at Jim's request, Long Hair rode to the American encampment and gave the letter from Dr. Todd to General Harrison.

CHAPTER 16

Marietta
February 1813

MARIETTA WESTERN SPECTATOR
8 February 1813

Slaughter on the River Raisin
Indian savages slaughter and torture the wounded and
helpless. British abandon wounded without protection.
All those who couldn't walk were killed.

American troops killed by Indians. General Winchester surrendered to smaller British force. Ohio regulars are victims.

A momentous slaughter of American troops occurred on
January 23rd and 24th of this year. Dispatches received report that
over 600 American soldiers were killed or captured by the British
Western Army under General Proctor. The Americans had set
up a defensive position on the River Raisin at Frenchtown in
Michigan Territory when attacked by a force of British and Indians
under Round Head and Walk in the Water, the evil Wyandot
chiefs. The Report indicated that Hundreds of Kentucky militia
and Ohio troops were carried off to Canada to be imprisoned.

Wounded who could not travel unaided were killed in a most vicious manner.

Some of the brave soldiers are reported to be from Washington County. Civilian citizens of the village of Frenchtown report that there were no survivors; the entire town has been burned to the ground by the wild savages. Gen. Winchester called a coward and surrendered when victory could be had. Currently no more information from the U.S. Army is available. The SPECTATOR will print more news as we recieve it.

It was market day and Anna was in town with Henry when she heard the news; the paper was posted in the square and at the Western Spectator. The town was abuzz and she listened to every bit of conversation she could to find out if there was any news of Jim. She had received a letter several days before that said he had joined the army of the North West Territories and was headed north to fight the British. *Was he in this battle? Was he killed or tortured? Did he survive?* The questions had no answers but she couldn't stop asking them or suppress the fear that Jim might be dead.

Life on the farm for these past six months had been most lonely. It was still operating, chores were getting done. All the hands had stayed after the general's death and looked for someone to take charge. The harvests were bountiful: corn, potatoes, squash, beans, wheat, and apples were both stored and sent to market.

The annual frolics of the harvest, hosted in the past by the general with enthusiasm and generosity, did not occur this year; no one seemed interested. The cattle drive to Pittsburgh and eastern markets along Zane's Trace, long a tradition, was called off.

Twenty cows and fourscore swine were taken to the new slaughterhouse in Marietta instead. Virginia spent every Sunday in Marietta with her daughter and friends at the Congregational church. Joshua and Virginia met with Rufus Putnam and other bank officials on November 12th to arrange for the annual payment on the farm's debt. Winter lumbering was scheduled to begin but, without any leadership, few trees would be cut. Everyone kept to themselves, going about their duties with caution and vigilance. They had little trust or confidence in Joshua's leadership and were hopeful that someone else would take over the farm. Virginia, who was in charge of preparing the dinner meal served to all hands at noon every day except Sunday, abdicated that responsibility to Anna. Not being as efficient or competent in the kitchen, she labored mightily with the new responsibilities.

Joshua, more sullen than ever, worked hard from early morning to late evening, laboring on projects where interaction with the farmhands was minimal. He provided little if any direction, and would explode unpredictably with rage. This manifested itself in verbal assaults and threats to all the farm hands within ear shot. So far, his outbursts had not resulted in any physical violence, but it seemed only a matter of time. After most of the harvest was complete, he began, on Saturday nights, to adjourn to the apple shed at the far end of the lane and take up with Elizur Kirkwood, who came onto the property with his mule, accompanied by several jugs of his whisky and the old blue hound. They would build a fire and carouse far into the night, continuing the drinking for most of Sunday. Elizur then took his leave and Joshua returned to the house and disappeared. This routine went on for three months, and the hands felt it couldn't last much longer before something bad happened. They watched and waited with great anxiety and trepidation. The four farmhands, together all these years, were afraid to leave and fearful of staying; needing someone to take care of them, they looked to Anna.

Mr. Putnam had come by twice to meet with Joshua and Virginia since the meeting in July. Anna knew that he was the only person holding the farm together and, without his oversight and supervision, Joshua would destroy Maggie's Hill and all those depending on it. She wrote two more letters to Jim at the trading post on the Wyandot reserve in hopes that they would eventually find their way to him. He needed to come home and take over.

Virginia continued to fulfill her obligations with little if any enthusiasm. On occasion, she would hug Anna and thank her for her loyalty and hard work. Anna's efforts to engage her in conversations regarding the future, however, were quickly avoided; discussions were limited to the immediate tasks at hand. It was indeed a lonely world and, in vulnerable moments, Anna would think about escaping from the sadness, fears, and ever-growing responsibilities on the farm. She knew, however, that Henry, Wendell, Charles, and Penelope, still working and hoping to last out the year to get their inheritance, depended on her; she couldn't leave as she had no place to go, and some day Jim would come back to her here.

On one cold and blustery night, her labor being done for the day, Anna stoked the fire in her small bedroom, poured a small glass of port from the liquor cabinet, lit her pipe, and alone in her thoughts, wandered back to the good times when the general and Jim filled her days with hope and happiness. This night, she recalled her first days on the farm.

Journal Entry
Jonathon McGuire
In repose
Maggie Hill Farm
February 1, 1806

> *"At last I am almost over a most pernicious and persistent battle with fever and congestion to a degree not recalled in my life time. I have been without humor or pleasant temperament since taking ill on the eve of the first day of this dismal year. Dear, dear Virginia now with child stayed*

at my side, the recipient of ill humors, violent retches, and soiled bed sheets. So devoted, she let no one into my chamber except for an occasional visits by Jim and others who would be allowed just a few minutes of my time. Two fortnights of illness have left me weak and without ambition. Only now can I turn to my sacred journals and recount the last several months of my life, the most recent, however, of little worth or value, best forgotten.

"We returned from the cattle drive two days after the holiday in miserable weather, exhausted and glad to rest. I was home but an hour or two when Virginia took me aside and said, 'I want you to meet someone. She is staying in the first floor bedroom and has been here for several days. I brought her here from the church last Sunday. She is in a sad state and needs our help.'

"I went into the room; it was well lighted with an excessive number of candles. I looked onto a face most abused and brutalized; only the poor girl's eyes were in a normal state of appearance. Without a word from me, she quickly said hello, regretted her looks at the moment, but was most thankful of my daughter's kindness. Her name is Anna Erikson from Varmland Sweden; she stated in a strong voice that she has been in Marietta since October last , 'working at Mineral's boarding house on the picket, doing the owners' washing and beds.' She stated that she worked most hard, and got room, food, and an occasional dollar for her labors. There are many rough fellows there and, Saturday last; two drunks were seeking her favors. When she refused they beat her most awfully. Mineral broke off the assault by the two ruffians and helped her to get to the church, where Doc True was called in to attend to her traumas. Virginia stayed with the girl and brought her here to mend.

"It appears that Virginia is taken with her, so that I

trust she will be with us for awhile. I will need to find out what first brought her to Marietta, apparently alone.

"The cattle drive most recently completed was most adventuresome and needs, in my humble opinion, to be recalled and recorded. This was to be the farm's 1st cattle drive and I left with much apprehension. It was also Jim's 1st journey outside of his small world. He marveled at it all. We left with 74 head of our freshest corn-fed young cows on the 1st day of November, north on the Muskingum trail to Cambridge east on the trace to cross the river at Wheeling and down the national road to the Pittsburgh market. With good weather and few setbacks, we hoped to return the farm better for the experience by the day of holly to celebrate with my precious daughter. Charles, Wendell, Jim, and Tom Wilbur from Belfry, an experienced driver hired on, made the journey. Everyone took to the labor and quickly learned the duties of a driver. Jim was eager and handled the long and weary days with nary a complaint. Our caravan had 6 of my horses and 8 mules hired out from Sideman's stables, well packed; they carried our necessities. The air at the start was most fresh and clear. We made 15 miles per day in good weather, and headed east out of Cambridge on our 7th day. Drove stands were available most nights, with ample forage and farmers welcomed our presence with grains at 20 cents per bushel and corn at 20 cents a shock. We were the last drive of the season but supplies were plentiful.

"The rains and sleet came the 3rd day out of Cambridge and we lay up for 2 days, a most uncomfortable time; with the stock unable to graze, they lost their weight. We crossed the Ohio at Wheeling with the lead cow crossing on a ferry and the remainder swimming behind. The river ran high and I was anxious for the welfare of the herd. They crossed in good order but much further downriver than anticipated.

We rested in fair weather with adequate forage for three days to regain the lost weight, and then proceeded with hard travel down a most difficult road not much improved since my last journey in '90. We paused again for several days at a drove stand 2 days out of Pittsburg to prepare the cattle for market. Buyers were plentiful and offered top value. We celebrated our good fortune by staying at a comfortable Inn and enjoying a generous amount of robust ale and a hearty meal. The outgoing young maiden who served our table enjoyed the good looks of young Jim and proceeded to pull his face into her full and fetching bosom on several occasions through the course of the evening. There was great hilarity; I must admit I envied his position and would have enjoyed such a provocative feast. We left the next morning after filling the packs of the mules with supplies and necessities. I negotiated a price of $32.00/head and, with the loss of only 2 cows on the drive, my purse was amply full with a most tidy sum even after settling the many debts incurred on this endeavor.

"The return home was cold and wet, with severe weather that held us up for several days. We then tarried not at all, looking forward to our own hearth and beds. In spite of our best and determined effort, we missed the holiday.

In the spring of that year, the general used the proceeds from the cattle drive and lumber harvests to purchase free and clear two hundred acres of unwanted thicket lands that bordered his north and east boundaries. Most speculators saw this land and all land to the east as mostly worthless, rugged, impenetrable, and an endless terrain of ridges and hollows with swamps and wetlands that produced hordes of mosquitoes every summer. Deep in the thicket, away from the wanderer's eye, were several large stands of giant hardwoods, suitable for the mainmasts of the world's largest sailing vessels. In his travels with Jim, he also came upon a formation of dark rock that followed the contours of a ridge line for almost a mile. He knew this to be coal and saw a possible future with this new fuel.

It was also his custom and the fervent wish of his departed Maggie that each spring, they would take whatever funds that were available and donate them to a Quaker mission in Pennsylvania that arranged for the purchase of slaves at auctions at various sites in the slave state of Virginia. The Quakers received funds from many donors and would ensure the emancipated slaves were given the opportunity to lead a stable and productive life. It was their mission to free and provide sanctuary to as many black friends of the south as they could afford. In years when sufficient proceeds were not available from their farming operation, the McGuire's would borrow funds from the Washington County First Mercantile Bank, using the farm as collateral. As their mission grew, so did their debt. They were quiet but busy and determined organizers of a free slave movement in the new state of Ohio.

Virginia gave birth in April; she and Anna, already close in friendship, shared the joys and labors of a newborn girl. For the moment, the general avoided inquiring about Anna's history, but strongly suspected her to be a runaway indenture. *A problem that will need to be dealt with in the future,* he thought.

CHAPTER 17

Wyandot Encampment
Maumee River
Ohio Territory
February 1813

Small Tree, the young Wyandot healer, watched Long Hair and his warriors bring the wounded soldier to his small, makeshift medicine lodge and lay him on a deer hide on the ground. He looked closely at the wound and felt Jim's head. The white man's was burning up and he was talking with the spirits. The healer had helped his father treat many an arrow and gunshot wound; *if he can get past the fever he will live,* thought Small Tree with some confidence. He stripped the soldier of his clothes and made a smudge fire inside the small lodge. The dark smoke curled out the opening at the top, and Small Tree knew that the smoke from his fires and his chanting would soon bring the blessings of an animal spirit. This was critical for the survival of his patient.

Jim remained in a feverish sleep. Filled with bad dreams and visions, he had little awareness of the circumstances and events that were swirling around him. The shelter was cold, even with the fire; the healer gathered water from the river and proceeded to wipe the body down with the cold water to reduce the fever.

He continued in this effort over many hours and several days. On the third day, the fever lessened, and Small Tree pulled out his sucking tool, the hollow wing feather of an eagle. He cut the crust from the festering injury, inserted the feather into the wound and slowly began to suck the infection out. He worked tirelessly for most of this day, rotating the rub downs and the sucking tool. The next day, the healer searched through his basket of dried herbs and prepared a poultice of slippery elm, lobelia, and poke root. He added water to the mixture until it reached a sticky mass and applied it directly to the wound; he would leave it on for twenty-four hours. The young healer kept the smudge fire going and repeated his call for an animal spirit to provide life. He rested little, paying close attention to Jim's condition. If he lived it would bring honor to the young shaman; both his father and Tarhee would boast of his skills at many fires. Small Tree would not give up.

Jim slept a fever-induced sleep, on occasion calling out and murmuring. At several times during this critical period, he was clear enough to ask where he was. On the fifth day, Small Tree went outside to collect more brush and branches for his fire. It was mid morning of a cold, clear day and he saw a chattering crow perched on a barren branch of a nearby oak tree. *This is a good sign,* he thought as he went back to his medical duties; he wiped Jim down with cold water, felt the poultice and it was warm, drawing the infection of the still festering wound. Another would need to be prepared soon.

Small Tree tried to recall if there was anything else his shaman father had taught him about healing this type of wound; nothing came to mind, so he continued the rituals: relit the smoking fire, did his chants and incantations to the spirits, and asked for the life of a departed animal to claim this young warrior and bring him life. The young healer would now fast until his patient was safe from death. He made Jim drink cold water several times each day and, when sufficiently awake, helped him to consume a gourd of venison stock. Jim's body accepted the nourishment and soon entered a more peaceful rest.

With his fever diminishing, the dreams softened and the patient dreamed of a new life without the violence, emptiness, and isolation. When he was awake and his mind alert, he felt an immeasurable distance from Maggie's Hill where he was a welcome member of a large and generous family. He yearned to be embraced and cared for again, but would have to do without. This was not the time, place, or circumstance for vulnerable thoughts.

The next morning, Small Tree observed the crow perched on the same branch as it had been the previous day. It stayed for some time, chattering continually; Small Tree smiled, thanked the spirits, gave a blessing to the noisy bird, and knew that his patient would survive. Late that afternoon, Jim's fever broke completely and he returned to the living. The young healer was pleased, and shared his success with Long Hair and the others.

Jim, still very weak, rested in the camp for several days, eating an occasional sparse meal and gradually gaining strength. His wound was sore to the touch, but the fever and infection were gone. On the eighth day of his recovery, an officer from General Harrison's command rode into Long Hair's camp and, staying on his horse, approached Jim sitting next to an outdoor fire, hunched over with his British blanket around his shoulders. He saw the officer, gradually recalled that he was in the army, and made a feeble attempt at standing at attention; however, he had to sit down again after several unsteady moments.

"The general asks of your health," the messenger said, looking down at the wretched image of a soldier.

"I am recovering well, sir," Jim said.

"In that case, you need to report for duty in twenty-four hours," said the officer. He turned his horse and rode away.

The next morning, on a thawing late February day, Jim said goodbye to Small Tree. He wanted give his benefactor something to express his gratitude for saving his life, but had nothing to offer. The small band of Wyandotte had to find some new clothes for him to wear; his dirty louse-filled and blood-stained garments had been burned when they were removed from his body on arrival. He was not very soldier-like with an oversized hunting shirt covering to the knee a very old pair of filthy deerskin breeches. He kept his winter moccasins, as they were still somewhat useful. Jim looked to thank Long Hair, but he had left earlier on a hunting trip to the dark swamp in an effort to keep his small band from starving and to find forage for the horses.

Now with a ferocious appetite, Jim quickly became aware of the meager rations: watery soups made from various plants, jerked venison and parched corn were the staples. There were no government rations distributed from the fort and Long Hair had mentioned the day before his departure that his party of Wyandotte would return to their land on the Sandusky if the Army of the Northern Frontier failed to supply provisions.

Jim began his walk of four miles to the American fort to report to duty, as ordered. He was tired, hungry, and under strength as he trekked slowly to his unwanted destination. The cawing of a crow followed him for most of the journey.

Jim knew little, nor did he care much about what the new routine of army life would be like. Since he had enlisted in late December he had been shot, captured, escaped and watched the slaughter of good men and the incompetence and cowardice of many officers. He found himself on this day, as all days since his enlistment, tired, hungry, cold, dirty, and angry. After several hours of walking through the melting snow, he paused before crossing the still frozen and treacherous Maumee River. He saw his immediate future as quite dismal but had no idea what to do about it. Thoughts of continuing down the river, away from the army, to find a better life somewhere entered his mind; instead, he cautiously crossed the thawing river, climbed the steep ridge on the south bank, and entered the bustling profanity of Fort Meigs.

Jim observed the chaotic beginnings of a fort where the outer stockade, block houses, and buildings were in various states of completion. The land surrounding the fort had been stripped of all life; all the brush was cleared and every tree had been cut down for a mile in all directions. The barren ground was a sea of semi-frozen mud, ankle to knee high, caused primarily by the numerous teams of mules, oxen, and horses that were hauling logs, lumber, dirt, and supplies in every direction while eight hundred soldiers so covered with mud as to be unrecognizable were laboring mightily in the construction of the new fort. Several large piles of branches, brush, and vegetation were breathing anemic columns of smoke; efforts to burn the excess in these wet conditions were going poorly.

Forlorn and pathetic in the southeastern corner of the half-built perimeter were the canvas shelters of the enlisted men. There was row upon row of small four-man tents; their white coverings were caked with mud and grime, victims of the terrible conditions. Smoke from several cooking fires was rising skyward where the noon meal was in various stages of preparation. Noise was everywhere; the loud and never-ending cursing of the teamsters, yelling of the officers, and angry shouting of the wretched enlisted men. The occasional bellow of an ox and the braying of a tired and mistreated mule contributed to the pandemonium of what appeared to be a most dispirited encampment.

Jim reluctantly asked for the officers' quarters and was directed toward the southeast corner of the stockade where, on higher, drier ground, several large officers' tents were located. He struggled through the mud to present himself; he walked barefoot, holding his moccasins and leggings so they didn't get lost in the mud.

His borrowed clothes were filthy and tattered; a knife stuck in his belt, a British blanket, and a small pouch strung with rawhide was his only other possessions. He approached an officer standing outside the largest tent and was told to wait, standing, ignored in the mud. A soft snow began to fall, which soon turned to drizzle.

His meeting with General Henry Harrison took almost an hour to occur. Jim stood outside the officers' tent while the commandant and several officers sat comfortably inside; they had a wooden floor with a large rug, and sat around a small wood stove. He was introduced by an adjutant and was told to tell his story. The officers asked many questions about the battle of Frenchtown, the behavior of General Winchester, his encounter with Tecumseh, the slaughter of the wounded, and the treatment by the British. The commandant reread Dr. Todd's letter aloud and asked the private to comment. The general was thoughtful and courteous, and seemed interested in Jim's version of the events. In closing, Harrison stood and directed Jim to make a statement to a scribe so that it would be recorded as an official record. Jim replied that he would prefer to write it himself. The attending officers stood silent for a moment in the face of this suggestion of insubordination. The commandant asked about Jim's writing skills and then agreed.

As Jim turned to leave, the general asked him of his impressions of Tecumseh. Jim said, "He is strong, brave, and believes in the native's place as the keeper of the land and his superiority over the white man. He has a strong dislike for you, sir. He also allowed the massacre at Frenchtown and I cannot forgive him for that, sir."

The general thought for a moment then said, "Thank you, private, you're dismissed." Jim sat in the corner of the officers' mess tent and wrote his report quickly and simply.

He handed over his four pages of parchment and the orderly instructed him to get a work clearance from the doctor. An hour later, Jim appeared for duty with his first hair cut in five months and with an ample dose of potash and gunpowder to kill the infestation of fleas. He was a disillusioned, grieving, and lonely youth who was still not ready for army life.

CHAPTER 18

Fort Meigs
Ohio Territory
March 1813

*D*ear Anna,

This be a most miserable place, mud everywhere and rain and snow all week, no food, nor fire as we work and sleep in squalor. We await the supply trains that never come.

The officers know not what to do and tolerate no good advice offered by men wiser than they. We do make progress on the building of the fort. I labor with some Kentucky Militiamen building storehouses and other buildings inside the picket walls. We hope for spring, drink mountain whiskey when possible, smoke terrible tobacco, and hope the British and the Indians don't come too soon. Much has happened since my last letter. Will tell all when time is more abundant.

The Army is insufferable; I enjoy it not and do not expect any improvement. I hope our dear General will understand that not all do well with the abuse and regimentation. I regret but will suffer my enlistment.

My wound has healed and I will be in better health as soon as stores arrive. I think always of Maggie Hill and wish soon to return. How are your health and circumstances? I worry some of my mother and hope she will

prosper. Please give my wishes to all.
  A courier is leaving this moment to the south and will take mail.

Best to you
Jim,
Private
Army of the Northern Frontier

February had turned into March and continued in its desolation; the building of the fort progressed from sunup to sundown. Cold and rainy weather throughout the month and the lack of provisions placed hardship on all the men. The population diminished as troops from Virginia and Pennsylvania whose enlistments were up left for home; desertions were also high, particularly with the Ohio troops, who left and returned to their homes. Some said they would return when the weather and conditions improved. Jim had many opportunities to leave but stayed on, deciding for some reason, the lingering devotion to the general perhaps, to honor his enlistment. He hoped against all odds that things would get better. Long Hair and his small band came by early in March and said goodbye; still without supplies or direction they left for Crane town on the Sandusky. Long Hair said he would be back in the spring if there was still a fort and a war to fight.

Jim sadly watched them leave; they were the only friends he had found during his short enlistment. He recalled his short stay with the Wyandot Nation and thought he might return there when his enlistment was up. He wondered for a moment how Labithia was doing and if Mr. Walker had found a way to get her to Canada.

Jim's work ethic kept him out of trouble during the long days. The harsh conditions and endless hours of work on the fortifications did not allow him the time or the energy to do anything but sleep when he was not laboring. Morale was very low and rebellions occurred on a regular basis. Most of the officers were young, with little if any experience, and were ineffective in maintaining control over the defiant enlisted men. Orders were ignored or ridiculed. Skilled and experienced craftsmen—carpenters, lumbermen, teamsters, wheelwrights, iron workers, and several engineers—provided the necessary skill, experience, temperament, and pride in their work to keep the construction going forward. Captain Woods, the competent officer in charge, was away for most of this time visiting his ill wife.

Amid the confusion, large hardwood trees were felled from the dark swamp that bordered the fort on the south and east. The trees were cut to eighteen-foot lengths and hauled from the woodlands by teams of oxen. They were placed vertically three feet into the ground. Ramparts were built to support the stockade walls and provide protection for the sentries and riflemen. Seven blockhouses, standing two stories high and double built of rough-hewn logs with a reinforced roof, were the strength of the construction. The bottom floor had ports for various sized cannon while the second floor harbored slots for the marksmen who would take the measure of British officers who carelessly came into range of the long rifles. Several well-protected artillery batteries were being completed to cover the exterior of the fort for up to four thousand yards. Inside the enclosed walls, many buildings were being constructed to harbor supplies, armaments, stables, and living quarters for the officers. Jim's experience growing up, where working with wood and lumber was a common activity, served him well in his labors. He was assigned a variety of tasks: digging post holes, cutting timber, working as a carpenter's helper, and doing odd jobs wherever he was needed. Unfortunately, Jim was not formally assigned to a specific regiment and, as a result, he drifted like an orphaned soldier; he bunked and mustered where he wanted, was unattached and had to make his own way.

Most of the militia and regulars came in groups from small rural communities where everyone was kin or knew of each other. They stayed together as units and were resistive and suspicious of outsiders. Jim did tent with a company of Kentucky volunteers, who reluctantly accepted him only because he was a veteran soldier who had been with the Kentucky boys at Frenchtown and his surprise winning of a shooting contest with the borrowed Kentucky rifle of one of the volunteers. His status was also enhanced by his resistance of authority and his outspoken frustrations over the living conditions and the incompetent officers at the fort.

Jim did not belong to the Kentuckians in any meaningful way, however, and so he roamed the camp looking and hoping for a friendship and a place to belong. It was a lonely life.

The troops were always hungry, tired, and cold as they worked from early morning to dark in rain and snow, barefoot and threadbare. Homemade liquor called moonshine by the Kentucky volunteers would appear whenever there was a moment of leisure. Jim developed a taste and looked forward to the numbing effect of the lethal alcohol that took his mind off his day-to-day misery.

April, however, brought a brighter sun and dryer conditions. Several supply trains arrived from the south, up the Hull Trace from Dayton to Fort Defiance and down the Maumee River. The trains were filled with the necessities of army life: food, armaments, uniforms, medical supplies, tents, spirits, forage, and fodder. The days of scarcity were soon forgotten and the workload also slackened as the fort was coming closer to completion. Several regiments of regulars and militias from Ohio and the Kentucky territory arrived.

General Harrison returned from a trip to Cincinnati in mid April. He took charge upon his arrival, and discipline was quickly imposed on the many unruly rogues who now would have to become soldiers.

Jim's ongoing indifference to army life and disrespect for the officers continued and actually worsened as the workload lessened and he found more time to complain and resist the new order. Rules were now strictly enforced and disobedience was not tolerated. Jim resisted; trouble started and he quickly became part of the problem.

Order of the Commandant
Court Marshal of Pvt. Jim Morgan
April 17th 1813.
Fort Meigs, Ohio

From the list of grievances submitted to the commanding officer by the undersigned, it has been determined that said Private James Morgan is guilty of serious crimes, misbehaviors, and acts of insubordination as stated, and stands charged with the following.

April 9th, refusing close order drill,
    Threatening an officer,
    Drunkenness.
April 11th, assaulting a teamster
April 14th, improper uniform,
    Failure to muster for parade,
    Disobeying a direct order,
    Threatening an officer,
    Drunkenness.
April 16th, refusal to approach officer when so ordered.

It was General Harrison himself who was standing at the court marshal this Saturday morning, and listened with some interest to the reading of the complaint by the young provost officer. The court was held in the newly constructed commissary building, which was only half filled with the recently arrived supplies. Private Morgan was one of many to be tried on this day. The commandant, with two other officers, sat at one side of a large table; at a smaller table sat the prosecutor, who called the men to stand before the court.

Upon reading of the charges, one of the officers asked him of his plea. Jim said, "Guilty, sir." He stood at attention but felt indifferent to his fate. Although circumstances had improved in the six weeks since his arrival at Fort Meigs, he still had nothing to look forward to and certainly nothing to lose. He was surprisingly calm.

The general spoke quietly. "Private Morgan, with all your experience I expected more from you. You obviously have little discipline or interest in a soldier's life." Jim said nothing, standing erect. The general looked at his papers. "You have a one year enlistment," he said. "We have seven more months to make you a soldier. You are reported to be disrespectful, defiant of officers and standing orders; you ignore instructions and appear in a drunken state on many occasions. What say you to these charges?"

"I admit to the charges as written and reported, sir," said Jim. General Harrison stared hard at the young recruit, trying to decide if he was worth keeping in the army.

"Tell me," he said, "why did you assault the teamster?"

Jim said, "He was mistreating a mule, sir."

"But it was his mule," the general said.

"I don't take to any mistreatment of animals, sir," said Jim.

"Do you have any interest in this army; private?" asked the general. I could drum you out immediately, send you home a coward." He waited for a response.

"I prefer to finish my enlistment, sir," said Jim.

General Harrison was quiet for a moment, looked again at the written report and then looked directly at Jim. "The colonel reports that you are a strong worker and that you shoot a Kentucky rifle quite well."

"Yes, sir," Jim said.

The court hereby finds Private Morgan guilty of all charges heretofore presented and orders that the defendant receive the following punishment and restrictions for his disobedience, insubordination, and injurious behavior.

Confined in isolation with one leg tied to a log for 12 hours of each day.

To ride the wooden horse twice a week for 1 hour each time.

Endure the shaving of one eyebrow and half of the head.

Nourishment limited to bread and water only.

All punishments for one month commencing this date and to cease if and when hostilities commence.

"Sergeants at arms, take him away."

Jim was marched to the disciplinary tents to begin his punishment. He was confident that he could do anything for a month and the fact that there were other soldiers with similar sentences minimized the hardship.

Two weeks into his punishment, he was awoken at dawn's light by the disciplinary officer, who said that the British and their Indian allies had arrived and they needed all men to muster. Jim, dirty and disheveled, was ordered to report to Captain Hover of the riflemen company. He was released from his bonds and glad to be freed although, all things considered, the punishment was not as severe as he had anticipated. He had no particular animosity or resentment toward the officers who ordered his punishment. He accepted his sentenced, recognizing that his behavior had consequences. The rebellious culture of the enlisted men provided him with some status and acceptance for his misbehavior among the riotous volunteers of the Kentucky militia.

With the exception of riding the wooden horse a most

uncomfortable contraption that resembled a small horse and when sitting on it caused great discomfort. his biggest problems were boredom and idleness. The weights he carried were tolerable and it minimized the isolation that there were other men sharing similar punishment. Other rogue soldiers with friends doing punishment would find ways to sneak food and, on occasion, whiskey to the men in the disciplinary tents.

Jim was sore and walked with difficulty with swollen and abused ankles, slowly adjusting to the freedom of movement, somewhat awkward in his gait. Mostly he wanted to forget the previous two weeks and was curious to see what was on the other side of the stockade.

Drums were rolling muster, officers were shouting orders, horses were being corralled, and men were running to their formations; 2,400 officers and men were preparing for war. Jim reported to Captain Hover, who was assigning two score Kentucky militiamen to their sharpshooter posts on the walls and inside the blockhouses.

As the captain finished giving his instructions, he turned to Jim and said, "I'm assigning you to blockhouse 1. It faces the river and you will have a good chance to pick off British officers. Are you finished with your shenanigans? Do you still have a steady hand and clear gaze?"

"Yes, sir," Jim said. "Yes, sir."

"Report to the magazine keeper and select your rifle, powder and ball on my order," said the captain. "And attend to your post."

The scene outside of the walls in the early morning light brought fear to many of the untested troops who would soon see their first combat. Jim climbed to the second level of the block house and looked out through the gun port. All around the fort there was activity. Downriver, near the old Fort Miami, which had been abandoned years ago, the British army was disembarking from a flotilla of boats that had sailed from Fort Malden. Troops were busy unloading several batteries of cannon and moving them to positions of tactical advantage. Horses were carrying supplies and officers to encampments set up at various locations on the heights overlooking the fort. Drums and bugles sounded instructions as the British army prepared for battle. Cannons and mortars, munitions, tents, food, and fodder were being stored and moved throughout the west bank. Thousands of red coated soldiers and an equal number of Indians were busy in their preparations. Most ominous were the four separate artillery companies building their batteries. It would only be a matter of hours before the infamous cannonades were to rain down on the beleaguered fort. Directly across the river in the woodlands, hundreds of Indians allied with the British were making camp and painting their faces. Jim knew that somewhere in their midst was Tecumseh, organizing his men, preparing for the revenge of Tippecanoe and the destruction of his hated enemy, General Henry Harrison.

Jim watched the ever-changing goings-on around him with both amazement and curiosity. His vantage point provided an opportunity to see how an army organized to do battle. Heavy showers began at mid morning and would last throughout the day, but would not slow down the activities on either side.

British engineers built two batteries opposite the fort on the west bank and two on the east bank facing west into the fort. Through the day and into the rainy evening they made ready six twenty-four pounders and three howitzers. Several rounds were fired that evening for effect, with no damage to the fort or its inhabitants.

The British preparations continued unabated and, by nightfall, still at his post in the block house, protected from the rain, Jim awaited the dawn. It would not be a long night. Behind him and inside the stockade, Jim looked down from his vantage point and observed several hundred men quietly digging and building a wall of earth that ran parallel to the east-west angle of the fort. The men worked hard throughout the night and, by early light, a traverse of dirt twelve feet high, twenty feet at the base, and over three hundred yards long dominated the parade ground and interior of the fort. The soft dirt would absorb the shot and shell of the British cannon, as well as providing protection for the men and horses.

The rains continued as the British began their devastating cannonade early that morning. The artillery attack would last with minimal interruptions for five horrendous days. Additional enemy batteries were brought on line throughout the day and over five hundred rounds of solid shot, preheated cannon balls that were designed to start fires and blow up magazines, and the mid air explosions of howitzer shells poured down on the beleaguered fort.

The fort survived the initial assault; there were few casualties, the traverse performed its duties as intended, and the hardwoods of the nearby swamp that reinforced the block houses withstood and resisted the explosive force of the aerial bombardment. It was clear by the end of the first day that the fort would stand.

A British company with Indian support had crossed the river during the first night and was now building siege trenches and fortifications for artillery closer to the fort; the long-range cannonade of the previous night had been ineffective. Jim watched the British, in their carelessness, move closer to the fort and into the range of the sharpshooters. One young officer, resplendent on his horse, was supervising the construction and not particularly attentive to his location; cocky and preoccupied, he was now close enough for a try. Three hundred yards with light wind, intermittent rain, and patches of smoke challenged the shot. The marksman lifted his rifle, rested it on the gun port, and waited. Time went by and other riflemen were whispering to Jim, who had the best shot: "Shoot the bastard." Jim cocked his long rifle, forced himself to relax, and waited for the right moment. Time went by. The lieutenant fell from his horse and lay motionless on the ground; a small column of white smoke flowed from Jim's rifle. Cheers went up from the soldiers and officers on the parapets.

Indians were also moving across open spaces and surrounded the fort, waiting for the cannon fire to break open the barricades. Captain Hover passed the word to refrain from shooting Indians and to wait for the officers. "Shoot the officers," he said. Jim's first shot made him a marksman and his battle for Fort Meigs began. Over the next five days, he stayed on post, moving about in the block houses and on the ramparts. He looked for targets and providing protection to artillerymen exposed to enemy fire. Through the long days of incessant artillery barrages and skirmishes, he would patiently wait for a target, and was successful at shooting and killing a handful of British officers. He became well known as a deadly sniper and wages were placed on his accuracy.

The defenders slept and ate at their posts, mostly after dark or whenever a lull in the barrages allowed. Fatigue was ever present; there were few hours of uninterrupted sleep. Rain showers brought cold nights but refreshing drinks for a parched army. The days ran into each other and exhaustion dominated. Jim didn't have the energy, time, or interest for idle thought or contemplation; killing had become most of what he did and he was getting good at it.

During his time on the parapets, he looked for targets and had several opportunities to take aim on Tecumseh, who was continually moving about the perimeter, actively leading his warriors in numerous assaults and feints to find weaknesses in the fortifications and access the interior. He would occasionally come into range of Jim's long rifle; he chose not to pull the trigger, but didn't know exactly why. A lingering respect for his mission, the time they spent together on the Hock hocking River, and the long-ago friendship with the general may all have influenced his hesitation.

From his vantage point, through the smoke and rain, he would watch and appreciate the chief's leadership as he organized, directed, and led his warriors, always fearless and with little regard for his own life.

The siege of Fort Meigs continued for five days. With an unlimited supply of munitions brought down by boat from Fort Malden, the British bombarded the defenders with over five hundred rounds per day. The Americans had a much smaller supply and responded more judiciously. Still, the fort held; as the days went by the men began to take a great pride in their handiwork. The fort had sufficient supplies of food, but water was rationed as it was dependent on rainwater. A well under construction when the assaults began was not completed until the fourth day of the siege and, under a continual barrage, provided only a limited amount of water.

The American army was not without tragedy. The garrison watched a regiment of newly arrived Kentuckians float down the Maumee River on flatboats; one company landed upstream a mile on the enemy side and attacked several minimally defended British batteries, destroying eight cannons. The elation from the American officers and men watching the attack changed quickly to horror as Captain Dudley pursued a handful Indians into the forest and found an awaiting ambush by Tecumseh's Indians. Only about a hundred of the six hundred men would survive the massacre.

Tecumseh was tired and discouraged; in spite of the recent capture of Dudley's company, things were not going well. The inability of the British cannons to breach the sturdy, reinforced walls of the fort, and General Proctor's reluctance to initiate a serious assault, were causing a loss of enthusiasm among the many chiefs of his alliance. The promise of great plunder and land by the British if they could defeat General Harrison was wearing thin and there was much talk of abandoning the effort.

Having arrived late for the ambush, Tecumseh talked with some of his chiefs and observed at the spiked cannon as the captured American troops under Captain Dudley were led to the partial ruins of old Fort Miami, where they were to be secured until arrangements were made for their movement to Fort Malden and imprisonment.

Within a few minutes, the whoops and yells of his men and screams of the prisoners were heard coming from the old fort. Tecumseh immediately pushed his tired body onto an idle horse and rode hard, entered the old front gate at full speed and saw the slaughter that was underway. Many of the Kentuckians were already dead or fatally injured and the Indians, with scalps in hand, were dancing about the killing ground. Tecumseh grabbed the Indian nearest him, pulled his hair, and put a knife to his throat. "Stop now. Stop," he said. The men stopped the slaughter and began to leave the fort and carnage behind them.

Many British officers were standing by and did nothing to stop the killing. Tecumseh looked about quickly and saw General Proctor amongst the officers. He walked quietly, knife in hand, and stood face to face with the general. "What say you to allow this to occur?" he demanded

Proctor stepped away from the enraged Tecumseh and said with little conviction, "I cannot control your hordes; they defy all civil orders."

"You are a coward," said Tecumseh, "a disgrace to your King. Remove that red coat; put on your petticoats and leave this land." He looked about and walked past the frightened, milling prisoners. He went back to his camp, disgraced and betrayed. Jim was unaware of the great chief's honorable behavior on this battlefield.

THE END AND THE BEGINNING

On the fourth night, under a bright moon, Jim and hundred or so off-duty volunteers dug out unexploded British cannonballs that had lodged into the soft dirt of the traverses. In order to secure the much-needed shot to reuse against the British, the armaments department offered a glint of whiskey for every round turned in. It wasn't long before the singing, cursing, and stumbling of drunken soldiers filled the night air for both sides to hear. The next day, Jim suffered from a brutal hangover.

General Proctor gave up his siege on the sixth day, the glory he dreamed of for himself no longer a reality. He ordered his men and weapons to the boats and returned to Fort Malden. Tecumseh, irate over the general's incompetence, called him a coward and predicted failure in the battles to come.

CHAPTER 19

Marietta
June 1813

Journal Entry
Jonathon McGuire
June 3rd 1804
In residence

'*It is with tragic reason that I have not taken pen to any correspondence since Sunday last. Violent events occurred in our county that I expect will generate serious repercussions for our efforts. Joseph Tomlinson II, son of the patriarch of Williams Station in the Virginia territory, brought himself and four of his offspring across the river to Marietta landing: Thomas, Carpenter, Ezekiel, and the youngest and failing Benjamin. The word went out that they were seeking 2 of his runaway slaves who had absconded into Ohio country several weeks prior. Madelyn Moody sent young Orlando Beverage to the farm to alert me to this event. I immediately saddled and proceeded on the thicket trail to head to the Craig farm, a long day's ride. Before my arrival, terrible events had already taken place. The good William Craig had seen the Tomlinson's on horseback coming off* the Trail and, heading directly to his homestead, he called the alarm to Mike and Jacob, who in great haste ran to the forest to escape again from their brutal masters.

"Mike, most regrettably was caught by the fleet Thomas, who began to beat the slave unmercifully and without let up. Mr. Craig and his tenant Simon were held at bay and under the gun of the Tomlinson clan were witness to this horrible event. The slave Mike was clubbed repeatedly with the butt of Thomas's weapon. The assault was vicious and Mike nearly succumbed; however, he was able to pull out his bull knife and stab the young Thomas in his abdomen. He bled most profusely and died in his father's arms. The family wailed in their grief, threatened Mr. Craig and his indenture with repercussions if they did not return Jacob, who was now well hidden in the marsh north of the farm. After some time and with great debate over how to proceed, the Tomlinson's placed young Thomas's body on his horse; they roped the slave by the neck to the last horse and left heading south on the road. I feared young Mike would not survive the day.

"I arrived in time to comfort the gentle Mr. Craig, who was extremely distressed over the events. Martha Craig insisted that I immediately take Jacob to another sanctuary, for they no longer had any liking to participate in this most noble cause. I did my best to relieve and reassure the Craig's, but they were determined that I take Jacob with me. I rested the evening in a most sorrowful house and slept but little. Simon and I went to the marsh at first light and spent all the morning encouraging Jacob to show himself and to trust in our protection.

"In due time, I lifted Jacob and his belongings onto the back of my horse and took him away from the Craig's, who were very fearful that the Tomlinson gang would return and

*wreak vengeance on their peaceful family. Regrettably I was
unable to offer much reassurance. Jacob and I traveled the
day and, with the remaining light, had bedded down near
a swamp when we were surprised by Carpenter Tomlinson,
who must have stayed behind and followed us. He now at-
tempted to take Jacob into his custody. Jacob ran into the
swamp in great fear; Carpenter followed and pulled his gun
to shoot the wailing Jacob. I, being close at hand, grabbed
a fallen branch and hit the Tomlinson boy over the head.
I heard his skull crack and he fell face down in the swamp.*

*He was soon to drown if not already dead; I did noth-
ing to save the young man. We buried the body with rocks
in about 3 feet of water and in great haste left the site and
proceeded on a long night's ride. On the new day, we found
a temporary shelter with the McCray's. Jacob and I continued on after a brief rest and proceeded north to take Jacob
to his freedom, far away from the scene of such a violent
crime. After a hard week of travel and continued vigilance,
I dropped good Jacob off at the blessed family in Ashtabula
for his trip across the great lake. Jacob and I vowed to never
speak of this event in our lifetimes. I journeyed home and
arrived most tired and desirous of rest and refurbishment,
fearful that the Tomlinson's would discover the events of
that tragic day and seek revenge. There is such a need for
sanctuary and shelter for these unfortunates, who travel such
a long and dangerous road. I will revisit the Craig's in due
time. I regret deeply the events that occurred but not at all
my actions. A slave's life is most precious. There is more
work to do.*

Anna and Virginia went to church services together on this
Sunday morning in early June; this was an unusual occurrence
since the general's death almost one long year ago. Joshua, as

usual, was nowhere to be seen and appeared to be indifferent to his wife's frequent trips into Marietta. The day was sunny, with the promise of high humidity and afternoon showers. *The corn could use a good soaking,* Anna thought as the friends enjoyed the morning. The Marietta congregational church was filled and a rousing sermon was delivered to the parishioners. Reverend Robert Moody, a large man with a rugged countenance, spoke loud, long, and with passion regarding the many evils and sinful ways of his fellow man. His large, booming voice softened as he introduced the issue of slavery.

"Only a river separates Gomorrah from the free land of the blessed," he said. "We look across that river and see damnation, God's children slaving in perpetual bondage on the farms and fields of our southern friends who promote the devil's work."

Anna was invited into the parish parlor after the dinner the congregation shared on the lawn on the fourth Sunday of every month. There were eight members of the church and two strangers, a married couple by all appearances, sitting in chairs in a makeshift circle in the large parlor of the parsonage. All windows and doors were open to catch the cooling breeze that often precedes rain showers. Anna was familiar with most everyone present.

The reverend introduced William and Martha Craig and said, "All of you here, except for young Anna, are aware of the wonderful work that the Craig's have done these many years in providing shelter and sanctuary to the runaway slaves who have passed our way, seeking freedom and salvation in the great land to our north. Mr. Craig reports that difficult times have presented themselves and he is in dire need of assistance." The reverend turned, sat down, and with a nod gave the floor to Mr. Craig. He remained sitting, a small man with a small voice, causing the listeners to lean slightly forward.

"For some eight or more years," he said, "Mrs. Craig, my two oldest boys, our freeman and my self have provided safe passage for many unfortunate souls who have come unto our state to find freedom for themselves and their families. We have provided shelter and safe passage to Canada for many. Now, however, we are fraught with worry. With the passing of the great general who provided us with the support, resources, and protection necessary to do our work and the closing of the northern border by the British government it has become more difficult to secure safe harbor in the north. The unfortunates continue to come, unannounced, with no escort or sponsorship. In addition, the slave catchers, knowing of our work, visit our farm continually without fear or challenge. We are unable to continue this effort." Mr. Craig paused for a moment; the room was silent, the bustle of handheld fans the only motion. Mrs. Craig wept quietly into her kerchief. "We will be leaving after the harvest for the Indiana territory to join up with my brother and his family."

Anna listened to the talk, led by the parson with many conversing at once, of the loss of the Craig's, and how this handful of quiet and caring people would be able to continue the mission started by the general and his wife more than a decade earlier. By listening to the various conversations, Anna learned a lot more about the general's involvement in the sanctuary and transport of runaway slaves. She recalled clandestine, shadowy visits in the night, missing food and commodities from the pantry, and the unspoken understanding that these nocturnal events should not be discussed. She wondered why she was invited to this meeting and looked to Virginia for clarification; for the moment, however, Virginia seemed to be avoiding her. After an hour or so, Rufus Putnam, the leader of Marietta, and his wife entered the meeting; apologies were offered and introductions were made. Mr. Putnam, Reverend Moody, and several others went onto the porch for a private conference. Upon their return, the conversations softened and eventually ceased. Everyone looked quietly at

Anna. Rufus Putnam, standing, hands folded together began to speak.

"My dear, close and most secretive allies of our noble cause," he said. "I have asked you here this day to discuss the difficult times we are faced with in carrying out our mission. With the Craig's leaving for Indiana, we no longer have a shelter to hold and protect our dark friends who risk their lives to seek freedom. The slave catchers have become more active; they frequent our public houses and benefit from the words of those in opposition to our cause. We have no place unknown to these evil men and, regrettably, our last three passengers have been apprehended and returned to captivity.

"We can no longer continue our noble effort without the availability of a sanctuary that unknown to everyone except those trusted few in attendance today. This is why I have asked Virginia to invite Anna Erikson to join us."

Anna sat stunned, looking again at the general's daughter; she held Anna's hand and pressed it gently. Rufus paused for a moment and moved closer to the confused house keeper. "You see, Anna," he said, "we know of your affection and respect for the general, and Virginia assures us that you have a most confidential nature; we seek your assistance."

Anna, looking at the general, quietly asked, "What would you want of me? I have no way to be of help."

Rufus returned to his chair, leaning forward slightly. "Our beloved general and wife Maggie were most active and enthusiastic in their efforts to assist runaway slaves in securing freedom," he said. "The general would, when necessary, hide slaves deep in the thicket for days and sometimes weeks until their passage to Canada could be arranged. We know not of this place but are aware that young Jim Morgan used it as his sanctuary during his days hiding in the forest. Perhaps he showed you where it is."

Anna, now appreciating her value to the group, said, "Yes,

Jim did show me a secure hiding place deep in the thicket. But I would never be able to find it again." A slight pause as everyone waited for her to finish her thought... "I know who could, though: Water Bird."

Anna, quickly and quietly made arrangements. The following Tuesday morning, she and Digger walked the path to Council Keeper's village, which was overgrown and quite rugged, with several steep climbs to ridge tops and then down again. After two hours of hard walking, she came out of the tall trees and into the sunlight of the village. Little had changed, Anna thought; a handful of native dwellings, teepees, lean-tos, and a poorly maintained long house were scattered around on an open meadow of about twenty acres. The mounds of corn, squash, and beans were knee high and prosperous; several women and their young children were engaged in cultivating the vegetables. Dogs barked upon Anna's entrance and challenged the entry of Digger who, being much wiser, ignored the growls and snarls. Water Bird approached and welcomed the visitor.

Chief Council Keeper came over to greet Anna and asked of the farm and its operation. He said how much he missed the general, then went back to a small stand of maples near the corral and relit his pipe.

Anna and Water Bird spent the rest of the day in conversation, walking about the village, and sitting by the small creek that flowed through the meadow and down to the Ohio. Anna then discussed the purpose of her visit. Water Bird listened and mentioned that she knew of the hiding place, as it was she who took Jim there and made it his home during his summer in the forest. She had also assisted the general in hiding escaped slaves at the cave for over five years, up until his death. She described how he would bring the passengers to the edge of the village meadow and Water Bird would take them to the hiding place, staying with them if necessary.

The general would then pick them up when arrangements were made for their continued travel and take them on the trail that went north. She thought that, over the years, they had helped thirty to forty slaves find their freedom; the sanctuary had never been discovered. They went on to talk about the general, Virginia, and the farm; Water Bird asked about Jim and reassured Anna that he would return soon.

She also mentioned the generosity of the general, in the fall after harvest and the spring starving season when he would deliver several cows, pigs, and mules packed with apples, corn, and flour. No one had brought anything this year and it was difficult for the clan without the assistance. Anna said she would find a way to fix that, and Water Bird was very happy to assist again in the general's mission.

The shadows were long when Anna walked up the apple lane; Virginia was sitting on the porch, awaiting her return.

"How did it go?" she asked. Anna sat down, weary from the long day, and took off her bonnet.

"Very well," she said. "Water Bird will help. She helped your father for many years. She is a good, strong woman and we can count on her. I learned so much about the general's work with her clan and the many runaway slaves that came their way. They helped a lot of people together. She misses him also." Virginia listened without speaking. Anna, enjoying the rocking chair, went on to say, "The farm did not provide the village with any beef or supplies after harvest last year, and Water Bird's people suffered greatly." Virginia responded that Joshua did not allow it; nevertheless, a way would be found this year.

"She will come with her sister and niece to help with the wheat harvest next week," said Anna. "The hiding place will work for the summer. I don't know about winter. Do the slaves come in winter?"

"Daddy always said a bitter climate does not stop the taste

for freedom," said Virginia. "We will have to find something else for the hard months." They both sat silent, looking out over the orchards.

Anna asked, "Do we really want to do this?"

"Yes. We need to," Virginia said quietly.

"Did your day go well?" Anna asked.

Virginia thought for a moment. "Wesley got the wagon fixed," she said. "Joshua is gone again today, and I don't know when he will be back." Anna didn't respond and they sat in silence for a moment. "Come inside, your dinner is waiting." They went into the kitchen.

The following Sunday they went to church services and listened intently to Reverend Moody's ongoing condemnation of the slave culture. After the service, they were invited into the parish parlor, where the same people were gathered as had attended the previous meeting. Rufus Putnam introduced them to Jacob Hicks, who was introduced as a friend of the movement; he would be the primary escort for slaves seeking assistance. Virginia reported on the progress made with Water Bird and the sanctuary. She also expressed a warning that the slave catchers had been hanging out at the farm and extreme caution would be required when bringing fugitives to the farm for safekeeping. After the formal meeting, Jacob told Anna about Jim's work on his mother's farm, transportation of the slave Labithia to safety and the unusual nocturnal meeting where they had encountered one another. Jacob and Anna liked each other instantly and took more time than needed to work out the procedures to pass on to their runaways. Anna began to appreciate the dangers involved in this effort, but found Jacob to be confident and courageous. Mostly she was thankful for the information that shed a little light on the mystery of Jim's life since his departure.

CHAPTER 20

Fort Meigs
Ohio
July 1813

The garrison, enjoying the victory, spent the rest of May and June repairing the damaged fort and had quickly developed a sense of pride in their mighty edifice, even considering it invincible. Morale was high for the most part; good feelings between officers, regulars, and the militia were the norm. It was a busy place. Reinforcements and supplies arrived almost on a daily basis. General Harrison had left immediately after the British withdrawal to arrange for security along the Ohio shore of Lake Erie, anticipating and preparing for another British invasion. Patrols reported an ongoing Indian presence north of the Maumee. Most men expected the enemy to return.

Jim was recognized for his lethal skills with the long rifle; his willingness to stay at his post through explosions, shrapnel, and the noise of the enemy's cannon endeared him to his superiors. Along with some others, he was presented with a commendation for bravery while under fire. To a degree, he enjoyed the newfound attention; however, he was still unassigned and did not officially belong to any military unit. This allowed him more freedom in selecting daily duties and tasks, but he struggled with the isolation and loneliness.

Jim still did not care for army life, but now he kept his feelings to himself and did not protest as much. He hoped for a letter from Anna, thinking more each day of his past life at Maggie Hill, wondering whether he would find a place there for himself some day.

Jim began to count the days of his enlistment and tolerated the boring daily routine. He eventually took up and tented with a company of volunteers from Pennsylvania who called themselves the Pittsburg Blues. Having grown up together, forty men under the command of a Captain Butler had volunteered en masse in Pittsburg the previous September; they were now skilled artillerymen who manned two twelve pounders. They shared the east block house where Jim carried out sentry duty and protected them from sniper fire. They were appreciative of his marksmanship and invited him to bunk in with the company.

Proctor and the alliance reappeared at the fort in late July and tried to draw the American troops out of the fort and into an ambush without success. Without heavy artillery, the British were unable and unwilling to lay siege. They quickly moved on to Fort Stephenson, a small supply fort twenty miles southeast on the Sandusky River. Efforts to take this fort were also unsuccessful. On July 24th, the British gave up on this halfhearted effort and boarded their boats in Sandusky Bay to return to Fort Malden.

Jim spent most of his time on sentry duty watching for an enemy that never appeared in strength or approached the fort. His short time with the Pittsburgh Blues ended, however, when the company's six-month enlistment terminated on August 1st and General Clay approved their departure. Jim was once again unassigned; he bunked alone with little to do and no responsibilities.

Jim was almost a man now. The last six months of his life had exposed him to the cold brutality and cruelty of war. His long rifle was the tool of the executioner. His calm indifference in killing others and lack of fear in the near-death heat of battle left him with the strange confidence of a man who could take care of himself in any situation, a ruthless warrior who cared little for the honor or trappings of war. Inside the soldier, however, was the desperation of a haunted and hungry child. He couldn't define his feelings but, to himself, he admitted to being lonely, wanting somewhere, someone to belong to. But he worried that others wouldn't want him now. Thoughts of his future generated uncomfortable feelings of anxiety and loneliness. Who would want an angry, drunken killer?

Time was idle but went by fast. Jim wrote another letter to Anna while hoping for word from her and worrying for her welfare. His thoughts drifted back to the farm more often now, and he wondered whether she still cared for him and if she would welcome him back. Jim knew that he wanted to go home and eventually decided to petition General Harrison for an early discharge.

The military units that had been there in the difficult days of February were gone, and others were leaving on a daily basis. The few friends Jim had departed with their units. He had no reason to stay.

Life at the fort was tolerable, however: the meat was mostly fresh and there were an ample number of pigs and cattle for future consumption. Flour was sufficient for a daily ration of bread and this season's corn and potatoes would be arriving soon. Candles and soap were distributed twice a week and a ration of whiskey was there for the asking. The routine was relaxed, and drills and musters were sporadic.

Jim now began to spend most of his time at the stables and in the corral, helping the civilian teamsters who transported the supplies for the army to make their camp. It was a busy place; several wagons would arrive or leave almost every day. Jim enjoyed

the work and being with the livestock; the familiarity of cleaning, feeding, and managing the horses, mules, and oxen recalled
a more enjoyable time. He was also attracted to the civilian envi-
ronment with their generous offerings of whiskey, profane and
careless ways, and relaxed demeanor.

Jim continued to break some of the army's rules, particularly
related to his appearance, as he found it difficult to wear the heavy
wool uniform with its useless hat. Officers, knowing his history,
were now more tolerant of his oppositional disposition, and allowed some leeway when it came to his compliance with military
structure. Working at the stables kept him out of sight and mind,
and allowed him access to the spirits that he consumed whenever
possible. Everyone seemed to prefer it this way. Jim submitted his
petition in early August and hoped that the commander would
make his decision quickly.

Two days later, the drums rolled again: something important
was about to happen.

Jim walked up from the corral. The 1,200 officers and men
still remaining at the fort gathered in loose formation in front of
the commandant's headquarters. It was several minutes after the
formations were in order that General Harrison walked onto the
porch and opened a large dispatch. Holding it with two hands, he
announced a great victory by Admiral Perry over the British fleet
commander Barclay on Lake Erie off Point Pele, near the British
fort at Amherstburg.

"The victory was total," he said. "The western sea lanes belong to the U.S. Navy and the road to Canada is now open. We
begin our march in twenty-four hours. Initiate all necessary preparations. The order of battle will be available to officers shortly.
Hail to Admiral Perry and his men for this great victory." A cheer
went up and the commander dismissed the formation. A new
flurry of activity spread throughout the fort.

Jim went back to the corral and helped the teamsters load the wagons for transport to the ships anchored down river. Most of the men and supplies would be going by Lake Erie and up the Detroit River to attack Fort Malden. Jim spent most of the day working with the teamsters and with nothing more to do he went to clean up his locker and await further orders.

It was early the following morning when Long Hair and forty warriors entered the fort. Among the riders was the great Tarhee, leader of all the Wyandotte, sitting tall in the saddle. Jim went to greet his friends and helped translate to senior officers as to the role of the warriors was discussed. It was quickly decided that they would be assigned to Colonel Johnson's Kentucky mounted regiment, who would follow the Armada up the Detroit River via a land route and protect its western flank. The Wyandotte would serve as scouts for the regiment. At the request of Long Hair, the commandant approved Jim's assignment to the Wyandot scouting party. It took most of the day for the army to complete the paperwork to permit the transfer.

The infantry left the fort with all the supply wagons the following morning, heading the boats awaiting them at Put in Bay Harbor. The mounted infantry would leave in a week and roughly parallel the flotilla, riding up the west shore of the Detroit River.

There was great activity and excitement all around. Almost everyone wanted a chance to leave the fort and pursue the enemy. Jim was also excited; he was with Long Hair again. The Wyandotte provided him with a horse and the armory master allowed him to keep a long rifle. In addition, to Jim's surprise, Long Hair brought several letters from Anna; he read them quickly and placed them in his pack to read again when there was more time. Being with his friends, and with the anticipation of battle, his loneliness faded away.

CHAPTER 21

Amherstburg
Upper Canada
September 1813

Tecumseh heard the intense firing of many cannons and
watched intently from his vantage point at the southern
tip of Bois Blanc Island. Neither he nor his allies could see any
of the ships as they engaged in battle; the heavy smoke settled
over the lake and for most of an hour they patiently awaited the
outcome. Eventually the cannons stopped; as the smoke quietly
cleared, they still could not see any ships, and wondered who had
won the great sea battle. At first Tecumseh was told by General
Proctor that the British were the victors, but when he saw the
British making arrangements to leave the fort, he barged into
the pavilion with several of his chiefs, where Proctor and his officers were preparing to leave. Tecumseh stood in front of the
commandant.

"Is it true your admiral Barclay has been defeated?" he asked.
"And you are abandoning us to our fate?" The general didn't answer. Tecumseh, accepting his silence as truth, looked upon the
now quiet room and spoke directly to the cowering general.

"Father, listen to your children. You have them all before you. You have always told us that you would never move a foot off the king's ground, but now you are leaving without seeing the enemy. We are sorry to see our father doing so. You are so much like the fat dog that carries his tail on his back but, when fearful, drops it between his legs and runs away. You possess the arms and ammunition the great father sent for his red children. If your intent is to retreat, give them to us and leave and welcome. The Great Spirit is with us, and we are determined to defend the land that belongs to us. If it is his will, we will choose to leave our bones upon our land."

Tecumseh and his warriors returned to his island encampment and debated what to do in their desperate situation; anger and bitterness dominated the debates over the future of the Indian alliance. Tecumseh stood tall and, talking quietly now, said almost with resignation, *"Great warriors hear me. Will we ourselves be destroyed without a struggle, give up our homes, the country bequeathed to us by the Great Spirit, the graves of our dead, and everything that is sacred to us? Do we go home to never fight again? I know you will cry with me: Never, never."*

It was early afternoon when they saw columns of black smoke drifting up from Amherstburg. The British were burning the shipyard, fortress, storehouses, and all the supplies they could not take with them.

Colonel Elliot and several officers rowed to the encampment and implored Tecumseh to go with the British army. He conveyed Proctor's promise that they would stop and fight the Americans somewhere on the River Thames. With the promise of a battle, the officers were eventually able to convince the embittered Tecumseh and the other chiefs to join the retreat.

With only a few days' provisions, one thousand dispirited warriors and several thousand women and children from seven tribes began the march north to the final encounter.

Colonel Johnson's mounted regiment remained impatiently

idle at Fort Meigs for the better part of a week as they awaited the final embarkation of Harrison's main army from Put in Bay on Lake Erie. Eventually, the mounted regiment of six hundred Kentucky volunteers and the forty Wyandotte scouts rode out of the nearly abandoned fort, crossed the Maumee, and rode up the west bank of the Detroit River.

The weather was balmy for late September as the scouts watched the American flotilla of over six hundred boats stop at Hartley's point across from the southern end of Bois Blank Island.

The invasion force found Fort Malden, the boat dock, and several supply buildings burned to the ground and abandoned by the British and their Indian allies. Harrison's troops continued to sail up the Detroit River, heading for Sandwich, Ontario, chasing the retreating enemy who were going north by land. The pursuit of the British was in earnest and would continue until they agreed to stand and fight.

CHAPTER 22

Thames River
Ontario, Canada
October 1813

Journal Entry
Jonathon McGuire
Brigadier General
Army of the South
Camden, North Carolina
General Nathanael Greene
Headquarters
January 5th, 1782

"*Great events this day; my humble contribution to the great American war is about to expire. General Greene, my commanding officer since the dark days of Valley Forge, has accepted my resignation and I will soon return to my beloved Margaret and our Pennsylvania home. But first permit me to describe this day's events.*

"*Upon conclusion of a banquet for all the officers, families, and invited guests in the great hall, General Greene called me forward to stand at his side. He proceeded with great elegance, I must say, to describe how I have served him as his commandant of his Quartermaster Corps. His presentation went back to the desolation of Valley Forge where, upon taking command of the army's commissary at the orders of General Washington, he found me almost alone after the desertion of incompetent civilians, teamsters, and quartermaster officers, trying to feed and supply the beleaguered troops. He told of how he depended on me to organize and manage the duties of this critical but thankless assignment, and watched how, under me and others, through the years in New York and Pennsylvania, the quartermasters grew to be a well-run department. He enjoyed talking, describing with interesting anecdotes and some humor the general's army of the south. He told of how we evaded Cornwallis and caused heavy losses to his army and supply lines, and how by having his quartermaster march with the army, we were better prepared for the victories at the Cowpens Guilford court house and Eutaw Springs. He toasted my contributions to these victories and said that the efforts of me and my men will never be hailed but will always be celebrated by the officers and armies who go into battle. There numerous toasts and additional testimonials but, at the conclusion of the evening and to my great surprise, General Greene honored me with the braids of a Brigadier General. I was dumbfounded, for this was not anticipated or requested. Then, without pause, and with great emotion, he offered me a gift from him of a Kentucky long rifle, a most magnificent weapon of the highest quality, forged and built by the Moravian settlement in Christian's springs. I stood unashamedly for all to see, tears in my eyes, as he read the inscription so eloquently carved on the curly maple stock. I will never forget these words as he read them to all in attendance.*

To General Jonathon McGuire, forever indebted.

THE END AND THE BEGINNING

General Nathanael Greene 1781'
"This will be my most cherished possession. I leave to-
morrow, the Army generously offering a team, small wagon,
horses, and accompaniment by my two trusted and dedicated
aides, Corporals Wendell Petrol and Charles Summers, as
my escort home."

Long Hair and the Wyandotte scouts, ahead of Johnson's mounted infantry, moved faster now. In two days of steady travel, they arrived at Detroit, where they promptly chased a small group of marauding Indians away from the village. The regiment rested there for a day, awaiting the arrival of Harrison's army. Once this was in sight, they moved across the Detroit River to Sandwich, Ontario, and immediately lead the pursuit of the British up the River Thames.

Tecumseh and the British army were retreating chaotically, following the river north and east with the Americans less than a day behind. Jim was enjoying this adventure, the balmy weather and freedom of movement of riding with Long Hair and the Wyandot scouts ahead of the mounted regiment. They encountered several small bands of fleeing Indians who had abandoned the British cause and were either going back to their native lands or trying to make peace with the American forces.

On the third day they approached M'Cregor's Creek as it flowed between high banks, emptying into the Thames. A skirmish occurred as they encountered several Indians in the process of destroying the bridge that crossed the creek; rifle fire was exchanged with no injuries, and the defenders quickly withdrew. The scouts secured the bridge and held their ground, awaiting the arrival of Colonel Johnson and the mounted regiment.

It was late afternoon when the scouts, tending to their tired horses, observed a contingent of sixty or more Indians approaching from the east, walking out of the woods from the British lines.

Jim immediately recognized the tall, bent frame and long stride of Walk in the Water leading his warriors in retreat. There was some commotion and apprehension as the scouts and mounted regiment watched the Indians approach. An officer mentioned that they appeared to be abandoning the British and seeking a truce with General Harrison.

Jim observed Walk in the Water's arrival for several moments; then, with a mounting and uncontrollable fury he walked up to the chief and, with full force, hit the old man on the jaw with the butt of his rifle. The chief fell to the ground and lay there unmoving. Jim quickly looked at the chief's rifle, saw the inscription still visible on the burly maple stock, reached down, and forcibly took the rifle from his hand.

It was indeed General McGuire's long rifle; lost at the Battle of River Raisin when Jim abandoned his post and rifle and ran in mortal fear from the attacking enemy. Walk in the Water began to moan and several of his warriors approached Jim with blood hatchets drawn. He stood his ground and said to the gathering crowd of Wyandot scouts and Colonel Johnson's mounted regiment, "This be Walk in the Water who slaughtered the Kentucky volunteers at Frenchtown last winter. He has my long rifle. I was there, I saw him kill the wounded, and he needs to die. They all need to die."

Jim was grabbed and restrained by Long Hair and several of the scouts while he stood over the fallen chief, Colonel Johnson rode up quickly to disperse the menacing crowd that had gathered around the fallen chief. He ordered Walk in the Water's warriors to continue on to the army's headquarters, where General Harrison would determine their fate. Many of the Kentucky soldiers had friends and family in the regiment destroyed at the River Raisin and were seeking immediate revenge. A chant of "Kill, kill the red bastards" rang out from the soldiers as the Northern Wyandotte quickly marched away through the hostile crowd, taking their injured chief with them; a massacre had been avoided.

Jim continued to stand in place, his body shaking and his anger unresolved. He knew he would have killed the old chief if not restrained by Long Hair.

Later that night, long after General Harrison's arrival at the encampment on M'Cregor's Creek with the main body of 3,500 troops, and with preparations for the upcoming battle completed, Jim sat quietly away from the others, cleaning the general's beloved rifle, which he had thought he would never see again. To have it back was a rebirth that resolved the strong feelings of guilt and failure that had stayed with him since his cowardice on the River Raisin.

He worried, however, about his violent reaction earlier that day, and knew he would have killed the old chief if not restrained. All the men he had killed before had been strangers: distant, unrecognizable, and impersonal. *Is this what war does? Killing is too easy,* he thought. The concern didn't linger; he wrapped himself in his blanket and tried to sleep before the dawn.

Tecumseh, after an active night preparing for the battle, positioned his remaining five hundred warriors in a wooded area on the right flank of the British battle line. One young warrior asked his leader, "What do we do? Do we fight the Americans?"

The great chief paused, looked about at all his troops, and said, *"Yes, my son, we will be in their smoke before the sunsets. My body will stay where it falls, on the field of battle."* He was dressed in his deerskin hunting shirt, breech cloth, and leggings, with a kerchief wrapped into a turban on his head that held a white ostrich feather. He shook the hands of the white officers who were present, looked into the eyes of his fellow chiefs, and was heard to say in Shawnee, "The Great Spirit has a big heart." Tecumseh was ready.

It took most of the day for the Army of the Northwest Frontier to move into position facing the British line of defense. Five to six thousand young men, both white and Indian, prepared to do battle. The opposing lines crossed a front with the high bank of the Thames River on the British left, a marsh protecting their right flank, and a small swamp in the middle. The entire half-mile front was heavily wooded with sugar maple, beech, and oak trees, with little underbrush.

Once in position, the bugles blew, the drums beat, and the battle promptly began. The British regulars defended the left flank; after suffering several shots from the two cannons and two volleys from the rifles of the American infantry, they quickly broke and ran from the battle, desperate and in chaos.

Officers, including General Proctor and his staff, led the shameful retreat; others surrendered, standing quietly with their hands in the air. The battle on the left lasted less than ten minutes.

Tecumseh and his warriors, on the right of the British, protected by a thicker landscape, held their fire. They watched the dispirited rout of their allies through the smoke and fire. The bugle blew again; the Wyandot scouts and the mounted regiment, following orders, rode across the shallow swamp and into the trees to engage the Indians. They dismounted, as the trees hampered the horses' movement, and found firing positions behind fallen trees, waiting. There was a momentary silence before the warriors, faces painted now in red and black, began to charge the awaiting Kentuckians. The field of battle was suddenly overwhelmed by a deafening crescendo of violent yells, whoops, and an occasional premature rifle shot from the anxious militia. The men ran irregularly between the numerous trees on a two-hundred-yard front. Positioned next to Long Hair, Jim watched the movement in the trees as Tecumseh's five hundred warriors moved forward.

Tecumseh saw the panicked collapse of the British and now knew for certain that this was to be his last battle. His dreams were broken. He had been betrayed again by the white man. He wanted his father to be proud and he thought tenderly of his mother and the good years of his childhood on the Piqua. His hesitation was brief as he led the charge through and among the trees to the awaiting enemy, tomahawk and pistol in hand. He searched desperately for Harrison but, as he was nowhere in sight, pursued another officer on horseback. Several chiefs and clan members were by his side.

In less than two minutes, the forces collided with each other; the roar of rifles, the smell and smoke of gunpowder, the cries of the wounded and wailing of the horses added to the battle. Among the smoke and through the trees, Jim saw the white ostrich feather leading the others and moving quickly and courageously toward the Kentucky regiment. He sighted the long rifle and waited for a clear shot. He experienced the familiar recoil and discharge loud in his ear.

He was immediately surrounded by the advancing Indians. Violent, chaotic, and intense hand-to-hand combat commenced all around him; a brief flash of Frenchtown passed through his memory as he used his rifle as a club to fight off a young Shawnee warrior whose tomahawk barely missed his head.

In the midst of the struggle, he heard the whoops of war turn to wails of sadness and cries of despair. Suddenly, unexpectedly the Indians disengaged and retreated from the battle almost en masse; all were disappearing into the woods on the far side of the marsh. Jim knew why. Family members picked up their fallen leader and carried him into cover.

The smoke of many fires hung low over the celebrations of the victorious Army of the Northern Frontier. Tents had been quickly put up and supply wagons were gathered a mile or two back from the battlefield. A small contingent of disciplinary troops were finishing the burial of the dead. The injured of both sides were receiving medical attention. Soldiers rummaging through the spoils of war had found several kegs of brandy and rum; the liquor was quickly taking affect.

It would soon be a wild night for the victorious, with little attention paid to military discipline or the orders of officers; rations of food, tobacco, and spirits were generously distributed. Some distance away from the main body of troops, a hundred or so warriors from several tribes were gathered around a large fire, chanting their thanks to the Great Spirit for a great victory and homage to the few who were killed. Alcohol would not reach this body for another hour or so. Above the dark ceiling of smoke, a bright and crisp autumn night blessed the gathering.

Tarhee, the great chief of the southern Wyandotte and spiritual leader of all tribes in attendance, rose from those sitting and, silhouetted in front of the bright fire, held his arm high. It was expected that he would speak this night. The drums and chanting stopped and the warriors moved closer to hear the shaman.

"Great warriors of the Wyandotte, Shawnee, and Seneca. Great Chiefs Black Hoof and Black Snake. You have done well this day. Our fires are filled with the Great Spirit and the redcoats of the king have run like rabbits from the wolf. Brave warriors, it is a great day for us but a bad day for the peoples of the lakes and forests. Forest Boy, white friend of the Wyandotte, shot and killed forever Chief Tecumseh of the Shawnee and leader of all the brothers. He will be known as the man who killed Tecumseh and will carry his spirit until the Dancing Tail clan sets it free. He will walk with that name for all time.

"Let me tell you, great warriors, Tecumseh was my friend and my enemy. The Wyandotte have fought with him and against him. I fought with his father Pucksinswau against the white men of both empires.

"I honor his life; he fought for all red peoples everywhere. We now stand without the power to defend ourselves from the white man and his greed; great warriors, know now that the sky, trees, and water no longer belong to the Great Spirit. We will soon be discarded by our white father as he takes our land, burns our villages, and destroys our way of life. We fought this day against the great Tecumseh and we fought against ourselves. Hear my

words, great chiefs. He was the last warrior that could protect us from the white man's evil. My warriors leave tomorrow and return to our land on the Sandusky to await in time our own destruction."

The Indians gathered around the fire knew this to be true and were saddened. Once the Tarhee sat down, other chiefs said their piece. Gradually and in small numbers the warriors left the group to find the spirits amongst the white soldiers.

The battle and a way of life were buried on the banks of the Thames this day and the victims celebrated.

The next morning was chaos and many were miserable in the aftermath of the alcohol consumed throughout the night. By early morning, the officers regained control of the remaining liquor and secured it. The victorious American army and the rapidly disappearing British made it clear to all that the war on the western frontier was over. Many battles remained to be fought in this war, but they would move east, not to return to the western territories. The need for troops greatly diminished and the excitement mounted as units from all states prepared to return to their homes. General Harrison and his staff were sending couriers in all directions—east, south, and west—with announcements of his great victory and plans for the dismissal of most of his troops. Many units were being discharged and returned home; several were sent to Sandwich and Detroit to take up garrison duty. Two regiments followed the British on their retreat eastward. The encampment appeared in disarray; men and animals were going in all directions, supplies divided up and horses allocated and reallocated. The first to leave were the Kentuckians, including the mounted regiment. On their way home, they would stop on the River Raisin and bury the bones of their fallen comrades who had been without burial or ceremony since that cold day in February. Jim, busy elsewhere, was not there to wish them well.

Jim stood at attention in the presence of General Harrison

and many of his aides; it was busy in the four-room house of the commander's headquarters. Harrison saw Jim and turned his attention away from his officers. "Well private," he said, "we meet again. Reports indicate that you fought bravely with Colonel Johnson and the scouts. Be at ease, sit over here." Jim took a seat as directed. The general stared at Jim without speaking for a moment, as if deciding how he would approach the young soldier.

"I have your application for an early discharge," he said. "It says you want to return to your home in Marietta."

"Yes, sir," said Jim.

Another pause, the general continued. "It says in this report that you shot Tecumseh and the claim is supported by the Wyandotte scouts. Is that a fact?"

Jim said, "Yes, sir, it is a fact."

"How can you be sure that it was him?" the general asked.

"I have met him several times and I had him in my sights quite often at Fort Meigs, sir," said Jim. "I recognized him."

"Why didn't you shoot him at Fort Meigs when you had a chance?"

"I thought him to be a great man, sir," he said.

"What made you shoot him yesterday then?" the general asked.

Jim said, "Sir, I knew he was the only person who could defeat us and keep the war ongoing. I wanted to go home."

"I see," said the general. "There is another report that states that Colonel Johnson shot him. What say you to that report?"

"I know what I did, sir," said Jim.

The general sat for another moment, leaned across the table. "Be advised that the officers and men of Colonel Johnson's command will be most adamant that he, not you, fired the shot that killed Tecumseh," he said. "I will not be able to support your claim."

"I know not of what they say," said Jim, "nor do I care for

any attention or celebration. I know what I did, sir."

The General picked up the quill, signed the discharge application, and handed it to Jim. "See the pay master for a voucher and the quartermaster for your mustering rations," he said. "You are a good soldier, Private Morgan, and a free man. Good luck. Dismissed."

Jim, Long Hair, and the Wyandotte warriors left the next morning for the Sandusky.

The last desperate, hopeless effort to save an entire civilization died along with Tecumseh on the River Thames. Except for several rebellions in the Deep South and isolated skirmishes in the Northwest Territories, the native populations of a third of a continent were no longer a threat or challenge to the white man. The aboriginals who prospered on this land for thousands of years were now subservient to a larger, more powerful society. They were dependent on its charity and victims of its inhumanity. A proud race of red men was now enslaved. Jim thought of none of this as he rode south with his Wyandot friends through the black swamp and on to the Sandusky River Valley. Soon, however, he would be a witness to another episode of the white man's evil, and play a role in the beginning of the struggle to free another race already enslaved.

As one culture dies, another will be born.

End of Part 1

PART 2
THE BEGINNING

CHAPTER 1

Ohio Constitutional Convention
Chillicothe, Ohio Territory
November 6ᵗʰ, 1802

*D*ear Friends and Members of the Ohio Constitutional Convention,

I would like to thank the honorable Edward Tiffin for allowing me a few moments in your deliberations to petition this distinguished body to consider the burdens of slavery and how it will define the future of this great state. It is with great appreciation that you have and will honor the directives of the North West Ordinance who, under its authority, permits the petition for statehood and mandates the formation of a free state. I must, in my appeal to you, appeal to a greater calling, and reference the status of dark fugitives from the south who become residents in the free regions of our land. I request that this body ignore and abandon the requirement in the same ordinance that calls for the legal reclamation of any person whose labor is lawfully claimed in any one of the original states. Beyond the words is a more humane calling. On our border to the south is the great river that our unfortunate friends will always see as the river of freedom; with more and more frequency, they risk their limb and life to cross over to this land of ours and secure the liberties they so desire and deserve. There are many in this territory and I say proudly that I am one who seeks the abolishment of the vile institution and practice of enslavement of our fellow human beings. My request, however, is more humble: that you determine as is your right to prohibit the forced return of any fugitive seeking our shores and the freedoms therein, and refuse to allow any legal representative of any of the slave-holding states to physically remove these refugees from our state. I also ask that you permit so-inclined citizens to assist these refugees in ways that protect and promote their freedom and protect said citizens from any judicial prosecution or sanctioned persecution.

This is the only opportunity that this state will have to honor and abide by the highest and most sacred principles so dedicated in our constitution: "that all men are created equal and endowed with the rights of life, liberty and the pursuit of happiness." Many of us in this room were in the company and presence of these men who wrote and spoke these noble words. Most assuredly, it was their intent that these principles have dominion over all others.

Let these be the words of Ohio.

You're most obedient and humble servant,
Jonathon McGuire

The Ohio Constitutional Convention ignored the general's plea and allowed fugitive slave ordinances to be part of the laws of Ohio.

Ferry Landing
Marietta
September 1813

A large, active, and somewhat cheerful crowd had gathered to see the Putnam's off on another journey to Washington City to convene the national conference of surveyors. President Madison had appointed Rufus Putnam to chair the year-long conference, and most of his close friends seeing him off this day knew how important it was for the aging patriarch of Marietta to gain back a national presence that had been idle ever since President Jefferson shamefully dismissed him as the Surveyor General of the United States some eight years before.

They were much older now; Beth and Rufus, and the long ride to the capital via the Virginia Pike would mean four weeks of hardship, even in good weather. God knows how long it would take if a wet spell settled in over the Appalachians. Rufus, however, was not thinking of recapturing his reputation at this particular moment. He was much too busy with last minute details of the journey and saying goodbye to family and friends. The flatboat was docked at the Ohio River ferry landing, awaiting the Putnam's carriage and supply wagon, crammed with household items, food supplies, dry goods, and horse feed to come aboard. Thomas Merchant, the Putnam's manservant and teamster on this journey walked the horses onto the ferry to cross the Ohio to Parkersburg, where the land journey would begin.

Beth knew that his last meeting two days prior with the Board of Trustees of the First Mercantile Bank had not gone well; she was familiar with his agitations and preoccupations, and could tell from his demeanor that there was a serious rift between Rufus and the board.

Mr. Putnam's resignation as chairman of the board was accepted as expected, but little else happened to his satisfaction. Most upsetting was the management of the heavy debt that was left by General McGuire, mortgaged by the Maggie Hill Farm. The board was in no mood to continue to tolerate missed deadlines, interest forgiveness, and the refinancing that had been an annual occurrence for the last ten years.

His true friend would soon lose his legacy and the general's dear daughter Virginia would suffer the loss of her inheritance. She would become a common woman with a no-account husband and nine-year-old daughter living, in all probability off the Christian charity of her friends. *Such a sad ending,* he thought as he rechecked the load on the wagon and walked over to the carriage.

Rufus was angry that no one, not even Myron Johnson, his strongest ally, supported carrying the debt another year. Everyone anticipated that the farm's harvest would again be insufficient to meet the loan coming due in January. Rufus wished that he could have been more forceful in explaining to Virginia the serious financial situation that she was facing. His warnings and dire predictions seemed to have had little impact and generated little if any alarm. He sometimes thought that she might want the farm to be taken from her, to absolve her of responsibility and allow her to escape her husband and the desolate existence in which she was mired. He hoped that she has some financial reserves hidden away because she was about to lose everything; there would be nothing of value left. He cringed with the image of several of the board members talking loudly and arrogantly, looking forward to taking over this valuable property, reselling it for twice its debt, and perhaps securing a mining claim to capture the rights to a large vein of coal on the east boundary that looked very large and easy to extract. "Coal is the fuel of the future," trustee Silas Cole repeated several times during the heated but one-sided debate. The board clearly wanted the farm to fail. *So much for loyalty and compassion for their fellow man,* Rufus thought as he said his goodbyes to the well wishers and family.

Rufus was equally concerned that his meeting the previous week with Joshua, Virginia's husband, had not gone well. Several times in recent years, Rufus had protected him from prosecution for serious crimes that he had committed. Joshua seemed unresponsive to the threats of disclosure and prosecution that had in the past resulted in a modicum of responsible and compliant behavior. Knowing that Rufus was leaving, Joshua responded to him with an air of indifference and defiance never seen before.

The Marietta Drum and Fife Corps had finally showed up

and its twelve members were filling the active and noisy water-front with patriotic songs and sound that only their families could enjoy. Rufus and Beth hugged their children, in-laws, and grand-children one more time and boarded the ferry, both with tears in their eyes. Their entourage of two helpers and their twelve-year-old grandson felt the boat pull against the current, carried toward the Virginia side.

"I'm sorry, dear friend Jonathon; I have left you and your family down," Rufus said aloud. He pushed the bitterness away, thinking about the journey and his return to politics and the pomp and ceremony he enjoyed so much.

Anna and Virginia had also come to the send off on the river-front on this first day of September, 1813. It had been an active summer for the two ladies. They had provided sanctuary to sev-eral fugitives. Anna, in particular, spent much of her time bring-ing food baskets, clothes, and other necessities to the runaway slaves.

She remembered them all with fondness. The first to arrive was a tall but very thin mulatto named Thomas, who said he was twenty-four years of age but didn't know where or when he was born. He was a gentle person who had been in hiding in the wil-derness south of the Ohio River for over a month, on the verge of starvation, until he was found by Jacob. Thomas belonged to a Mr. Martin Smith of the Virginia Territory; he had worked in the tobacco fields every day for ten years. He had a hard time not working during his time at the sanctuary, and continually pestered Water Bird for things to do. A few weeks later, Jacob arrived with two more fugitives: Sam, a large, middle-aged man of very dark skin and wooly hair, who was owned by a J.B. Bean, a tobacco farmer from Greenup, Kentucky; and Nance, tall and thin, whose body had the scars of numerous whippings and beatings. This was Nance's third escape and his owner, a Mr. Beckwith of Wood County, Virginia, had put up poster offering an ample reward for his return, dead or alive. Both had been fugitives for several months and met accidentally, hiding in the woodlands near Portsmouth, Ohio, and being fed on occasion by a kindly farmer who would leave food out behind his barn. It took two days for Jacob to gain their trust and a week of moving and hiding, as slave catchers were actively on their trail.

The most recent fugitive was a Ms. Ehlive Moss, a pretty young lady who had left Kentucky several weeks ago with her husband and two young children; they were nearly caught by a group of white farmers who had come upon them unexpectedly and, in those terrifying moments, she was separated from her family. The rest of the family's fate was unknown. Ehlive was forlorn; her passion for freedom had been diminished by the loss of her loved ones. Jacob returned to Kentucky to find that her family had been captured and returned to their owner.

Water Bird stayed with them and Anna provided food, clothes, and blankets. They all left together on a late August night when Jacob and two associates led them on a dangerous and long journey to a Quaker refuge in western Pennsylvania, and then hopefully to Canada, if and when the war would allow it. All except Ehlive were eager to go; they were thankful for the care and comfort that was provided them. Jacob promised that he would do what he could to free Ehlive's loved ones.

On her trips to the sanctuary, Anna got know her guests quite well, understanding their personalities and dispositions, hearing of their hopes and dreams. She listened as they told the stories of the terrible conditions in the tobacco plantations south of the river.

All had been brutalized in various ways; their treatment always lacked dignity and humanity. Anna quickly began to feel rage and understood completely the passion and determination that drove the General and Maggie to fight against this ugly institution for so many years. She also got to know Jacob, a handsome, serious, and determined man who had committed his life to providing sanctuary for the ever-growing number of refugee slaves who would find their way across the river.

She regretted that they didn't spend more time together so she could get to know him better. It was a tearful day when they all left; the sanctuary was now a very lonely place. She was looking forward to more visitors, but realized that Jacob would be gone for some time.

Three days prior to the Putnam's leaving they invited Virginia, Anna, and several others to their house where a dinner was held for the ladies to thank them for their wonderful work and encouraged them to continue to serve God in this way.

On this day of departure, they both feigned good wishes and happy spirits to the generous travelers who had done so much for them in so many ways this last year. They hid their fears from each other and everyone else. Fear, however, was the only thing on their minds.

Just recently, they had noticed Lucas Williams and his half-breed partner Palitah Moon associating with Joshua at the McIntosh Tavern on the point. They also loitered at the farm under Joshua's invitation, watching the daily activities. It was an unwanted feeling, knowing that they were being surveyed by evil men who would do evil things.

Joshua watched the procession from the outdoor tables at McIntosh's, enjoying the beer and the companionship of the two slave hunters, who had reappeared in town several weeks before. It was almost noon and the spectators were becoming jovial; Joshua was enjoying the moment, had great plans and expectations for the future, and was pleased as hell that old man Putnam was gone and good riddance. *The old bastard has been holding a lot of crap over my head for a long time,* he thought. First there were the forged checks and then theft of money from the bank. Most worrisome was the problem of that barmaid squatter, who seduced him in the back alley of the tavern house a year past and then proceeded to falsely accuse him of rape and abuse. *It's a good thing that bitch left town,* he thought. These crimes had been kept secret by the intervention of Mr. Putnam to protect his friend's proud name, as honorable as Marietta itself.

Once the ferry pulled out, the citizens started to disperse and the bar filled with town folks who would take some refreshments before continuing their labors. Joshua and his two friends moved to a corner table, ordered more ale, and began to discuss a promising future.

Anna and Virginia had returned to the farm after the Putnam's' sendoff in late afternoon. They gathered the hands on the front porch of the big house to share the events of the day and speculate on what it would mean for all of them. The hands stood or sat in quiet but anxious anticipation. Wendell Petro and Charles Summers sat close together. Henry Pennmeter, as usual, stood apart, his arms wrapped around his chest, saying nothing. Virginia spoke calmly; explaining that with Mr. Putnam leaving for an extended stay in the capital, the farm had lost its benefactor and protector, and that there was no one else in Marietta that would be willing or able to confront and control Joshua or to manage the financial difficulties with the bank. Wendell asked about Joshua's brother, who had brought him home from Elizur Kirkwood's last summer.

Virginia went on to explain that August was doing poorly and did not appear interested in his brother Joshua any more. Neither Sheriff Micah Miller nor Judge Theodore Commons had the fortitude to take on the rogues and ruffians that were Joshua's partners. Reverend Moody would do what he could, but they shouldn't expect too much. The discussion was dispiriting; Penelope asked " What is going to happen to all of us? Do we have to leave? Virginia said "you are free to go and I will do what I can to get you the money the general left in his will but the bank has frozen all of the farms funds; Anna and I have decided to stay and work the farm as best we can, we hope that you will stay", she paused for a moment then continued "I do not know where Joshua is or when he will return, and can only guess at his intentions." More discussion and expressions of their fear and anxiety followed; eventually they all decided to continue on and hope for the best. Eventually they left in silence to finish their afternoon labors.

That evening, Anna, Virginia and Penelope moved into the general's cottage, where Virginia took the large bedroom and the others the smaller back room. Digger slept by the door, listening for any threatening noises. The apple harvest would begin in the morning. Anna said her nightly prayer for Jim to return.

CHAPTER 2

Washington County
September 1813

Journal Entry
Jonathon McGuire
Maggie Hill Farm
September 1806

"I write this night most tired but satisfied, as the apple harvest just finished. The cider will be fermenting until early January. We enjoyed a full harvest with all of our 12 acres free of the dreaded blight. The Roxbury Russets are now fully matured with fine cider apples. The bellflowers had a more modest production, suffering somewhat from a worm infestation. In all, we expect to take to market in the New Year 400 barrels of fine hard cider. The winter price as speculated by the Putnam's to be $10/barrel. Funds sufficient, I dare say, to help satisfy the farm's mortgage and Mr. Connor's greed full disposition for another year. There is sufficient surplus to produce a few gallons of vinegar, many pies, and spoilage to provide fodder for the livestock for the best part of the winter.

"Allow me to share some bemusement and pleasantry

that occurred two days prior. All hands were hard at work in the pressing shed, preparing the final load of the Bellflowers, when Wendell asked me to look down the lane toward the house and we all observed a most peculiar man walking towards us. He was small, thin in stature, and dressed rather poorly with old britches that fitted high above his ankles, a coarse flower sack with holes cut out for his head and arms for his blouse, hatless and barefoot, his feet thick with dirt. He carried few belongings: a bible, cooking pot, and large leather purse that fitted around his neck.

"He introduced himself as John Chapman, recently from Pennsylvania, and asked if we had any apple seeds to spare, a most unusual request, I must say. I offered all that had been brushed aside from the last pressing. He immediately began to inspect them and indicated that russet seeds would be preferable. He continued talking while he filled his sack with several hands full of our best seeds and stated that he collected seeds from wherever he could to plant in the spring in plots wherever conditions were good for growing; he would return to cultivate his seedlings each year until he could sell them to farmers and settlers as they took up land around his plantings. He admitted upon inquiry that he owned no land and did not appear to be offended when I stated that he be a squatter. He was most pleasant of disposition, in spite of his forwardness. He supped at our table, ate no flesh but consumed large amounts of our scalloped potatoes and corn meal mush. He did enjoy numerous cups of last year's cider apparently unaffected, and suggested that if I added crabapples to the fermentation I would enjoy a heartier beverage.

When Maggie asked of his modest dress, he proclaimed that he gave most of his clothes away to people needier than he. He was irritating at times, pushing some form of a

Nordic biblical religion on to his Protestant audience.

   "Mr. C. slept on the hearth and left early, without words, taking a pan of yesterday's corn bread with him. A friendly if not peculiar man whom I trust will have difficulty prospering in his bizarre enterprise."

Jonathon McGuire

Anna and the hands were busy with the apple harvest. The prosperous twenty-acre orchard was steady cash crop that the general had depended on every fall to help pay off his debt to the bank and leave funds to see him through the winter. This year, there were only five hands instead of the usual eight working twelve hour days for three weeks, doing the picking hauling, pressing, gleaning, and filling the barrels to an anticipated final product of eight hundred barrels of hard apple cider. Once the barrels were filled, the apple juice would be allowed to ferment for two to three months to increase its alcohol content; it would then be sold to an apple buyer to be shipped downriver to market. The farm's cider had become quite popular in recent years, particularly since the general added crabapples to his cider mixture.

Virginia rode into town after harvest to ensure her that her daughter, who was staying with the Moody's to attend school and be with other girls her age, would not be bothered or harmed by Joshua. She also made inquires around town to find a suitable foreman to manage the farm and hopefully stand up to Joshua if that were necessary.

"All the good men have gone off to fight the war. The only ones left are a bunch of sorry asses," said Millie Gilhausen, the proprietor of the feed lot and long time Marietta widow. "Now, if Tom were still alive, he would help you out in a minute." The answer, although more politely stated, was the same from all of the people she visited. Discouraged, she went to the bank and asked to talk to Willford Conner, the new president, to discuss the release of the employees' inheritance and the farm's financial status. She was quite surprised when he was too busy to see her. She was successful in purchasing an old rifle and several pistols with ample ammunition from Ekiah Cooper, who served as the village blacksmith and gunsmith. Her ride back to the farm the next morning was depressing, Joshua had disappeared since the Putnam's' departure, but Virginia was expecting him at anytime.

That evening she got together with Anna and Penelope and sitting around the kitchen table drinking dark tea Virginia unexpectedly shared her thoughts. "I knew Joshua growing up but didn't notice him much, he stopped going to school early; twelve I think. I don't think we ever talked. Then Mother died and my life fell apart and I remember being so angry mostly with Father who spent his time weeping and writing by himself. I was so all alone then. Joshua came to work on the farm that summer. He was older but paid a lot of attention to me. I was attracted to his rugged looks and reckless behavior and when Father disapproved I spent more time with him. Then the night we had the corn frolic and I had to much cider and he had his way with me, not only did I lose my innocence but was impregnated with his seed, it was terrible time I didn't enjoy anything about Joshua lovemaking and knew nothing about child birth. I finally confided of my condition with Madeline and then dear Anna. We got married before I showed and the wedding as I recall was a most dismal event; he was an angry man from the beginning and developed an immediate dislike for Jim who had caught everyone's eye. Joshua was not all bad and even nice when he wanted to be and we did have some good moments; he was always was nice to our daughter and she feels so torn because of all she hears. He began to carouse and engage in all his tomfoolery after Elizabeth was born and the town started to talk right away. It was most humiliating for father and me but I cannot regret my decision because it brought me Elizabeth. I knew about his embezzlement, drinking and gambling debts and his assault on the poor indentured barmaid even though father tried to protect me from it. Rufus held a hard rein for a long time but now that is gone and he is under the influence of some very evil people. We are all alone I am afraid".

The kitchen was quiet and the fire had burned low. Anna finished her tea, got up to clear the table. "We will do well" was all she said.

Now began a time of upheaval where the very life of the farm and its inhabitants were put in serious jeopardy.

CHAPTER 3

Wyandot Nation
October 1813

The first breaths of fall floated on a clear sky as Labithia, letting the warm sun provide her comfort as she moved among a large stand of wild raspberry bushes that were overweight with a bountiful harvest, awaiting the birds, animals, and humans that would take their fill of the sweet and nutritious berries. The slave girl had never seen such a thick patch; she carried a woven basket around her neck, quickly filling it with the red and plumb fruit. She enjoyed being alone, doing her work at her pace with no one to answer to. Every day, she celebrated her freedom: the joy of a quiet walk, banter with her emancipated family, and a sense of worthiness that grew a little every day. Her body had grown and filled out with the promise of womanhood. Canada seemed far away now; there was little talk of her continuing her journey until the war in the north ended. She reached over to continue picking, when a large unseen hand, reeking of tobacco and feces, quickly and silently covered her mouth. The fear and shame known to all slaves returned. She instantly knew her fate. A nauseous and devastating grief filled her belly as she was dragged from the tranquility of the berry patch to the violence of a leather strap tied about her neck. She cried quietly.

Millie and Lebanon Parker would not notice her absence for another hour and, with trepidation, they went to the patch to find the evidence of the kidnapping and signs of three horses going in a southerly direction. Their worst fears were realized. Lebanon rode the mule to Walker's Trading Post several miles distant to share the terrible news.

The slave catchers rode the horses slowly and with arrogance. They were in no hurry; Lucas Williams knew that all the Wyandot warriors were in the north fighting with the Americans, and that there were few, if any, tribal members available to challenge their authority. Labithia had stopped resisting after she was severely beaten with a horse whip that Lucas carried for moments like this. Her horse was between the two slave catchers, with Lucas in the lead. She was now in great pain, semi-conscious, with a leather rope around her neck and her wrists bound and knew that if she fell off the horse, she could easily be strangled. Her only thought after the severe beating was to stay awake and alive. She reached deep inside herself to find the strength to persevere. Her old instincts returned; survival was one of the things slaves were good at. *Someone will help me again,* she thought as they left the nation, going south on the Sandusky river and heading for the Scioto.

The return of the warriors from the great victory on the Thames was less than celebratory; an early arctic storm blew down from the north on the second day of their return. Heavy rains, sleet and snow followed them across the Maumee and into the dark swamp where high waters flooded the traditional trails. The horses and men suffered the two days in chest-deep and freezing swamps with nowhere to rest. They kept going as best they could and, on the third day, frozen, exhausted, and hungry, they staggered out of their misery and headed for Crane town and sanctuary. Jim was one of the first men to reach their destination.

He turned his exhausted horse over to a young Indian and went into the warmth of the long house, where the early arrivals were already receiving dry clothes and refreshing food and drink. Jim planned on staying here for the night and proceeding to Walker's Trading Post in the morning. As he was nourished with hot stew, he looked forward to spending several weeks in leisure and conversation at the trading post with Charles Walker, as well as visiting with Labithia.

It was late evening. The wind and rain had finally stopped, the fires in the long house were burning low with smoke drifting up and out of the openings in the roof, and most of those remaining were sleeping or in quiet conversations. Jim was huddled with Long Hair around a fire pit; they smoked pipes and discussed how hard the return trip had been on Tarhee, the great chief, who was resting with fever and quite weak. Charles Walker entered, looked around, and walked over to the fire pit. He greeted the two men and Jim noticed the seriousness in the trader's demeanor.

"What is wrong?" Jim asked.

"Libithia is gone. The slave catchers kidnapped her four days ago. They headed south, two men on three horses. They were seen leaving the reservation and, by their description, it was Williams and Moon." Walker paused.

Jim stared at the fire for a moment and said, as if talking to himself, "I will have to go get her." He paused again. "I will leave in the morning." He looked at Long Hair and asked, "Is there a horse I can borrow?"

"All the horses we rode are too exhausted to continue," he said. "You will have to take the blue eye. He is fresh but will need to be ridden easy; he can make it if you don't push him too hard. He will be our gift to you and we will ask the Great Spirit to ride with you." They sat for some time without talking; the trader sensed Jim's desire to be alone and got up to leave.

"A letter came from Marietta," he said handing it to Jim. He sat in silence for some time before he opened it.

September 12ᵗʰ, 1813
Dear Jim,

I pray you get this letter in time. So much has happened. Mr. Putnam and Elisabeth left for the capital city on President Madison's bidding some three weeks ago. He will not return for at least a year. Joshua now fears no one; Elizur and the two slave catchers have taken over the farmhouse and Virginia, Penelope, and I have moved to the cottage and fear for our lives. There is much drunkenness and debauchery; they threaten us but so far have done nothing. They come and go as they please and do no work. Virginia purchased some weaponry and we are vigilant and determined, but will not be able to hold them off. We are so afraid. The men are still here, staying away from the house when Joshua and his ruffians are present. We work the farm as best we can, but little is getting done. Yesterday morning early these devils rode to Council Keeper's village and set it afire. They ruined their harvest and drove everyone off. Council Keeper and his brothers have gone to the Indian encampment at old fort Harmar and Water Bird has gone into the thicket with her sister and niece. Virginia has gone to town to get help, but no one has come to our aid.

This summer we did the general's work and provided sanctuary for some escaped slaves. The slave hunters left this morning, but I suspect they will soon return. We fear greatly that terrible things will happen.

You, dear Jim, are our only hope. Come quickly if you are there.

With hope and affection,
Anna

Jim had said his good byes the prior evening and left before daylight. he rode slowly and steadily south out of the treaty territory. By midday the blue eye was starting to labor, so they rested for several hours and the horse rallied. Jim agonized over the slow pace. The long days, uneventful for the most part, gave Jim ample time to assess his situation and think about the future. His life seemed much more complicated now; he didn't know what was expected of him or what he would do when he returned to Maggie's Hill. He found some comfort in deciding that he would do whatever needed doing and he was confident of his abilities. First, however, he had to find Labithia. Although he wanted to pursue the kidnappers aggressively, he talked himself into patience. He needed to take his time, find out where they took her, and figure out how to rescue her.

He recognized with some satisfaction that all the fear he had felt a year ago when he was being pursued by the slave catchers had disappeared; he would do whatever it took to find and free the young captive. The world had changed and so had Jim.

He followed the Sandusky River south for two days and then went overland to the Scioto. He decided to stop at the Hicks farm, as he was curious to see the lady he spent such an interesting summer with so and to find out if Abigail had heard anything of Labithia. On the journey south, Jim stopped at a farm each evening and asked for feed, food, and shelter. Once the suspicious and reluctant farmers learned that he was a war veteran returning home, they were eager to accommodate the traveler and listened intently to his description of the historical events on the River Thames. The Blue Eye, with proper rest and nourishment was able to put in a good day's labor.

On the morning of the fourth day, he saw the two large oak trees and followed the small creek into the farm. Little had changed.

"Mr. Morgan, what a surprise. What brings you here?" said Abigail. She held a small child in her arms and watched Jim come slowly down the path, stopping the horse few feet from her. He looked at her carefully and his mind began to calculate as he noticed the size and apparent age of the infant.

"Hello Mrs. Hicks," he said. "I am discharged from the army and heading home to Washington County; I thought I would pay my respects."

"Most kind of you Mr. Morgan," she said. "Please dismount and take rest at the table under the oak; I will bring you some cider and biscuits." Mrs. Hicks, still very formal in her speech and demeanor sat on a bench as Jim enjoyed the provisions. "You have changed, Jim," she said. "You're much older. Did you fight with General Harrison against the British?" Jim said, "Yes, ma'am, I did," and said no more. More silence followed as he finished his cider.

"Don't bother to ask about the child," said Abigail. "There is nothing you need to know or do."

Jim remained silent, looking at the infant squirming in Abigail's lap, now fully understanding the circumstances. "What is the child's name?" He asked. "Margaret," she said. They continued to sit in silence, not knowing what to say. The tension and awkwardness of the moment continued; then Abigail said, without solicitation, "I have a man who is kind and careful and works hard; I am satisfied as to my situation. He is on the river tending to his catfish lines and will return this afternoon. Jacob is away fulfilling God's mission to find salvation and comfort for God's black creatures."

Jim, noticing her nervousness, smiled slightly and said "can I be of assistance for you and the child in any way?" Abigail shook her head and said "no we are fine but thank you for your charity". Jim then asked about Libithia; Abigail's formality and reticence disappeared upon hearing her name.

"Oh Jim," she said, "The slave catchers were here four or five days ago. They had labithia and camped near the road, well in sight; Lucas made a point to ride down the path and show us the poor girl. She was so whipped and beaten as to be unknown to me. She was bare of breast and back and most abused. I offered

to provide the two devils with ample cider, chicken, and cornbread if they would allow me to tend to her needs; I helped her
eat some chicken soup, gave her warm cider, and put some palm
bark ointment on her festers and wounds. All she could whisper
was, 'Thank um, help me.' It was so distressing; I am still haunted
by the sight and her sad voice."

They sat sharing a mournful silence for several minutes. Jim
briefly told Abigail about the journey north with Labithia and
her time with the Parkers. He asked if she knew where they were
taking her. "They made a point to tell me that they were going to
Joshua Sprout's homestead in Marietta," she said, "to your general's farm and then to her owner in Kentucky."

"I must go, I have to go," was all Jim said and he got up from
the table. "My horse is old and worn thin. Do you have a horse
that

She looked toward the pasture and said, "Why don't you leave
on the horse you came with?" Jim turned toward the corral; the
buckskin stood quietly, her neck and head extended over the
wooden fence, watching her old friend, wondering why it had
taken him so long to return. Jim calmed the old horse, talking
softly. He then brought the Blue Eye into the corral and took the
time to feed, water, and groom him. He was retrieving his old
saddle and bridle in the tack room when he noticed a neat and
orderly living space in the barn, in the same corner where he had
resided two summers ago. He smiled quietly.

Buckskin and Jim left within the hour. He asked Abigail to
get word if she could to Jacob and have him come to Marietta.
"I will need his help," he said. He got on his horse and headed
towards the oaks. "I will find Labithia, if you are ever in need of
assistance?" He said to Abigail. "You need to go" she called in
parting. She was pleased to see that Jim had become a confident
and capable man. *This bodes well for young Margaret,* she thought.
The blue eye had earned his rest and pasture and would spend the

time he had left well fed and cared for.

The buckskin, glad to be under a familiar saddle and rider, traveled well and long on the road home. Jim retraced his steps from the journey north two summers prior and rode into the October nights. He felt a growing urgency to be home; he wanted to see Anna, care for his mother, and find Labithia. The slave catchers were four days ahead but traveling slowly.

The young girl knew little of her life since her abduction in the raspberry patch on the Sandusky. After the initial shock and trauma, she shut down her emotions as well as she could. Lucas Williams and Pelitha Moon were brutal men. They whipped her back to shreds, pulled her off the horse and tossed her to the ground, kicked her to wake her, pulled back her hair, and urinated on her when she asked for water. These were the agonies she endured on a daily basis. Labithia expected to die but hoped that she would somehow survive; she had little awareness of her surroundings and felt the intense pain in her back, the bruises about her body and the stiffness of riding for hours with a leather rope about her neck and hands, tied to the saddle horn. One day rolled into another and it was all she could do to stay alert. One cold night, however, she heard a gentle voice giving her food and softly applying a soothing ointment to her raw back; a blanket which provided a moment of comfort before it was ripped away. The keepers gave her only enough food and water to keep her alive; she slept on the ground tethered to a tree, with only a small horse blanket to protect her from the autumn nights. The very long and cold nights were the worst of her suffering.

Labithia did remember one dream: her mother holding her in her arms while talking quietly about her African homeland. She desperately tried to hold onto this and recall the memories so dear. On occasion, she saw silent white bystanders as she was paraded through village after village. No one offered comfort. They only stared. She wondered at times where her rescuers Jim and Jacob were, and if they would search for her. As time went by, she let this hope fade from her thoughts.

She was near death when she was dropped on the front porch of the large house on Maggie Hill.

CHAPTER 4

Maggie Hill Farm
October 1813

Joshua had felt invincible since the Putnam's departure. There was no one left to threaten him with criminal charges and punishment; the sheriff was too timid to challenge his misdeeds. He now spent most of his time in town with his rogue friends at McIntosh's Tavern in rowdy, drunken, and bullying behavior; most of the establishment's regular customers would leave whenever Joshua appeared. He enjoyed a new sense of power and would walk about town with a swagger, intimidating many of the citizens. Joshua made no effort to work the farm any more, and tolerated Virginia and the hands as they made an effort to sustain the many necessary activities. He no longer tried to please his wife and actually enjoyed her growing helplessness and frustration. The Marietta community of hardworking and well-meaning citizens observed his behavior and those of his cronies and became concerned. No one, however, was willing to intervene. It was more convenient to avoid the troublemakers.

It seemed that Joshua's strength was his collection of hangers-on with no visible means of support; they encouraged his behavior and hung about as long as there was plenty of rum and the occasional woman available. This was the world into which

Joshua had welcomed the slave catchers and their property. He fell easily under their influence and celebrated a lifestyle that was a culture removed from the McGuire's heritage. His only problem was the ever-increasing need for funds to keep his friends in alcohol, refreshments, and women.

The bank would no longer accommodate him; the officials told him that all accounts had been frozen due to the debt owed. Efforts to secure loans from his family and other community fathers were either rejected or ignored.

Thus, after the Putnam' departure, Joshua began to sell the possessions of value that he could access. He was able to round up twelve pigs to take to market and sold a fine team of horses, the general's pride, to an itinerant horse trader. Wendell and Charles watched with great concern and, upon the instructions and encouragement of Virginia and Anna, released the pastured beef cattle and the remaining pigs into the thicket, where they would join other feral life stock and survive quite well in the wild.

Joshua then took Maggie's highly valued antique silver collection to Lydia Mouton's Gold and Silver Shop on River Street, where the proprietor offered pennies on the dollar. With no concept of the collection's value, Joshua accepted the first offer of $50.00. Lydia, a long time Marietta shopkeeper and friend of Maggie's for many years before her death, put the valuable collection in safe keeping, waiting to see what the future held.

Two days before Jim's arrival in Marietta, Joshua Sprout and his three colleagues, the slave catchers Lucas Williams and Palitha Moon, recently back from their successful trip to the north, and Elizur Kirkwood the whiskey maker, left the house and walked to the pasture where the dairy cows were congregated. They intended to take Henry Pennmeter's prize Guernsey's to sell at the market in Marietta.

Henry heard the laughter of the men and looked out see them approaching his prize cows. In an instant, he grabbed his shotgun and ran out of the barn toward the intruders; he roared "NO!" His gun went off in the air and, within an instant, a second shot echoed through the farm. Henry fell face down in the mud of the previous night's rain. He lay without moving; Anna, looking out from the cottage, saw the entire event and ran across the lane to Henry, ignoring the threat of his killers. She fell to her knees next to him.

"Henry, Henry," she cried, but seeing the blood covering the back of his skull knew that a terrible event had occurred. She sat in the wet ground holding the poor lonely man; the killers continued to the pasture, rounded up the rest of the cows and, with their horses, herded them down the path to town. Elizur went back to the house to stand guard over the slave girl, who was still tied to a post on the front porch. Moon reloaded his rifle, looked at Anna and, deliberately pointed the gun at Digger, who was at her side, growling at their enemy.

She quickly grabbed the defiant dog and covered him with her body. The shooter paused for a moment, looked about, and shot a rooster's head off. He said as he left, "You're next, scrub woman."

All the residents walked quietly from their hiding spots to the sobbing Anna, who was still holding Henry, with Digger leaning against her in an effort to comfort her. Wendell went to Henry's bed in the barn and returned with his blanket to cover the lifeless body. Virginia, the last to arrive, encouraged everyone to go into the barn. There was no conversation for some time, everyone hiding in their personal fears, knowing that the danger to them was very real. Virginia was the first to speak

"We need to stay together," she said. "I want us all to remain together, but we can't stay here. I need to go to town and report this killing to the judge; he will have to do something this time."

"I will try to find somewhere for all of us to stay until we can return," Anna stated quietly, thinking. "Water Bird is at the sanctuary she and her family are planning to stay the winter. We could stay until the danger passes or Virginia finds something for us." Penelope began to cry. "They will find us there," she said.

"They are too lazy to go that far into the woods. We would be safe until—"

"Jim's not coming, Anna! you're dreaming!" Penelope said. She continued to cry; everyone else sat in quiet contemplation.

"I need to bury Henry," Wendell said, getting up and going to the tool shed. Charles followed close behind.

"Shouldn't we wait until the sheriff comes?" Penelope asked.

"No one's coming," Anna said, and went to help with the burial.

And so it came to be. The small group of frightened but determined friends made the arrangements. Virginia rode to town that afternoon, carrying a loaded pistol under her shawl, worried that she might encounter her husband and the evildoers. She went first to Judge Commons and reported the crime.

"Your husband, Mr. Sprout, has already been here and signed a statement testifying that Mr. Moon shot Mr. Pennmeter in self defense, that the old man shot first," he said. "I will send Sheriff Miller up to the farm as soon as he has some time to investigate the situation. Would you like to make a statement, Mrs. Sprout?" Virginia turned and walked out without saying another word.

The rest made arrangements to pack up necessities and head for the sanctuary at first light.

Anna took food and another blanket to Labithia and demanded to attend to her needs. Elizur, the sole custodian at the time and well into his drink thought for a moment, smiled menacingly, and waved his arm in a motion of approval. Anna approached and quietly kneeled over the slave girl. She gently helped her eat a bowl beef stew, encouraged her to drink from the small jug of well water, and left the blanket with several days' worth of biscuits, jerked beef, and the rest of the water. Anna talked quietly, avoiding the gaze of Labithia's keeper.

"Hide this as best you can," she said. "Listen close. We have to leave but I will be back. You will be safe soon. I promise you we will be back." Anna wiped her warm, bruised face, quietly brushed her hair, listened to her labored breathing for several minutes, said goodbye, and then turned and left.

"Thank ye," Labithia said, but Anna did not hear.

Wendell picked up Henry's shot gun, retrieved his shot and powder, and said to no one in particular, "I will protect us."

They left next morning, leading the two mules that had been dear to Henry, and which he used for almost everything and let the two remaining horses go into the thicket. They had piled the mules and themselves with all sorts of material needed for their existence: blankets, canvas tarps and coverings, smoked meats, bags of corn meal, potatoes, crocks of cabbage, vegetables, tools, nails, the rifle, and the pistol recently purchased by Virginia. Anna led the way for the group of vagabonds hoping for a safe harbor. It was mid morning with several hours of hard walking behind them when Anna called to Water Bird and asked to enter the sanctuary.

CHAPTER 5

Marietta, Ohio
October 1813

Marietta Western Spectator
October 10th 1813

Great victory in Upper Canada. General Harrison
routs British forces on River Thames. Slaughter at
River Raisin revenged.

Tecumseh Killed

First Reports in from Sandwich, Upper Canada.

General William Henry Harrison and his brave troops from
Kentucky and Ohio routed the shameless General Proctor, who abandoned his troops in the heat of battle and ran away like the coward
that he is.

On October 5th, the American army defeated the British regulars and
Indian alliance in a day-long battle. British retreat up the Thames River.

Soldiers from Washington County fought in the battle. Tecumseh
killed many Indians surrender or retreat. Unofficial report states that
a local soldier shot the great chief. Much confusion during the battle.
Private Jim Morgan recently of Marietta said to be the shooter.

The general's report states that fighting in the North West territories is now finished. The citizens of Ohio are safe.

Joshua and his bullies saw the commotion at the news board in front of the Spectator office. He pushed his way through the small crowd, ignoring the complaints of the others.

"That no good upstart, saying he killed Tecumseh. Best he don't come back here," Joshua said as he made his way back to McIntosh's.

It was night and the village was quiet with just enough moonlight to ride the Muskingum River trail into Marietta, past the campus, toward the First Congregational Church. Jim had decided to stop at Reverend Robert Moody's parsonage to find out what had happened to cause Anna to write such an alarming letter. The Moody's had always been trusted friends of the general. Jim walked quietly on to the porch and saw a lamp burning in the reverend's study. He knocked quietly on the door, knocked again, and saw the reverend's shadow cautiously approach.

"Who is there?" he asked.

"It is Jim Morgan, sir," said Jim. "I have come back from the army"

The door opened quickly. "Jim come in, come in," said Moody. "Virginia, Madelyn, come down, hurry, hurry, we have a visitor."

The four of them sat through the night and into the morning around the kitchen table; eating biscuits, cold chicken, apple turnovers and cider. They initially talked about Jim's adventures but the conversation soon turned to events in Marietta. Virginia conversed calmly and quietly about Joshua and the slave hunters. Jim learned early in the conversation that Labithia had been brought to the farm five days before and tied up on the front porch; she had been badly bruised and near death. Virginia talked about how she and Anna asked permission and then risked their lives to go to Labithia once or twice each day, to feed and comfort her as best they could. She recounted how she had purchased several weapons; one woman would cover the other with the recently purchased musket when they went to assist the slave girl. Jim was saddened and intensely angered when Virginia described Henry's murder. He wanted to make sure that it was Pelitha Moon who had fired the shot. Jim only asked a few questions as Virginia told him almost everything he needed to know without being prompted. He inquired mostly of how Anna and the rest of the helpers were doing, having lived in the sanctuary for two nights and three days. He wanted to know of Virginia's attempts to find a living space for all of them to get them through the winter.

There was hardly a pause as the reverend began to talk animatedly of how Rufus Putnam was holding information about Joshua Sprout's criminal behaviors to protect both the McGuire and Sprout families from embarrassment. Once Mr. Putnam left, the threat of prosecution was gone and this freed Joshua to rampage and terrorize both the farm and the community.

Virginia mentioned tonelessly how he had beaten her severely on several occasions and threatened Anna. It was only a matter of time until one or both of them would be brutalized by his gang of ruffians. This was the primary reason they carried a pistol with them at all times.

The Reverend said that the farm was heavily indebted to the First Mercantile Bank and that Willford Connor, the bank's president as well as members of the board wanted the farm to fail so they could resell it at twice the mortgage value and sell the rights to the coal formation in the northeast corner of the property which they could sell as fuel for the developing steamboat trade. "These are corrupt men without Christian values," the Reverend said. Once Mr. Putnam left town the bankers had encouraged Joshua to abandon his labor. Without cash from his harvest of corn and apple crops and the annual fall slaughter of livestock Virginia would not be able make the loan payment. The bank could foreclose in January when the next payment was due.

Joshua and his cronies had stopped the timid sheriff from taking any action on any complaints that related to them. He did not even investigate the killing of poor Henry Pennmeter.

Madelyn also talked about Jim's mother and Daisy who, after returning from the harvest festival two weeks ago, found their humble homestead burned to the ground, with ashes still warm and everything lost. The sheriff made no effort to investigate, saying, "Squatters don't get any service from me."

"They are rebuilding with scraps and are determined to stay on their lawful land. The church is helping as much as it can," Madelyn said, choking back tears as she began to pick up the last of the dishes. Jim was mostly silent throughout this night, asking a few questions for clarification but fully understanding the terrible circumstances to which he had returned.

He asked of the report that the general had willed the Thicket to him. "Free and clear of any of the farm's debt, in your name; the deed is on record at the land office," said Moody. "All you have to do is identify yourself, sign the deed and the land is yours." He asked if they knew where Joshua and the slave catchers were at this hour. "At Flora's Boarding House and they won't be up early," the Reverend commented. Virginia looked straight ahead; she had not felt any humiliation or shame over her husband's action for a long time.

By morning they all still sat around the table, emotionally drained and physically exhausted. Their heads were bowed, deep in their own thoughts; they all wondered without asking what, if anything, Jim would or could do. After several minutes of deep thought, Jim got up, gave Virginia a long and deep embrace, hugged and thanked Madelyn for her hospitality and kindness, and shook the Reverend's hand firmly, expressing his appreciation for his assistance.

Moody then asked if he had indeed shot Tecumseh. Jim

assented and added, "I don't know what I will do, but I do know Labithia needs my assistance." As he opened the door to leave, little nine-year-old Elizabeth, Virginia's daughter, came out of the bedroom, rubbing the sleep from her eyes. She saw Jim standing in the door way and ran to him with arms outstretched. He picked her up, gave her a kiss on the cheek, set her down, and left through the open door into the grey dawn.

"Mommy," said Elizabeth, "Jim is back. Will things be better now?"

Virginia put her arm around her shoulder, thought for a moment, and said, "I think so. Yes, Elizabeth. I think things *will* be better now."

It was a perfect Indian summer morning: bright, still, the fresh smell of fall, the brilliant orange, yellow, and red leaves of the hardwoods densely covering the forest, awaiting a wind to begin the cascade of colors to their rest on the forest floor. Water Bird was preoccupied. She was kneeling, repairing a tear in the blanket that served as the door to her shelter. She noticed Digger, who was sleeping nearby, lift and tilt her head for a second; she scrambled up and trotted through the camp toward the north path. Water Bird watched Digger for a second and then said, somewhat casually but loud enough for Anna to hear, "Jim is back."

Digger ran out of sight, down the path. Jim kneeled to greet her and she jumped into his arm, licking his face. He embraced and petted his good friend for several minutes and then they walked side by side into camp. Anna was standing and watched Jim approach. They both paused. She reached out and gently caressed his cheek with moist eyes and gentle tears. Jim stood silently; his eyes clouded, and said, "I am back."

"Yes, you are, Jim," she said, "and it is about time." They embraced for a long moment; everyone gathered around with quiet excitement and anticipation.

The refugees spent a glorious day in their camp, all of them asking and wondering what Jim would do. They all felt as Anna did that Jim would somehow make things right. They hoped that this teenager who, when last seen, was just an overgrown child, would somehow rescue them from their struggles and make everything better. A world of feelings and worries swarmed over him; everyone, excited, tried to wait patiently as he embraced each of them. He was most glad to be with Anna again, and knew that they would be alone soon; he was particularly happy to have the wise and competent Water Bird for counsel.

Anna offered Jim a mug of hot sassafras tea as he sat on a fallen log near the cave entrance and looked about the camp; the shelters were poorly constructed and wouldn't withstand the first winter storm, which could roll in at any time. Clearly they did not want to stay here, with the exception of Water Bird, her sister and niece, who had built an impressive shelter around the cave opening. Everyone wanted to talk, to share their experiences and fears with the one they placed all their hopes on. Jim was only beginning to understand the responsibilities on his shoulders. Other than finding a way to save Labithia, he didn't know how to begin to help these people.

Finally, Penelope, the most impulsive of the group, burst out, "What are you going to do, Jim? When can we go back to the farm?" He glanced at Anna, who he knew also wanted answers.

"I don't know," he said. "I don't know yet." It was not the response they had been waiting for all these months, but they were satisfied that he would do something to help them. Wendell went to take care of Buckskin; the rest continued to do their duties, but watching Jim for any sign of action. He spent the rest of the day listening to all the stories that needed telling. He also succumbed to a short, refreshing nap.

An hour before dark, he picked up his rifle, a pistol, and his recently sharpened long knife and said to Anna, "You need to come with me. I'll tell you what we are going to do." They walked together to see Water Bird. "We are going to get Labithia," said Jim. "I am told she is deathly ill."

"I know," said Water Bird. "I am ready."

CHAPTER 5

Maggie Hill Farm
October 1813

The sky had darkened as they entered the farm from the thicket. They saw the lights of the farmhouse and heard loud voices. They listened for a moment.

"They all are back," Anna whispered; "all four of them and a whore or two." A quarter moon was beginning to rise, allowing for some contrast in the black sky. Anna pointed out a dark, motionless pile on the porch. "That is Labithia. She is wrapped in the blanket we gave her. She is tied to the post by her ankle with a leather strap." Jim handed Anna his rifle and reminded her to shoot the first one who came out the door. They moved closer so that Anna would have a better shot as she positioned the rifle on the split rail fence that surrounded the farm house. She recalled all the shooting practice they had enjoyed as youths; she would shoot to kill.

Jim moved across the yard quickly and quietly, moving from one tree to the next until he was within ten yards of the porch. He paused to control his breathing and calm his fears. The dark pile moved just a little. *She is still alive.* At that moment, the door opened and Jim could see the profile of Lucas Williams against the lantern light coming from inside. He stumbled a bit as he urinated off the porch and, when finished, walked over to the pile, kicked it twice, and said in a slurred voice, " "This little nigger is going to Kentuck tomorrow, back to her owner, to be nothing but piece of shit all of her life." He laughed and went back inside to join the frivolity. Jim moved quickly and stepped onto the porch. He listened briefly to her breathing and quickly cut the tether and the strap that bound her wrists. He picked her up in his arms, surprised at how light and thin she was. They retreated quickly past Anna.

"Let's go," he whispered. They proceed at a fast walk through the orchard, pasture, and onto the path that led back to the thicket. "Labithia, this is Jim. You're safe now," he repeated several times. There was no answer, but Jim could hear her breathing. He was glad for the moonlight. It would be a long and hazardous journey to the sanctuary.

It was at least an hour before Joshua noticed the slave girl missing and raised the alarm. With lanterns and torches, they searched the farm, all of it, everywhere. Lucas was in a rage, cursing everyone; there was no sign of her rescuers. He saw the cut tether and bonds and knew she was not alone, but didn't know who she was with or where. He rode his horse hard several miles down the road to Marietta. Upon his return, Lucas, calmer now looked out over the farm and into the darkness to the east. "This won't be easy," he said to himself, "but I'm damn well gittin my nigger back."

Jim found the sentry tree as he remembered it, a large, tall, straight black oak standing dominant amongst a dense stand of virgin hardwoods, which had looked out over the endless ridges and ravines to the west for more than a hundred years. It was here that Jim, during his summer in the forest, would climb and scan the wilderness that was his home. He could see in several places where the ridge-top trail descended into the ravines and then climbed out again. As a child, he had seen it as a lonely and hopeless tree; now it would be one of opportunity. Jim was certain they would come this way. He settled into a comfortable branch, still heavily protected by the colorful palette of changing leaves, and waited. He took his time and sighted his rifle onto an opening that allowed a clear but very long shot onto the trail. There was no wind and the forest was very quiet; Jim thought only of the sounds and visions of war as he prepared for this mission: the explosions of howitzer shells, whishing of bullets, and frantic screams of men and horses were sounds he knew. The silence was disconcerting but it would not affect his concentration.

When Jim brought the almost lifeless body of Labithia to water bird, it was still in the dark of early morning. It had been a long journey and even her frail body became heavy; they rested several times and were relieved not to hear any indications of being pursued. Water Bird had prepared a palette of furs and a blanket on the ground and started a smudge fire that was beginning to fill the cave with a dark smoke. She had carried a large bucket of cold water from the spring, a collection of herbs and seeds in her medicine bag. She would do what she could. With her sister helping, they removed the blanket and the rags from the slave girl's body. In the light of the small fire, she almost cried. It was a horrible sight to look upon and to smell: a starved, frail body covered by the abuses of beatings and neglect. Labithia, hot with fever, could only moan. Without saying a word, the women went to work.

Labithia didn't know at first what was happening. She felt arms around her and felt movement. The arms were strong and without violence. She heard a familiar voice but not the words. She was moving quickly now, away from the light, her body hurting with the movement. The voice she knew, it was Jim's; she began to cry without tears. *I just might live,* she thought, *I just might live. Praise the Lord."* She had no strength and could not speak. She remembered being placed on a soft bed and people removing her rags and cleaning her beaten body. She knew that she was safe for now and could sleep in peace.

For most of the previous year, Jim had killed at his pleasure as an army sharpshooter and was rewarded with accolades and celebration. He carried that style into this battle and saw it as his duty. He did not think about the restrictions and regulations of civilian society; did not anticipate any repercussions or cared about any consequences. As far as he was concerned, he was on the ramparts of Fort Meigs, doing his job.

The men rode into sight slowly and cautiously; Jim saw them first on a far ridge and waited for them to reappear much closer. The riders paused and talked for a moment, then proceeded. At the next opening they would be in range. Jim was very calm and confident, focusing on the job at hand. They rode up the next ridge—Lucas, Moon, Joshua, and Elizur in single file. Moon slowly came into view; the forest was quiet, anticipating. The shot echoed, a few birds flew, and Moon fell backward off his horse.

He lay face up. The ball had made a large hole through his forehead, ending his life. His horse jumped and ran a few steps. Lucas looked up and searched the trees, detected a small puff of white smoke slowly rising in the still air several hundred yards away. He was impressed with the shot. Elizur did not dally; he turned his mule around and was over the ridge and out of sight. Lucas dismounted cautiously, observing his long time companion.

"Let's get the hell out of here. I'm not getting killed for some nigger," Joshua said as he spurred his horse and followed the whisky maker. "I'm getting the sheriff," he commented half heartedly as he retreated. Lucas looked all around, searching for clues. *Who is the enemy?* He wondered. *It will take a lot of manpower to retrieve this slave,* he thought as he reached for the reigns of Moon's horse, mounted his and rode over the ridge. He didn't look back at his fallen partner.

Jim was pleased with his shot. "This is for Henry," he said

out loud. He watched them leave, waited a few minutes to see if anyone would be returning, then climbed slowly down the sentry tree and made his way to the path where the body still lay.

Anna and the others heard the single shot of a rifle as it echoed through the thicket. Everyone looked up and at each other silently. *Please let this be good*, Anna thought as she returned to her labor. Labithia was still asleep and breathing well; this was a good sign. She forced herself to be hopeful.

Jim looked around in all directions at the top of the ridge, nearest where Moon had been shot. He had taken a long time to get there and was very cautious. He saw no signs of the intruders and went down the path to where Moon's body remained. He decided to remove it and with a lot of effort, he carried it on his shoulder deep into a ravine and covered it with fallen timbers, dead branches, rocks, and underbrush. Disposing of the body was difficult and took most of the day. It was getting late when Jim left the ridge line and returned to the sanctuary. He did not know what Joshua and Lucas would do, but was confident that no one would return in the darkness to search for the hideout. There was quiet excitement and relief when Jim walked into the sanctuary; the others gathered around and wanted to know what happened. Anna stood back, reading his face for any signs of the day's events. He reassured them as best he could that everything was all right and there was no need to worry. Anna handed him a gourd of cool water. They would have their time together later.

Labithia was sleeping soundly with heavy breaths when Jim looked in on her. Water Bird, tending to her needs, whispered that she had awakened several times during the day, accepting water and some beef broth. Her fever was still high and they would continue to cool her body. Jim asked if there had been a sign and she responded that the owl that screeches had appeared for a moment in the afternoon. "All the signs have been good," she said as she motioned for him to leave the tent. This was not a time for visitors.

It was dark when Jim sat down with Anna, away from the others; they shared some biscuits, smoked pork, and hard cider. He had not eaten all day and ate hungrily. When he had finished, he spoke quietly.

"I shot and killed Moon," he said. "The others went back toward the farm but did not return. I buried his body down a deep ravine, some distance away. They won't find it unless they bring dogs. I have no idea what they will do next or what I will do…" His words drifted away with his thoughts. Their hands met and held each other. Digger came over and lay between them.

Anna said, "First you get some sleep. We will deal with it in the morning." They sat together in silence for a long time, holding hands and three bodies touching, staring into the fire with the flames dancing across their faces. Being together was a great comfort for two young people tired, scared and overwhelmed with responsibility; problems beyond their abilities to solve.

"Will Labithia live?" Jim asked.

"Yes," said Anna.

CHAPTER 6

Washington County
October 1813

Jim awoke early and went back up the ridge. It was another clear day and he searched the ridges to the horizon with no sign of his enemies. Sometime during the morning search he decided what he would do. Upon his return to the sanctuary, he brought everyone together and told them what had occurred in the last twenty-four hours, leaving out the shooting of Moon. Anna and Jim would be the only ones to carry that secret. He reassured them that they were safe but wouldn't be able to return to the farm for now; Virginia was getting help from friends in Marietta to try to have Joshua removed from the farm.

Jim spoke with competence and confidence. "I am going to leave now to see my mother, assist Virginia, and try to convince the others to leave us alone," he said. "You will be safe and I will be back in a day or two." Anna and Jim had talked earlier and agreed that she would stay at the sanctuary, managing any problems that might come up.

Jim rode off the road and up the long path to his mother and Aunt Daisy's well secluded farm. He observed a most desolate place: both the house and barn had burned to the ground, with just the rock chimney standing witness to what had been a busy, active, and happy home. Daisy, Molly and Jim's little sister Amy were working at repairing a section of roof on the small storage shed that was only partially burned and where they had built a small shelter.. The reunion was warm and welcoming in spite of the devastation that surrounded them. They made some coffee and biscuits while Daisy shared the recent catastrophe. "We had come home from the harvest festival in Marietta two weeks ago Sunday; we could smell the ashes before we saw them. The house and the barn were done burnt to the ground, everything gone, the chickens were scattered but lived somehow as the coup was ashes" Daisy started to cry and turned away; Molly continued; "nothing was left, it all burnt, some dishes and two pots. The food in the root cellar was all we eat since. We have no clothes except what were wearing, even the bible was burnt. The cow was taken to the widow Larsen down the hollow for milking when we were gone. She is staying there till we get a roof up. The cat came back two days ago." Daisy recovered now; put an arm around Molly and Amy and continued in an angry voice "Look over yonder; that whiskey jug was sitting on the chopping block. Elizur will not chase us off, we stay no matter what happens.

"I have a deed to this miserable plot of land and no one will take it from me. Without land we have nothing. We're not going anywhere; nobody is chasing us off our land." She spoke angrily and with conviction.

They all worked until dark, turning the meager shelter into a more livable space, repairing the openings in the roof and walls.

They would at least have a dry shelter that would do until Jim returned to rebuild their house. They shared a small dinner of fried potatoes and more biscuits over an open fire. Molly mentioned that Elizur was back on his plot, making whiskey. "He done came back yesterday," she said. "Hadn't been there for awhile."

Jim rested for an hour after dinner, he re saddled the buckskin while telling his mother that he would be back in a day or two to help them rebuild their life and not to worry about Elizur. "Mr. Kirkwood will cause you no more grief or discomfort," he said. It was near dark when he rode off. The family huddled together, tears of joy and relief falling openly as they watched Jim ride off.

"Good evening, Mr. Kirkwood."

Jim walked out of the shadows toward Elizur, who was profiled in the light of the fire and preoccupied with throwing more logs under the boiler. He looked up and jumped backward. "Well, Mr. Morgan, you be back from the war," he said. "Some say you killed that Indian chief. What say you?" He was talking fast, quickly sizing up this threatening situation. He saw both a rifle cradled in Jims arm and a pistol in his belt; he looked about for his musket and realized it was too far away and not loaded.

"Where is the old blue tick? She didn't welcome me," Jim said.

"Done up and died in the spring," Elizur said as he noticed the long-handled ax within arm's reach. *It was his only hope he thought.* "What be your purpose coming on my land?"

"I come to kill you," Jim said quietly.

"Oh, kill me, why, damn, you be the one who killed Moon two days back," said Elizur. He became nervous and agitated as he quickly realized the danger he was in. He started to stammer, fidget, and walk in small circles; looking down like he was talking to himself, edging toward the ax. "Why me? Why kill me? I don't do nothing". Damn."

"You burned down my mother's home, left my family homeless," Jim said.

"No I didn't, Jim," he said. "It were an accident." He quickly reached for the ax, heard the click; his hand stopped inches from the handle. The cold rifle barrel was touching the back of his head. "Oh, Jesus, Mister Jim, Jesus, don't kill me." He dropped to his knees. "Don't kill me." Jim stepped back and lowered his rifle.

"You did harm to the slave girl," he said.

"Not me Jim, no, not me, it was the slavers that had their way with the nigger, not me. Take my whiskey, Jim, it's good and fresh. Take it all. Don't kill me, oh Jesus, don't kill me." He continued to speak in an agitated manner.

"You're going to die," was all Jim said as he motioned with his rifle for Elizur to sit down on the ground away from his still and cabin. He moved and sat without challenge or resistance, talking to himself in gibberish.

Jim picked up a burning branch from the fire underneath the boiler and walked over to Whiskey Makers living quarters—a small, one-story, dilapidated, and cluttered old wooden cabin—and set fire to the house in several places while keeping his eye and rifle on his captive.. The dry wood and materials burst quickly into flames. Jim then went to a crude shed that stored most of Elizur's supplies— corn meal, sugar, yeast, and several jugs of corn liquor.

"No Jim, no." Elizur was on his knees, watching in horror as his world burst into flames. The heat made both of them back up, the brightness of the flames giving an eerie light to the area and the trees beyond.

Jim wasn't done. He picked up the ax and, with powerful swings and in a rage of his own, destroyed everything that belonged to the whisky maker. This was the second time in his young life that he had taken an ax to the squatter's property; this time however, he was much more effective. In a few minutes, everything was destroyed: the coiled copper pipes, fermenting containers, pots and pressure cookers, numerous jugs and casks filled with alcohol. His energy spent, Jim dropped the ax and stood looking at the total destruction. He then turned to Elizur who had not moved, sitting in a trance-like state, talking and crying nonsensically. The fire was still raging, several small explosions adding to the conflagration. Jim stood and looked at the devastation for a minute, then motioned Elizur to walk to where the frightened mule and Buckskin were tied and told him to get on his animal.

Elizur had made no move to run, attack, or resist; he stood nervously, still gibbering unintelligible words and phrases. Jim watched him closely, suspicious of what to make of this odd behavior. Elizur continued his nonsensical speech as they left his burning home and headed down to the Little Muskingum River Trail. The flames of the burning encampment lit the night sky for several miles in all directions.

The Little Muskingum entered the mother river several miles north of the Ohio. A well-trodden path went north. They stopped without getting off their mounts, and Jim pointed the long rifle at Elizur's face. "Don't come back to Washington County," he said. "If you do, I will kill you." He stared into wild eyes that did not respond and appeared to not understand anything that was said. Incoherent and confused, the Whiskey Maker turned and went north on the river road, riding his mule, talking nonsense to himself and without any worldly possessions. It was a lonely scene. Jim resisted feeling any pity for the man and watched him disappear in the gray light of a promising day. Jim and the buckskin headed south. Elizur had appeared to have lost his faculties and Jim wondered where he would go and what he would do; he had several families of cousins that lived in the hollows a long day's ride north of the confluence. While growing up, Jim had often heard people say that squatters always survive. He hoped it was a wise saying.

It was late, and cold in the sanctuary, all the occupants were doing their best to get some sleep in a small shelter of branches, bushes, canvas, and animal skins that was not cozy. The winds would drift through easily and everyone prayed that it would not rain this night. Penelope, who had gone outside to relieve herself, saw far to the east a yellow and orange glow that stood strong in the dark sky. She woke Anna, who wrapped her blanket around herself, climbed out of the structure, and gazed toward the light.

She stared in silence and knew that Jim had found Elizur. She worried and wondered what else Jim had done. *Killing seems to come easy to him. He acts like he is still in the army and it is okay to kill people; does he plan on killing all of them? Is there no other way to solve these problems? What else is there? The sheriff does nothing; what did we expect from Jim?* The questions had no answers. *Who is this man? How much has he changed?* She was anxious to be alone with him. There was so much to hear, to understand; she wanted to explore his feelings, to know him again. It seemed he had lost all of his youth—his humor, playfulness, affection. *Such a burden he has taken on. Have I—have we expected too much from him?* She became quite fearful as she realized that there may be a terrible ending to all of this.

She also noticed the glow of a fire in the cave where Water Bird her sister and niece were tending to the frail Labithia in their ongoing effort to keep her alive. Anna returned to her bed in the shelter. *I hope he returns soon.* She moved an uncooperative Digger over several feet to get some room for her legs.

Jonathon McGuire
August 2nd, 1804
Marietta, Ohio

> *"I must record a most unusual event that involved me and my good friend Rufus Putnam. Maggie and I were houseguests of Rufus and Elisabeth P. three evenings past. A dinner guest was a tall and well-dressed man who hailed from Frankfort, Kentucky territory. His name as introduced was Nathaniel Berkshire; he had come to Marietta to seek an agent for his superior Tobacco product to sell and distribute in the Ohio Valley. He had interviewed several*

*merchants this day. The other guests were the Reverend
Robert Moody and his charming wife Madelyn. Most of
the early evening conversation was about the unfortunate
duel of Alexander Hamilton and Aaron Burr, which
occurred on the New Jersey shore across from Hamilton's
residence in Manhattan in early July. The lack of civility
between the antagonists was well known to the public. The
death of Hamilton, however, was most unfortunate; I had
met the distinguished patriot several times during the Great
War, when serving under General Greene. In any event, the
duel was discussed in great detail and Mr. Berkshire seemed
to belabor the topic, which both Maggie and Elizabeth at-
tempted to change on several occasions. The gentleman was
most fond of Putnam's Madeira and it had a deleterious
affect on his arrogant countenance. Toward the end of the
evening he engaged in a most unsuitable discussion of his
slaves, or property as he called them, and how he managed
his property with a cruel hand. The conversation was most
disagreeable to me and the others; I lost my civility at one
point and pointed out his inhumanity to his fellow man
with some passion. He took great exception to my opinion
and, at that moment, challenged me to a duel with pistols.
Of course I accepted the offer, much to Maggie's dismay,
and the arrangements were made for an early a.m. event
at the Indians' mounds near Colonel Stacy's gravesite. The
evening ended abruptly on that note, and Mr. Berkshire
departed for his boarding house. There were no dueling pistols in Marietta, so it took some effort to secure reasonable
facsimiles. Maggie refused to sleep in my bed that night, to
my disappointment...*

*"In the morning, Rufus and I were waiting at the des-
ignated site and, after some delay, a messenger arrived from
Mrs. Cooper's Boarding House with a note addressed to*

Mr. Putnam. Rufus chuckled as he read the communiqué. It seems Mr. Berkshire had an emergent situation back at his tobacco plantation that needed his immediate attention. He asked to reschedule at a time more convenient. We enjoyed a hearty breakfast at Bracket's with much mirth included. Maggie is still not in a mood for conversation. A long summer, I suspect.

Jim, very tired now, rode into Marietta as the morning commerce began to come alive. He stopped in front of the land office on Front Street, a small log cabin located next to the Mauritius Campus. He had to wait for an hour before the clerk opened the door for the day's business. Jim announced himself and requested to pick up his deed. The thin, crooked, and elderly clerk listened to Jim's request, muttered that he knew where it would be, and walked to rows of files in the back behind a large waist-high counter. The clerk returned in a few minutes with a folder in his hand and asked for proof of person. Jim showed his discharge paper, which he had folded several times and put into the leather pouch he carried around his neck. The clerk mumbled approval, opened the folder, and reviewed the deed. He showed it to Jim and had him sign and date the document. An official seal was imposed and the deed was officially his. The old clerk lowered his voice and said to Jim, "Don't give this document to anyone, particularly the bank. They want your land." Jim somewhat confused and not understanding all the implications in the clerk's words said "thank you sir". As the clerk turned and walked away he said in passing, "The general was a friend of mine."

Jim was now the sole owner of the land he occupied. He wondered why the general was so generous. A wave of sadness engulfed him as he felt the loss of his champion. How he wished he was here to tell him what to do. Jim led the buckskin to the courthouse a block away.

The Washington County Court of Common Pleas and Sheriff's Department shared a one-story log building located in the Campus Mauritius enclosure on Washington Street. It comprised a courtroom and two small offices, one for the judge and one for the clerk. The sheriff's office was in the back and contained two rickety cells that held prisoners awaiting sentencing or court hearings. Jim walked into the court, identified himself, and told a bailiff present that he wanted to see the judge. Theodore Commons was sitting in his office when he heard the request; he, in turn, instructed the bailiff to get a message to Sheriff Micah Miller and the president of the Mercantile Bank, Willford Connor. He noticed that a small crowd was gathering outside and thought it best to be on the bench when he talked with this young man who was generating such interest in the community.

"State your name and your business," the judge said in a most formal manner.

"Sir, my name is Jim Morgan, and I have most recently been discharged from General Harrison's Army on the Northern Frontier." The judge knew of this young man, but did not reveal this.

"And what is your business with the court?" he asked.

"Sir, I have come here to clear my name," he said. The judge remained silent and Jim continued. "A year ago last June; after I had left Marietta to join the American army, I was informed that charges had been filed against me by the sheriff of this county. I have come to have those charges dismissed."

The sheriff came into the courthouse as Jim was speaking and the judge asked him what memory he had of this event. The small courtroom was quickly filling up with a dozen or so curious citizens, some of whom recalled the events surrounding the general's death and Jim's disappearance. The judge noticed that Willford Conner had quietly walked in and taken a position on the far wall, where he could make eye contact with the judge but not be noticed doing so. .

The judge, a decent man who enjoyed his family, his brandy, and the comforts of his position, was indebted to the bank and in many judicial situations, followed its trustees' instructions, particularly in relation to financial litigations. He was instructed to proceed with a slight nod of the head.

"If you are prepared, Mr. Morgan," said the judge, "we can conduct a preliminary hearing to determine only if a crime was committed." Jim agreed and the judge ordered the clerk to find and present the documents. While they were waiting, Judge Commons asked Jim if he had indeed shot Tecumseh.

"Yes, sir, I did," Jim said without further comment.

"You must tell us about it some time." The clerk presented the document and the judge read the charges aloud.

To the Court of Common Pleas
June 19th, 1812

Upon the testimony of one Joshua Sprout, a landholding citizen of Washington County, State of Ohio, the following criminal charges were filed against one James Morgan, present residence unknown: Felonious theft of property, livestock, and currency belonging to one Jonathon McGuire, a citizen and landholder of Washington County now deceased.

Signatures of the complainant,
Judicial authority evidenced.

Judge Commons leaned forward, looked down at Jim, and said, "There is no plea at this hearing. We are only here to find probable cause that these crimes have been committed. Do you have a statement to make at this time?" Before Jim could respond, a loud and profane disruption was heard in the back.

"The bastard is guilty of these crimes; I saw it with my own eyes. He stole the horse and the rifle. I saw them missing when he disappeared in the night. Lock the criminal up." The judge gaveled several times and the crowd settled down.

"You disrupted these proceedings," he said. "One more outburst and you will be denied a presence in this courtroom." Jim turned and noticed that Joshua Sprout and Lucas Williams, both clearly influenced by spirits, were standing together near the doorway. He was also pleased to note that Reverend Moody and Virginia had joined the spectators. "Proceed, Mr. Morgan," said the judge. "Pray tell us why these felonious charges should be dismissed." Jim told the story of his last meeting with the general and his instructions to him. The retelling of this moment made speech difficult for him and he halted several times.

"It's a lie, it's all a lie. I tell you the stupid old man had no faculty—" The gavel came down again. The judge realized he needed to end this quickly; it was getting out of control and the bank would not be pleased. The commotion quieted down and the sheriff was holding Joshua, prepared to remove him, when Virginia moved quietly through the crowd, made her way to the front and stood facing the judge.

"Your Honor, may I speak?" she asked. The judge nodded an affirmation "I am the general's daughter, Virginia McGuire Sprout. If I may have a moment, I have some information that might be helpful in your deliberations."

The judge quickly looked at Mr. Connor and got the approval to proceed. "This is somewhat unusual, but it is not a trial, so continue. Virginia took a large notebook out of her purse.

"This is the general's personal journal, she said. "It is in his handwriting with signatures. Please refer to his last entry, your honor," she handed the manuscript to the judge, who looked at it briefly.

"Mrs. Sprout," he said, "be so kind as to read the entry that

THE END AND THE BEGINNING

you refer to."

She cleared her voice, and read. *"I have done my work, it is late. I fear this will be my last entry. Young Jim is on his way. It was difficult but most prudent, he knows little and I have protected him so. He is ill equipped to take on his enemies here. He was given old Buckskin, my Kentucky rifle, plenty of shot and powder, and twenty silver coins to see him through the hard times. He will determine his prominence on the northern frontier, war is near; he will grow to be a man. I worry he is not well prepared...I do expect and it is my hope that he will return one day to this land of ours. I have not talked with Virginia. I will miss her so. I am so tired. I rest my pen. Jonathon McGuire."*

The court room remained quiet as if respectful of this very personal and difficult moment. Virginia's voice had faltered as she read and recalled that terrible day.

The judge looked for Willford Connor and he was gone. *Distressing,* he thought, *I have to decide on my own.* He came to a quick, if hasty decision. "I find the reading of the general's entry to be sufficient evidence," he said. "The petition against Mr. Morgan is dismissed."

"Your honor, Jim Morgan killed my half-breed and stole my nigger. I want my nigger back."

Lucas Williams had made his way to the front of the room and was now standing face to face with Jim, aggressively staring him in the eye and ignoring the judge. This was the first time the two antagonists had met face to face; their mutual animosity overwhelmed the court room.

"That is not for this court to decide," said the judge. "Proceedings are finished." Commons slammed his gavel one more time, hurriedly left the bench, and went into his office.

Lucas still looking directly at Jim, said, "I will get my nigger back." He turned and left the courtroom, pushing people aside. The spectators began to filter out. Joshua was outside waiting; Jim, Virginia, and the reverend walked out onto the courthouse steps together.

"You no good bitch," said Joshua. "I'm sick of you and your friends." Virginia looked straight ahead, passing her husband without acknowledgement heading for the Moody residence with Madelyn. Joshua followed Virginia for several steps, and continued to yell abuses at his wife for several minutes as she quickly moved away. The square was now crowded with curious onlookers.

Jim stepped forward and spontaneously called to the angry husband, "Joshua Sprout, hear me. You have challenged my integrity, humiliated your wife, and dishonored General McGuire; I hereby, in front of these witnesses, challenge you to a duel to the death."

Joshua, who was walking away, stopped, turned, and said, "What say you?"

"A duel," Jim said, "I challenge you to a duel. It is legal in this state and you are a coward if you decline.

Joshua paused for a moment, and then sneered. "A duel it will be," he said. "It will give me great pleasure to watch you die."

"Tomorrow, early, pistols," Jim said. Saying nothing more, Joshua and Lucas turned and walked in the direction of their favorite tavern.

The observers were silent, everyone's eyes on Jim in anticipation of what would happen next. He stood for a minute and asked, "Who wants to be my second?" A young apprentice at the Spectator volunteered and asked what he needed to do. Jim said, "I have no idea."

The reverend, Jim and the apprentice had moved to the parlor of the parish house, a few close friends of the Moody's were invited. They were mostly in a celebratory mood. Virginia, however, was sitting in the visitor's rocking chair, looking out the front window, rocking with little motion and very slowly. Jim noticed and asked her of her mood. "Jim," she said, "you cannot shoot everyone. Tomorrow you will kill my husband and you know he will be sodden with liquor. This is not a time for merriment."

"But he has mistreated you so," Jim said, confused at her response. Virginia continued to rock slowly.

"He is still my husband and Elizabeth's father. In spite of his behavior we still hold him in affection; I do not relish his death." She said still staring out the window. Jim, not knowing what to do or how to respond, asked if he should call the duel off. "That is not a decision I should or will make. It will be a sad day in any event." She desired no more conversation.

Jim was very confused and asked of everyone and no one, "What do you want me to do? That is all I know. You all want me to help you. Tell me what to do. Why am I all alone?" He was shouting now, with desperation on his face and tears in his eyes.

Reverend Moody observed the interaction and, with a hand on Jim's shoulder, directed him into another room. He presented a wise and paternal figure, and offered Jim both counsel and understanding. "Jim," he said, "please understand. We are folks who are unfamiliar with violence and destruction. It is against our nature and beliefs. In every matter that is important, there are risks; your challenge cannot be undone, and no one can say whether your action was right or wrong. It would cause greater harm to you, Virginia, and this community. The general would be proud of all you have done both in the army and since your return. Honor was important to him, and he was so hopeful that you would inherit his character and courage. You need to move forward. Do not hesitate."

Jim said, "But I don't know what else to do. All I learned was to kill; I know nothing else. It seemed to be the right thing. I remembered the general was in a duel a long time ago." The reverend responded to Jim's desperation with a reassuring pat on the back and they rejoined the gathering. *This boy needs to stay strong,* he thought. Virginia had gone to her room.

After the crowd drifted away, Madelyn Moody arranged for water to be boiled in large quantities, ordered Jim to remove all his clothes so they could be thoroughly washed, and told him to bath himself in the wooden tub in the wash room. "Jim," she said, "your heroics are commendable, but your stench is unbearable. We will wash and dry your clothes in front of the kitchen fire and you, my young hero, will clean all of yourself." This took most of the late afternoon and evening. Jim ate dinner with the family with a large blanket wrapped around him. Madelyn also found time to cut and sew a pair of the reverend's wool britches to fit the thinner Jim.

The young apprentice from the Spectator had taken the job seriously and tried to make arrangements. No one could remember a duel except the one that had almost happened in 1804; they did not know of the protocols for such an event. "They are for eastern elite, not a bunch of frontiersman," someone said. "We had a lot of killings, but no duels," another old timer ventured. The apprentice finally went into the Spectator archives and read the accounts of the Hamilton and Burr duel, from which he took detailed notes. He found a set of matching pistols, unused for many years, volunteered by Elva Brackett.

The early morning was brisk, with a sharp north wind. Jim had stayed with the Moody's, his sleep sporadic. Anxiety over the day's events and concerns over the previous day kept his mind working most of the night. Virginia's response had been surprising and bothersome. He wanted her to be his friend; most of what he was doing was intended to help her. He was tired and unsure of upcoming events. This morning, he hoped that Joshua would not show up; yesterday, he had wanted to kill him. Jim fought urges to run away himself on this restless night; they were effectively resisted. He didn't know where to go or what else to do, in any case. *At least I will look good and not smell so bad,* he thought.

Reverend Moody, who would be the referee, was already up

and starting a fire in the kitchen. He did not invite anyone else to the event and the dueling site was kept secret. The reverend was impressed with the apprentice, a new lad in town who took care of all of the details and prepared the day's event, and who was even now knocking on the parish door.

I need to get his name, Moody thought as he welcomed him in.

Jim, the apprentice, and the reverend arrived as scheduled at 6:00 a.m. at Ogden's Pasture, a long meadow along the east shore of the Muskingum some distance from the picket. The wind picked up and began to blow in random gusts that chilled the body. With no overcoat, Jim felt the cold through his now clean hunting shirt. The apprentice had loaded the pistols before they left the house, and they were now covered in their case. The new boy in town asked politely if he could have an interview with Jim if he survived. "Only if I die will you have that pleasure," he said, half joking.

Joshua arrived looking very unkempt, with a jug of corn liquor hanging on his thumb and forefinger. He did appear sober, however and walked with balance to the Reverend. No words were spoken; he did not look at or acknowledge Jim. With him were Lucas and a man not known to Jim or the reverend. There were no introductions. The reverend asked if they were prepared to proceed. Both parties nodded and the pistols were presented, with Joshua getting the first choice. They looked at their weapons and accepted them.

The apprentice handed the reverend a piece of paper and he began to read from it, apologetic because he had never been involved a duel before, "From this point, stand backwards facing away, your weapon in your right hand facing up, arm bent straight at the elbow. Each of you on my count walk five paces, stop, turn, and fire at will. If the first shot by one of the parties does not disable the other and the opponent's weapon is not discharged, he then has a count of three to shoot or forever hold his weapon. This is a single firing; there will be no second shot. Your second will be responsible for securing medical assistance if needed. He stopped reading the instructions and dropped them to his side, paused, and asked if everything was understood. Both opponents nodded.

The reverend continued. "Take positions, weapons ready, and pace at my command. One, two, three, four—" A shot rang out. Joshua had turned on the count of four and fired his pistol. The smoke cleared quickly in the wind; Jim was standing, looking back at Joshua. Realizing that his shot had missed, Joshua dropped to his knees, arms at his side, head down, awaiting his departure. Jim, who until this moment was extremely calm, aimed his pistol slowly and deliberately at his enemy's bowed head. He was now intent on killing. *This is easy,* he thought. Somewhere far away he heard someone say, "Three seconds." The trigger was eager in his finger.

He is Elizabeth's father, Jim thought. He lowered his weapon and let Joshua live. "You have a daughter," he said. Jim handed the loaded gun back to the apprentice and started walking back to town. Coming toward him at a brisk pace on the river road was the reverend's one-horse surrey with Virginia tall in the seat, working the reins. She didn't look at Jim as she rode by. Joshua was still on his knees, head bowed; his occasional sobs were carried on the breeze. Both Lucas and the stranger left Joshua where he was and walked back to town in a different direction from what Jim had taken. Virginia got out of the surrey, walked over to Joshua, and placed a blanket around his shoulders. She leaned over; whispered to him for several minutes, and finally kissed him on the head. She got back in the buggy and asked the reverend, who was now standing by himself, if he needed a ride. The apprentice was running to catch up with Jim to get his story.

Madelyn was busy preparing a breakfast: pork sausage, eggs, corn mush with maple syrup, and dark flour biscuits. Jim was the first to return; nothing was asked and nothing was volunteered as he warmed himself at the kitchen hearth. Elizabeth came in from the coop with a basket of fresh eggs, saw Jim, and asked, "Is my daddy all right?"

"Yes, Elizabeth, your dad is fine," he said. She gave Jim a hug, said thank you, and went to wash and boil the eggs. Madelyn, listening to the conversation mouthed the words "Thank God" and continued with her labors. The apprentice knocked, came in, and asked Jim if he would be able to answer some questions for the newspaper.

"Please join us for breakfast. There will be no talk now," Madelyn said as she offered both of them a hot mug of coffee. The reverend and Virginia arrived together; she asked Jim to go into the parlor, where she gave him a brief kiss on the cheek,

"Jim," she said, "you were a brave and gentle man this day. My daughter and I are in debt to you for your kindness. We thank you."

"Elizabeth already has," Jim said, not knowing what else to say. Being somewhat uncomfortable with the intensity of Virginia's feelings, he turned to the safety of the kitchen.

Virginia continued to hold his arm and held him back, saying, "Joshua is leaving Marietta this day. He is going on horseback to his cousin's farm near Portsmouth and won't return for some time. It is safe now for everyone to return to the farm."

Jim said, "That is good news."

"I will go to the thicket right away and bring everyone back. They will be so pleased,"

Virginia then said "We can stay on the farm for several months at least—" Jim interrupted her; "One problem at a time was something your father always said. There is much to do." Breakfast was ready.

It was mid afternoon when Jim tied Buckskin at the small, well hidden corral where the two mules were staying and walked the steep path into the sanctuary. Digger greeted him before he was in sight of the camp. Jim had borrowed a blanket to stay warm on the trip to the thicket; the day had become overcast with wind squalls that suggested snow flurries. His friends stopped their labors and moved to the fire where Jim had gone to warm his hands. Anna and Jim's eyes met; he didn't notice the great relief in her eyes.

They stood in silent anticipation, waiting for Jim to tell them of their future. "Much has happened since I left two days ago," he said. "There is still much to do, but it is now safe and we can go back to the farm. Get your things; if we leave soon we can get there before dark." A collective cheer was heard as they went about packing up their belongings.

"Come with me to see Labithia," Jim said to Anna, as they embraced for a moment. The cave was warm; a small fire was going as they entered.

"Well, Forest Boy, you have returned," said Water Bird. "I hope your journey had a good ending."

"Yes, Water Bird. Things are better. How is our friend?" Jim leaned over and looked carefully at Labithia. She was covered with soft animal skins and appeared comfortable. Her eyes opened; she smiled when she saw Jim's face, and squeezed his hand. Her eyes stayed with him for several minutes, and then quietly closed.

"She is better," Water Bird said. "The spirits are pleased. The owl that screeches has returned to give her life, and watches over her. She needs more rest." Jim asked if she could be moved. "Her journey cannot begin today. Her life is brittle and we need to stay here with the spirit. Her fever returns often and is not cured. We stay here today. This is our place; she will heal here. We have all we need for now." Water Bird looked away, dismissing him.

It was a motley crew of refugees that walked up the path. It would be dark soon and everyone wanted to be home. Dealing with the destruction and neglect could wait till the morning. It was close to midnight before Anna and Jim were alone in the cottage; it felt natural to melt into each other's arm. It was home and nothing needed to be said.

It was late morning when Anna and Jim arose, refreshed and optimistic. Jim knew that to keep Labithia safe, he would need to find Lucas; he was determined to do whatever it took. He worried that Lucas might show up at the farm, and had everyone lock their doors and keep a firearm ready just in case. *I need to finish this business, whatever that means,* Jim thought. He and Anna had talked in the early hours of the morning and decided that the farm was safe, at least for now, and everyone could enjoy their return.

Everyone worked this day: cleaning the house was the most formidable job. Furnishings were destroyed, and there was rotting food, feces, urine, tobacco, and alcohol everywhere. The smells were atrocious. Anna and Penelope opened all the doors and windows, and began a major clearing and cleaning. Both agreed that it was best that Virginia was not there to witness the utter destruction of a once proud home. Wendell and Charles salvaged what was left of the livestock; many chickens had died and those that were left had gone feral. Several of the roosters were the obvious victims of target practice. The pigs, except for two that had been crudely slaughtered and left to rot, were in good shape. The cattle and pigs were running feral in the thicket and, upon inspection of several of them, they seemed to be faring well. The two men took a wagon full of hay to various sites in the open pasture to make it easier to gather the cows. It was a hard and busy day, with everyone in high spirits. Anna fixed a hearty meal and served it at the kitchen table. They had worked on the room all day to make it presentable. For Jim, it was the first day since his return that he was free of worry. He recalled the wonderful days in the past when he had worked around the farm, and began to appreciate why he missed them so.

CHAPTER 7

Old Fort Harmar
Marietta
November 1813

In the late afternoon, Lucas Williams rode the ferry across the Muskingum River to an area near old Fort Harmar where, in recent years, dislocated and vagrant Indians had taken over the parade fields and pastures to make a home of sorts. As Lucas walked through the community now referred to as Sotville by the disapproving white community, he was surrounded by many once proud Shawnee, Pottawatomie, Delaware, and Ottawa people, offering their bodies or panhandling for a jug of spirits or a few coins.

He was in the middle of a settlement of rags and refuse; shelters consisted of lean-tos and an occasional teepee. It appeared that a hundred or so Indians had taken refuge on twenty or so acres. There was garbage everywhere, and carcasses of pigs, deer, and cows were being picked over by the feral dogs and vultures that seemed to be ubiquitous. Several horses were seen, underfed and idle, doing the best they could on the overgrazed pastures. Lucas ignored the solicitations and begging and asked where he could find Council Keeper. After several inquiries, he was pointed to the far end of the encampment, where a fire warmed an open-sided structure. It had been two days since the ill-fated duel and the disappearance of the pathetic Joshua, who was no longer useful to Lucas.

Lucas knew from over hearing gossip at Brackets that Labithia was still in the thicket.

He had tried to get the sheriff to secure volunteers with bloodhounds to go to the thicket, find the sanctuary, return the nigger to him, and arrest Morgan for murder. Micah Miller did not make any effort to respond to the slave catcher's lawful requests, only saying he would act in due time. Lucas gave up in an angry rage, and looked for another way to get his nigger.

Council Keeper appeared to be sober when Lucas found him sitting at a fire, eating a tepid stew and getting ready to leave Sotville to hunt deer in the river bottoms.

He was quiet, looking Lucas over as he made his introduction. He said in his broken English, "You destroyed my home and sent my families to the winds, broke the Shawnee Treaty of the Harmar. You enemy to Council Keeper, no business with me."

Lucas, ignoring the challenge, said, "I bring you treasure and ask for the great chief's help."

"I make no trade with my enemy," said Council Keeper. "Say your business and leave."

Lucas pulled out a leather pouch. "Here are many pieces of gold; they are yours if you assist me in finding my nigger. She is being sheltered in the thicket at a place that you know of and can lead me to." Council keeper showed little interest, looking at the pouch that was set in front of Lucas.

"You seek your slave girl who is protected by Forest Boy deep in the thicket where you cannot find him." he said. "He has killed the half breed and will kill you if you seek him."

"I will kill Forest Boy if he tries to stop me," said Lucas. "I need you to show me where he has hid the nigger; the gold is yours if you take me to it." Council Keeper paused, filled his pipe from his tobacco pouch without offering any to Lucas. He puffed several times.

"Forest Boy killed the great chief Tecumseh and has his spirit in his heart," he said. "He can only be killed by a member of Tecumseh clan that will come soon to claim the Great Spirit back. Forest Boy can only die at the hands of the Shawnee."

"I seek not your help in gittin my nigger," said Lucas. "I want you to show me where they're hiding. I will give you half of the coins when we depart and the rest when you show me." They both sat for awhile, saying nothing.

"I know of the thicket and the dark places," said Council Keeper. "I know of where they hide. I will show you but not help you. You come, we go, no one else. Show me your pouch. We go in the morning."

It was late and everyone was in their rooms. The farm house was dark. Someone standing outside called for Forest Boy. Wendell responded first, picked up his musket, and had cautiously approached the stranger when Jim appeared outside the cottage and recognized Council Keeper's twelve-year-old nephew, No See One Eye. He was standing in the middle of the path, unsure of where he should go to find Forest Boy. Jim walked up to him and spoke in Shawnee, asking him his business.

The boy said, "Council Keeper is taking the slave catcher to the thicket by Blue Creek at dawn. He will only show him the way and not help in killing you. He sent me to tell you this."

"Thank you, No See One Eye," Jim said. Before Jim could offer him a place to rest, the boy had disappeared in the darkness.

He walked back to the cottage, where Anna was standing, her arms crossed in the cold. "He is coming to me," Jim said. "I don't have to go looking for him." Anna's fear returned. *When will it end?* She thought as they went back inside the cottage. As she returned to her bed, she worried at how excited, even enthusiastic

Jim was at hearing the news and the upcoming encounter with his enemy. *Why is he so anxious to kill people?* She asked herself.

Lucas wrapped his heavy blanket around him as he watched No See One Eye's shadow come down the path from the farmhouse and then disappear in the darkness. He felt confident now. *Morgan will come looking for me in the morning and I will be waiting for him. Then council keeper will show me the sanctuary and I will get my nigger.* He waited for several minutes, then returned to his horse and headed to the warmth of town to prepare for the morning's deadly visit.

Jim left the comfort and intimacy of his bed well before dawn, collected his rifle, pistol, and the general's binocular, which had been hanging unused since Jim's departure so long ago. He raised the tired buckskin from her sleep and with Digger by their side began the ride to the sanctuary on the path they all knew so well. Today would be the end of this war.

"I am in need of peace, without worry. I am tired," said Jim.

"So am I," said Buckskin.

"Me, too," Digger growled

Jim reached the sanctuary at first light. Water Bird was brewing some tea over a small fire; the cave was cozy and warm. Jim explained the message brought to him by No See One Eye.

"Council Keeper is no threat," she said, "He will not harm you. You have the spirit of Tecumseh; only his clan will do you harm. Kill only the white man." Water Bird paused and, in anticipation of Jim's thoughts, said, "The slaver will not find us. Go without worry." He looked closely at Labithia, who was sleeping soundly. "She is much better," said Water Bird. "She will soon be strong enough to move." Jim and Digger walked out of the sanctuary toward the Blue Creek Spring; the terrain was too difficult for horses and they had a difficult hike ahead.

Anna could not sleep; the fear and doubt pressed hard on her mind. Only in the few wonderful moments alone with Jim, when they escaped into each other and shut the outside world out of their life, did she find promise and hope. She tossed and turned in a confusing cascade of worry and questions. *This is not the Jim I remember; he seems distant, cold, and without humor. What has the army done to him? Why does he keep on killing? Isn't there a better way? Why doesn't anyone help him? The town doesn't care. Why is he fighting this battle on his own? Where is Virginia? Jim cannot do this himself.* The thoughts never stopped; she was fearful now than ever before, and so helpless. *I just want the old Jim back.* Anna stayed up after he left. Sleep would not return on this night.

Jim and digger paused, exhausted, and rested a minute before they climbed over the ridge that looked down on the clearing. A spring bubbled out of the ground and formed blue creek meadow, an open marshy area one hundred yards wide and four hundred yards long. The creek at the opposite end of opening flowed into a heavily wooded canyon and began a long descent, eventually ending in the Ohio River flood plain, where it slowed down and flowed quietly into the river.

Dense forests on steep ridges bordered both sides of the marsh. Jim surveyed the open area and saw nothing as they quietly went over the ridge and walked on the east side of the meadow, away from the Indian path on the opposite side. *If they are here, they'll be near the path,* Jim thought with confidence. The deciduous trees standing tall and bare on the steep slopes in the late October wind offered no hiding places. Digger, walking behind Jim she had for so many years, growled low. *"They're here,* Jim thought as he dropped to one knee, partially protected by several bushes. Only his eyes moved as he scanned the meadows opposite side. Digger's very low growl reinforced the reality that they were being watched. He didn't like his location; there was no place to aim or fire, and he would have to move. He looked around and settled on a fallen tree about twenty yards higher up on the slope. Before he went there, however, he needed to locate his enemy and he would not move until then. The forest was still, only sporadic breezes stirring the dead leaves generated any noise. Digger continued to lie still, not moving. How well she remembers our hunting days, Jim thought. Nothing and no one moved for an hour. Jim's eyes systematically searched the path on the far side and the bordering forested slopes from near too far. He had to assume that he had been seen, or there would be movement. Jim didn't know what type of weapon Lucas had or how good a shot he was.

The sun broke from the scudded clouds for just a moment, and Jim saw a movement illuminated in the new light in some low brush near the path right before it disappeared off the ridge and down to the valley. It moved again: a horse's tail. Jim quietly thanked the Council Keeper, who he was sure knew that he would be able to see the horse. Slowly, deliberately he brought his eyes back along the trail; finally, he saw a very faint silver circle with a dark interior, and knew he was looking into the front end of Lucas's gun barrel. Adrenaline began to flow: *three hundred and twenty five yards, a long shot but possible. He doesn't have a long rifle or he would have fired by now.* These observations flowed quickly through his mind. Jim needed a better shot; either he or Lucas would have to move. He didn't worry about Council Keeper, believing, as Water Bird had told him that he would not participate in the deadly showdown. Jim needed to move to the better location, where he would be higher and twenty yards closer, hopefully with a better line of fire. He decided to stay where he was for awhile, as Lucas did not appear to be a patient man. He could wait him out.

Jim watched the gun barrel; Lucas was very well hidden and remained motionless for a long time. Finally, the barrel moved slightly; Jim and Digger ran to the fallen tree and quickly jumped behind it, getting into a protected position. He saw that the rifle was again pointed at him. Jim had a better shot now, a clear line of sight to his target's exposed left shoulder. He was now ready to shoot, but wanted a head shot; he moved his body slowly but was unable to improve his line of sight. "I never miss from this range," he said to himself, as he settled in and waited for Lucas to move and hopefully expose something more than a shoulder and the rifle. He was much more confident now as he settled in for his shot. After several minutes, he observed a quick flurry of movement out of his sight line; Jim was not distracted and stayed on his target. In a second, Lucas moved; Jim now had his shot and pulled the trigger. The target fell forward. Jim turned and saw Council Keeper running very quickly down the path toward the horses. As Jim began to reload, Lucas's gun went off. Jim ducked instinctively as he heard the ball hit a tree many feet short and below his location.

Lucas was now running bent over, with one shoulder drooping, following Council keeper toward the horses. Lucas was still alive. This was surprising and disappointing; Jim had hoped that his shot would be fatal. He finished reloading as he saw the Council Keeper get to his horse. "Take both horses, take both horses," Jim yelled, his voice echoing through the forest. The chief got on his horse, leaving the other, and disappeared down the path towards the river. Jim began to run through the marsh toward Lucas. To get a second shot, he had to run through knee-high water and marsh grass, which slowed him down. The slave hunter ran hard; he stumbled at times but got to his horse, mounted, and rode away, slumped in the saddle. He too disappeared over the ridge. Jim was still in the marsh, rifle to his shoulder, a few seconds too late and fifty yards too far.

They left the marsh, crossed the meadow, and followed the trail. Digger smelled blood and directed Jim toward it; looking closely, he saw several drops and became more hopeful that the wound was mortal. "I don't want to go searching for him," he said to Digger as they walked to the ridge where the path worked its way down the side of the bluff. Jim climbed onto the low branch of a large hemlock that looked down to the river valley far below and focused his eyes on the trail that led to the Norburg landing and ferry crossing, sitting almost empty alongside the Ohio River.

It didn't take long for him to see a diminutive horse and rider, far away, heading toward the ferry. He took out the binocular and watched Lucas riding, slumped in the saddle, holding his shoulder; when he got to the landing he stopped at the ferry operator's shack, slowly slid off his horse, and went inside. He reappeared in several minutes, his shoulder now wrapped tight to his body. Lucas walked his horse onto the ferry and Jim could see him holding a pistol and the reins in the same hand; the gun was pointed in the general direction of the ferryman. They slowly crossed the river to St. Mary's Settlement on the Virginia side. Lucas upon landing rode west finally disappearing into the trees.

Jim watched with disappointment, knowing now that his battle was not over. A harsh, cold breeze blew suddenly across the bluff. "C'mon, Digger," he said. "Let's go home." They began the long hike back to the sanctuary.

Labithia was awake, alert, and sitting up. When Jim entered the cave, she placed her tiny hand in his and held tight. "Lordy mistr Jim," she said, "yous don save me."

CHAPTER 7

Ohio River

Jonathon McGuire
Journal Entry
October 22, 1811

"*A* most remarkable day. It was mid morning and,
out in the middle of the Ohio a loud and persistent, whooshing noise caused me to look and see with my
own eyes a most bizarre contraption that could only be the
"steam boat" that many of the river travelers had been
talking about of late. Most unusual in appearance, it made
a god awful noise from the steam machine, which somehow
moved a series of large paddles placed on its stern. These
seemed to push the boat forward at what appeared to be a
fast pace. It passed two flat boats and even a keel boat using
its sail.

"The boat in question had two large compartments
both forward and aft; in between was a large funnel-shaped
pipe that went straight up for 10 to 15 feet and from the
top came out a continual pouring of smoke, fire, and ash.
It went downriver to the Harmar point and then turned
around and, to my perplexity and amazement, returned

upstream at a good pace and with little effort. Most remarkable. It then came around and, with a great uproar, turned into the Muskingum and tied up at the point. Virginia and I watching, I must say, in disbelief, rode the surrey in haste into town to see this new machine. The entire town was in an uproar. It drew a great crowd to the riverfront; horses were most frightened by the noise and smoke, and there was great fear among the citizens, most of whom stayed a safe distance away fearful that this contraption would blow up at any minute. Most folks' only knowledge of steam machines was the one that worked Ginley's Grist Mill, which did not seem any way as dangerous as this contraption. We were invited on board, with dear Virginia fearful but willing; we met the owner, a Mr. Roosevelt, and his wife, who appeared most relaxed and without fear. Virginia was most concerned that Mrs. R. was with child and would place such risk on herself.

"The boat is named the New Orleans and it left Pittsburgh only a day ago. It is heading to its namesake city and hopes to arrive in 3 weeks.

"I'm told by the crew member attending the boiler that it requires an enormous amount of wood and coal to feed the fire that turns the water into steam, and the crew was busy buying up and loading all the lumber that was present. I did notice a large bin of coal on board that was used for the same reason. I thought it unusual that Mr. Conner and Cole, my enemies from the bank, were in conference with Mr. Roosevelt and the captain for the best part of an hour. I must say that it confirms my suspicions that they desire my land because of the black rock formation that runs along one of my ridges. I have been told by others that it is a field of good burning coal.

"The steam boat stayed but three hours and its smoke

could be seen long after it disappeared downriver. A most remarkable day that will forever be remembered by our community. I can't imagine this steam contraption having much of a future, however."

Jonathon McGuire

"Welcome, Mrs. Sprout and Mr. Morgan. I do appreciate your visit." Willford Connor was coldly civil in his welcome. The conference room seemed much smaller now than it had when Jim came here with the general for social and ceremonial visits with Mr. Putnam and other war veterans; then, it had been a warm and enjoyable place. He felt none of that this day. They sat around the well-worn and shiny maple wood table. Virginia and Jim sat on one side, looking at the silent, dull faces of two bank officials. A clerk had brought in glasses of apple cider. "Mrs. Sprout, I believe you know Mr. Silas Cole." Connor didn't acknowledge Jim's presence. "This is a difficult but necessary meeting, as it pertains to the indebtedness of your property, commonly known as the Maggie Hill Farm, to the First Mercantile Bank of Marietta. I will turn the meeting over to Mr. Cole, who will go over the figures with you."

He was a very thin, unattractive man with slicked down hair and a long thin neck. His business suit seemed much too big for him, and his high-pitched voice had a screechy quality about it. He began without any greeting. "I have prepared two documents for you," he said. "The first is the statement of indebtedness, which defines both the history and current state of your mortgage account on said property. As you can see, it is quite substantial. Please note the signature of General McGuire, now deceased, attesting to the accuracy and authenticity of this account. Paragraph six indicates that a payment of 8,221 American dollars or gold equivalent is due no later than 5:00 p.m. on the 31st of December, 1813.

"The second document is a demand letter that acknowledges that if the payment is not presented in full and in a timely manner, said property will foreclose with all goods, materials, improvements, and livestock surrendered to the bank. In addition, the demand letter requires the immediate removal of yourself and all other inhabitants residing on the property." Silas Cole sat back and smugly added. "Please, Mrs. Sprout, read the documents carefully and then place your signature where designated. May you also note that the conditions and directions of the general's estate allow yours to be the only signature necessary."

Jim could only imagine how Virginia felt at this moment; she sat with her back straight, looking forward with a distant expression on her face, showing no interest in the man or documents before her. She remained silent for some time then said quietly and calmly, "Gentleman, you will have your money." She rose from her chair and walked out of the room; Jim followed, looking at the thin, frail, despotic Silas Cole.

Before leaving the room, he said calmly, "We will meet again in different circumstances." There was no response.

Virginia walked out of the bank; Elizabeth and Madelyn were waiting to go with her to a quilting session at the Meigs house on Front Street two blocks away. Jim watched them leave, still in an irritated and agitated state, and wondered if Virginia was as outraged as he was. In a discussion two days previously, Virginia had told Jim that there was no money in any account that would be sufficient to make the pending payment; when he offered his deed to pay the debt, he was informed that he could not sell his land in the thicket until his majority two years hence. When asked, Virginia told him that there was no other plan to save the farm at this time. Jim, agitated at Virginia's apparent indifference, felt quite forsaken. "What the hell am I doing this for if no one gives a damn?" he had asked.

"Excuse me, would you be Mr. Morgan?" Jim turned and looked at an elderly man of rugged features, well dressed in business clothes and the wide-brim hat that was becoming popular with the local cattle and livestock dealers. "I am Felix Renick of Chillicothe," he said, "and this may be an opportune meeting for both of us. May I invite you over to Bracket's as my guest for lunch? I can tell you of my business there." Both the name and the face were familiar; Jim agreed and, as they entered the establishment, the three ladies watched from Ohio Street a block away.

Virginia smiled just a bit, and said, "Let's go a-quiltin'."

Bracket's was in a bustling mood with the fireplaces crackling, smoke hanging low, and the din of many voices. They exchanged greetings with Elva, who had been the establishment's sole proprietor after her husband's death in '07. "Welcome back, Jim," she said. "I hear you're a hero." She showed them to a booth and they sat for a lunch of scalloped potatoes with ham, bread, and a hot tin cup of hard cider.

Jim said, "I do remember you. You're the cattle drover from the Scioto River."

"Yes," Felix said. "We met on several occasions in your youth. The general and I were great friends and had mutual dealings in the livestock business; we had many good years and a few less productive. The general was a man of great integrity whom I both admired and trusted." He paused for a minute as the food was delivered, then continued. "I am aware of Virginia's financial difficulties and I would like to discuss an opportunity that might be helpful to both of us." He again stopped; Jim's silence gave him the approval to continue. "I have recently brought over from my Scioto farms forty head of two-to-five-year-old corn fed cows with the intent to sell them to the army cattle and hog buyers. They, however, left this market most hastily a week before when the word of the disbursement of General Harrison's army after the great victory on the Thames was received in Marietta. They have moved east to purchase beef closer to the Army of the Niagara. I am told they are in Pittsburg, where they are buying up all the beef available at top prices. We were selling our summer cows to the army at fifty dollars per hundred weights, a most profitable sum, I must say."

Jim, beginning to understand where the conversation was going, said, "No one has ever driven cows to the east in December."

"That is true," said Felix, "and there is great risk of course, but if the weather is good it could be done in four weeks without hogs. The road has much improved since your last drive several years ago and, if you go north along the Muskingum trail to Cambridge, there is a new, shorter trail north of the trace that takes you to Steubenville. The Ohio crossing is better there than at Wheeling." He paused and started on his lunch; he thought the conversation was going too fast, and that it was best to slow down.

Jim, however, continued without hesitation. "I think we could round up sixty to eighty cows that are roaming free on the general's open pasture and in the thicket," he said, "but even with top prices it would not be sufficient to meet the debt."

They had both stopped eating and were looking at each other. Felix, pleasantly surprised at Jim's quick comprehension, pushed his plate away, wiped his mouth, ordered more cider, and nodded at several acquaintances. Then he continued. "I do have a proposal," he said.

Anna, another long, hard day over, took a minute, sat by the fire with a glass of port and a warm pipe in a now quiet house, and tried to get a handle on her life. There had been so many events and activities in the last three days that Anna had had little time to reflect. What a joyous day it had been when she and the others watched Water Bird, her sister and niece, riding the mules and buckskin toward the house. Jim had carried Labithia, wrapped snugly in a blanket, up the thicket trail, through the yard, and into the main house. It was a most wonderful celebration that evening—a bountiful meal, with all hands in attendance around the large kitchen table and much cider, wine, abundant laughter, and the telling of many stories of recent events. Only Virginia, who had come to the farm that morning, was somewhat somber.

The night she had spent with Jim, she had felt only lust and the quiet strength of her lover. Only in the morning did she become concerned when, in the quiet of the bed, Jim shared his frustration over his failure to kill Lucas, and his determination to finish the job. *There is still a part of him that is cold, at odds with the compassion he shows to his friends, animals, and particularly Labithia.* Labithia, even now, as Anna got up from her chair and stoked the fire, was sleeping in the large bedroom she was sharing with Water Bird.

The farm was again a busy place, with Wendell and Charles fetching the pigs back to the sty, repairing the chicken coops and recapturing the chickens, putting hay out in the pasture to encourage the cows that were let out to return, and repairing the various dwellings that were vandalized by Joshua and his crew. She enjoyed watching everyone return to a life that had almost been lost. Still, she felt left out as Jim and Virginia, in their haste, seemed to exclude her from conversations regarding day-to-day activities and the myriad of decisions that seemed to be made all around her. Yet, everyone, including herself, seemed to be filled with hope for a bright future and a return to a life that was similar to what it had been when the general was alive.

Her day had overflowed when, in mid morning, Jacob Hicks had appeared out of nowhere. He was returning from a trip to Pennsylvania, where he passed along two fugitives that he had picked up in Cambridge. The three of them had made a difficult journey to the Quaker sanctuary where safe transport to Canada would be arranged. Jacob was very tired but enjoyed the refreshments that Anna provided. He and Labithia shared a most tender reunion. The rest of the day was spent in conversation, with the two of them sharing all the events that had occurred since their last meeting in late summer. Jacob and Anna had embraced on meeting, and she was warm to his touch. She thought this evening about her attraction to him and chose not to force the feelings away.

Jim was riding Buckskin up the hill to the farmhouse at a slow trot, his mind racing with the events of the day. He was excited about the proposal and was solving problems and organizing the adventure in his mind. One ominous cloud remained: what to do with Labithia? *She will have to come with us,* was his only solution.

It was late when he opened the door to the main house after stabling Buckskin and quickly talking to Wendell, who had unexpectedly assumed the role of farm guardian and spent several hours every night roaming the property. Jim looked forward to Anna's bed and received a warm reception but with less enthusiasm than he had recently experienced.

The morning brought Jim and Jacob together for the first time since their meeting on that dark night in the middle of the Scioto River. They were sitting in the kitchen, being served boiled eggs, biscuits, jam, and coffee, searching for a place to start a conversation. Anna looked at these two attractive men: Jacob, older it appeared by several years, taller by several inches, and handsome in a traditional sense, quieter in speech. Jim was of stronger build; his beauty was in his presence, his confidence and strength. Both were educated and well spoken, and they were beginning to enjoy each other's company. It was a breakfast that she would always remember: two determined and competent men, the three of them together for a moment in time.

Labithia, still weak and frail, helped by Water Bird, walked out of the bedroom and into the parlor where she gestured for

Jim and Jacob to sit down on either side of her. She then quietly placed her tiny dark hands on their large, strong hands and pressed them to her. The three sat for some time together without words; the only conversation was the tears shed by all, expressing a profound message.

Water Bird gave the three of them their time and went into the kitchen to smoke her pipe. She, too, worried about the farm, Labithia, and her own family's future.

Anna watched Jacob and Jim from the windows of her kitchen as they spent several hours after breakfast, conversing as they strolled around the farm. She noticed that Jim was particularly animated, and it was clear from their postures and gestures that a strong bond was developing. She found herself uneasy about the two of them being together; she was disappointed that she wasn't invited to join them.

Virginia was waiting for the two of them when they returned to the house. She invited Anna and Jacob to discuss the proposal offered by Felix Renick and agreed to by Virginia.

"The farm is in great debt and it will be lost to the bank if we do not make a payment by end of this year," she said. "Presently, we have no liquid assets, and will not be able to clear the debt. We agreed, Jim and I, to drive our cattle to the eastern market to raise the necessary funds. Mr. Renick, a Scioto cattleman and a good friend of my father, has offered to send some forty head of his cows, which are presently waiting for slaughter at the packing house, with our drive. He will defer payment for twelve months, so we could include his with ours. I expect we can round up eighty to a hundred cows from the pasture and those grazing wild in the thicket, drive them to Pittsburgh and, with a good price, secure funds sufficient to make the payment and save the farm for another year."

She paused and Jim, anticipating their many questions, tried to answer them before they were asked. "Yes," he said, "it is dangerous this late in the year with the winter storms. If the weather holds, the roads will be dry and we will be able to make twelve to fifteen miles per day and get there in three to four weeks. That should give enough time to sell the cows and get back here by end of the year. We leave in six days and will start rounding up our cows tomorrow. Mr. Renick has offered to allow his stockman, Jasper Cutler, to join us. He is very experienced and has driven the Steubenville road. We will be taking only cows, no pigs. I am told there are enough drover stands along the way with plenty of feed, as there has been a scarcity of drives this fall; we should have adequate forage and shelter for most of the trail. We will be using pike boys to help us for much of the drive. In Pittsburgh, the army buyers are offering top dollar for good beef. I expect to return with hard riding and get back a day or two before the New Year." Jim paused for a moment and then said, "We have to do this. It is our only chance."

"Who is going?" Anna asked.

"Me, Wendell, and the stockman."

"That is not enough. You know that," she said. "I want to go"

"Anna you are needed here," said Jim, "and so is Jacob if he will stay." Jacob nodded. "It's not right that I don't go," she said. "I can do the work, and I want to be part of this."

Anna was angry now, left out again. Jim repeated, "You are needed here."

"Bullshit," said Anna, and turned away with feelings .

"What about Labithia?" Jacob asked. There was no response. No one had a good answer.

At that moment, Water Bird stepped into the kitchen. She sat down on the rocking chair near the hearth, took out her tobacco pouch, and prepared her pipe. The others watched her intently and waited for her to speak.

"I must talk and you must listen," she said. "I will take care of Labithia. She is of Shawnee blood now; I am her keeper. She is to be known as Little Bird. We must do what I say. She is not strong enough to travel hard or long and cannot be safe in this house. Jacob, you are not a warrior, and cannot protect her from Lucas Williams and his clan, who will soon be seeking vengeance. Lucas is now in Kentucky and was near death with fever; soon he and his brother will return to get the slave girl and kill Forest Boy. I will take Little Bird to the home of Jim's mother. Elizur is gone?" The question was directed at Jim.

He nodded and said, "He is now of feeble mind and is not a danger."

Water Bird continued. "The farm home is secluded and unknown to Lucas. I shall know when they cross the river and will be able to find other places to hide if need be. No See One Eye is my eyes and ears, and will warn me of any dangers. When Little Bird is strong and can travel, I will take her to a better place." Water Bird paused, relit her pipe, took several draws, and looked up at Jim, who was standing behind the table.

"Forest Boy, be warned," she said. "You are in great danger. The Williams family will seek revenge no matter Lucas's fate. They will come and soon." You killed the great chief Tecumseh; you have been told of the Shawnee law. When a warrior chief is killed in battle, his victor receives the great chief's spirit into his heart. The chief's clan will then seek out and return the great chief's spirit. Soon, the dancing tail clan's work with the English king will end. They too will come. No one can help you; it is their way. You know of this?" The room was deathly quiet. Jim stood silent, nodding. "Jim," said Water Bird, "I fear for your life."

There was a long pause. Water Bird was done speaking; she looked off into the distance, smoking her clay pipe. Jim responded quietly, "I know of this, and have been warned by Chief Tarhee of the Wyandotte. I know not the fate of Tenskawatawa or Cheeksauhaloa, Tecumseh's brothers, or the rest of the clan;

when I left the army, they were still fighting with the retreating British. They may stay for a long time as the war continues in the east. I also suspect that Lucas will be unable to ride for another month and I don't think his kin will come without him."

Jim had listened to Water Bird's warning but the danger seemed far away. He was focused on the present. He looked at Anna, who was looking down at the floor, and felt his own anger rising at her hostility. "I know not what to do about my enemies," he said. "All I can do is what needs to be done now and I believe we should save the farm if we can. Is that what you want me to do? I have taken many risks and endured many hardships, and am willing to do more. If my efforts are not what you want, I will stop." He was speaking mostly to Anna, who continued to look away.

Virginia, however, walked over to Jim, touched his elbow, and said seriously, "Jim, we are most beholden to you and proud of you and all you have done."

There was a long quiet pause while Jim calmed his feelings, then continued. "The cattle drive will leave on Saturday," he said. "There is much to do. I now go to my mother's to repair their burnt-out house, which they refuse to leave and provide them with a simple and dry dwelling. I will take one mule with tools and supplies and fix it up as best I can. I expect to be back late tomorrow. I don't think that Lucas or his people will leave Kentucky any time soon. Little Bird will be safe here for two more days. Jacob, Wendell, Charles will be here to protect the farm. In the meantime, bring the hay out to the pasture, open the fields where the corn is harvested, and round up all the cows that are in the thicket. They need to fatten up and should weigh at least nine hundred pounds before we leave.

CHAPTER 8

Washington County
Ohio
December 1813

Cloudy skies, cool temperatures, and brisk winds accompanied the drovers north out of Marietta, on the Muskingum trail past South Olive and then following the Duck Creek trail to the Cambridge post road. Everything had been going well since the drive's departure three days ago. The cows were in good shape; the road was hard, with no rain and a few subfreezing days; and there was no dust or mud, at least one of which was always present on previous drives. Jasper Cutler was a pleasant surprise; he knew his cows and how to manage a drive. Wendell was enjoying his duties and free of all the complaining of previous trips to Pittsburg. Breaking him and Charles up seemed to have helped his disposition.

Jim, riding straggler behind the herd, gave him time to think back on the previous days; he was surprised when Digger, who in past drives was a most eager participant, sat on her haunches, when the herd was formed up and taken out of the pasture. He looked down at his best friend and expected her to fill with enthusiasm. She didn't move, just looked up at his master without expression. Jim dismounted and went to Digger, where he spent several minutes petting and holding her, telling her it was okay. "You stay here and take care of everyone," he whispered. Once the herd was out of sight, Digger returned to the house and lay on the porch, looking out over the farm. Jim missed him now as he thought about their many trips together. The final count was 154 cows, all in the eight hundred to one thousand pound range. Jim was determined to bring all of them in; hopefully, they would be sold at ten cents per pound. He had done the math many times and it always came out at 13,000 dollars. On previous drives, the general always took care of the business. And Jim had paid little attention to all the responsibilities.

Being in charge, Jim now worried about everything: the health of his cows, costs to feed and pasture, the condition of the Ohio when they needed to cross. So far, the drive was orderly; the cows were content to follow Black, the lead oxen, which belonged to Felix and had been used on many prior drives. He figured he had been making twelve to fifteen miles per day. Drove stands were available three of the four nights, and adequate fodder and pasture were available. He expected to be in Cambridge in another day and give the cows a day to rest and feed. All three of the drovers had been on this road many times and, with the cows under good control, they had no need for a pike boy. Observers and passersby had expressed concern about driving this late in the year, but they wished them well.

Jim felt some relief in being alone and away from Anna. He wondered about her changing attitude; she had been welcoming upon his return from the war, but now seemed irritated, moody, and resentful when they were together. Her bed had grown cooler.

She said nothing about her change in mood and, when Jim would inquire, it seemed only to worsen. He couldn't help but notice her interest in Jacob and wondered if she would be going to his bed; he was surprised when he didn't feel any jealousy or anger over that possibility. Several cows drifted off the path and Jim let Buckskin redirect them back to the road and the herd. Jim knew that every drive has its problems, but two days out of Cambridge, it couldn't be better.

The farm settled down to a routine. Jacob stayed on as promised, working hard to rebuild the smoke house and chicken coops, which had fallen into disrepair. He also spent time each day with Little Bird, who was more alert but tired very quickly. During the evenings, he enjoyed the general's library, which was a treasure of literature; he would read to Anna by candlelight. They spent many hours together and she enjoyed his companionship and responsiveness to her attention and interests. She would listen to his essays on the evils of slavery and the sanctuary movement in Ohio, as well as how he and others were carrying forward the abolitionist movement that had been the general's passion.

A week after the drovers left, No See One Eye visited Water Bird and reported that Lucas would live and was recovering. He might reappear soon to threaten the farm. Virginia continued to spend most of her time at Reverend Moody's with Elizabeth, but would ride the preacher's surrey to the farm when the weather permitted for day-long visits. Penelope and Charles continued to look to Anna for directions in their daily labors, and the farm began to run again, although it had been scaled back considerably.

Two days after the cattle drive left for Pittsburg, Water Bird, her family, and Little Bird left for their new residence. Jacob offered to act as an armed escort, but was turned down by Water Bird. The mules were piled high with supplies, food, and dry goods. As she watched them leave, Anna immediately felt a sense of loss and purposelessness; her role seemed further diminished. She would miss her friend the little slave girl, but she would have more time with Jacob.

In town at the First Mercantile Bank, bets were laid on Jim's return, with the odds heavily favoring his failure to reappear on time. The first day of December brought pleasant, almost balmy weather.

CHAPTER 9

Pittsburgh, Pennsylvania
December 1813

Jim walked impatiently outside the fenced pasture where the cows had been sitting for several days, fattening up on hay and corn silage. He was becoming quite concerned about time: They had had to seek shelter for two days to wait out an ice storm, and it took an extra day to ferry the cows across the Monongahela. As a result of Jim's decision to rest them an extra day where there was good fodder and shelter, he was left with only eight days to return.

They only lost two cows on the journey, and the weight loss was acceptable. They should get top dollar.

The army agents were supposed to have arrived the previous day; it was now mid morning and there was no sign of them. Time was becoming critical; Wendell wondered what they would do if they didn't show up. Jim wondered the same; he hadn't seen any other buyers in the vicinity. "They will be here," was all he would say.

"Guess we would have to go further east, Baltimore maybe," Wendell said, talking mostly to himself.

This would be the first time Jim negotiated a sale. He had watched the general do so on previous trips, and wished he had paid more attention. It appeared to be easy, and the general was always in a good mood when it was over. He tried to remember everything Felix had told him. "Don't be afraid to walk away," he had said several times. Jim had decided to ride into town and look for another buyer when two men rode down the path to the pastures where the cows and drovers were waiting.

The four of them celebrated at Hoosier's Tavern and Inn that night. The negotiations and weighing took all day. The Army buyers initially behaved with arrogance, trying to bully Jim into five cents per pound on the hoof. Jim stayed firm, even after several ultimatums, with his original offer of ten cents; he had observed early that, in spite of their dismissive manner, they wanted his cows. Negotiations were at a standstill when Wendell mentioned that Jim was a war hero and had shot Tecumseh at the Battle of the Thames. At first, the buyers didn't believe his boast, but Wendell showed them a newspaper article from the Western Spectator that he kept in a shirt pocket, and they became more cordial and respectful. This seemed to move the sale along. After more dickering, Jim came down to nine cents and the deal was sealed.

The drovers enjoyed a hearty meal, ample beverage, and a warm and soft place to sleep the night. Jim would leave at first light after taking care of the finances at the First Bank of Pennsylvania, with assistance from a banker friend of Felix. He was most impressed when he held in his hands a check for $11,624.00 American. Following his instructions, he purchased a federally secured draft payable to the First Mercantile Bank of Marietta for $8900.42. When the bank business concluded, he hastened to the stables and purchased a strong and durable horse for a quick return. He only had seven days to cover two hundred miles and be at the bank before closing on December 31st. Good weather and a good horse would allow him to go thirty to forty miles a day, but if anything went wrong however, the effort to save the farm would fail.

He said goodbye that night and provided funds and instructions to Jasper and Wendell, who would follow behind, bringing Black the oxen, the two mules, and the tired buckskin with them at a more casual pace. They would stop at the drover stands to pay for the shelter and feed that were provided on the way to Pittsburgh. On early Christmas morning, Jim rode to the end of Liberty Street and crossed the Alleghany on the Jones flat ferry; he stepped out lively on this cold but clear December day.

CHAPTER 10

Maggie Hill
December 24 1813

The day of Christmas Eve was quiet at the farm; chores were done early, Charles worked in the shop most of the afternoon, carving small animal figures to give as gifts, Jacob cut a small spruce for a Christmas tree, and Penelope and Anna trimmed the tree and prepared a holiday dinner. Everyone was preoccupied; they were worried, but hopeful that Jim would make it back in time and with enough money to pay this year's mortgage and keep the farm going. No one talked about the future, but it was on everyone's mind. The meal was served in the early evening; smoked ham, mashed potatoes, scalloped corn, hot biscuits and two apple and two mincemeat pies. The meal was jolly and warm, with everyone sharing humorous stories of previous Christmases. The enjoyable evening was over by 9:00 p.m., when Charles and Penelope went to their separate rooms to be with their own thoughts.

Anna was still preoccupied with her attraction for Jacob. Over the last four weeks, they had spent many hours together; she found herself deeply infatuated with this handsome, strong, and attentive man; her strong feelings for Jim were still alive, but when she was in Jacob's presence another set of feelings seemed to overwhelm her. She was aware that Jacob didn't respond equally to her feelings and avoided being alone with her; she sometimes orchestrated a meeting with them so that the two of them could express their feelings and intentions. His lack of response only seemed to make him more desirable. Infatuation began to dominate her life.

Anna would lay awake deep into the night with Jacob sleeping only a bedroom away; she got up on many occasions and stood silently outside his door, hoping he would call to her, but he never did. The time they were together was becoming more difficult for both of them; recently, Jacob had deliberately been going out of his way to avoid her, particularly when they were alone. She continued to seek his attention at every opportunity.

That evening after the Christmas party, when the house was quiet, he asked Anna to sit on the couch in the parlor with him and held her hands in his.

"Dearest Anna," he said, "please listen to me. My words will hurt you, but I know of no other manner to tell you this. I am most aware of your affections for me and honored to be the recipient. I am unable, however, to harbor the same affections and attractions for you. You see I am a man who neither seeks nor desires a women's lust or love. I care only for men, and seek my affections in their company. I have been of this nature for my entire life, or as long as I remember and have no desire or ability to change." He paused for a long moment, and then continued. "I hope you understand." Anna did not respond, staring only into Jacob's eyes. "I am sorry, Anna, that I have caused you so much pain, and regret that I did not share my condition with you when I first noticed your interest in me. Nothing can or will happen between the two us, except friendship. Jim has risked his life for you and you were prepared to betray him. This troubles me greatly, for I too love Jim in a way that only one man can for another. I ache for him as you do for me. If he returns to the farm and seeks your continued affection, I hope that you will find a way to accept him for who he is and be devoted to him. Anna did not respond, and Jacob waited patiently for several minutes. When a response did not come, he continued to speak.

"I now need to move on," he said, "and I will be leaving on the New Year's Day to visit my mother and then continue the mission that we have talked so much about. There is so much to do." Anna pulled her hands away from Jacob, grabbed a shawl, and stepped outside; the sky was clear, with a multitude of stars overwhelming the night. Far below in the valley, a few lights were still burning. "What have I done? Oh my God, what have I done?" She walked down the path toward the apple orchards, hardly noticing the brisk, chilly night. "What a fool I be" The tears turned cold on her cheeks. Digger did not follow.

Three nights before the new year, a weakened but determined Lucas and his brother, Craven Williams, crossed the river from the Williamsburg landing to the Marietta ferry dock and rode their horses to a clandestine rendezvous with representatives of the First Mercantile Bank. Lucas's wound was still sore to the touch and he tired quickly, but the fever was gone and he was feeling stronger each day. In spite of his condition, he could not resist the invitation from Silas Cole to meet him this night at the ceremonial mounds north of town.

CHAPTER 11

Muskingum River Road
Washington County
December 30th 1813

J im was feeling very confident; the return trip, first on the Steubenville post and then on the Duck Creek road, was going very well. The streams were low and easily forded, the roads were dry and hard, as the winter freeze had settled in with no rain to challenge it. The horse he had selected, if treated properly, would ride for up to ten hours a day at a solid pace; he was able to stable and feed him each night at farms and inns that were spaced about ten miles apart to accommodate teamsters and slow-moving cattle and hog drives. It was now almost dark on the sixth day of the return trip. They had been riding steadily since morning with only a rest stop. Jim had recently crossed the ten-mile bridge on the Muskingum River Road. Both he and the horse were exhausted from the hard pace they had kept for the last week, but Jim figured they would keep going this night, walking the horse after dark, which would be falling in an hour. He looked forward to being in Marietta in early morning with an entire day to turn over the funds to Virginia and then get some rest.

The horse leaped as Jim heard the first shot. He was thrown

high out of the saddle and they both fell down a six-foot embankment that dropped from the road to the river. Jim was also
conscious of a second shot that whizzed past his ear; the horse
was gurgling blood and drawing its final breath as Jim recovered
and knelt down for protection behind him. Fatigue had been immediately replaced by life-protecting energy; he was alert and
thought quickly. They could not be more than a hundred yards
away. It would take a minute or two for them reload. Jim's rifle
was strapped to his back and there would not be time to uncase
and load; he pulled his flintlock pistol from his belt and quickly
loaded and set the prime. He then moved around the horse to be
able to see the road and his attackers and hoped there were only
two. His breathing was heavy and his hands were sweating. The
light was almost gone when he saw two silhouettes about ten
feet apart, walking slowly up the road toward him, muskets at the
ready.

Jim was quickly going over his options. He would wait to respond as long as possible, as darkness would be his friend. The
figures coming toward him were quiet, slow moving, and unidenti-
fiable; they approached, cautiously peered over the embankment.
They were no more than 15 yards away. Jim shot the nearest one
in the head and then quickly ran upriver several yards, into some
thick bushes, to reload. There were no shots, only silence, and no
sign of the second assassin. Where was he?

Jim continued to kneel behind his bushes, silent and with little
movement He waited until darkness reduced visibility, and then
slowly climbed the embankment, anticipating that the partner was
waiting in ambush. He first observed the body, silent and dark on
the road where it fell; the dead man's partner was nowhere in
sight. Several minutes elapsed and Jim became more confident
that the partner was gone; he stood up and went to stand over
the body, which was lying face down. He rolled the body over;
It was Lucas, there was just enough light in the darkening sky to

identify him. Jim's shot to the throat left a large pool of blood under his body; Jim felt little; other than some relief that his enemy would no longer be a threat in his life. Jim moved quickly still concerned of the whereabouts of the other assassin. He grabbed the body by the back of the collar and pulled it to the side of the road then rolled it down the embankment where it rested next to the still warm carcass of his horse. Jim continued to look all around and seeing no sign of the Lucas's partner went back down the embankment to the horse. He untied his heavy blanket from the saddle, took off the bridal, cut the saddle at the cinch, and placed them near a tree. He covered the horse's face with the saddle blanket, thanked it for its sacrifice then placed Lucas's hat over his face and began to walk south to Marietta. He could still be there by morning.

Jim soon found himself in conditions as terrible as any seen in the Ohio River Valley in memory. The northwest wind, bothersome in gusts most of the day, exploded in gale-like force several hours after his deadly encounter. A snowstorm of blizzard proportions was steamrolling in horizontal waves across the darkened landscape. The temperature dropped sharply and Jim, who had been walking along the road, knew he was in dangerous conditions and would have to find some type of shelter from the blinding storm immediately. There was barely enough light to distinguish the road from its tree-covered borders. The river to his right was lost in the blowing snow, and he quickly lost his sense of direction. He walked toward the darkness, reached out and touched a large tree, moved around it to get away from the wind, and decided that this would have to do. He felt and found a small depression at the base of the large oak and sat down, getting as small as he could be. Jim was scared. He had been in cold, windy weather many times, but nothing like this; he knew he would have to stay here until daylight. By crouching very low, he was able to stay out of the force of the wind; the snow, however, was swirling around, and quickly covered everything with a heavy white blanket. Drifts were beginning to build. The howling wind in the treetops was terrifying; branches began to break and crash. Breathing hard and fighting a sense of panic, Jim assessed his situation.

In order to stay alive, he would have stay awake and out of the wind; he worried that he would not be warm enough to survive and decided to use his long knife to cut five-inch strips from the bottom of his heavy wool blanket to put around his face and into his winter mittens.

He dared not take off his leggings or deerskin-lined boots; his feet would have to survive without additional help. He stayed low in the depression as he struggled to cut the blanket. He was encouraged by a large snow drift that was beginning to form on the south side of the oak; this would offer more protection from the deadly wind, now blowing in gale force. Jim hoped desperately that the blizzard would blow out this night; it would be five or six hours before there would be enough morning light to continue the long walk into Marietta. To stay alive, he needed to fend off the overpowering desire to sleep that was already calling him. "I need to keep my mind alive," he said out loud as he forced himself to stay awake. The night took forever with the roaring wind and endless snow continuing unabated, huge drifts building up in unpredictable fashion; the continual breaking and crashing of branches high in the trees turned the forest into a profane and angry world. Jim was cold, very cold; he had not moved from his protected but fragile space; his body shook and he felt the cold deep inside. He did everything to fight the deadly sleep: reliving his life, planning the future, singing every song, and reciting every poem he knew. The cold eternity eventually passed and the long night began to wane; the ferocious blizzard however continued unabated. Jim could now see his outstretched hand in front of his face and decided it was time to move. He stood up, rearranged his blanket, hat, and scarf, and stepped out from his shelter and into the deadly blizzard. It was worse than he could imagine. The wind was so fierce that it blew him backward as he struggled to stand upright; the snow blinded his eyes and he had look down at his feet to see his direction and to protect his sight from the intense driven snow. The cold tore at his core and he knew he needed to move. He immediately walked into a drift and then another; some were waist high, others chest deep. He plowed through as best he could; the wind pushed him sideways, the drifts seemed endless. On occasion, wooded areas protected the road and the snow was only knee high, giving him a brief reprieve. It was impossible to set a course and, on numerous occasions, he drifted off the road. The exertion warmed his body and he could soon feel the cold sweat on his skin. He continued on but within an hour he was exhausted and hardly able to move; the never ending drifts and relentless wind; destroying his energy and the will to go on. Lost in the blizzard and making little headway, he decided that if he could find any kind of shelter, he would stop and wait out the storm and abandon the mission.

He kept hoping that the storm would soon diminish in its ferocity and permit Jim to see enough to know where he was and find shelter. In the meantime, he continued on for a second hour, followed by a third; eventually, he came upon a stretch of road where the drifts were less frequent and the wind less ferocious. The snow, for the most part, came to below the knee. He hoped that he was walking through Putnam's apple orchards, which were only several miles from the center of town. Visibility was still low and he couldn't be sure; he plodded on, concentrating only on staying alive and on the road in front of him. Suddenly, out of the wind and snow, a large, dark object was coming right at him; as quickly as his exhausted body allowed, Jim rolled to one side, looked up, and was able to make out a team of horses leading a red sled with a driver bent over the reins, covered in snow. Jim called out, but knew that he had not been heard or seen. "Why would anyone be out in this weather?" he asked himself.

Jim forced his body with all of his energy he could muster to rise and keep moving; he knew that if he fell again, he wouldn't get up. He continued on, one foot after the other, one drift to another, overwhelmed by fatigue, walking endlessly. His mind was in a fog, harboring little awareness or memory. He would go until he could go no more. At one point, he became very thirsty and could think of nothing but a cold drink of water; knowing that eating snow would destroy his energy, he ignored his body's demands and continued on; another hour, perhaps two. He thought about nothing; the need to get to the bank and the harrowing events of the night before were no longer part of his memory. He walked in a frozen trance; death was no longer his enemy, becoming more of a friend as he struggled on. Exhaustion called to him to rest and find peace. More time went by. The wind, still very cold, blew with continued intensity and the snow moved horizontally across the landscape. Jim was wrapped in a blanket of white, indistinguishable from his surroundings. Eventually, after many hours, the wind seemed to lessen; he was now able to make out objects further away: trees, fence posts, a barn provocatively calling him to her protection. He ignored them and continued moving, finally seeing a light off to his left, vague and barely visible. He plodded on. The drifts were smaller now and walking seemed easier; he saw a second light closer than the first but he continued on. He knew now he was in town and he began to believe he would survive. Soon the Campus Mauritius loomed out of the snow on his right. He knew he would make it now. He was within blocks of his destination, his long ordeal soon to be over; then he could rest. *Go to the bank, conduct my business and sleep.* He saw a figure hunched over, walking in front of him into the wind then quickly disappearing from sight. More lights were now visible and he could make out several other foolish pedestrians walking hunched over to unknown destinations. Soon, he could identify the snow-covered buildings of downtown Marietta. The bank was just ahead. The deadly New Year's Eve blizzard continued with great intensity, but it would not claim him as a victim.

Jim opened the door of the warm, well-lit bank, and was overwhelmed. He stood in the middle of the small lobby, taking off the frozen scarf that covered his mouth and nose; he felt weak in his knees and fought hard to keep his balance. The warm air drawn into his cold lungs stopped his breathing and he took several large breaths. Unable to see, he tried to remove the ice-packed snow from his eyes, but that seemed to make it worse. The almost empty bank stopped its business and everyone stared. No one spoke: there was complete silence. He continued to stand in the same place, waiting for his sight to return. His entire body was covered in thick snow, frozen to his clothing, giving him the appearance of a white, unrecognizable polar monster. The snow began to thaw almost instantly, quickly forming in puddles around him. He took off his hat and the cold water flowed down his face. "May I help you sir?" asked a small voice close to him. Jim could barely make out the timid teller asking him his business.

"I need to pay a bill," he said. If he could have seen clearly, he would have noticed Willford Conner, Silas Cole and others coming out of the conference room, staring in disbelief. As the clerk showed him toward the teller windows, he asked, "And what time would it be?"

"It be 3:15 on New Year's Eve, sir," replied the clerk.

"Good. I made it with time to spare," said Jim as he continued to the window. He used all his strength to continue standing. Slowly and with difficulty, he opened his very wet blanket and deerskin coat to find the waterproof pouch inside his money belt that held the precious bank draft.

The parsonage was a gloomy place. Fires in the kitchen and parlor and burning candles throughout the house gave off the image of a warm and comfortable home riding out the ferocious storm. Several times this day, Reverend Moody had shoveled snow off the porch, looking nervously toward the north but unable to see to the end of his walk. The cautious optimism of the previous evening had sunk to despair when all awoke to the blizzard. As its ferocity continued into daylight, they feared the worst. If Jim was caught in the storm, he would not survive. Madelyn cried and prayed openly for God to intervene and save her young friend's life. Anna, who had arrived from the farm the previous day in an optimistic mood, confident that Jim would return, was now wrapped in a shawl, staring out the snow-blown window. Virginia was in the kitchen, quietly reading to Elizabeth who had stopped asking when Jim would return because everyone had stopped answering. Any hope to save the farm had been dashed as the day and the storm crept along.

The front door flew open and the snow-covered apprentice charged into the house.

"Mr. Morgan is at the bank, I seen him myself, he made it," he said. "He is at the bank right now." Madelyn, nearest the door, collapsed onto the second floor stairs and continued her praying. Virginia, Anna, and the reverend immediately grabbed their coats, hats, and shawls and ventured into the storm, bent over into the wind, moving single file, following the apprentice and walking as fast as the deep snow and brutal winds allowed.

They were shocked at his appearance. He was wrapped in a heavy sodden blanket, hair and beard drenched in melting snow, barely standing. Employees and customers were staring at this forlorn figure; he appeared confused and disoriented. "Jim, dear Jim; are you all right?" he recognized the reverend's voice and turned slightly and slowly toward it. "Is Miss Virginia here?" he asked.

"Yes, Jim, I am here," she said. He slowly removed a document wrapped in waterproof sealskin and handed it to her. He began to talk, his voice raspy, barely audible, and slow.

"I have your funds," he said. "One is a secured draft to the bank for the exact amount of your debt; you have time to pay it now if you like." Virginia nodded, holding her hands out to Jim, who began to stagger just a bit. He paused. "The other is federal notes for the rest of your profit. Wendell has kept four hundred to pay off debts incurred on the trail and I have forty dollar in my possession for expenses on my return. There is a bill of sale and itemized expenses; it is all accounted for."

Virginia held Jim's hands to keep him steady, then reached out and accepted the pouch. Anna, hands to her face and tears rushing down her cheeks, moved toward Jim. He held up one hand and said to all of them, "Stop, I can't do any more. Don't ask me. I am done, I need to rest." He then took several wobbly steps toward the two bank officials, stopped, staggered again, and said in a raspy whisper, "Your mercenaries failed you." He then walked past everyone, opened the door, and went back out into the blizzard.

His friends stood in confused silence, not understanding what had just happened. Virginia opened the letter, looked at it, and went to the teller, ignoring the bankers. "Please deposit this federally insured draft and apply it to my outstanding debt, which I understand is due today," she said. "I will wait for my receipt. Thank you."

"He went to Bracket's," the apprentice yelled to everyone as he reentered the bank after following Jim to his destination. The reverend put his arm around the near hysterical Anna.

"Let him be now, Anna," he said. "God knows what hell he went through to get here and he needs to take care of himself. Give him his rest, he has earned it."

Anna fell into his shoulder and asked "What did he mean? Is he leaving us?"

"Time will tell. Yes, time will tell. I will go later to see to his welfare," the reverend said to calm Anna's fears. "As soon as Virginia is finished with her business, we will go home."

The tavern lamps were lit and the two fireplaces were roaring in anticipation of the traditional New Year's frolic which, this year, would be severely hampered by the inconsiderate storm. Only a few customers were sitting about; Elva the owner and matriarch of all her customers heard the door open. She watched Jim emerge out of the swirling snow and move slowly to the bar.

"You're back," was all she could say, shocked at his appearance and knowing his situation.

"Elva, may I to use your fire to dry off?" he asked. "Also, get a large pitcher of fresh water and a big bowl of your venison stew, if it be available, and some corn meal biscuits and hot buttered rum. My thoughts for two days have been only of that and you Elva." His satire went unnoticed; the proprietor and customers watched in silence as he slowly and with difficulty took off his heavy blanket, deerskin long coat, and hunter's shirt, hung them on the large pegs on the wall next to the hearth, then sat down and removed his deerskin-lined leather boots and both the heavy woolen and lighter linen socks. He was mostly worried about his feet and the shape they were in. He was already beginning to feel pins and needles in both feet. They were swollen, red in color, and painful to the touch: they were frost-bitten but not frozen. He knew the difference intimately from the cold and miserable days of the winter season in the northern army,

"A lot of pain tonight and swollen feet for a couple of days, if I am lucky," he said to no one.

Elva brought the provisions to his table; Jim saw the large pitcher of cold water and became thirsty again. He drank heartily of the pitcher. He rested for several minutes sitting at the table; Elva insisted that he take off his woolen pants, bringing him a large clean blanket to wrap about himself. "Jim, you're a sight for sore eyes for sure," she said, "but you're not ready for the ladies. I will clean up these clothes of yourn and I am burning these pants. I will bring you my dead husband's attire, which should fit. You need now to get some food and rest while I attend to those feet."

Jim devoured a bowl of the best venison stew he ever had; in a few minutes, however, exhaustion finally overwhelmed him and he started to nod off. Elva brought a pan and gently poured warm water over his feet for several minutes. Then, very carefully, she wrapped them in thin cotton gauze. Jim was barely awake, mumbled something incoherent that Elva ignored. She then arranged for a sleeping mat next to the corner hearth, walked him over, laid him down, and told the customers not to bother him.

"He is in for a hard night," she said. "Does anyone want to go fetch Dr. True on this miserable night? He's going to need some medicinal assistance." The apprentice volunteered.

The morning was bright and the world of snow sparkled in the sun's welcomed rays. The storm was gone and the town was wrapped in a heavy blanket of new snow. Reverend Moody shook his boots off as he walked into Bracket's; it took him a minute to adjust his eyes as looked upon the dark interior. "Preacher; you here to lay a sermon upon us sinners?" The reverend ignored the smattering of laughter as Elva tilted her head toward the back corner where Jim was sitting, wrapped in a blanket, his feet up on a bench and covered with gauze.

"He got some laudanum from the doc," she said. "Slept all night; a case of frost bite and exhaustion. He isn't talking much." The reverend nodded his thank you as he walked by.

"I just ordered up some breakfast. Would you like to join me?" Jim said as the reverend approached.

"Don't mind if I do," the reverend said. He sat at the table across from Jim; they didn't speak for awhile as coffee and then a skillet of scrambled eggs, blood sausage, potatoes, and corn bread were served. Jim asked if the snow had stopped and what had brought the reverend this way.

"I came to ask after your welfare. How you be?"

"Feet frosted, expect to be walking today," Jim said. They finished the meal in silence and Elva filled their cups with coffee and dark chocolate. Jim continued, "They will find a body up north, past the orchards, with the thaw; Lucas Williams; along with my horse," he said, looking at his coffee.

"Come to the house and rest up," said the reverend. The people that love you are there."

"Might need some help," said Jim. "I will need some new footwear; I can't get into my boots." Elva secured a large knife and cut off the tops of his boots, then gently wrapped his feet in the deerskin lining. She then cut up his old blanket, covered the feet with strips, and wrapped them tight.

"This should get you there," she said.

"Thanks, Elva. You're one good woman. I will be back to cover my expenses." They embraced for a moment while the reverend nodded his appreciation.

"Come back when you can dance, Mr. Morgan," she yelled as they stepped out of the dark tavern and into the light. They both squinted.

The second day after the great New Year's Eve storm was also sunny and with no wind. Commerce returned to Marietta as its citizens began the job of clearing sidewalks and storefronts and moving snow off the roads. Several teams of strong horses pulling sleds filled with emergency supplies were going to the country to provide assistance to any rural families that had had a hard time of it. Virginia went to Woodall's Stable early and rented a fine team with a sled for Jim and Anna to take to the farm. She then had it filled it with food, coal oil, blankets, and some warm clothing that Virginia knew was needed. Jim felt much better after spending all of New Year's Day and night in an exhaustive sleep, and was eager to move about. His feet were still swollen and sore, but he could walk with the cane provided by the reverend. Jim and Anna, who had not talked or not spent any time together since his return, would leave immediately to go to Maggie's Hill and make sure that everyone had survived the storm. On the following day, Jim would continue on with the team and sled to Daisy's and see how they were all doing. Jim wasn't too worried, knowing that Water Bird was there and would see to everyone's welfare.

The horses made good time getting through the deep snow and drifts. On several occasions, they would get out of the sled to lighten the load and make it easier for the horses. They avoided any conversation about themselves, and kept it light and incidental, commenting mostly about the weather. Conversation about the events of the last six weeks, and particularly the last five days, would wait.

"How do you like my new boots? Four dollars at Holden's."

"You look almost civilized," Anna said. "Soon you will be wearing store-bought pants." They could see the chimney smoke before they came around the last bend; the horses, working hard up the hill would be in need of a good rest. Jacob, Penelope, Charles, and Digger came onto the porch to welcome them home.

The arrival of Jim and Anna turned the farm into a frenzy of happy activity: cutting fire wood, shoveling walkways through the snow, distributing new blankets and overcoats for Charles and Penelope, and restocking the pantry shelves. Jacob and Jim removed the snow from the woodpile and spent most of the day cutting and chopping firewood to size. Jim, hampered by his frostbite, insisted on splitting the wood. They conversed like old friends; Jacob was an understanding listener and Jim was eager to share his adventures with someone who understood. He recounted the events in no particular order and quietly shared the events of the cattle drive, the blizzard, the ambush, and the shooting of Lucas Williams. This triggered a discussion of what the future would hold without the slave catcher.

Jim said, "Others will come to seek their bounty. I have no tolerance for those who seek to profit from the miseries of others. If my fortune is to stay here, I will do my best to ensure that no slave catchers will do their miserably business in Washington County."

They agreed that, when there was money to be made, there would be many more to take Lucas's place. Jacob, in turn, talked about how settled in Water Bird and Labithia had become with Molly and Daisy. "They share duties without complaint; converse eagerly and laughter abounds. The slave girl's health has improved, but she will always be a frail woman. I must say, she has regained her curiosity and is becoming downright sassy."

Jacob said that it was time for him to leave and he would go late this day to his mother's farm near Chillicothe and assist her for the rest of the winter, then continue his work in the spring, building a secret network of hidden roads, trails, and sanctuaries for the slaves who would find their way to Ohio and freedom.

Coffee and biscuits were brought to them by Penelope and they took a break inside the woodshed, among the smells of coffee and freshly cut wood. A small fire brought a sense of comfort as they lit their pipes. Jim sat with his sore feet resting on some uncut wood while he sharpened his ax with a handheld whetstone. Jacob said he needed to say some things before they parted. Jim nodded his head.

They sat silent as Jacob seemed to struggle for words; he hesitantly mentioned Anna. "I know not of your interest in the actions of Anna and I in your absence," he said. "I must say that nothing of a carnal nature occurred. Let me explain that I am not interested in the intimate companionship of a woman, any woman. I am..." Jim looked directly at Jacob, who paused for a moment. Jim took up the conversation.

"I know of men with your peculiarity," he said. "They were frequent at Fort Meigs and one, I must say, was most obnoxious in his pursuit of me. Be who you are, but do not impose your interest or intentions and we will be the most trusted of friends. I have no claim on Anna and must confess I am not bothered by her interest in you; the future of Anna and I is uncertain. I care for her as much as a sister as I do a lover." He paused; ran his finger down the sharpened blade of his ax, and seemed satisfied. He had a sip of coffee and looked again at Jacob.

"I am both an old man and a young man, and I have done and suffered much these last two years. This has left me weary and tired; for the present, I seek only comfort and rest. I am, however, of but twenty years, and I have for as long as I can recall looked upon the Ohio River and wandered in my mind down its course to its destination and sought to explore all of its wonders. My youth, I hope, is still with me." Jim said nothing more of his future, knowing not what it would be; this didn't seem important at the moment.

There was another silence, as if everything had been said and they searched for another subject dear to both of them.

"Jim, I must say to you that all of us dedicated to the freedom of enslaved peoples understand that the cause may require extraordinary efforts. Bravery such as yours, in this most difficult time will forever be remembered and indeed celebrated. We welcome you and hope that if so disposed you will continue to fight the battle with us. Our road is dark and poorly traveled as we strive to provide shelter, protection, and transport for our refugees to their promised land."

"My friend Jacob," Jim said, "be assured that I will always be part of this cause so beloved by the general, no matter my place or position, and I do believe our paths will cross often and we will have ample opportunities to travel this underground road together."

Jacob appeared relieved that all the difficult conversation was over and he continued to talk eagerly of his grand design: the people involved, potential recruits, new contacts in Canada, and interesting stories of close encounters with the slave catchers.

They cut and split firewood for several hours and then, with the help of Charles, loaded it high on the wood pile. Anna was waiting with a warm and generous dinner, which they ate in a subdued manner, anticipating Jacob's departure. Immediately thereafter, he saddled his horse and left with an hour or two of light so as to arrive in Marietta by dark. He would spend the evening at the Moody's'. Sad goodbyes were quickly said and he left with just a wave.

The fire in Daisy's reconstructed farm house was warm and bright as Water Bird and the rest of her new family settled in for the evening. She was smoking her pipe. "Jim will be here in the morning," she said quietly. Everyone smiled and looked forward to his return.

Molly said, "So, my son is safe." She didn't question how Water Bird would know such a thing. Labithia, who was partly dozing, became alert.

"Jim be cmin in de moning," she said. "Glory be, he be safe. Praise the Lord, glory, glory. Bout time dat Jim cme back."

It was late. The fire had burned low and a gusty wind began to pick up and blow snow across the windows. Jim and Anna were now alone in the chairs around the hearth; the conversation was subdued and in a contemplative way Jim wondered what the general would say about these recent events.

"The general would say come to my bed and never leave," she said. Jim smiled, banked the fire, and limped on sore feet to the warm glow of the candlelit bedroom. Digger, roused from her sleep, stretched and followed.

CPSIA information can be obtained at www.ICGtesting.com
Printed in the USA
LVOW081253130112

263662LV00002B/35/P